REGENCY

Innocents & Intrigues

Lose yourself with two gorgeous
Regency romances from Helen Dickson

Helen Dickson was born and lives in South Yorkshire with her retired farm manager husband. Having moved out of the busy farmhouse where she raised their two sons, she has more time to indulge in her favourite pastimes. She enjoys being outdoors, travelling, reading and music. An incurable romantic, she writes for pleasure. It was a love of history that drove her to writing historical fiction.

REGENCY
Innocents & Intrigues

Helen Dickson

All the characters in this book have no existence outside the imagination
of the author, and have no relation whatsoever to anyone bearing the same
name or names. They are not even distantly inspired by any individual
known or unknown to the author, and all the incidents are pure invention.

Mills & Boon, an imprint of Harlequin (UK) Limited,
Eton House, 18-24 Paradise Road, Richmond, Surrey TW9 1SR

REGENCY: INNOCENTS & INTRIGUES
© Harlequin Enterprises II B.V./S.à.r.l 2011

The publisher acknowledges the copyright holder of the individual works
as follows:

Marrying Miss Monkton © Helen Dickson 2009
Beauty in Breeches © Helen Dickson 2011

ISBN: 978 0 263 89594 0

052-0212

Marrying Miss Monkton

Helen Dickson

Chapter One

The day was wet and blustery. Charles had slept little, and uneasily, for the problem of going out of his way to call at Chateau Feroc was an added irritant he could do without. He lifted his lean face so that trickles of water ran down his cheeks. The weather suited his mood.

He rode into a small village with one main street. It was no different from any other village in France, with its huddle of poor cottages, a church tower on the outskirts, a windmill and a tavern. A particular stench arose from the gutters to assail his nostrils and touch like icy fingers upon his deepest fears. It was the stench of poverty, the foul, unacceptable smell of humanity at its lowest.

The wind had risen and the fallen leaves went whipping along the ground and collected in roadside ditches. The road along which he slowly rode was narrow and crooked and paved with cobblestones, glistening with the rain. There were few people about, and the few he saw were ragged; when they turned to face him on hearing his horse's hooves, he could see raw hunger in their eyes, and every time he saw it he wanted to curse.

These were troubled and dangerous times in France. The country was suffering financial difficulties, which stemmed from the heavy costs incurred by France during the war with America, which had left the Treasury bankrupt. But the ordinary masses were of the opinion, and rightly so, that France's troubles were not helped by lavish court spending. To pay the heavy taxes imposed on them, people starved while the nobility were busy at the elaborate idleness in their grand chateaus or at the palace of Versailles, in the swim of the gay life of Louis XVI's artificial paradise. Revolution was already apparent in the minds of the masses.

On the edge of the village Charles saw an old man and a child of no more than five or six, a boy, he thought, stooping and carefully picking up sticks and placing them in a sack. It was, he knew, their only means of warmth and to cook the meagre rations that came their way. Stumbling, the old man dropped the sack and his precious kindling tumbled out. The child bent to retrieve them, his fingers young and nimble compared to those of the elder. Charles stopped and dismounted and helped them in their task.

When the sticks had been retrieved, the old man smiled at Charles out of his lined face.

'My thanks, *monsieur*,' he said.

Charles looked at him, wondering how old he was. He knew he was probably many years younger than he looked, but when he asked him, his answer shocked him.

'Thirty-two.' His smile broadened when he saw shock register in the stranger's eyes. 'Hunger makes old men of us all, *monsieur*.'

The distant sound of carriage wheels rumbling on the cobbles reached their ears, an impatient drumming that came slowly nearer, growing louder and sounding clearer. All three looked ahead and stepped aside to avoid being run down by the coach and four bowling towards them. The uniformed coachman was lashing the horses, the black coach careering so fast that the wheels were almost lifted clear of the ground, the horses' hooves making sparks against the cobblestones.

Charles caught a glimpse of its occupant, an elegantly attired young gentlewoman wearing black. The coach was travelling so fast that it was impossible to see her face properly, but his sharp eyes caught a glimpse of a pale face surrounded by black hair.

'Look at her,' the peasant growled. 'Aristocrat! Ere long we'll make an end to the likes of them and their arrogant breed—and good riddance is what I say. They'll get what's coming to them—had it coming for a long time, they have. They'll be shown no mercy on the day of reckoning.' So saying he spat on the ground and wiped his mouth on his sleeve.

'You pay your dues to the Seigneur?'

'I give him everything. I pay to grind my corn at his mill. I pay to transport it across bridges not once but a hundred times. I pay to press my own grapes for wine. When winter comes we go hungry and we have to feed the children on bran and roots, which swell their bellies up; one of my daughters died last winter—a painful death. My wife is too weak to work. We killed the oxen for food, and the bailiffs come to search my house for salt.'

'They found some?'

He nodded. 'They fined me all the money I had left.

The taxes are eating us up. We have decided to leave the house and take to the road. We shall leave everything— the furniture, the land—everything. Let them take it. With nothing we can't be taxed.'

'I am sorry for you,' Charles said with deep sincerity. Shoving his hand in his pocket and bringing out a *louis,* Charles handed it to the man. 'Here, take this. Buy yourself and your family something to eat.'

The man shook his head, making no attempt to take it. 'Where would I spend a *louis?* Have you nothing smaller, *monsieur?* Were I to present such a large coin at the baker's or the grocer's or anywhere else, it would raise suspicion and attract the attention of the bailiffs. They would demand to know where I came by such a coin and my assessment would be increased.'

Charles took back the *louis* and gave him some small coins, not worth as much, but the man was satisfied and stuffed them into his pocket. They would enable him to feed his family for days, if not weeks, if he and his wife were careful.

'There are terrible times ahead for France,' Charles said, hoisting himself back into the saddle. 'There is a great fear. All over the country, the lines are crumbling.'

The man nodded. 'Aye, *monsieur,* you are right,' he said, his voice hoarse with real emotion. His sunken cheeks already wet with the rain, became more so when the tears that gathered in his eyes spilled over. 'I doubt I shall live to see it.' Taking the child's hand, he nodded his thanks and went on his way.

Charles rode on slowly, unable to shake off his meeting with the man and boy. He had seen much suffering since he had come to France. The peasantry was in debt, increasingly resentful—and suffering from the catastrophic effects of the previous year's bad harvest. The populace blamed the nobility for the high price of grain and was enraged against them.

Since the recent storming of the Bastille in Paris, revolution had spread to the countryside. Mob violence had broken out in many regions. The whole of France was like a tinder box. One strike and there was no knowing what would follow. He knew the temper of the mob. If they saw blood they became like mad wolves. It was the kind of violence that gave Charles many a qualm about the rightness of their cause, for some of the mobs were made up of villainous, evil-smelling brutes, who, he swore to God, had never been starving peasants or anything else but brigands.

He had seen it all, recording it all in his mind, so that he could set it down when he put up in some inn or other, where he would rest for the night before setting off again on his journey back to England. But before embarking for his home country, he had a slight detour to make. To the Chateau Feroc, here in Alsace.

Coming to the next village, Charles had a feeling of unease. Crowds were gathered in the cobbled square in little knots, having suspended their operations to watch a young woman who, against all reason and judgement, with a large basket on her arm was distributing food to a small group of scrawny, hungry children. A carriage, the one that had passed him on the road, waited across the street, the driver seeming uncomfortable and clearly wishing he were somewhere else.

Charles reined to a canter as he rode slowly into the square. He could feel the pulse and panic of the people swirling about him from the very atmosphere beating down on him. There was an ominous silence as he passed and a menacing mutter that rose at his back, and the faces that watched him were questioning, insolent or uneasy.

His progress became slower as he rode towards the woman, fighting down his apprehension and his fear. There was a danger that he could get himself involved in a riot, and he might have to draw his pistol and shoot, for the mob was like an animal, and like an animal it could sense fear.

The woman was perfectly calm, and quite uninterested, he thought, irrationally swinging from the extremes of fear to the limits of exasperation, in the dangers of the situation. She paused in her work and looked up, frowning a little at the sight of him. Dismounting, holding the reins, he moved closer, the children stuffing bread into their mouths with dirty little hands as they scuttled away.

'What are you doing?' he demanded, taking her arm and drawing her aside.

'And who, may I ask, are you?' the young woman enquired, looking him up and down with icy disdain and shaking off his hand. There was insolence in the way he stood, in the lean, rangy line of his body, that gave the impression of dangerous vitality, and in the firm set line of his well-shaped mouth. Even the slender brown hand that had gripped her arm recalled the talon of a bird of prey, while the look in those pale blue eyes was unnervingly intent. She was very lovely, but she was maddened by his interference in something she considered none of his concern.

'It doesn't matter who I am,' he snapped, deliberately keeping his voice low. 'Have you no sense? Take a look around you and then maybe you will understand my concern.'

She did as he told her and studied the groups of people. They were watching her, glaring, the men brutish, openly hostile, quiet and threatening. She looked again at the stranger. 'These people know me— I do not believe they will harm me.'

'If you believe that, then you are more foolish than I thought. The quality of your clothes and the mere fact that you have access to food represents authority, and that sets you apart.'

She raised her chin, smarting at the rebuke. 'The children are hungry. I wanted to bring them food. I'm trying to help them.'

'By putting yourself in danger?'

'I know the dangers, but they are more likely to harm you than me.'

This was precisely what Charles himself had thought, and his anger against himself for not having had the moral courage to leave her to take her chance kept him silent.

'It was kind of you to concern yourself. Thank you.'

'You have nothing to thank me for,' Charles said brusquely, 'but what the devil did you think you hoped to achieve? Can't you see that it was the height of folly for a lady to bring food to the village at a time such as this? It's small wonder you weren't mobbed—it's still not too late.'

Suddenly the young woman couldn't answer, for she knew he spoke the truth. Having overheard the servants at the chateau talking in subdued tones as they cleared away the remains of the dinner the night before, saying what was left would have fed the people in the village for a month or more, and how everyone went to bed hungry, especially the small children who did not understand the suffering they were forced to endure, on impulse she had instructed cook to fill a basket of food and come to the village to distribute it to the children. Now, looking around at the hungry, hostile faces, with a quiver of fear she saw her mistake.

'You are right,' she said, finding it hard to defend herself because she knew she was in the wrong. 'Maybe I shouldn't have come, but I've distributed the food now so I'll leave.'

They stood face to face.

Charles saw a slender young woman of medium height. Her forehead was wide, her chin slightly pointed, her skin the colour of ivory and she had startling translucent green eyes. They were surrounded by long, thick lashes under delicate black brows that curved like a swallow's wings. Her skin was flushed at the cheekbones, whether with her indignation or perhaps where the sun had tinted it.

Her raven-black hair was drawn from her face and hidden beneath her bonnet, and yet it still managed to look unconfined. Wisps of soft curls peeked out from beneath the brim, and he had the strangest need to put up a hand and smooth them back. Her jaw was strong, clenched to a defiant angle, and her whole manner spoke of fearlessness, a fearlessness that told him she was afraid of no one, and certainly not of him.

Wearing a black woollen cloak over her black dress, she could not be mistaken for anything other than what she so evidently was, a lady of quality.

She saw a man dressed in a black frock coat, black trousers and black leather knee boots, a white silk cravat wound and knotted round his neck. He was tall, lean and arrogant as men of consequence often are. His narrowed eyes were pale blue and penetrating, with silver flecks in them. They were surrounded by long, curling dark lashes. His hair beneath his hat was a shade lighter than her own and just as thick. It was drawn from his handsome face and secured with a thin black ribbon at the nape.

Charles looked sternly at her. 'I don't suppose you told anyone you were coming here—what you were doing?'

She shook her head. 'They would have stopped me.'

'And they would have been right to. Your family ought to punish you most severely for this escapade and curtail all your outings in future. Go home, and should you have any more noble intentions, I advise you to think again. Shall I escort you?'

She stepped back, her look telling him that she deeply resented his high-handed attitude. What right had he to criticise and chastise her? 'Certainly not,' she answered tightly. 'I can take care of myself. I will go my own way.'

Charles watched her carriage drive off before mounting his horse and riding away to find an inn where he could stay the night.

It was a subdued Maria that rode back in the carriage to Chateau Feroc, her empty basket on the seat beside her. Putting the obnoxious stranger out of her mind, she stared wide-eyed out of the window. Even though the scenery was marred by the lowering clouds, it was hard to imagine the turmoil that beset France when such a beautiful landscape unfolded before her eyes. But how she wished she were back in England, at Gravely, her home, where she had spent the happiest time of her life.

Maria's father, Sir Edward Monkton, had expressed in his will his desire that she be made the ward of the Countess de Feroc, his deceased wife's sister, until she was of an age to marry Colonel Henry Winston. Colonel Winston had obtained a well-paid administrative post in the ranks of the East India Company, which was where he had become acquainted with her father. It was six years since Colonel Winston had been home to England, six years since he had visited Sir Edward at Gravely Manor.

Having contracted various ailments whilst in India, her father had suffered greatly from ill health. Aware that his time was limited and desperate to settle Maria's future before fortune hunters began presenting themselves at Gravely, when Colonel Winston approached him as a possible suitor for her hand—his tanned face and colourful talk of India reviving memories of his own years spent in that country—he had accepted his suit, satisfied that his daughter's future would be secure.

Maria, though just thirteen at the time, had not objected, for she had become extremely fond of the handsome, dashing colonel, who went out of his way to talk to her, to flatter her and to tell her of his exciting life he led in India. Of course the wedding could not go ahead until Maria was of age and by then Colonel Winston would have served another six years in India.

When Maria was fourteen years old, her arrival at Chateau Feroc had made an unfavourable impression— an impression that was equally unfavourable to her.

The chateau was so very different from her home in

England. The contrast was startling, the warm, happy and colourful environment that she had left behind so very different to the cold and stately French chateau. Here she was met with strict discipline and hostility from family and servants alike. Not even Constance, her spoilt cousin, had made her welcome. Driven in upon herself by the circumstances of this new life reduced Maria to a state of loneliness, despair and dumb misery. Her silence would have aroused compassion and understanding even in such a hard, dispassionate person as the Countess, but Maria's quietness and her desire for solitude was put down to petulance and resentment.

It was mid-morning when Charles approached the Chateau Feroc. On all sides of the magnificent house large formal gardens were enclosed by freshly trimmed box hedges, with long, elegant walks peopled with statues, and urns brimming with flowers, and ornate, soaring fountains. Arrogant peacocks displaying their full, colourful plumage strutted on lawns like green velvet.

An air of peace and serenity prevailed over it all— in marked contrast to the character of its owner who, he was told when he asked to see the Count de Feroc, was being interred in the family tomb in the local church this very day.

Turning his horse, he headed off in the direction of the church. The path leading up to the gates was lined with faces bearing every expression from sadness to sympathy, curiosity and hostility for the man whose demand for higher taxes had made their lives intolerable.

All eyes were on the church as people began filing out in a subdued procession. Charles dismounted and removed his hat as a mark of respect for the dead Count and his family. He stood apart, a quiet observer as they were handed up into waiting carriages. Mourners were few, for people of the upper classes were afraid to travel far in these troubled times.

His eyes were drawn to the impressive and stately figure that could only be the Countess. She was followed by two women, their heads bowed, and like the Countess they were dressed in deepest black, their black gloved hands clutching their prayer books. Veils fell from their bonnets' edges concealing their features, but failed to disguise their youth. Charles's eyes were drawn to the taller of the two. She was of slender build, and there was something about the way she moved that he found vaguely familiar.

Watching them drive away, he felt it was inappropriate for him to intrude on the funeral party and the Countess's grief, so he returned to the inn until the next day. But he would wait no longer. It was dangerous for him to remain in France, and if he were apprehended he would more than likely be hanged or shot or beaten by the mob. He must leave France without further delay.

As Charles followed the imposing servant in white wig and midnight blue livery up the great white marble staircase of the Chateau Feroc, he was surrounded by all the graceful elegance of eighteenth-century France. Here, it was gilded scrollwork, innumerable tall mirrors that seemed to double the house by reflection, exquisite porcelain, heavy silks and thick carpets and glittering chandeliers.

He went along a corridor and was admitted into a high-vaulted room, with all the elegance and luxuries befitting a family of the nobility. The furniture was in the mode of the present reign, Louis XVI, delicate and fine, the beads of the crystal chandelier catching the firelight and brightening the whole room.

Madam la Countess—an English woman who had met and married the Count de Feroc on a visit to France with her parents—received him alone. She was a stiff, thin, elderly woman with grey hair and very pale skin. In deepest mourning, she presented an imposing figure in a high-necked gown of heavy black silk. Grim faced, she rose from her chair when he entered and calmly watched him approach. There was no sign of grief for her dead husband on her face.

Charles stopped in front of her and inclined his head. When he straightened up it was to find himself looking into a pair of coldly critical pale eyes. Immediately he could see she was one of those aristocrats who had her feelings buried under deep layers of social propriety, the sort who might stare icily at someone, or turn away, affecting indifference.

'Thank you for receiving me so promptly, Countess,' he said in flawless French. 'May I offer my deepest condolences on your loss.'

'Sir Charles Osbourne! Welcome to Chateau Feroc.' The Countess spoke English to the Englishman, her voice clear and incisive.

'Please speak to me in French, Countess,' he requested with calm gravity. 'These are difficult times and servants hear and speculate too much.'

'As you wish,' she replied coolly.

'I apologise for my inopportune arrival. Of course I had no idea of the Count's demise until I arrived.'

'How could you? It was very sudden.' The Countess had never been particularly fond of her husband, and had regarded him with tolerance rather than affection. 'You are here on behalf of Colonel Winston?' she remarked, resuming her seat and indicating with a wave of her hand that was almost royal that he should occupy the chair across from her.

'That is so, Countess—to escort your niece, Miss Monkton, to England.'

'I know. I was expecting you.'

'Colonel Winston said he would write to you apprising you of my arrival and the nature of my mission. You have received his letter?'

'Yes, some weeks ago. We expected you earlier than this.'

'I did not come direct. The recent troubles make travelling difficult. I also had some matters of my own to take care of first.'

'You have been in Paris?'

'I have come from there.'

'And are things as bad as they say?'

He nodded grimly. 'The rioting grows worse by the day. Nobles are fleeing the city—and France, if they can manage it without being apprehended.'

'Then we can be thankful that we do not live in Paris, Sir Charles. So, Colonel Winston is no longer in India,' she said, folding her hands in her lap, her thin-lipped mouth relaxing slightly.

'No. He has been in England six months.'

'And eager to reacquaint himself with Maria, he informed me. He feels that to delay the marriage would be unnecessary and harsh. You must know him well. He must think highly of you to entrust you with the responsibility of escorting his betrothed to England.'

'We are not friends, Countess,' Charles was quick to inform her—Henry Winston was an unsavoury character and not a man he would wish to count as one of his close associates. 'We are—acquainted. No more than that.'

'I see.' The Countess studied him thoughtfully. 'Do you disapprove of Colonel Winston?'

'It's not a matter of disapproval, Countess. Our meetings have been infrequent.'

'And yet he asked you to escort Maria to England.'

'For reasons of his own he was unable to come himself. I was coming to see my own family—my mother is French, from the south. Everyone in Britain is alarmed by the news that crosses the channel. I was concerned for my family.'

'Your mother still lives in France?'

'No. She married an Englishman—my father—and chose to remain in England when he died. Colonel Winston was worried that Miss Monkton might become caught up in the troubles and wanted her to get out. When he heard I was leaving for France, he approached me to ask if I would see her safely to England.'

'And you agreed, without having met her.'

'My father and Sir Edward Monkton were close friends for many years. They were in India together. I remember him as being a very fine and noble man. I also owe him a great, personal debt.'

'Tell me.'

'When I was a boy my mother and I were washed away while crossing a swollen river. Sir Edward came to our rescue, putting his own life at risk. Without his bravery I would not be here now. It is for that reason that I agreed to escort Miss Monkton to England. While in India I came into contact with Colonel Winston on numerous occasions. He made no secret of how Sir Edward had been easily manipulated into agreeing to his betrothal to Miss Monkton. It was a matter of great amusement to him. I feel under an obligation to protect Sir Edward's daughter and I have made it my duty to try to stop her marrying Colonel Winston when the time comes. Will she have any objections to leaving France?'

'Not at all,' the Countess answered crisply. 'All Maria talks about is going home and marrying the Colonel.'

'She has not seen him for six years. She will find him much changed.'

'As he will Maria. She is no longer a child.'

'And you, Countess? Will you and your daughter not accompany us to England?'

The Countess studied him for a moment in silence, contemplating his question and curious as to what had prompted him to ask. 'Ah,' she said, narrowing her eyes on him. 'Would I be correct in assuming you are about to try to persuade me to leave my France?'

Charles's firm lips curved in a slight smile. 'You are, Countess. I sincerely hope I will succeed. I would be happy to escort you and your daughter, along with Miss Monkton, to England. France is in great turmoil and every day things get worse. There is no organisation in the country, only chaos everywhere. I believe you are in mortal danger, and that you are at risk of your life— I would not like to be a noble in France now. Very soon you will find yourself alone and friendless, and prey to all kinds of dangers.'

The Countess smiled thinly. 'I think you exaggerate. I hear rumours—most of it nonsense, of course. My husband was of the opinion that the fear is spread to provoke disorder so that it will bring about anarchy. Rumours of conspiracy and crime, reports of disaster, spring up everywhere, both by word of mouth and by writing. It is the panic mongers you have to fear.'

Charles's expression tightened. 'I shall hope very much to be proved wrong, but it seems—unlikely. I am staying at a local tavern and I hear things—that some of your own servants have run off and joined the people. The peasants are in such a state of revolt that they are ready to commit any crime. Indeed, in this very parish, they talk openly about setting fire to the chateau. I urge you, if you do not think of yourself, then think of your daughter.'

The Countess raised her head imperiously and gave him a hard look. 'Constance will remain here with me.'

'Being English will not save you, Countess. English law cannot reach you here. You were the Count's wife. The mob will not see beyond that.'

'Are you saying that we should all leave immediately, that you think I need saving?'

He nodded. 'You must leave quickly. I took the liberty of having false travelling papers drawn up for that eventuality.'

The Countess's brows rose with surprise. 'You did? How did you manage that?'

Charles's face remained closed. 'I know the right people.'

'I see. Well, I will not pry into the whys and wheres, sir, of how these things are done, but I must tell you that you have wasted your time. But is it safe to travel? If there is danger, would it not be safer to stay here?'

'There is no safety anywhere, least of all in the chateaus of France.'

'No one would dare attack the chateau. I know the people hereabouts. They have always looked to us for their livelihood and they will continue to do so.'

God give me strength, prayed Charles, setting his teeth. It was no use. She did not even now realise the magnitude of this terror that was overtaking them. He was tempted to ask—what livelihood would that be? The people you speak of are starving because of the likes of you and your exorbitant taxes, but instead he said calmly, as though reasoning with a fractious child, 'Because of who you are, I urge you to flee the country.'

'This is my home. I feel perfectly safe. I have no intention of—fleeing. If things do get worse then of course I shall consider leaving, but I am confident that they won't.'

A mildly tolerant smile touched Charles's handsome visage, but the glint in the pale blue eyes was hard as steel. Could there be any greater display of contempt for the hardships the people were facing? While ordinary people had starvation staring them in the face day after day, the Countess was blind to the offence the ordinary French people took to their self-indulgent plutocratic life style.

'If you don't wish to make mourners of your friends, Countess, I suggest you leave with us.'

'You do much to fan the flames of discontent with such foolish talk, sir. I am sorry. I have made my decision.'

Charles shifted in his chair impatiently, holding his

irritation in check. He could see he was wasting his breath—she had no intention of relenting. She was adamant, blinkered about the atrocities going on around her, and very foolish.

'I am sorry to hear that. However, I will leave you the papers—but you will have to make your own way and travel as peasants, Countess. It will be difficult, I know, and will need much planning on your part and assistance from people you can trust. You would never reach the Channel otherwise. You do realise that Miss Monkton will be very much alone when she arrives in England, and very dependent on Colonel Winston.'

The Countess raised her head imperiously. 'As her betrothed, that is the way of things.'

'And you are comfortable with that?'

The Countess looked a little taken aback as she met his steady gaze. 'Comfortable? But it is what the girl has wanted ever since her father died. Why should I be uncomfortable about that?'

'Because Sir Edward placed the responsibility for her upbringing in your hands. You are her guardian. Have you no wish to see for yourself the sort of man she is betrothed to?'

'I have no need to. I have listened to what you have said, but Colonel Winston is a gentleman, having seen long and honourable service with the East India Company. He is *eminently* suitable to marry my niece.'

'How can you know that, when you have never met him?' Charles persisted.

'Maria's father, my brother-in-law, knew him well. He liked and trusted him enough to agree to a betrothal between them. That is good enough for me.'

'I beg your pardon, Countess, but when he agreed to the betrothal Sir Edward was an ill man. I imagine he was ignorant of Colonel Winston's passion for pleasure—for drinking and gaming. I do not lie to you. Colonel Winston is almost fifty years old, old enough to be your niece's father.'

The Countess remained unmoved. 'It is not unusual for young ladies to marry older gentlemen. Of course all men drink, and on occasion drink far too much and behave accordingly. But wives must not make an issue of such things. My brother-in-law placed Maria in my care until the time when she was of an age to marry Colonel Winston. She is nineteen years old. She will be under your protection until you deliver her to her betrothed. When she leaves the chateau I shall consider my obligation to her discharged.'

Charles looked at her for a long moment. His eyes had darkened with anger and his mouth had closed in a hard, unpleasant line. He was unable to believe the Countess could cast her responsibility to her niece off so callously, to send her into the clutches of a man who would use her ill. It was like sending a lamb to the wolves.

Sadly Miss Monkton's father's judgement about the prospective bridegroom had been seriously impaired. His eyes were too dim to see what Charles would have seen—the calculating, dangerous look in the Colonel's eye. In those days he'd had the body of Adonis and the face of an angel, and was as full of vice as the devil.

'You must not forget the fortune Miss Monkton represents. The prospect of being able to retire a rich man and preside over Gravely appeals strongly to his vanity. He will go through your niece's wealth like water in a fast-flowing stream the minute he gets his hands on it. Colonel Winston left the Company in disgrace—an unsavoury scandal concerning his neglect of duty, which resulted in many lives being lost.'

'Then he must have had good reason,' the Countess replied, her tone falling just a little short of sounding flippant.

'He was found in a brothel, drunk out of his mind, the following day.'

'I see. I would appreciate it if you did not tell my niece of Colonel Winston's...unsavoury habits—although personally I wouldn't worry about it. You do see that, don't you?'

Charles did see, and he was sickened by it. He saw that the Countess had no fondness for her niece and that she was willing to send the girl into the lion's den without a qualm and impatient to do so, with no concern for her future protection. That she could do this was nothing short of despicable and had Charles quietly seething with anger.

'Then you must forgive me, Countess, if I say that you are being extremely naïve. I have given you the facts and you choose to ignore them. I can do no more. But by doing nothing to prevent the marriage of a young girl to a man of his sort, it will not be long before she is broken in mind, body and spirit.'

The Countess looked a little taken aback at the harshness of his tone and his blunt speaking and she stiffened indignantly. 'You exaggerate, sir. I know my niece,' she told him frostily. 'If you are worried about what she will do when she reaches Gravely, you need have no worries on that score. She is a sensible girl. Level-headed like her mother. When she reaches England she will see for herself and make up her own mind as to whether or not she will marry Colonel Winston—and she will. I have every confidence that Colonel Winston will lose no time in making her his wife.'

Charles, who had turned his head towards the door when he thought he heard a sound, spun round and looked at her again, thoroughly repelled by her attitude. 'It is precisely on that account,' he said fiercely, his eyes flashing, 'that I hoped you would accompany her. I know very little about Miss Monkton, but from what you have told me she appears to have cherished a romantic and childish attachment for the man. In your care you could protect and support her when she discovers, as she will, the impossibility of marrying Colonel Winston.'

The Countess returned his gaze with a coldly smiling blandness that told its own story. 'I think you should meet my niece. She will tell you herself how much she wants to return to England. It is six years since her father died. Six years since she left Gravely.'

'Over six years since she saw Colonel Winston.'

'That too, but as I said, in the end she will make up her own mind.'

'As I always do, Aunt,' a voice rang out from across the room.

The Countess and Charles looked towards the door to see a young woman standing there.

Charles rose to his feet, recognising her as the young woman he had met in the village the previous day distributing food to the children. Closing the door softly behind her, she moved towards him; he was struck by her proud, easy carriage, her clear skin and the striking colour of her blue-black hair, drawn from her face into a neat chignon. She was stately, immensely dignified, her face quite expressionless, but underneath he sensed that she had overheard some of his conversation with the Countess and that she was quietly seething.

'Sir Charles, this is Maria, Colonel Winston's future wife. Maria, meet Sir Charles Osbourne. He is to escort you to England.'

When Maria stood in front of him, Charles bowed his head and murmured a few words of conventional greeting. But when he raised his head a sudden feeling of unease caused him to look at her with a start, his scalp prickling. She was studying him with cool interest, her expression immobile and guarded. His eyes met the steady jade-tinted gaze, and for one discomforting moment it seemed that she was staring into the very heart of him, getting the measure of him, of his faults and failings. He had never seen eyes that contained more energy and depth.

It was not until she began to talk that he realised the depth of her charm. Her voice was low, beautifully modulated, and her French was a joy to hear. Everything about her fascinated him, drew him to her, and he felt a stirring of interest as he looked into the glowing green eyes, the passionate face of the young woman before him.

Maria found herself gazing into the eyes of the man she had seen in the village the day before. Her lips tightened ominously. 'You! So you are the man Colonel Winston has sent to take me to England?'

'He did not *send* me, Miss Monkton. He approached me and asked me if I would escort you when he heard I was coming to France.'

The light blue eyes rested on her tight face and she thought irately that he was aware of her dislike and amused by it. 'I see. I do not know what you meant when you said to my aunt that when I reach England I will discover the impossibility of marrying Colonel Winston and nor do I care to—and he will not force me into marriage. No one could do that, sir.'

'He—is much changed since you last saw him. You must be prepared for that.'

She smiled. 'As I am changed. That is only to be expected after six years. It is quite normal.'

'I do not speak lightly, Miss Monkton.'

Maria heard him with growing annoyance. There was much she wanted to say to him, but not with her aunt's eyes watching her every move and her ears missing nothing of what was said. She disliked his easy manner and the steady gaze of his light blue eyes, but his last words awoke an echo in her mind, of her own doubts about marrying Henry. When his letter had arrived informing them to expect Sir Charles Osbourne who was to escort her back to England, she had experienced a joy like she had never known—joy because she was going home to Gravely, a joy that had little to do with her becoming reunited with Henry.

Of late there was a doubt inside her mind concerning her betrothed, like a small persistent maggot nibbling away. Perhaps it was that she had got older, had read more into his letters, which had become shorter as time went on. The writing was scrawled as if hurriedly written—as if he found writing to her more of a duty than a pleasure. Whatever it was, the spell had begun to lose some of the lustre of its first potent charm.

But she would not expose her doubts to this arrogant Englishman and she thrust them into the background of her mind.

'You do not like Colonel Winston, do you, sir?'

'No,' he replied truthfully. 'I don't.'

'These are troubled times. I am sure you have more important things to do than assist a complete stranger across France.'

'I do have important matters that occupy me.'

'Then if you dislike him, why did you agree?'

'One of the reasons is because my father and your own were friends. They were in India together.'

'Oh—I see!' she faltered. 'I didn't know.'

'How could you?'

'And the other reasons?'

He smiled. 'There were several—which I shall tell you about on the journey. When I became aware that you were to return to England and the difficulties you may encounter, I was happy to offer my services. My father would have expected nothing less of me than to help the daughter of an old and dear friend.'

'Then I am grateful to you, sir. I will be pleased to avail myself of your protection and assistance on the journey. How are we to travel?'

'By coach.'

'Which Chateau Feroc will provide,' the Countess offered.

'Thank you, but I must decline your offer. It must be an ordinary equipage, nothing too grand, you understand. I will acquire the coach and two post horses. There must be nothing in your baggage to give you away,' he told Maria with a note of authority. 'All your fine clothes and any jewels you might have must be left behind.'

'I have no jewels, sir. Everything I have of value—jewels my mother left me—is in England in the strong room at Gravely.'

'Good. We shall travel as husband and wife—Citizen Charles Duval and his wife Maria, visiting relatives in a village near Calais. We shall speak French at all times. Consequences could be dire if we are heard speaking English. We are both fluent in French, so if we are stopped no one will suspect we are anything other than what we seem. Memorise your assumed surname if you will. You will dress in plain clothes as befits the wife of a cloth merchant of modest means. Good clothes are enough to brand a person, as the mob attribute fine dress to nobles and rich bourgeois.'

'And my maid?'

'Will remain behind.'

Her delicate brows rose. 'This is all very unconventional.'

His eyes sliced to hers. 'These are not ordinary circumstances.'

'Nevertheless Maria cannot travel alone with you without a maid. Why—it's quite unthinkable,' the Countess remarked, her expression one of shock.

'That is how it will be. I am not planning a tea party, Countess. I am trying to execute a plan to get your niece to England with her life intact. On this occasion etiquette and protocol don't count.'

'When must we leave?' Maria asked.

'In the morning. We must prepare for the journey at once. It is essential that we have food and warm clothes.'

He turned to the Countess. 'I must go. Have Miss Monkton brought to the inn at first light. I consider it safer that the servants should know nothing of her departure. For our own safety the driver will know us under our assumed names.'

After politely taking his leave, he went out, striding along the corridor to the stairs. On hearing the soft patter of running feet and the soft swish of skirts he turned, pausing when he saw Miss Monkton hurrying towards him.

Chapter Two

'There is something you wish to ask about the journey?' Charles asked.

'No, not that. It is about Colonel Winston. Why do you dislike him so much?'

Charles's face hardened and the perfectly amicable expression in his eyes disappeared. 'My dislike is neither here nor there. I am not concerned about Colonel Winston. Can you not at least show some gratitude towards the people who are trying to help you?'

Maria raised her head. 'Yes, of course I am grateful, and it was ill mannered of me not to show it. I apologise, but please do not abuse Colonel Winston to me.'

'I will not abuse him to you and nor will I offend your ears with matters that are beyond your comprehension, but I strongly urge you not to marry him.'

Maria's eyes were suddenly bright with anger. '*You* say this to me. *You*, a perfect stranger.' She saw the sudden anger flare in his eyes. Her chin lifted haughtily and she favoured him with a glance of biting contempt.

'My father was a good judge of character and thought well of him. He would never have agreed to the betrothal if he was not of good character.'

'And you, Miss Monkton? How well do you know your betrothed?'

'I have got to know him through his letters.'

'That is hardly the same.'

'It is good enough for me.'

Charles sighed, turning away. 'Who can claim to know what moves a woman's heart? At all events,' he went on in a harder voice, looking back at her, 'your betrothed is not a fit person to wed a decently bred girl, but it is none of my business, of course. I have said my piece. I can do no more just now.'

He saw the lovely face turn white with anger, and he knew a fraction of a second before she raised her hand what she intended. His own hand shot up and he caught her wrist before she could deal the blow to his cheek. She gasped at the quickness of his reaction and to her fury he unexpectedly laughed.

'I see I have misjudged you. Perhaps you will be a good match for Colonel Winston after all.' Releasing her wrist, he turned on his heel and proceeded to walk away.

Maria watched him go, the bright colour flaming up in her cheeks. 'One more thing, sir,' she said to his retreating back. 'I heard what you said to my aunt about me cherishing a romantic and childish attachment for Colonel Winston. How dare you presume to know that?'

Charles's jaw tightened, his humour of a moment before gone. So this girl thought she could impose on him with her queenly airs. Furious with himself, more than with her, he took refuge in anger. 'So much the worse for you,' he said grimly. 'I will not mention it again. I will escort you to England and Colonel Winston, but I will not go so far as to wish you joy in your union.'

Coldly furious, Charles had no intention of exerting himself further in this matter just now. Having seen much service with the army in India and returning to England on the death of his father, when a prominent member of the Whig opposition found him about to travel to France on his mother's bequest to see how her relatives fared during these troubled times, he had asked him to secretly collect and report information on the events in Paris. Happy to oblige an old friend, Charles had agreed.

With this and other things on his mind, he'd had little time to think about the problem of Colonel Winston's bride. Having fulfilled his commitments, travelling miles out of his way to Alsace to collect Miss Monkton, he had done what he thought was right by informing her guardian of certain aspects of Colonel Winston's character. As far as he was concerned he had discharged this office and his conscience was clear. But he was encouraged, for, despite her youth, Miss Monkton clearly possessed both character and courage, and was quite capable of breaking off the engagement at the last minute if necessary.

Maria arrived at the inn at first light. She rode her favourite horse, her intention being to leave it at the inn where a groom would collect it later. She was dismounting when she caught sight of the dark forbidding figure striding towards her with the silent sureness of a wolf. This morning he seemed even taller, lean and superbly fit. In fact, if it were not for the arrogant authority stamped in his firm jawline and the cynicism in his cold eyes, Maria would have thought him breathtakingly handsome.

Looking her up at down and satisfied that she would not attract any untoward attention in her plain black woollen dress, which she had obtained from her maid with another carefully packed with other items necessary for such a long journey in her valise, he said brusquely, 'Come. It is time.'

Their departure occasioned no remark. Once in the inn yard, they were caught up in a fierce gust of wind that blew rain into their faces. Maria breathed in deeply with a sudden exhilaration. The wind smacked of freedom, of England and home, and suddenly she discovered a new meaning to her flight.

Her initial thought when Charles Osbourne had told her of his plans had been undoubtedly to go home, but now as she felt the wind on her face it came to her suddenly that there was a fierce joy in severing all ties with Chateau Feroc and France. Impulsively she threw back her head and laughed, as if she were offering herself up to be carried away by it.

Her effervescent laughter caused Charles to look at her in fascination and curiosity. 'I imagined you would be apprehensive about the journey. It will be a hard flight.'

'I don't care,' she said, still laughing. 'I love the wind. And besides, I am happy. I am going home, which is what I have dreamed about for so long.'

The rigid lines of Charles's face relaxed. 'I know. Come—wife.'

His eyes twinkled somewhat wickedly in the grey morning light. Maria looked at him sharply. 'Only for the duration of the journey to Calais,' she quipped, quick to resent his easy dismissal of her grudge against him. And yet despite her attempt to remain cool and detached, her heart beat out an uncontrollable rhythm of excitement.

'I hope you don't harbour an aversion to being alone with me for such a lengthy period,' he said, taking her hand to assist her into the coach.

'Why should I?' Maria enquired quizzically, pausing with her foot on the step to look at him. 'Unless, of course, you are a rogue at heart.'

'I may well be,' Charles acknowledged, lifting to his lips the slender fingers of his assumed wife, letting his warm, moist mouth linger on her knuckles in a slow, sensual caress.

Maria became aware of a strange quivering in the pit of her body and realised her breath was being snatched inwards when his lips came into contact with her skin. Sliding her hand from his, she lifted her skirts to step aboard and immediately felt her companion's hand beneath her elbow aiding her ascent. She settled herself on the seat while striving to control her composure.

His eyes danced teasingly up into hers, his lips curved into a smile. 'You could be in danger. You are by far the most enticing female I have seen in a long time.'

As Maria listened to the warm and mellow tone of his voice, and her gaze lit upon that handsomely chiselled visage, her eyes were drawn into the snare, and for a moment she found herself susceptible to the appeal of that wondrous smile. She glanced at him reflectively, wondering if she should read anything into his statement, and raised her brows meaningfully.

'Perhaps I should warn you that if warranted, I am not above defending myself.'

Charles had the feeling that what she said was true—and her intended slap the day before proved that. He laughed to ease her fears, while his glowing eyes delved into hers. 'I am sure you could do so admirably, so be confident of my good intentions. I shall take care to treat you as I would a wife—with the utmost respect.'

Maria cast an apprehensive eye toward him as he climbed in, but much to her relief, he settled across from her. As he caught her gaze, he grinned.

'I fear the nearness of you would completely destroy my good intentions. It is safer if I sit here.'

Maria relaxed back in the seat. She could only hope that his restraint would continue and her resistance would not be tested.

The carriage was discreet, with no outward signs of wealth beyond a pair of post horses. The driver, Pierre Lamont, who knew them by their assumed names and had been paid an enormous amount of money to drive them to Calais, clicked his tongue as the whip curved gracefully through the air and the conveyance lurched into motion. When they had passed from the cobbled inn yard, the long journey back to Gravely had begun.

Maria had left Chateau Feroc without regret. However, despite the cold reserve with which her aunt and Constance had always treated her, she did feel a slight pang of remorse. Even at the last minute her aunt had refused to give way to sentiment and embrace her, but Maria was surprised to see how much distress Constance displayed.

Constance did embrace her, her eyes in her white face

wide and full of tears. Maria felt her tremble as she clung to her. It was only then that she realised how afraid her cousin was of remaining at the chateau and that she secretly wished she was leaving for England with Maria.

In that one brief moment Maria saw Constance not as the self-obsessed cousin, whose sole interest lay in her pretty face and her ability to attract the sons of the nobility as well-to-do as themselves, but as a young girl frightened for her life. Maria had held her, surprised to feel her own throat constrict with pain and tears brimming in her eyes.

'I wish I was going with you,' Constance had whispered earnestly, 'but Mama won't hear of it.'

'Then defy your mother, Constance.'

'I cannot. I could not go unless she came too.'

'I wish you were coming with me,' Maria had replied with heartfelt understanding. 'If you can persuade her and you manage to get out of France, you must come to me at Gravely. Do you promise?'

With tears running down her cheeks, Constance had clung fiercely to Maria for a moment longer, and then, tearing herself free, she fled into the house.

Maria had turned away, too afraid to think of her cousin's fate.

As the driver urged the horses into a faster pace, Maria braced herself against the sway of the carriage. Glancing across at her companion, she was suddenly reminded that she was going to be completely alone with a man for the first time in her life, a man who was as handsome of face as he was of physique—and with a boldness that gave her a sense of unease.

She knew nothing about him, and what, she asked herself, was he doing in France at this present time? She could not exactly understand what she was doing with him and why this stranger should have interested himself in her affairs to the extent of coming halfway across France to find her. Had he some ulterior motive? He might even be a spy—British or French, she had no way of knowing, since she knew nothing about spying.

During the journey perhaps she could turn the conversation to draw him out, to get him to talk about himself. In some strange way he both attracted and intrigued her. She looked into his light blue eyes and the expression there made her heart trip and beat a little faster. His long compassionate mouth curled in a slight smile.

'We have a long way to go,' he said, when they were settled, 'so don't make this harder on yourself than it need be. You're stuck with me for a few days so you may as well accept it. Shall we declare a truce for the duration of the journey?'

'Yes, I think we must,' she concurred.

'We shall also forgo formality and use our given names. It is for the best, you understand.'

'Of course,' she replied, removing her bonnet and dropping it on the seat beside her.

'I'm sorry the Countess and her daughter would not come with us.'

Maria felt a small tremor of misgiving. 'You fear the chateau will be attacked?'

He nodded gravely. 'It is only a matter of time. Your aunt is a stubborn woman.'

'Yes, yes, she is. I sincerely hope they come to no

harm.' Maria stared out of the window at the passing scenery. It was all familiar, but soon they would pass into fresh territory that was alien to her. In the grey light it looked dismal. 'I hate France,' she said in a small voice, her expression subdued.

'I sense you were not happy at Chateau Feroc?'

'I do not mean to sound ungrateful or uncharitable but, indeed, I could not wait to leave. It is a cold, joyless place with no laughter.'

'And you like to laugh, do you?'

'Yes, although I have been at the chateau so long I fear I might have forgotten how to.' Inexplicably the laughter rekindled in her eyes and she laughed again, just for the sheer joy of laughing, and when she looked into her companion's eyes, she experienced a sudden relief of tension.

Charles smiled a little crookedly, thinking her courageous and fresh and very lovely. Despite her youth and inexperience she was no vapourish miss who would swoon at the first hurdle. 'You should laugh more often,' he murmured softly. 'It suits you.'

She sighed. 'There is nothing to feel happy about in France just now. What will happen, do you think? You have been to Paris?' He nodded. 'Was it very bad?'

'I saw much blood shed by the mob. I have had to ask myself, where has the dignity, the self-control, the resolution gone in the France of today? But the people have their grievances—it would seem with some justification. The rise in prices and rents, as well as the taxes they have to pay, are increasingly burdensome. It is only right and natural that they want change.

'I agree absolutely and the demands of the people

must be listened to and acted on. Privilege must be abolished, and all men should be taxed equally, according to their wealth.'

Maria looked at him with interest. 'Anything else?'

'These and a hundred others.'

'You speak like a politician. Is that what you are?'

A cynical smile curved his lips. 'No.'

'Then what do you do?'

'Do I have to do anything?'

'I suspect you are not the sort of man who would be content to idle his days away doing nothing.' She looked out of the window. 'You have to do something.'

'I dabble.'

'In what?'

He shrugged nonchalantly. 'This and that.'

She took her eyes off the passing scenery and regarded him intently. 'You mean you're a businessman?'

He grinned. 'You might say that.'

'And is your business respectable?'

Her question brought a humorous gleam to his eyes, and a tantalising smile played on his lips. 'Perfectly respectable,' he declared, 'but if I were to tell you more of what I do, we will have nothing to talk about, and we have a long way to go.'

'You may not consider the question important, but it is to me. My life is very important to me. Since I have entrusted it to someone I know nothing about, it is perfectly natural that I want to know everything there is to know about you.'

He stared at her, one black brow raised interrogatively. There was a direct challenge in his eyes, which she found most disturbing.

'Everything?' he enquired silkily, and Maria could sense the sleeping animal within him begin to stir.

Her thoughts were thrown into chaos, for she had not expected such an uncompromising response to her hasty remark. She glanced away, trying to regain her composure, and then looked up to meet his eyes.

'I do not wish to offend you, but I do not know you, so how do I know I can trust you?'

'What exactly do you fear?' he asked. 'That I am not equal to the task of escorting you to England?'

'I am naturally apprehensive. If you were in my place, wouldn't you want some indication of your good faith? Since when did businessmen risk their lives by coming to a country torn by strife?'

'When they have family they are concerned about.'

She looked at him with interest, her green eyes wide and questioning, her lips parted slightly in surprise. 'Your family live in France?'

'In the south—the Côte d'Azure. My mother is French.'

'I see. So that explains why you speak French like a native. I did wonder. Did you manage to see your family?'

'Yes.'

'And are they all right?'

'When I left them they were in perfect health.' His eyes darkened. 'Whether they will remain so remains to be seen.'

'Why? What are you afraid of?'

'They are connected to the nobility. That connection could well bring about their death—and my own. Anyone found assisting suspected royalists will be ruthlessly condemned. The life of a noble is not worth a candle in France. I believe that every noble family and many of the richer bourgeois will suffer unless they flee the country.'

'And your mother?'

'She is safe in England, thank God.'

'Do you have siblings living in France?'

He shook his head. 'I have two sisters, both of them happily married in England.'

'And—do you have a wife waiting for you in England?'

He laughed easily and dusted the knee of his breeches. 'No. And were you always so inquisitive about others, or is it just me?'

She smiled and gave him a coy look. 'I'm sorry. I suppose it must seem like that to you. It's just that it's so long since I talked to another English person, apart from my aunt and Constance, that I forget my manners.'

Charles thought that Maria Monkton had a truly breathtaking smile. It glowed in her eyes and lit up her entire face, transforming what was already a pretty face into one that was captivating. He was intrigued, but he did not let it show in his face, for as much as he would like to taste and relish at first hand what was before his eyes, to throw caution to the four winds and dally to his heart's content, he had to consider at what cost he'd be doing so.

'Please don't apologise. I am not offended.' His chuckle sounded low and deep. 'Our journey to England will be long and arduous, but I can see that with you I will never be bored.'

She met his eyes. 'Like you said, we have a long way to go. Things change. Must we speak French all the time?'

'Yes. The less attention we attract to ourselves the safer it will be. When we are within earshot of the driver if we address each other as Charles and Maria he will be none the wiser.'

Maria felt comfortable with Pierre. There was a look about his square face that inspired trust while the steady gaze of his blue eyes compelled honesty. 'I think he can be trusted. What do you think?'

He shrugged. 'Who can one trust nowadays? One can never be sure. He seems trustworthy enough and was glad of the work. The coach belongs to him and I have paid him a handsome sum—with the promise of more if he gets us to Calais safely.'

'I would like to thank you for helping me, Charles. Is there a reason for this—apart from our fathers being friends?'

'I have reason to be beholden to Sir Edward.'

'Oh?'

'He saved my life—and my mother's. It was during the monsoon season, when my mother and I were going to join my father in Bengal. We were crossing a fast-flowing river when our boat went out of control—several people perished. From the shore your father saw what was happening and commandeered a boat to come to our aid. Not once while he was helping us to safety did he consider the possibility that he might lose his life. I fell into the river and was in danger of being washed away when he jumped in after me. Somehow he managed to get me back on board.' His features softened with remembrance. 'I owe him my life. You should be proud of him.'

'I am, and I realise how you must have felt honour bound to come to my rescue.'

'Something like that. I realised it was the least I could

do for Sir Edward—to see his daughter safely out of France. It is my way of saying thank you to an exceedingly brave man.'

'Yes, I can understand that. Thank you for telling me.'

'My pleasure.'

A familiar, slow smile played on his lips and he fell silent. He was relaxed, and there was no mistaking the provocative way in which his gaze lingered on her eyes, her hair and her soft lips.

Feeling his warmly glowing eyes devouring her as if he were strongly tempted to do more than just stare, a sudden flush mounted Maria's cheeks, and she said abruptly, 'I am sorry about—almost slapping you. It was unforgivable of me and I should not have done it.'

'But entirely understandable,' Charles answered gravely. 'Think nothing of it. It is forgotten.'

Maria waited, expecting him to apologise for the things he had said about Colonel Winston, confident that now she had given him an opening to do so, he would hopefully retract them, but he remained silent.

Beneath the shadow of her long lashes her eyes passed slowly over her companion. His broad shoulders filled his dark blue coat, and the grey breeches were close-fitting to display a superb length of firmly muscled limbs. It was obvious at a mere glance that he was an arrogant man, bold and self-assured, and much to her aggravation, she realised he would be the standard by which she would eventually measure her betrothed.

The clouds were suddenly swept away and the sun rose, bathing Maria's face in its soft, golden light. She knew Charles continued to watch her, for she felt the heat of his gaze more firmly than the warmth of the sun.

The countryside along the way failed to hold her interest, for his close presence wiped everything else from her mind. His gaze was persistent and touched her warmly. A smile was in his eyes and on his lips.

There was that quality about her companion that made her wonder if he were something more than what he appeared. It was as if his eyes could penetrate her flesh, and she wondered if she would ever cease to feel the unsettling vulnerability and wariness she experienced in his presence.

There was one time when the road was choked with peasants and vagabonds and carts and horses, when they had no choice but to go with the flow of things. At times the people were openly aggressive. Danger was in the air. Maria was a realist, knowing that they might be apprehended at any time. No one was safe. It was a relief to know that Charles was armed, with a plentiful supply of ammunition.

Thankfully they were offered no violence and their carriage went unmolested.

Halfway through the journey of their first day on the road, the carriage clattered and rocked over cobbles and Maria, glad of the opportunity to stretch her legs, descended stiffly to pace around the coaching-house yard while the steaming horses who had brought them so far were unharnessed and a fresh pair put to.

Getting back inside the carriage, she had to wait for Charles, who was in conversation with Pierre. Leaning a little closer to the window to study her companion when he was unaware that he was being observed, she gazed at him, her green eyes becoming darker, her soft skin a little pinker, her lips parting as she breathed faster, caught up in a sensation she herself did not understand.

As though somehow he had sensed her curiosity, he suddenly turned. And there was something about the way he looked at her that made Maria shudder before snatching her gaze away from him. He had no right to look at her in that way—that openly bold and danger-ous way. No right at all. There was something about him that made her feel odd and nervous and excited, tingling with the rush of unfamiliar sensations invading her body. That feeling made her angry with herself and even more angry with him for being the cause of it.

Then they were off again.

It was dark when they reached the inn where they were to stay for the night. Pierre followed his passen-gers inside, carrying the valises. The inn was serviceable and clean, the air permeated with a delicious smell of food. The public room was full of people, mostly men drinking and discussing the worsening state of affairs in Paris. Their entrance attracted looks—secretive, sideways looks, suspicious, unreadable minds behind expressionless faces. Maria shuddered, having no desire to come into contact with any of them. Charles managed to engage two rooms.

'I think I'll go straight to my room,' Maria said. 'I would like my meal sent up if it can be arranged. I've had nothing to eat since midday and I am dying of hunger.'

Charles smiled at this youthful appetite. 'I'll see to it. I'll stay and have supper with Pierre. Go on up. The maid will show you to your room. I'll see you later.'

As she headed for the stairs an untidily garbed

peasant who had imbibed too much rose from a table and came to stand in front of her as she followed the maid, his smile a lecherous leer. He swept her a low, clumsy bow.

'*Mademoiselle,*' he declared. 'And who do you belong to, pretty wench?'

'*Madame,*' she corrected him coldly, remembering her part and looking away disdainfully.

The man sought to move. His limbs refused to respond as they should and he teetered precariously on one leg before toppling on to a nearby stool. He raised his gaze, but, seeing only the tall, powerful and glowering figure of the young woman's husband where the daintier form had been a moment before, he blinked, his eyes owl-like.

The gentleman stood there, smiling his icy smile. 'The pretty wench belongs to me. She is my wife, so if you know what is good for you you won't follow her. Understand?'

The man glowered in sullen resentment and looked away. Charles watched Maria climb the stairs, and only then did he turn away to seek out the driver of their coach.

After eating her meal, Maria sat before the bright fire, her thoughts flitting between her aunt and Constance at Chateau Feroc and her home in England. Gradually the night grew quiet. After preparing for bed she slipped between the sheets, thinking it would take her a long time to fall asleep, but after the fatigues of the long journey, added to the comfort of the soft warm bed, she was plunged at once into a deep sleep.

* * *

When she woke up in the darkness, it took her a while to realise where she was. She lay listening to the wind rattling against the window panes, but underlying this she heard the sound of gentle breathing. Troubled and uneasy, she lay quite still. The sound came again—a low snore. Fear stirred inside her. There was someone in the room with her. She sat up swiftly, rendered motionless by the scene that confronted her, for in the light of the still-glowing embers of the fire she was horrified to see her escort stretched out in a chair, his legs propped on the chair opposite.

'Oh!' she gasped, deeply shocked by the indignity of this discovery.

She had not taken in the sense of his last remark to her when they had parted—that he would see her later, and in the confusion of their arrival, she had forgotten that people who were married shared the same room—and the same bed. She realised that although their marriage was a sham, to allay any awkward questions from suspicious travellers, it was imperative for them to keep up appearances—but he didn't have to take it so literally—did he?

Quite suddenly the numbness left her and gave way to sheer horror and panic. Scrambling out of bed, she crossed towards him. He had removed his boots and was attired in his breeches and white lawn shirt. She stared at him with disbelieving eyes, not knowing what to think or how to feel. His dark hair was ruffled and a stray lock fell across his brow, and the hard planes of his face were softer in sleep. Without the cynical twist to his mouth, he looked vulnerable and incredibly youthful, and she noticed how outrageously thick his eyelashes were.

For a man who was involved in the dangerous business of reaching Calais unmolested, each road they took beset with dangers, he seemed offensively at ease.

Sensing her closeness, he was suddenly alert and his eyes snapped open. As he met her hostile gaze, his brows arched in surprise, and a slow appreciative smile spread across his lips.

It was a disconcertingly pleasant smile, and the fact that even through a haze of social embarrassment she could recognise it as such, increased rather than diminished her hostility.

'You cannot be aware of the impropriety of such a visit to a lady's bedchamber at this hour, or you would scarcely have ventured to knock on my door, let alone admit yourself.'

'When I came in you looked in a state of delicious comfort and I certainly had no intention of disturbing you.'

Maria flushed. She didn't like to think he might have stood watching her as she slept. Not knowing how to deal with a situation of this nature, she tried to distract herself from her inner turmoil and avoid his gaze that seemed to burn into her by watching the occasional spark erupt from the glowing embers in the hearth, but she found it impossible when every fibre of her being was on full alert to Charles's presence.

When she saw his eyes sweep over her body, even though her nightdress was concealing, she felt her modesty, so long intact, was being invaded by this man's gaze, this stranger, who was beginning to alarm her awkward, unawakened senses.

Folding her arms across her chest in an attempt to

protect her modesty and fervently wishing she had a shawl or something else to throw over her nightdress, she glowered at him.

'Unfortunately I have nothing with which to cover myself.'

Charles chuckled softly. Even in these extreme circumstances she felt it unspeakably shocking that he should see her like this. If she knew how long he had ogled her during her sleep, she'd realise it was far too late for her to try to salvage her modesty.

'That's a bit like closing the stable door after the horse has bolted. I assure you, it would not wipe from my mind the loveliness I savoured when I came in.'

Maria gasped, her cheeks burning. 'Have you no shame? How long did you stand there looking at me?'

It took an Herculean effort for Charles to drag his gaze away from the shape of her body outlined beneath her nightdress in order to meet her gaze. 'Long enough to know that the sight of you in your bed was sufficient to waken the slumbering dragon in me that I fear will not be easily appeased.'

In spite of his unrelenting stare, his glowing eyes devouring her as if he were strongly tempted to do more than just stare, Maria was distracted and felt a *frisson* of alarm when she saw he had his long fingers clasped round the butt of a pistol by his side. Her throat went dry. 'Do you make a habit of sleeping with a pistol?'

'Only when I deem it necessary.'

'And is it—tonight, I mean?'

'I think so. I have no wish to alarm you, but it's as well to be on our guard at all times.' He placed the pistol on the table beside him.

'Charles, you must leave my room. You cannot sleep here. Not with me. It—it's just not right.'

He sat up, dropping his feet to the floor and pushing his hair back from his face. 'My apologies, Maria. I did not mean to startle you. As I said, you were soundly asleep when I came in. I did not want to wake you.'

'Well, you should have done,' she flared, unconscious of the vision she presented as her hair tumbled about her shoulders in loose array. 'How dare you take such liberties? You will certainly destroy my reputation if you continue to indulge in such foolery.'

A slow smile touched his lips. 'It is not foolery— anything but. If you could see past that pretty little nose of yours, you would realise I am only trying to help you. Do not forget that I am here to protect you.'

Mutiny still showed in her countenance. 'When we embarked on the journey I confess that I did not give much thought to what the sleeping arrangements would be while we are en route. Indeed, the matter never entered my head. My aunt would be aghast if she knew we were sharing a room.'

'I dare say she would be, and yet I made her aware you would be travelling as my wife. Your reputation is the last thing you should be worrying about right now. I believe,' he began solicitously, the humour in his voice disguised by a disapproving frown, 'that you are some- how trying my ability to protect you.'

'I am not—and I am indeed grateful—but… Oh,' she gasped in frustration, 'why could you not have made me your sister—or—or your cousin—anything— anything but your wife?'

'Because as my wife you have my complete protection at all times. Of what use would I be to you if that oaf who accosted you earlier should take it into his sodden head to seek feminine company and remember you? From what I recall of some of the overpainted, disreputable women I saw in the public room when we arrived, you are by far the most desirable, so who could blame him? You are a rare prize for any man, Maria.'

His gaze never wavered from hers, but when it dipped downwards, Maria saw the light that flared in his eyes, again making her conscious of her lack of modesty. When she glanced quickly down, her fears were realised when she saw the soft, rosy peaks of her bosom straining against the delicate fabric of her nightdress. Raising her head, she met his gaze. Her heart seemed to leap in her throat in a ridiculous, choking way, and she chided herself for being so foolish as to believe he liked what he saw.

'There is a lock on the door. He would not get in.'

'He would find a way if he wanted to.' The sight of her flushed cheeks and the way she had wrapped her arms around her waist in an unconscious act of self-protection brought home to Charles for the first time the fact that his proceedings might be considered shockingly unorthodox to a young woman who had been protected from the opposite sex and the ways of the world for the whole of her life.

Getting up, he towered over her, looking down at her apprehensive, upturned face. 'You have led a sheltered life under the harsh eye of your aunt, who has rigid rules when it comes to raising young ladies of breeding and class. May I give you a word of advice, Maria? Common sense will always stand you in better stead than a slavish adherence to conventions.'

The shamed colour faded from Maria's cheeks and the hostility in her eyes was replaced by interest. 'If common sense is preferable to convention, then it is a point of view in complete opposition to the teachings of my aunt and the many governesses who had charge of Constance and me over the years.'

'It is my point of view, and I know I'm right—otherwise what do you think would have happened had I not apprehended your drunken admirer when I saw him come up the stairs and approach your door?'

She stared at him in horror, her hand going to her throat. 'He wasn't! You mean he actually intended to come in here? But—no man would dare to come to a lady's room, knowing they might encounter an irate husband.'

Charles nodded gravely. 'He most certainly was—until I—persuaded him to think again.'

'And the pistol? Is that part of the remedy to use against that—that oaf?'

'If need be—which I doubt.' His eyes glinted wickedly. 'The man is no longer in any fit state to climb the stairs, let alone molest a young woman in her bed.'

Her eyes widened with alarm. 'Why, what have you done to him?'

'Let's just say that at this time he will be sleeping like the proverbial babe.' He looked at her through narrowed eyes, his firm lips curving in a gently mocking smile. 'You left your door unlocked, otherwise how do you think I got in?'

'But you should not be here.'

A crooked smile accompanied his reply. 'And where would you have me go—to sleep outside your door, perhaps, which would be considered by some to be most odd and raise more than a few eyebrows? And if you're thinking of your aunt,' he said, his voice a conspiratorial whisper, as if he expected the formidable woman to emerge at any minute, 'don't. She need never know.'

On consideration, Maria had to admit that he was right. 'I never had a very high opinion of my aunt. It never occurred to me to question her authority and her rightness on her view on behaviour and etiquette. It just wasn't done.'

'I understand that, and in an ideal France, as it is in England, it isn't the practice for young ladies to question their elders. But these are not ideal times—far from it. People are finding themselves in all kinds of different, often violent, situations. No doubt your aunt will look upon what I consider to be eminently sensible proceedings as entirely scandalous.'

'And she would have regarded me, as the recipient of them, as something close to a fallen woman. With her inflexible code of what is right, when placed in the balance against the strict preservation of the social conventions, she would rather you had abandoned me to the advances of that oaf downstairs than for you to spend the entire night alone with me in this room.'

'So you do accept that my point of view is infinitely more practical than your aunt's?'

A smile broke out on her lips that brought a dimple in the gentle curve of her cheek. She nodded. 'Yes,' she whispered, conscious of a sudden sense of being released from a kind of bondage, as though some mental steel thread that still tethered her to the Chateau Feroc had snapped.

Watching her, it was the first time that Charles had seen her really smile since she had left the chateau. But he did not return it. Gazing down at her, she seemed older somehow. Her face was gently flushed, and the shadows under the wide dark eyes made them appear even larger. The whiteness of her modest nightdress was stark against the looseness of her hair that tumbled about her in rippling profusion, glinting with blue lights in the dimly lit room.

Charles had a sudden and disturbing vision of her betrothed, of the degenerate *roué*, Henry Winston, of his moist fingers twining themselves in that soft, sweetly scented hair, sliding over her bare shoulders, his mouth devouring those soft lips. He turned from her abruptly, his head slightly bowed as he gazed into the hearth.

'Go back to bed. We have a long day ahead of us tomorrow and it is imperative that you get your rest. You have my word that you are quite safe,' he assured her.

'But what about you?' she asked hesitantly. 'It will be a long day for you also. You cannot be comfortable sleeping in that chair.'

He turned and looked at her, smiling crookedly, a roguish gleam in his eyes. 'Where else would you have me sleep? With you, perhaps?'

Charles searched her eyes for barely an instant before the dark orbs went chasing off in another direction. Smiling, he leaned forwards to speak over her ear. 'The idea of sharing your bed with me doesn't frighten you, does it, Maria?'

'No, of course not,' she denied in a frantic rush, stepping back in an effort to put some distance between them. Her retreat was necessary to cool her burning cheeks and to ease to some small degree the unruly pace of her heart. 'But that is out of the question.'

'It needn't be.'

'Forgive me for ever thinking you were a gentleman,' she derided. 'So far you've done much to prove yourself as big a *roué* as any I have met—in addition to your impertinence in ogling me and suggesting I appease your—your dragon.'

Charles curbed a grin. 'Worry not, Maria, you are quite safe. But if you should have a change of heart and take pity on me, I can promise you such delight as you've never before imagined.'

Maria was shocked to the core that he should be speaking to her like this. 'Will you please stop?' she flared irately, lifting her eyes to his face in time to see his eyes dip into her breasts. 'You seem to forget that I am promised to another. You behave as if you really are my husband.'

Charles chuckled softly. 'Who knows what will come from our association? I may just decide to forget that I am a gentleman, to forget about Henry Winston, and behave as your husband just to show you what delights can be had between a married couple.'

'Except that we're not. You engaged two rooms, as I recall.'

'I did—one for Pierre.' Tilting his head to one side, half frowning, half smiling, he peered at her. 'His room is big enough to accommodate me if you would like me to leave you to sleep alone. Is that what you want?'

She bit her lip. The moment to tell him to go and leave her in peace was at hand, yet for the life of her she could not do so, for the fear of that drunken oaf coming to her room remained.

'No. I would like you to stay.' Without a word Maria

went to the bed and removed one of the blankets and placed it on the chair.

'You might as well be warm while you sleep. Thank you, Charles,' she said stiffly. 'You are being very good to me—when you aren't trying to seduce me.' Why she wasn't outraged by his audacity was a mystery beyond her comprehension just then.

He looked at her, the firelight flickering in his light blue eyes. 'Why wouldn't I be? Our fathers were friends, were they not? There is no reason why we should be any different.'

'No, of course not.'

Standing in such close proximity, Maria thought Charles looked very appealing—and very handsome. A warm trickle of an unfamiliar sensation ran through her body, a stirring she had never felt before. Her heart quickened within her breast, and her blood seemed to melt, turning her insides into a river of heat. She shivered. Charles noticed.

'Are you cold?' he asked, a crease of worry between his brows.

He reached to clasp her hand, his fingers very strong and sure. There was a faint white scar on the back of his hand, and Maria wondered how he had come by it. At the same time she realised she knew absolutely nothing about him. How could she? And maybe it wasn't safe to know.

She withdrew her hand and turned her thoughts away from this new, dangerous direction. She felt a sudden stillness envelop them. Vividly aware of his closeness, the spicy scent of him, she was overwhelmingly conscious of him—and confused. She was slightly irritated by the way in which he skilfully cut through her superior attitude, the artificial posturing she often assumed to save herself from him. She knew she asked for it, but the magnetic attraction still remained beneath all the irritation.

'I'm not cold,' she said, her voice sharp.

'Then go to bed.'

She did as she was bade and crawled back into the warm softness, allowing sleep to overtake her and her troubled thoughts.

Charles sat staring into the shifting, glowing lights in the dying embers of the fire, his mind wandering back to his young charge between the covers. A picture of a tumbling mass of blue-black hair swirled through his thoughts, of dark fringed green eyes that glowed with their own light, the colour of their depths forever changing like richly hued jewels. A nose was added to the lovely vision, slim and pert and a feature of perfection. A pair of lips floated into mind, gently curving and expressive; in his recollection he remembered the moment when they had left the inn to begin their journey and her lips had turned upwards and parted with laughter.

Let it be for ever so, he mused, but he knew it would not.

Thinking of the long and arduous journey ahead of them, he hoped they would reach their destination without mishap. Maria was depending on him, he reminded himself. She trusted him to get her to England safely. He owed it to her not to fail.

Chapter Three

The following morning when Maria awoke, the sight of Charles standing half-naked at the wash stand, his shirt thrown over a chair and his trousers unfastened at the waist and falling slightly low over his hips, was almost too much for her virgin eyes to bear. The vision of his tall, lithe, wide-shouldered form with sculpted muscles as he hummed a military march, bathed in the golden glow of early morning sunlight, would be for ever branded on her brain.

Shoving back the covers, she knelt on the bed and stared at him. Never having seen the naked male form before, she stared in virginal innocence, thinking he was one of those rare men who looked like a Roman statue. Up close, in broad daylight, his maleness, the power, the strength of his body, seemed even more pronounced. Armed with shaving dish and razor, a towel round his neck and lather on his face, he continued to shave.

Curious, never having seen a man shave before, as she watched him she felt an unfamiliar sensation—a melting sensation that somehow made breathing difficult and made her heart race. He did seem to have a way with him, and she could not fault any woman for falling under his spell, for she found to her amazement that her heart was not so detached as she might have imagined it to be. As handsome as he was, she could imagine that he had grown quite adept at swaying young women from the paths their parents had urged them to follow.

Catching her eyes in the mirror, Charles paused and grinned, his eyes glowing in the warm light of day. 'So, you are awake at last. Good morning, Maria.'

'Good morning,' she murmured, trying to shake off the effects of his winning smile. Unexpectedly she found herself the victim of an absurd attack of shyness.

Charles saw that her face was a mirror of lovely confusion, and, taking pity on her innocence, he fastened his trousers and quietly said, 'Have you never seen a man shave before?'

'No—of course I haven't—not even my father, and Henry—' She stopped what she had been about to say, that she had been very young when her betrothed had gone away and it had never entered her head to find out how and when he shaved.

Charles paused to look at her, the razor in mid-air. 'Ah, your betrothed. I wondered how long it would be before you brought him into the conversation. How did you manage to allow yourself to become betrothed to Colonel Winston?'

His remark seemed to discomfit her and, as if stalling for time in which to compose an answer, she wriggled into a sitting position and drew her long legs up against her chest and wrapped her arms around them, perching her chin upon her knees and raising her brilliant green eyes to his in the mirror. Sitting like that, Charles thought she looked incredibly desirable—a delightful nymph with long curly hair. Her pose allowed him a view of small feet and trim ankles. From there, his gaze ranged upwards with equal admiration.

'Was that question too difficult for you?' he asked, his eyes never leaving hers.

'It was—impertinent.'

Her reply was accompanied by such a well-bred, reproving look that Charles chuckled in spite of himself. 'You're quite right,' he admitted, grinning at the delightful young woman who dared to lecture him on his shortcomings. 'But I would still like to know the answer.'

'And I do not choose to discuss it. It is most unchivalrous of you to badger me about matters which are of a most private nature—not to mention excruciatingly embarrassing.'

'Embarrassing for whom?' Charles asked, ignoring her jibe. 'For you, or for Winston?'

'*I* am embarrassed—to find myself in such intimate surroundings with a near-naked man. I dread to think what Henry would have to say—not forgetting my aunt.'

Charles's sudden grin was wicked. 'I can well imagine what a dreadful experience this must be for you, Maria. But fear not. It will be our secret. Colonel Winston will never know.'

'I hope not. Look at me. I'm not even dressed.'

'I have been looking—all night,' he averred with a broad grin, and was forced to marvel at how comfortable he felt with her in such an intimate situation. Two days ago, he would never have imagined such simple, yet totally gratifying pleasure.

Maria's face flamed. Beneath the consuming heat of his eyes as they ranged slowly over her, she felt thoroughly divested of what few garments she had on. The sight of those bare shoulders and broad, furred chest made her feel most uneasy. Unable to continue watching him perform such an intimate task, totally shaken and thoroughly amazed by what she was experiencing, to hide the crimson tide that swept over her face, clutching her precarious modesty close, she climbed out of bed and turned away. No longer facing him, she missed the smile that widened his lips.

Charles could not resist a glance over his shoulder. Maria stood facing the door, resolutely refusing to look at him. His eyes coursed down the fine curves of her stiff back, from the slim erect column of her neck to the beckoning roundness of her hips. Putting down his razor and wiping the soap from his face with the towel, he turned towards her.

'I'm almost done. As soon as I've finished my ablutions I shall give you your privacy to perform your own and to dress. We'll leave as soon as we've had breakfast.'

When Maria turned to face him he was already thrusting his arms into his shirt. His smiling eyes captured hers and held them prisoner, until she felt a warmth suffuse her cheeks. Never had she felt such burning heat or such quickening fires in the depths of her being as she did just then.

Moving to stand close to her, noticing a thick coil of hair resting in the curve of her neck, Charles stretched out a hand and rubbed the tress admiringly between his thumb and forefinger. 'You have lovely hair, Maria,' he murmured huskily.

Maria realised her insides were melting as they were prone to do when he touched her in some manner. His eyes shifted from beneath a fringe of jet lashes to meet hers, which were softly shining, and for what seemed an eternity in the heartbeat of a moment, their gazes gently mingled. If ever she had wondered what it would be like to be drawn out of herself, to be absorbed into someone else, she found herself experiencing that now. Never had she known such intense, consuming emotions that filled her very being with what she could only assume was desire.

Lowering her gaze from his openly admiring regard, she was strangely thrilled by it, but also confused. He should not be looking at her like this, not when she was betrothed to the man who trusted him implicitly to behave with honour and decency to his future wife.

'I would like to get dressed now,' she whispered, aware of the slight tremor in her voice.

For a moment Charles stood on the threshold of something life changing as he struggled with an overwhelming desire to toss her on to the bed and make love to her. As much as he yearned to caress her silken flesh and make her groan with longing, he knew it would be a dastardly thing to do in the light of her being betrothed to another and that she had placed her trust in him.

Yet she seemed so vulnerable, so trusting, so willing…

It might have been the hardest thing he had ever done, but he drew back, denying himself the solace he craved. 'Do you have any idea what a temptation you have been to me throughout this long night, Maria? I want to touch you, but I shall exert every measure of restraint I am capable of rallying in an effort to quell the instincts of desire that goad me. I must leave. Get dressed.'

Looking embarrassed, Maria hurriedly gathered her clothes and slipped behind the screen. Charles had gone when she emerged fully dressed. She was relieved, for it gave her a moment to gather her scattered wits. Were he to contrive such assaults on her senses, it might well mean the collapse of her resistance and her ultimate downfall. She tried to feel abused and angered, but thinking of the feelings he had stirred inside her, she felt something more akin to—what?

It was nothing but curiosity, she vowed. She had merely had a taste of something she wanted to taste more fully. It was nothing but what any woman would want, and in her state of undress she would seriously test that rogue's ardour. There had been no contact between them—only their eyes, which had been a simple contact, but the memory of it lingered far too long for her to be able to discount its effect on her.

Frustrated, she swilled her face with cold water. What manner of man was Charles Osbourne, who had crept into her mind and taken root? She was beginning to think he had entered her life with the express purpose of stealing her heart and perhaps even her soul.

Going in search of him, at the bottom of the stairs she paused, experiencing a feeling of alarm on seeing the man who had accosted her on her arrival going outside. Sober now, he threw her a sullen look, but made no attempt to approach her. The cut on his lip and blackened eye told its own story—Charles had obviously fought well in defence of his assumed wife's honour.

* * *

Charles was waiting for her, his expression impassive, and yet there was a knowing gleam in his eyes when they settled on her that made Maria avert her gaze. There were others in the room eating breakfast before setting off on their journey.

As Maria did ample justice to her breakfast, she only half listened to the conversation around her. When she heard how a chateau, the home of an eminent nobleman, had been burned to the ground just yesterday in the Ardennes, she stopped eating and raised her head.

Knowing precisely what thoughts were going through her head, Charles shot her a warning look, his eyes conveying to her the danger of reacting too much to this news.

'Did you hear what they said?' she said softly, her face stricken. 'I know the chateau they speak of. It is not far from Chateau Feroc. We often went there—such a lovely family. It can't be true! I won't believe it!'

Alarmed that her sudden distress would draw attention to them, Charles rose abruptly. 'Come, the carriage is waiting. Finished eating? I think we should leave immediately. I know what happened at the chateau. Such things are happening all over France.' Placing his hand on her elbow, he steered her outside to the waiting carriage.

'But—but what about my aunt—and Constance?' she asked, having to run to keep up with his long strides. 'What are we to do?' She was churning inside, her mind spilling with horrible thoughts.

'There is nothing we can do,' he told her briskly, handing her valise to Pierre to secure to the coach and assisting Maria inside. Sitting across from her, he said, 'I warned the Countess this could happen. I urged her to leave.'

'But what will happen to them?' Maria's eyes searched his, and for a terrible stabbing moment she knew a fear so strong it seemed to take the breath from her body. She strove hard to curtail it. 'How could I have left them? I should have stayed. Everyone has been talking about what was happening, but I didn't really know how bad things were.' She leaned forwards and gripped Charles's arm with her hand. 'Charles, we have to go back. We must.'

Astounded by her totally unreasonable request, Charles looked at her. She really was ignorant of what was happening in France. She really had been contained in some kind of bubble at the chateau, living in some kind of dream world, while chaos went on all around her.

There was a brooding, hopeless expression in his eyes. 'We cannot go back. It has to be faced.'

She stared at him, tense and white faced. People were milling about in the yard as the carriage began to move, but she did not see them. She said in a hard, breathless voice that she fought to control, willing him to comply to her wishes, 'Please, Charles. It is not much to ask.' She could not endure it and she could not bear to think about it. 'I have to find out if she is all right—help her if need be.'

'Stop it,' Charles said curtly, averting his gaze as they took to the road. 'You don't know what you are asking. It isn't as easy as that. There is nothing that can be done beyond what I have already done. We go on to Calais.'

She snatched her hand away. 'You mean you *won't* do anything? That's what you're saying.'

He turned his head and looked at the white face beside him. Her eyes were no longer hard, but wide and imploring, and there was pure panic in her voice. The change in that face was like a knife in Charles's heart. After a moment, he said, 'No. I'm sorry.'

She did not look at him and her own hurt made her desire to hurt him also. 'No, you're not. You don't care—and why should I expect you to? You don't know them. They mean nothing to you. You don't understand,' she whispered numbly.

'Oh, yes, I do,' he hissed fiercely, the frustration of his inadequacy to do anything to help her aunt and cousin increasing his anger. 'I understand only too well. You did not understand the dangers that threatened you all at Chateau Feroc, and now you do you are perfectly prepared to jeopardise your chances of escaping the troubles, and risk both our lives into the bargain, just so that you can do what? If the chateau has not been attacked, then nothing will have changed. Your aunt will be as indomitable and awkward as ever, so our return will achieve nothing.'

'At least I will know.'

'Know? Know what, Maria? When I went to the Chateau Feroc to see the Countess I had just come from Paris. I had seen with my own eyes what was happening—the riots, the violence, death and looting that was going on all over the place. I hope I am wrong and that Chateau Feroc is not attacked. I can only say that in the event of my timorous fears proving justified, I hope the Countess will obtain some comfort from the realisation that she has sacrificed the life of her daughter and jeopardised the safety of the chateau in order to demonstrate a confidence in the fidelity of her servants.'

'You speak harsh words. Do you forget that when you arrived she had just lost her husband? For her to contemplate leaving her home so soon was anathema to her.'

Charles's precarious hold on his temper had departed and his voice was raw edged with anger. 'I appreciate that, but this is no time for sentiment. She must have had doubts, but she would not admit it. It is all very laudable. But in the present crisis it is hardly practical.'

'And if the chateau has been attacked?' Maria asked, her eyes hard and accusing. 'What then?'

'As to that I cannot say. It depends on the mood of the mob.'

She stared at him, images of the chateau burning and her aunt and Constance at the mercy of those terrible, maddened people. 'Do—do you think they would…?'

'There would be nothing that you or I could do for them. I'm sorry, Maria, but that is the truth of it and you must face it.'

'I never will.'

Although her glorious green eyes were glaring defiance at him, they were sparkling with suppressed tears, shining with an inner pain, and listening to her breathless, pleading voice, Charles would have given anything in the world to take her in his arms and kiss her tears away. But he knew that he must not.

'I would never have left had I thought anything bad would happen.'

'You don't know that anything bad has happened,' he said, trying to temper his impatience. 'Plead their case all you like, Maria, but you will be wasting your breath. I have to be in London very soon and I cannot afford to let anything interfere with that.'

'And I am one responsibility you can't wait to be rid of,' Maria retorted ungraciously.

'I will not turn back, Maria. It is out of the question. We go on. Both of us,' Charles said pointedly. 'With any luck we'll reach the coast tomorrow.'

The journey continued with Maria quietly seething at what she considered to be his overbearing and unreasonable attitude. Charles did not attempt to draw her out. He wished that he did not feel so responsible for her. It was an absurd feeling. It annoyed him and there was no reason for it. Nevertheless he could not rid himself of the feeling.

Glancing across at her, at her sad face and her small hands clasped together on her lap, he frowned. He was aware of a disturbing tug at his heart, and thinking again of how fortunate she was to be leaving France, he knew that should they be apprehended she was going to be a devilish responsibility.

Aware of Charles's penetrating gaze, Maria looked at him at this point in his reflections. She noted the frown and it brought back her courage and a sudden spark of anger. Sitting straight-backed, she said in a cool, composed voice, 'I apologise for my lapse in composure. It won't happen again.'

'There's no need to apologise. Just as long as you understand why I had to refuse your request to turn back.'

'I do. Of course we can't go back. It would be madness. I am just so concerned for my aunt and Constance.'

It was almost dark and they were about to stop for the night at the next hostelry when they saw the flames rising from a large villa on the outskirts of a nearby village. The fire was licking upwards, a thick plume of smoke curling into the darkening sky.

On his perch with a loaded blunderbuss beside him, Pierre stopped the coach in alarm when they were approached by a noisy, bedraggled band of people heading away from the fire. Many of the excited villagers had poured out on to the streets to view the spectacle, amid a great deal of howling and buffoonery. The men approaching the coach, their confidence already heightened with bloodlust, were armed with sticks, poles and spades and anything else that constituted a weapon.

'What is it? What do they want? Why have they stopped us?' Maria asked in alarm.

Charles looked at her. In the glow from the carriage lamps her face was white, her eyes enormous but quite steady. 'No doubt we'll find out soon enough.' His eyes were anxious and alert, but his voice was neither. He spoke to Maria in an entirely matter-of-fact tone that somehow carried complete conviction. 'Whatever happens, trust me. Unless they order you to get out, stay in the coach. We'll get out of this.'

'I wish I had your confidence,' she murmured fearfully, her eyes on the ever-increasing rabble.

Charles did not answer. It was as if she was not there. He was watching the men saunter towards them. There was an odd, still look on his face. His eyes narrowed suddenly. The abstraction left them and his hand closed round the butt of his pistol on the seat beside him, concealed by a fold in his coat, and Maria, watching him, as she always watched him when he wasn't looking at her, was all at once aware that behind that casual gesture his nerves were tense and alert, as if he were waiting for something to happen.

The leader of this band of unsavoury, hostile peasants was a man in a green-caped coat, his complexion the colour of ivory. His hatchet face with the thin lips and heavy, drooping eyelids was a curious mixture of alertness and perturbability. The chin that rested on the abundant folds of his untidy and soiled neckcloth was long and resolute. He peered inside with a somewhat suspicious glance at the coach's inhabitants.

'What is this?' Charles asked calmly. 'We have done you no harm and most certainly intend none.'

'Well, now,' the man drawled. 'It's simple enough. We've got no reason to see you and your lady—uncomfortable, but we've got no reason to trust you either.' He squinted one eye at Charles. 'Why, I don't know you—not at all.'

'It is a simple enough problem to cure,' Charles returned. 'Duval's the name. Charles Duval. I am of the people—of peasant stock on both sides.'

'But now you walk and talk like a swank.'

'I've bettered myself, I admit. Do you find something wrong with that?'

The man nodded slowly, without taking his eyes off the stranger. 'No—I was right. I don't know you.'

'The fire? Whose house is it?' Charles asked, appearing coolly unruffled by the interruption to their journey and the threat this band of miscreants posed to their safety.

'The house of the Seigneur,' the man growled. 'And the Seigneur is feeding the flames this very minute.'

Apart from a darkening of his face, Charles was

careful not to show the horror and revulsion he felt. 'What precisely did he do?'

'What's it to you?' he snarled. 'But I'll tell you if you want to know. That rich bloodsucker said that a man with a family could live on ten *sous* a day. That's never right, don't you agree, eh?'

Charles shrugged. 'What is that to me? I'm a stranger in these parts. I was not acquainted with your Seigneur, but he sounds just like any other I have come across.'

The hatchet face thrust itself further into the coach. 'Are you sure he's not a friend of yours?' He turned and roared, 'Look, boys! I don't think we can trust this man who calls himself one of the people.'

Obscenities were loudly uttered and sticks were raised, and, before the echo of their shouts had died away, to Maria's horror Charles opened the door and climbed out, the pistol he held concealed in the folds of his coat. Taken unawares, the crowd backed away. Charles stood before them, smiling his icy smile.

'You're the leader of this rabble, are you?' he said quietly, addressing himself to the hatchet-faced man.

The man hesitated. 'I might be.'

Charles started walking straight towards him. The rabble were at the man's back. The crude weapons wavered. This was unusual. They were not prepared for this. Nothing in their experience had prepared them to deal with a man who wouldn't turn and run when confronted.

Pierre had scrambled down from his seat and stood close to the window. 'Savages,' he murmured, just loud enough for Maria to hear. 'Savages, the lot of them, that's what they are. The devil's own. God save us.'

Pierre voiced Maria's own apprehension. The horses

were uneasy, their eyes alert, ears pricked and tremulous tails.

That was the moment when Charles took positive action. When he was close enough his hand shot out and he caught the leader by the coat front. Then his arm stiffened and he shoved the man backwards to crash into his comrades. The impact knocked several of them down into the dirt. They got to their feet, shouting and cursing, only to stare straight into the muzzle of Charles's pistol. The mob had no stomach for gunfire.

'A man's a fool to wander through France unarmed today,' Charles said, hoping it would discourage these madmen from inflicting harm and allowing the incident to degenerate into wholesale brigandage, as it threatened to do.

Inside the coach Maria watched the whole terrifying proceedings, the howling of the village's inhabitants loud in her ears. An odd shiver tingled down her spine at the sound and she set her teeth and tried to shut her ears.

Until that moment she had admired Charles's utmost forbearance in his dealing with the crowd, but she uttered a gasp of horror when she saw him brandish the pistol. Knowing that one man armed with a pistol didn't stand a chance of surviving against an angry mob, thinking quickly, inspiration struck. Opening her reticule, she pulled out a small pot of rouge.

Shrouded in her cloak, her hood pulled well over her head and holding it together so that only her eyes showed, she opened the door and climbed out. All eyes except Charles's became focused on her, but he knew she was there and silently cursed her idiocy for disobeying him.

Moving closer to Charles, Maria could almost feel

the effort he was exerting to keep his rage under control. She knew that relaxed, almost indolent stance of his was only a surface calm, beneath which was a murderous fury which he would no doubt unleash on her later.

She was numb to every emotion save a gnawing fear that feasted heartily upon what courage she could muster. She set her mind not to appear frightened beneath the hideous stares and bold leers that were directed at her, yet her knees had a strange tendency to shake beneath her. Despite her show of self-control, she was desperately afraid, not knowing what lay in store for them, but convinced now that the miscreants planned some hideous fate.

Disconcertedly she moved her gaze to Charles. His dark hair was stirred by the light breeze. Standing stiff and appearing to be in complete control of his actions, he seemed like a stranger, a man she did not know, distant, frowning.

Suddenly a bearded rough standing to one side of the leader nudged his neighbour with his elbow.

'Nice, isn't she?' he said. 'But I'd like to see more of her, eh?'

'Lends a bit of a swank to our company,' said another.

Another ill-favoured, toothless individual shrilled his assent to the statement, lifting his stick to emphasise his words.

Beneath Maria's blazing glower, the bearded man made a turn about her, a careless swagger in his walk. He gave her a lusty perusal, his mind holding lewd thoughts. Reaching out with his gnarled hand, he gave her hood a firm tug with a gesture that was at once peremptory. 'I'm Handsome,' he said.

She slapped down his hand with ill temper. 'That's a matter of opinion.'

A roar of laughter shook his audience.

'That's got nothing to do with his looks,' snarled the hatchet face. 'It's his name. Handsome, that's what he's called.' He scowled at her. 'Going far, are you?'

'Yes, as a matter of fact. To the coast. The doctor recommended it for—my health, you see.' When the bearded rough made a move to touch her again, she glared at him. 'I wouldn't do that if I were you. You might have cause to regret it. I've been ill, you see, and I'm not completely recovered—smallpox, it was.'

The leader's eyes narrowed as they flicked like a rat's from Charles to Maria and back to Charles. 'Is this true? She doesn't look like she's got much wrong with her.'

As if on cue, Maria calmly folded back her hood, relieved that they stood some distance away from her and that it was almost dark so they would just be able to make out the occasional spots of rouge she had dabbed on her face, hoping fervently they resembled pock marks.

The rabble gave a collective gasp and backed away, each and every one of them having a horror of contracting that often fatal, disfiguring disease.

Apart from a slight raising of his eyebrows when he looked at her, Charles's expression didn't alter. 'My wife does not lie,' Charles remarked, joining in the pretence. 'As you see, she is not marred quite as severely as some are, but the doctor advised her against coming into direct contact with others for fear she might still carry the infection. Maria, get back inside the carriage.' He issued the order without taking his eyes off the rabble. She hesitated, but only for a moment, for there was a steely edge to his voice she would ignore at her peril.

'Now, gentlemen,' Charles said pleasantly, 'you will have the goodness to go home to your wives and children. If you refuse, you will leave me with no alternative but to blow your brains out.'

The pistol levelled at them, and one other held by a steady hand in the doorway of the coach, was persuasion enough.

'From the look of the Seigneur's home, you have done enough mischief this day,' Charles said, softly. 'I have not done any hunting lately, which is a sport I always enjoy, so do not follow me.'

Then he spun on his heel and walked back to the coach, moving calmly and without haste. The rabble didn't follow him. He had known they wouldn't—although he didn't know whether that was down to the fear of being shot or contracting Maria's feigned smallpox.

'Are you all right?' he asked when he had settled himself across from her and ordered Pierre to drive on, putting the beacon of the burning villa behind them.

She nodded. 'When you got out of the coach, I counted each breath as though it were my last.'

'It could well have been. I told you to stay inside the coach.'

'I know, but I had to do something. I was terrified.'

'It took courage not to show it. It was also ingenious of you to feign smallpox.' He handed her a handkerchief. 'You can wipe them off now. They have served their purpose.' He glanced down at her hand. 'You found my other pistol, I see. Can you use it?'

'Yes, if I have to,' she replied, rubbing hard at the rouge on her face. 'One of the grooms at the chateau taught me how to shoot.'

'Which may come in useful, who knows? But hear me well, Maria.' His voice was like ice and his eyes held a terrifying menace as very quietly, very deliberately, he said, 'Unless you have a death wish, don't ever do anything like that again. By your reckless action you could have got us all killed. It was stupid. How dare you disobey me?'

Feeling the frigid blast of his gaze, reflexively, to her consternation and fury, Maria felt her cheeks grow hot and found herself shrinking into the upholstery, then checked herself and met his look head-on.

'Disobey you?' she repeated, indignant. 'If I did that then I am very sorry, but I think it was my quick thinking that saved us, not your pistol.'

'However it may have looked to you, I had the situation under control. How can any man make a cool-headed decision that he knows may involve grave risk, while the woman he is trying to protect has ideas of her own—ideas that could have jeopardised everything?'

She wanted to shout at him, to tell him how frightened she had been for him, but the words froze on her lips; instead she said, 'I wasn't thinking.'

'Obviously. When I give an order, I don't expect it to be questioned. That's a matter of principle with me.' His voice rang with authority. He saw Maria stiffen with angry confusion. 'Don't you dare defy me again.'

Before Charles's eyes, Maria's expressive face went from shock to fury, and then she coldly turned her face away from him. He stared at her profile, furious because, by her actions, the situation could have turned very ugly. But most of all he was furious with himself for failing to anticipate that such a scene with the rabble might occur, and for not taking steps to avert it by instructing Pierre to take the longer route to avoid the village, such had been his haste to get to the hostelry before nightfall.

He wondered grimly how it was possible that he could intimidate those he employed into doing his bidding with a single glance, and yet he could not seem to force one young, stubborn, defiant girl to behave. She was so damned unpredictable that she made it impossible to anticipate her reaction to anything. But then again, he thought, a feeling of admiration for the courage she had shown coming to the fore, the idea of feigning smallpox had been clever.

As they neared the inn where they would spend the night, he glanced at her, belatedly realising how terrified she must have been on finding herself confronted by a band of miscreants who had just set fire to a house with its inhabitants still inside. With a twinge of pity and reluctant admiration, he admitted that she was also very young, very frightened and very brave. Any other woman might well have given way to hysterics, rather than coolly confronting the rabble and implying that she could infect them all with smallpox as Maria had done.

On reaching the inn, Pierre drove the coach through the arched gateway and brought the steaming horses to a halt. Charles was the first to alight. Turning, he reached up and held out his hand to assist Maria, noting as he did so that her lovely face was stiff, and she was carefully avoiding meeting his eyes.

His gaze swept the bustling inn yard. 'Unfortunately we have not reserved rooms so we will have to take what's on offer.'

Maria turned to him. 'I would appreciate it if you would engage alternative accommodation for yourself tonight, Charles,' she said coldly. 'I don't care what interpretation Pierre or anyone else puts on a husband and wife having separate rooms—make any excuse you like, but tonight I would like my privacy.'

'As you wish.'

Maria was relieved he didn't object, but then Charles seemed to have a trick of wiping all expression from his face when he wished, and it was difficult to know what he felt or thought.

Noise struck them as they entered the main room. The inn appeared to be full, but Charles managed to engage rooms.

'This way, *madame,*' the innkeeper said, picking up her valise and heading for the stairs.

Charles stayed to drink a much-needed tankard of good, cool ale with Pierre in the common room.

Relieved to have some time to herself, Maria followed. In a moment he had thrown open a door and ushered her into a cramped chamber with bare whitewashed walls. Dimly illuminated by a single oil lamp, it was furnished with a long narrow bed covered with a flowered counterpane, a wash stand with a jug and basin, and a pair of upright chairs near the window set in the eaves. The innkeeper went out, promising to have dinner sent up.

The long day of undiluted tension and anxiety had taken its toll. The fire and the horrific images of what the people must have suffered in the flames had affected Maria profoundly. A ragged sob escaped her, and she flung herself away from the door in a desperate attempt to keep her mind from thinking of the many things that did not bear thinking of—of what might have happened to her aunt and Constance. Had the chateau been burned like the villa she had seen? Were they dead, or were they hiding and hunted, with no refuge?

Pressing trembling fingers against her temples, she sat on the bed. Tears flowed easily and the sleek lines of her body shuddered with each racking sob. She could not believe what had happened. The nightmare had come true at last, just like Charles said it would—noble houses were burning all over France, and this was far worse than any of the dreams had been, because she knew that she would awake from it to find herself trembling with fear.

Much later, Charles came to her room. Knocking softly on the door, he waited until he was told to enter before turning the handle, surprised, after what had occurred the night before, to find it wasn't locked. He found her sitting by the tiny window, her fine-boned profile tilted to one side. The forlorn droop of her head went to his heart. He could not help but wonder at the courage of this young woman. He had known no other quite like her, and the disturbing fact was that she seemed capable of disrupting his whole life.

'Maria,' he said softly.

She looked at him directly with her clear green eyes, without smiling.

Crossing the room, he went down on one knee in

front of her and took her hand. He longed to take her in his arms and soothe her as he would a frightened child, but her rejection of him would only make matters worse between them. It would be a step too far, too fast, and he didn't want her to withdraw into the protective shell she seemed to have built around herself and shut him out in the cold.

He could read nothing on her closed face. Her eyes were downcast, the thick lashes making half-moons on her cheeks. He could not tell if she was welcoming the touch of his hand or grimly enduring it.

'Maria—I'm sorry. I can't tell you how sorry I am. That you, of all people, should have had to go through that. What I said to you was harsh. I apologise for my tone. As you know, I was not in the best of moods when we came upon the rabble. My temper had been well tested earlier, and I stood very near the edge of losing it entirely.' A slight, crooked smile curved his lips. 'Am I forgiven?'

Maria nodded her acceptance of his apology, but the expression on her face remained impassive.

'If you're thinking of what happened earlier, forget it. It is behind us now.'

'Perhaps my memory is clearer than yours. Perhaps I cannot forget as easily as you. I can still see that fire, imagine those poor people who must have been—'

'Don't, Maria. Don't torture yourself this way. Violence is only one aspect of life.'

'I don't agree.'

'Yes, you do. Violence has always been hidden from you. It has been done by people far from sight. Now you have been made aware of it, and it will not go away.'

'Do you really think the Seigneur, and perhaps his family, perished in the fire?'

'It looks bad, I'll admit. But in the absence of any conclusive evidence to the contrary, why not believe that at worst the Seigneur and his family may have been hurt, and afterwards managed to escape?'

'That,' Maria said, 'is what I want to believe.' But there was no hope in her voice. 'I also want to believe things have not changed at Chateau Feroc. I pray my aunt and Constance are all right. When I remember how I laughed on leaving, of the joy I felt because I was going home—to Gravely.' She looked at Charles, unable to hide the guilt she felt and the self-disgust.

'Why do you look like that?'

'Because I am ashamed of myself. I ran away and left them to face a terrible fate. How could I?'

'You don't know that anything has happened to them. Besides, it was their choice to stay.'

'I should not have left them. My aunt took me in when my father died. There was no one else, you see. I was under an obligation to stay and help.'

'The way I see it, you had no alternative but to leave. Colonel Winston was most insistent that you left France while it was still possible. And besides, I had travelled a long way to fetch you. I would have been none too pleased to find my journey had been in vain.'

Realising that he still retained her hand in his, self-consciously Maria withdrew it, and immediately mourned its loss, its strength. Suddenly she was aware of his proximity and what it was doing to her. When she gazed into the pair of penetrating pale blue eyes levelled on her, her heart turned over.

Charles stood up and looked at the food she had left untouched. 'I see you have not eaten. You should eat something.'

'I haven't much of an appetite at the moment.'

'Then a glass of wine.'

'No—I…'

'I insist.' Charles poured some of the wine from the decanter into two goblets and handed one to Maria. She took it reluctantly and sipped it slowly. He sat opposite, watching her, and he sensed rather than saw her relaxation of tension.

'Feeling better?'

She nodded. 'When do you hope to reach Calais?'

'Tomorrow—hopefully before dark, which means an early start. I can only hope we get there without incident. Before I went to Chateau Feroc, I wrote to Colonel Winston informing him of when we hope to reach Dover—providing everything goes to plan. He will make provision for you after that—unless things change.' She gave him an enquiring look, but he did not enlarge on this, for it was his dearest hope that after taking one look at Winston, she would send him packing. 'I have made my own arrangements. We shall part company at Dover, but I will not be at ease until I am assured you are taken care of.'

Charles looked at her now. 'I suppose you are looking forward to meeting your betrothed again after all these years, Maria.'

The unexpectedness of his words took her by surprise. 'I—I am apprehensive—not knowing what to expect. It has been a long time.'

'Are you afraid?'

Maria met his steady gaze. 'I suppose I am—in a way. My dread of meeting Henry again actually intensified rather than abated as time went on,' she confessed quietly. 'You know as well as I that my father was a man of keen intuitive intellect and he was adamant in his belief that Henry would make me a good husband—and I will do all I can to honour his memory.'

'I know you will, and if you decide you cannot go through with it, I'm sure your father would understand.'

'You needn't try to assuage my feelings, Charles. I've realised for a long time the limited possibility of my marrying Henry. So please spare me your concern. There really is no need. In days from now I may decide to take a different path from what my father intended.'

'It is you that looks concerned, Maria. Will it disappoint you to walk away?'

'In a way. You see, at Chateau Feroc there were times when I was afraid. It seemed that everyone I had been close to had died—my parents, my brother who died in infancy, my maternal grandparents, who drowned when their ship went down in a storm in the English Channel— and there was no one at the chateau I felt really close to. In the early days I pinned all my hopes on Henry.

'When I came to France, knowing that he was waiting for me, my heart and soul longed for the years to pass so he would come and take me home. But as I grew older my feelings changed. He wrote seldom—the content forced—as though he wrote out of duty. I became apprehensive and even afraid of him. Determining his character for myself is vital in making a prudent choice before we speak our vows. Whatever his faults, I am committed to seeing him—whatever may come from it.'

'It could be the end—or the beginning of something.'

Maria looked at him steadily. 'Yes, it could.'

She was wearing the woollen dress she had worn when she had left Chateau Feroc, which she had unfastened at the neck. Her face glowed in the light of the lamp, and her black hair falling loose about her shoulders gleamed with flickering blue lights. With a rush of emotion Charles thought that she was the most beautiful thing he had ever seen. At the end of two days, he was captivated by her. She seemed to have taken up occupation in his mind. She was an intoxicating combination of beauty, an exhilarating intelligence and disarming common sense.

And if she severed all ties with Henry Winston, so much the better.

Chapter Four

Stretching his legs out before him, Charles leant his head against the high back of the chair to enjoy more leisurely what had become his favourite pastime since going to Chateau Feroc—watching Maria. She could not guess the depth of torture she put him through, for beneath his calm facade and silken words, he burned with a consuming desire for her. Last night he had sat sleepless in his chair while visions of her in all manner of disarray—laughing, angry as she had been in the coach earlier, sleeping or awake, but always paramount in his imagination—floated teasingly in and out through the shadowed fringes of his mind, enslaving his thoughts like some impish sprite with dark luminous eyes, leading him into fantasies no virginal maid could even imagine. He was ever conscious of her and painfully aware that she was a woman, and he wanted her.

The silence lengthened and drew out and filled slowly with sounds of the inn, and the monotonous fluttering of a large moth that had found its way in and was battering its wings against the glass of the oil lamp.

Maria dragged her eyes away from the window and looked at Charles's relaxed, unguarded face in the flickering light. His mouth was firm and unexpectedly sensitive. She looked at his hand holding the glass—slender and long-fingered, a hand possessed of an unexpected strength and an equally unexpected gentleness. Just being with him was beginning to cause her moments of painful confusion, yet just as often pleasure that lightened her heart and made it soar—and made her forget Henry.

'Why don't you like Henry?' she asked quietly.

Charles looked at her and shrugged. 'There are many reasons,' he repeated quietly, wondering how she would react were he to tell her the true nature of her betrothed—that he was utterly vicious and corrupt, rotten to the core, and without principle and honour, and the only reason he wanted Maria to return to England was because, if anything were to happen to her, he would lose sight of her fortune.

'Why? What has he done to you?'

'Nothing to me personally,' he replied at length.

'Then has he done something to someone else?' she asked, wondering why he looked so disconcerted. 'Is that why you dislike him?'

'If he has, then that is his affair.'

'And you're not going to tell me.' She sighed deeply, sensing his reluctance and decided not to press him. She would find out the true nature of her betrothed in due course. 'Don't worry, Charles. Whatever he is or whatever he has done, I shall find out for myself soon enough.'

'I'm very much afraid you will,' he said softly.

Not for the first time, Maria felt at a loss to understand him. Suddenly his presence was vaguely threatening. Whenever he stopped playing her escort he became a passionate companion, a predator set on unsettling her equilibrium, or a dark mysterious stranger. She didn't know whether he was a spy, although she was certain he was involved in some shady business, and that visiting his French relatives was only a cover-up. But that was his affair and she wouldn't pry. Pushing her hair off her forehead, she glanced out of the window.

'It is late. I think I would like to go to bed.' She got to her feet, smoothing her skirts. 'You—have a room that is comfortable?' she asked awkwardly.

'It is—adequate.' Standing up and noting her sudden discomfiture, he was encouraged by it. 'At least I have a bed to sleep in tonight,' he murmured with a slanted, meaningful smile. He crossed to the door where he turned to find she had followed him. He raised a brow.

'I—I thought I'd lock the door.'

'Very wise.'

'I—don't want a repetition of last night,' she said desperately. 'I didn't see any undesirable characters when we arrived, but I'm not taking any chances.' A roguish gleam suddenly entered Charles's eyes and with a touch of alarm Maria recognised her amorous companion of the night before.

'If you are afraid, I would be willing to—'

'No,' Maria was quick to reply in alarm, knowing he was about to suggest that he stayed. 'That would not be wise.'

Uttering a regretful sigh, he said, 'Then no doubt I shall find warmer companionship in other parts of the inn.'

Maria's eyes shot to his. The idea that he might seek out solace from one of the tavern wenches upset her and filled her with a fierce jealousy. An image of his long, muscular body stretched out alongside one of those women made her heart sink sickeningly. She was surprised to realise that she could not bear the thought of him making love to another woman, even though she was still officially betrothed to another man. Her cheeks flamed with the conflict that raged within her.

As if reading her thoughts, Maria watched Charles's gaze turn warm and sensual and she was aware of how close they were standing. Suddenly his manner bore an odd touch of threatening boldness as his gaze dwelt on her face.

'Worry not, Maria, the only woman I yearn to be close to is here now. You must find the subterfuge of travelling halfway across France as my wife strange— and dressed in such plain attire—used as you are to wearing elegant clothes and jewels.'

'It is no great sacrifice,' she replied softly, relieved that he had set her mind at rest. 'As for jewels, my aunt was forever telling me that I was too young to wear them. When I reach Gravely I shall have rubies and diamonds enough. Whether I wear them is a different matter.'

Charles looked at her from beneath lowered lids. 'Diamonds—for you? No. I think pearls would suit you better. They are less harsh—soft, soothing to the touch. Nothing vulgar—small, creamy ones.'

'You—you make them sound nice,' Maria said. 'But if I marry Henry, he might like me in diamonds.'

'I wasn't thinking of Henry,' Charles said. 'I was thinking of you. I would like to attach some pearls here—' he reached out and almost touched her ear '—and more—there.' He picked up her hand and laid it at her throat, close to the valley made by her breasts.

Maria's heart stirred, for it was an oddly sensuous and erotic gesture—far more so than if he had touched her himself. There was a silence as he continued to gaze down at her flushed face and time stood still.

'Please don't look at me like that,' Maria whispered, her voice quavering. 'It makes me excessively uneasy.'

He smiled. The light of the lamp behind her fell upon his face and hers in shadow, and the soft wavering flame threw an aureole about her, glinting on the long ripples of her black hair and outlining her small head.

'You are very lovely. Has anyone ever told you that?'

She shook her head. At Chateau Feroc she had been drilled in the habits of strict decorum and not, as some might think, given the beautiful chateau and the Count's fabulous wealth, in the glittering, fashionable world in which flattery and flirtation were commonplace.

'Maria,' Charles teased, gently touching her cheek with the back of his hand, 'you are blushing.'

'And I think you are quite mad.'

'My thoughts exactly,' he whispered, and, bending his head, he pressed his lips to her forehead, placing his hands around her upper arms and drawing her against his chest, holding her as if he knew she would struggle if he tried to do more than that. 'When we set out on this journey, you were not in my plans, Maria.'

'Oh, please,' she implored helplessly. 'I don't know what you want of me. Please don't do this.'

He took her chin between his thumb and his forefinger and lifted it, forcing her to meet his steady gaze as he quietly said, 'A kiss would not go amiss.'

'Nevertheless, I think you should proceed with caution.'

'A little kiss here and there is quite harmless.'

'A little kiss here and there is dangerous,' she countered, thoroughly convinced of that premise where he was concerned.

She turned her head away. The powerful force of sensual persuasion that he was capable of launching against her could reap devastating results. She must guard her heart. She was very susceptible. But when he placed a finger against her cheek and brought her face back to his, when his eyes delved into hers, he all but burned her heart inside out, and touched at its tender core.

'Have you ever been kissed, Maria?'

She shook her head, her breath coming quickly from between her softly parted lips. 'No, of course I haven't.'

His lips quirked. 'Then perhaps it's time you were.' A wicked gleam entered his eyes. 'It won't hurt. I promise.'

Maria's entire body started to tremble as his lips began to descend to hers, and she sought to forestall what her heart knew was inevitable by reasoning with him. 'Please, Charles. I am betrothed to another. Do you forget so easily?'

'Would that I could, but with a little gentle persuasion I might succeed in making *you* forget.' He laughed softly at her appalled expression. 'Don't look so shocked, Maria. Your betrothed will never know.'

His warm breath stirred her hair and warmed her cheek. 'Don't—I cannot do this.'

'Yes, Maria, you can.'

His lips brushed back and forth across her lips, and Maria shivered with the waves of tension shooting through her. The instant he felt her trembling response, Charles's arm tightened, supporting her. She did not struggle or utter one word of protest. Perhaps she knew it would do little good to do either. She stood entirely still. His hand curved round her nape, sensually stroking it. He began trailing scorching kisses down her neck and back to her lips.

'Don't be afraid. I'll stop whenever you tell me to.'

Imprisoned by his protective embrace and seduced by his mouth and caressing hands, being totally ignorant of such matters and not knowing what to expect, Maria helplessly raised her head to fully receive his kiss.

The sweet offering of her mouth wrung a groan from Charles and his lips seized hers in a kiss of melting hunger. His tongue traced a hot line between her lips, coaxing, urging them to part, and then insisting. Even though she was braced for it, the shock of his parted lips on hers was indescribable sweetness. She touched her tongue to his lips, and when she felt him shudder, instinct told her she was doing something right. The moment she yielded he deepened his kiss.

Too naïve and inexperienced to hide her feelings, her body jerked convulsively with the primitive sensations jarring through her entire body, and she surrendered mindlessly to the splendour of the pagan kiss. It was deep and, when Charles finally pulled his mouth from hers an eternity later, feeling almost bereft, Maria surfaced slightly from the sensual place where he had sent her. She forced her eyelids open and looked at him, the confusion she felt and her sudden awakening to the desires of her body in their soft depths.

But with the cold onrush of reality the passionate spell was broken and Maria pulled back in his arms. 'No, Charles, I cannot.'

He pulled her back and looked down at her, letting his eyes sweep the flushed cheeks and the roundness of her breasts rising and falling beneath her dress. 'Then speak a lie, Maria, and say you want no part of me.'

Though her mouth opened, no words formed, and she could only stare up at him, helplessly caught in the web of her own desire. Again he placed his lips on hers to possess their softness leisurely and languidly. He met no resistance and, with a low moan, Maria let him gather her to him, their mouths melded in warm communion, turning and devouring, until their needs became a greedy search for more. His hand slipped to her breast, caressing and kneading its swelling firmness, and the white-hot heat that shot through her was a sudden shock that made her catch her breath and drag her mouth from his.

'Charles, we cannot do this,' she whispered in desperation, tearing herself from his arms, shaken to the core of her being. 'You haven't enough honour and decency to stop yourself kissing another man's future wife.'

Charles's jaw tightened. 'So much the worse for you,' he said grimly. 'At all events, when the two of you finally meet up, he will see that he has lost you.'

'That will be for me to decide, not you, although I am touched by your concern—if that is what it is. If the chivalrous feelings you possess towards me are indeed genuine, then you may prove it simply by not taking advantage of my vulnerable and defenceless state by kissing me again. What am I to think—only that you are so-liciting me for my favours?'

Seeing a deep hurt underlying the anger in her flashing eyes, his anger melted. Lifting his hand, he tenderly brushed a dark lock of hair off her cheek. 'I am not trying to pry into what your feelings might be, and I am not soliciting you for your favours, Maria. It's just that after being alone with you for two days now and getting to know you better—you're like a potent wine that has gone to my head. I just cannot bear to see you in the thrall of a man who is unworthy of you—a man who aspires to be your husband.'

'I am not in Henry's thrall, Charles—never that. To the man I marry I shall gladly yield all I have to give—as well as all the love and devotion and passion I am capable of feeling. In return I shall want from my husband love, honour—and fidelity. But whatever happens, I will make up my own mind in the end.'

'I know you will, and I hope your decision will be the right one. And now I think you should go to bed. And don't forget to lock your door.' He turned in the open doorway and looked back, a smile curving his lips. 'Sweet dreams, Maria.'

Walking away from Maria's room the smile remained on Charles's lips. The kiss had proved what he sus-pected, that she had not the least idea of the mechanics of sexual intimacy between men and women. The suf-focating prudery of her life at Chateau Feroc under the stern, autocratic eye of the Countess had kept her in complete ignorance of such matters. He had seen it re-flected in the shocked and appalled expression on her face when he told her he was going to kiss her, and he had sensed it in her body's lack of response when he had.

But he was encouraged by the fact that her lips had answered his kiss. They had been soft and sweet and pliable beneath his own, and he would have liked to stay and educate her further, but seducing Maria Monkton was not in his immediate plans. For the time being, somehow he would have to cool the lust gnawing at his very being and try to forget how soft and sweet she had felt in his arms, to ignore the fact that she had set her hooks into him, and to control the strong attraction that seemed to bind his heart and mind to Maria.

Maria stared at the closed door in a waking dream. How was it possible that after just two days Charles Osbourne could stir feelings she had never felt before? She was fearful of what might happen if he came to her again and seeked to finish what he had started. She had escaped this moment—not entirely unscathed, but nevertheless with her virtue still intact. That state, however, was most tenuous and would not withstand another persuasive, unrelenting assault.

His kiss, his forceful persuasiveness, had been her downfall. He had known full well what he was doing to her, and the memory of what she had experienced in his arms made her plight all the more unbearable and she feared she was destined to remember his embrace for the rest of her life.

And Henry? She had given no thought to him while allowing her mind to dwell on romantic thoughts about another man. Her emotions were torn asunder, and she could find no peace in the depths of her thoughts. What her heart yearned for went against everything she deemed honourable, and yet she had no control over it.

Maria awoke to the sound of someone knocking on the door. Still drowsy with slumber, it took her a moment to remember where she was. When the knocking came again, startled, immediately she was out of bed, her heart slamming into her ribs, her knees turning to jelly. Pushing back her hair, she padded across the room.

'Who is it?'

'Charles.'

Maria stared at the door, reluctant to open it, reluctant to look Charles in the eyes after what had happened last night.

'What's wrong?' he asked, hearing the tiredness in her voice.

'You—you startled me. I didn't expect you…'

'Really,' he mocked from the other side of the door. 'Whom did you expect? It's late, Maria. If you remember, I told you I wanted to make an early start.'

'I'll get dressed. I'll be down in a moment.'

Charles was already doing full justice to his breakfast when she arrived downstairs. He raised his brows when she slipped into the chair across from him, his expression oddly impassive.

'You slept well?' he enquired coolly.

'Eventually,' Maria answered quietly, focusing her attention on the food the innkeeper's wife placed in front of her and pouring coffee into a mug. She took a sip of the steaming beverage gratefully. 'I'm sorry I'm late. I was more tired than I thought.'

Charles wished he could have let her rest a little longer. But there was no help for it. They must press on if they were to reach Calais that day.

'You can sleep in the coach. I promise not to wake you,' he teased gently.

Maria trembled at the gentle confidence she heard in his smiling voice.

As she climbed into the coach for the final stage of their journey, she found herself alone once more with this man who was beginning to have such a powerful effect on her. She had become a bewildered young woman with an added problem and an upbringing that convinced her that what she had let happen and enjoyed with Charles was unforgivable.

'Maria,' Charles said, dragging her from her thoughts. 'Is something wrong?'

Her eyes flew open and his unfathomable light blue eyes locked on to hers. 'Wrong? I…'

'Perhaps you'd like to talk about it?' he asked calmly. She shook her head. 'You're afraid. Is it me you fear, Maria? Or something else?'

The way he spoke her name in his rich deep voice had the same stirring effect on her as the touch of his lips. 'It—it's about last night when—when you…'

'When I kissed you.'

'Yes, that's it.'

'And?'

'I'm afraid of the things you made me feel,' she

admitted desperately. 'I don't understand them. I—realise that to you this is merely a—a dalliance…'

'Is that so?' he teased, a lazy, seductive grin sweeping across his handsome face. 'And you know that, do you, Maria?'

She swallowed nervously. 'Do you mean it isn't?' Visions of being kissed whenever he felt like it rose to alarming prominence in her mind. Hoping that by speaking in a calm, reasonable voice, rather than heatedly protesting his intentions, she said, 'It's not that I'm afraid, it's just that you shouldn't have done it. It was quite wrong of you, and I would appreciate it if you refrained from—from doing anything like that in the future.'

With a mixture of amusement and admiration, Charles noted her request. With any other woman, such a request would only add to his determination to taste her response to him again—and Maria was no exception. Of that there was no doubt. Maria hadn't any notion how much control he had to maintain over himself to keep his hands off her, and if the situation arose again his actions would be exactly the same—and Henry Winston be damned.

'The kiss was harmless, wasn't it?'

'I think so.'

'Neither of us was hurt, were we?'

'No.'

'Well, then, there is no reason why we should mention it again, is there?'

'No, I suppose not.'

'Good.'

The coach made rapid progress despite the dreadful condition of the roads—the combination of this and the badly sprung coach was punishing for both occupants. As dusk began to descend they were approaching the coast. Already Maria could smell the sea and she knew they could not be far from Calais.

They entered the medieval walled town, the wheels of the coach rattling over the cobblestones of the narrow, twisting streets. Reaching the Place d'Armes, the main square of the town, with its thirteenth-century watchtower, they veered off down a side street and Pierre halted the coach outside a small tavern that catered for the fishermen of the town. The doorway was low and a red light shone through greasy curtains.

Climbing out, Charles took Maria firmly by the arm and drew her inside. She found herself in a dimly lit, low-ceilinged room where the atmosphere was like a dense fog, reeking in equal parts of liquor and tobacco smoke. There were sailors and fishermen drinking and talking, some breaking out into ribald shouts as the serving girls passed among them, their hands groping and clasping softly rounded parts.

'Do we have to stay here?' Maria whispered, terrified in case someone should reach out and molest her in the same way.

'Stay close beside me and you'll come to no harm.'

When his eyes lighted on the newcomers, a man rose from his seat at the far end of the room, hoisting a basket on to his back. Maria gasped when she saw him pushing his way towards them through the fog like some weird and menacing Neptune, for he was the most fearsome man she had ever seen. He was a giant of a man with enormous shoulders and fists like hammers. A battered red-and-green cocked hat sat jauntily sideways on his pigtailed head and a bushy black beard sprouted from his chin. He had a broad face, a wide, fleshy nose that might have been flattened by a blow at some time, and bloodshot eyes.

'You're early,' the man said to Charles in a deep and powerful gruff voice, dropping the basket at his feet. 'I didn't expect you for another day.'

'We made good progress,' Charles said coolly, taking the man's arm and drawing him aside, out of earshot of anyone who might be interested in their conversation, which was doubtful, since most had their eyes fixed on a pretty and extremely well-endowed serving wench as she served them with ale.

'Did you encounter any trouble?'

'Only once. It could have been worse.'

'Never mind. You are here now.'

Charles drew Maria forward. 'Maria, this is Jaques.'

Jaques pulled his hat off and grinned down at her. 'Honoured to make your acquaintance, *mademoiselle.*'

'*Madame,*' Charles informed him quietly. 'For the time it takes us to reach England. Can you take us across tonight? If you can, there will be no need for us to find lodging. I have no desire to remain in Calais kicking my heels indefinitely.'

'Not till daybreak when the tide's full. Stay here until the early hours and then come aboard. You won't be alone. There will be other passengers.'

'I thought there might be. We'll be down in the harbour in plenty of time.'

Taken by surprise, Maria gave Charles a startled glance. Was this man expecting them? And if so, how could this be? 'Charles, there are boats crossing all the time to Dover, and then there's the packet. I'm sure we would have no difficulty obtaining passage on one of them.'

'Jaques brought me out from England. Not wishing to draw attention to myself, I asked him to be here to take me back.'

Maria stared at him in amused amazement. 'Not draw attention? Charles, have you had a good look at the man? No disrespect to you, Jaques,' she said, meeting Jaques's eye, 'but you can't help but draw attention. You are the most terrifying individual I have ever seen.'

Jaques looked down at her and laughed out loud at her outspoken honesty, not in the least offended by it—in fact, he was openly amused by it. 'Worry not, little lady. Appearances aren't always what they seem. I am but a simple fisherman here to sell my mackerel,' he said, giving the basket a kick with his foot, 'and as meek as a lamb and quite harmless.'

Maria gritted her teeth and forced herself to look this fearful new acquaintance in the face. 'I am obliged to go to England, so I will have to take your word for that.'

'You may rest assured that my boat is seaworthy. I've things to do before we put to sea,' Jaques said, drawing his bushy eyebrows together and addressing himself to Charles in a low voice. 'I'd be obliged if you told no one you're to sail with me on the tide.'

Charles inclined his head gravely. 'I know better than to do that, Jaques.'

Sticking his hat back on his head at random and hoisting the fish basket on to his shoulder, with a final wave of his hand Jaques headed for the door where he turned and looked back at them. 'The sea is rough tonight. I advise you to drink some grog while you wait. It's pretty cold down in the harbour in the early hours.'

Charles turned to his companion and smiled, aware of her trepidation. 'Jaques was absolutely right. He really is quite harmless unless provoked.'

'Are you sure about that? Forgive me if I do not share your opinion, Charles. The man bears a striking resemblance to a pirate.'

Charles chuckled low in his throat. 'The difference being that he has no eye patch or wooden leg—although I suppose on second thoughts he does bear some resemblance to a pirate in that he is a—gentleman of fortune—as well as being a fisherman.'

Something registered in Maria's mind and she frowned. 'These people who are to sail with us? Who are they, Charles, and why the need for secrecy?'

'Because they are aristocrats, *émigrés* already fleeing the country in fear of their lives. For a price, Jaques is willing to take them to safety in England. It's a good living in these times. Dangerous, yes, but good.' He glanced around. 'Now I have met up with Jaques I can send Pierre on his way—although he will probably remain here for now. Apparently he has family living further along the coast and will be glad of a spell of inactivity.'

Outside the inn they were caught up in a fierce gust of wind bringing with it stinging drops of rain and a strong smell of the sea. After they had said farewell to Pierre they went back inside. After partaking of a dish of steaming mutton, taking Jaques's advice Charles ordered hot rum.

'Drink some of this. It will be cold on the boat and you'll be glad of it.'

Maria was not so sure when she eyed the pungent beverage suspiciously. She had never tasted spirits and was on the point of refusing, but Charles bent forwards so that his head almost touched her ear, and he said quietly, 'Don't make a fuss, Maria. You'll get us noticed.'

Bravely Maria swallowed down the hot rum. She gasped and began to cough, which brought a broad smile to Charles's lips and he slapped her between the shoulder blades, which almost knocked her off her feet.

'I should have warned you. It takes your breath at first, but it will warm you.'

Maria was coughing too much to reply, but once she got her breath back she discovered that this assertion proved correct. An agreeable warmth infiltrated her body and she found it to her liking. She took another sip, cautiously this time, and seated herself on a settle before the fire to wait until it was time for them to leave.

The deserted harbour under the town walls was just coming to life. Fishing boats were getting ready to leave, and the now-empty fishing baskets heaped on the decks would be brought back filled with plaice and sole, wet and shiny, and granite-coloured crabs.

Jaques's boat was a small fishing vessel plainly crafted. It looked small and insignificant alongside a brig and two tall-masted frigates, but her very insignificance was a safeguard, as was the single, modest riding light at her masthead.

Jaques was beckoning to them on the deck, and seconds later they crossed the plank connecting her with the shore and were aboard. Maria wrinkled her nose.

The boat smelled nauseatingly of fish. She looked at
Charles, suddenly aware of how tense he had become.
Jaques moved out of the dawn shadows across the deck
towards them.

'We'll get off now. The tide's all but full. Escort the
lady below,' he ordered, keeping his voice low.

'Below?' Maria asked hesitantly, extremely reluctant to enter the bowels of the boat. She had a dread of
ships and would rather be on deck in the fresh air than
down below.

'Yes, Maria, down to the cabin,' Charles said, taking
her arm with a firm grip.

She held back. 'May I not stay here?'

Charles's grim expression as he met her gaze boded
ill. 'No, you may not. Until we have left the harbour you
must remain below.'

'But I don't—much care for ships,' she confessed,
ashamed of her weakness, but she couldn't help it. She
hoped her request to stay on deck wouldn't sound like
cowardice and that he would understand her fear.
'They—frighten me.'

His jaw hardened in annoyance. 'This isn't a ship,
Maria, it's a boat, a small fishing boat in case you
haven't noticed.'

Maria flinched. He spoke to her as he would to a
naughty child. 'I do know that, but they're one and the
same to me. My grandparents'—my mother's parents'—ship went down in a storm in the Channel when
they were returning to England after visiting my aunt.'

That made Charles pause. 'I'm sorry,' he said finally.
'I recall you telling me. I should have known. Nevertheless, Maria, for our sake and for those already below, it

is essential that the coastguard and the harbour authorities don't see us. If they should spot us, the consequences don't bear thinking about. No one saw us board. As far as anyone is concerned Jaques is embarking on one of his regular fishing trips. Do you understand?'

She did not persist. 'Yes, and I'm sorry. Of course I'll go below,' she said bravely. She hesitated, reluctant to go without him, she realised with a vague sense of surprise. 'You will come with me?'

His voice softened. 'Of course. We'll come back on deck when we're out in the Channel.'

So she allowed him to lead her below to the small cabin. In the yellow light of the lantern they saw they were not alone. Six shapes—the *émigrés,* two women and four men, who had smuggled themselves aboard during the night—all sat close together, clutching their few possessions.

Dressed in plain, shabby clothes, with caps covering their heads and pulled well down, they looked far more like the rabble who pursued them for their lives than aristocrats.

That was the moment when Maria was made forcibly conscious that she was just like them, a fugitive, because she was obliged to hide and flee. She had no choice but to humbly accept in silence what fate might send her, even to being ordered about by someone like Jaques.

Taking her hand, Charles drew her down on to a bench away from the others, just big enough for the two of them. Sensing her fear and feeling her body tremble next to his, he leaned towards her. 'Maria,' he said gently in her ear, 'you needn't fear the boat will go down. Jaques hasn't lost one yet.'

She glanced at him and then away again, conscious of the intense physical awareness she felt at his nearness. She wanted him to put his arms around her and calm her fears. She could hear the wind getting up. Down in the cabin it seemed to be blowing with a force that was terrifying.

Something in Charles's chest tightened. 'Maria,' he murmured, 'are you all right?' Placing a gentle finger under her chin, he compelled her to meet his gaze. 'What is it? Are you really so frightened?'

She swallowed and nodded. 'Would you... Do you suppose you could hold me?'

Wordlessly he put his arm around her and drew her close. She placed her head on his shoulder and he could feel her body trembling. 'There's nothing to fear,' he murmured gently, stroking her head. 'We'll soon be out into the Channel and then we'll be able to go up on deck.' He pressed his cheek against her hair and repressed a smile, suspecting her docility was a measure of her fear and fatigue—and maybe the belated effects of the rum she had consumed.

The moment he drew her into his arms, Maria was instantly conscious of the warmth and potential power of his body against hers, and felt an answering spark in him. She tilted her face to look at him. His hair fell in an untidy sweep over his brow. He had an engaging face. She saw something she had not seen in him before, the sweetness and humour of his firm lips, the quiet amusement behind his alert gaze. She paused, holding her breath as her heart turned over. To her at that moment, he was quite simply a beautiful man. Something stirred inside her. Something was happening, something that shouldn't be happening—something she didn't want to happen.

Her body began to soften. It was a melting feeling, one her body liked. For what seemed to be an age she really looked at Charles. Even though she had been alone with him for three days, it was like coming face to face with a stranger. It frightened her, especially when his eyes locked on hers. It was all she could do to face his unspoken challenge and not retreat from him. Measure by measure the realisation dawned that this was a man she did not know.

Nothing had prepared Maria for the thrill of quivering excitement that gripped her now. Her heart swelled with an emotion of such proportions she was overwhelmed. She was aware that this was a moment of great importance yet didn't know in what way.

Quite suddenly, and with stunned amazement, she was conscious of an overwhelming impulse to reach up and take his dark head between her hands and draw it down to her own. For a moment it was almost as though she could feel his thick hair under her fingers.

Against her will and against all common sense, something stirred deep, deep within her, something dark and soft and treacherous. A hot tide of incredulous horror engulfed her mind and body in a wave of burning shame, and she lowered her eyes, hiding them with her long black lashes. They had looked at each other deeply, a look that spanned no more than a few seconds and yet seemed to last for an eternity.

She shivered in anticipation, then almost shyly she pulled away from him. His eyes on hers were very bright, very tender.

'I'm all right now. You must think I'm very foolish.'

'No, Maria. To be afraid is nothing to be ashamed of. It often takes courage to admit it.'

Charles was not immune to the unresisting woman he had held close. He was a virile man, a very masculine man, who was accustomed to the women in his arms allowing him whatever he asked of them. He was well used to the lusting pleasures that were always available to him. He had not, until he'd kissed Maria, held a woman in his arms who was not only young but innocent. Not until she had met him had she encountered the closeness, the intimacy and power of a man's body close to her own, of desire that inflamed the flesh and confused all coherent thought.

The vessel slipped slowly out of the harbour and bounded forwards running into the Channel. On a word from Jaques, those below were told it was safe to come up on deck.

Clinging on to the rail next to Charles and with Jaques at the helm, as the vessel rolled on the swell already making itself felt in a choppy sea, the waves capped with curls of foam, Maria was filled with confusion. She could not understand herself. She realised that Charles was becoming very dear to her, but how could this be when she didn't really know him? Just a few moments ago, if he had made the slightest movement towards her she would have been in his arms.

Breathing deeply of the night air she looked back at the receding French coast shrouded in early morning mist. The wind was getting stronger, causing the sail to crack and the little vessel to lurch alarmingly.

'We're running right into a storm,' Maria gasped fearfully.

'This isn't a storm.' Jaques laughed, his voice booming over the noise of the wind. 'If you saw a real storm, you'd never forget it.'

'Get back from the rail,' Charles ordered, taking her arm and almost dragging her away. 'I'd hate to see you tossed overboard. I'd be forced to jump in to rescue you.'

'And I would expect nothing less,' she laughed, glad to be out of the claustrophobic confines of the cabin and the threat of being in such close proximity to him always posed to her susceptible heart.

'Are you all right?' he shouted above the wind.

She nodded. 'Yes. I am now. Don't worry about me. I'm going home and that's all that counts.'

Drawing her cloak tightly about her, she looked up at Charles, at his profile etched against the lightening sky. Indomitable pride was chiselled into his handsome face, determination in the arrogant cut of his jaw, intelligence and hard-bitten strength etched into every feature of his face. There was an aloof strength, a powerful charisma about him that had nothing to do with his tall, strong-shouldered physique or that mocking smile of his. There was something else, a feeling she got that he had done and seen all there was to do and see, and that all those experiences were locked away behind an unbreachable wall of charm, a handsome face, and piercing light blue eyes. Beyond any woman's reach.

Daylight had broken as the boat gently nosed its way towards the English coastline. It was a sight Maria would never forget. The boat was rolling gently now, the wind having dropped mid-channel. Gradually the land came more clearly into view, with its white cliffs and the castle overlooking the harbour. What a relief it was to see England again.

Ever since she had left she had wished to return. Now there was no need to wish any longer. At that moment she saw the sun rise in a ball of crimson on the horizon— just like an omen, she thought, marking the start of a new life, a happy life. Would Henry be a part of it?

Before Charles had arrived at Chateau Feroc she had had her doubts about marrying Henry, and now, after the short time she had spent alone with Charles and the sensations he had awakened inside her, sensations and womanly desires far different from anything she had ever experienced before, as arduous as the task promised to be, she saw no help for it. Already the decision was beginning to form in her mind that she would have to tell Henry she would not marry him.

Chapter Five

Maria was returning to a country under the reign of King George III, a man who was devoted to Queen Charlotte. The court of King George was irreproachable, respectable and formal. Unfortunately of late he had become mentally unsound. The malady had precipitated a political crisis and making his son George, a man who was totally self-indulgent and as incapable of curbing his spending as of governing his passions Prince Regent, was being considered.

In the coming days, and the more familiar Maria became with England and its politics and the royal family, she would realise there were many similarities in the man who would be Regent and the man to whom she was betrothed.

Once the boat was tied up to the quay, after thanking Jaques and bidding him farewell, Charles and Maria headed for the town. As they approached the inn where they were to meet Henry, Maria walked stiffly beside

Charles, her back ramrod straight, unable to forget what had taken place between them on the boat, and the profound effect those moments when they had looked at each other as if for the first time had had on her. She noticed how quiet Charles had become, how tense.

On the point of meeting her betrothed at long last, she masked her trepidations by an extreme effort of will. Whether Henry was as unworthy as Charles said he was, was yet to be determined.

With these thoughts she went inside the tavern. There were few people about. Her eyes scanned every face for the one she remembered. She turned to Charles, who was just behind her.

'I don't see Henry. Maybe he arrived ahead of us and has gone out—for a stroll, perhaps.'

Charles's expression was one of cynicism. How little she knew Henry Winston. He was not the type to waste his time strolling.

'Or perhaps he's been delayed on the road,' Maria suggested hopefully.

'I didn't expect him to be waiting, Maria. We have arrived a day ahead of schedule. I would imagine he is still in London. I'll go and order refreshment while we decide what to do.'

Maria seated herself at a table in a window recess so she could see the road and not miss the moment when Henry arrived. Now the moment had come, she was so scared and utterly unnerved that she knew she could not have moved a muscle to flee if need be. She waited as one transfixed, not knowing what to expect of the man her father had chosen for her to marry.

She turned and looked at Charles when he approached the table. Meeting his eyes she sensed that all was not as it should be. He was holding a letter in his hand, a hard, angry look on his face.

'Charles? What is it? Is something wrong?'

He held out the letter. She took it, her hand shaking a little. Seeing that it was addressed to him and strangely reluctant to open it, she offered it back to him, her eyes wary.

'It's addressed to you.'

'It concerns you. Read it.'

'Who is it from?'

'Winston. It would seem that he's unable to come to meet you—something about unforeseen business. He won't be coming to Dover.'

'You mean he can't get away?'

Can't or doesn't want to bother, Charles thought furiously. 'Now why is it,' he mocked, pacing the floor in exasperation, 'that letter doesn't surprise me? I had my doubts about him travelling to Dover, which would have been a true test of his merit. I can only thank God that he had the foresight to inform us, otherwise we might have been kicking our heels here for a week, waiting for him to arrive.'

Maria read Henry's brief note. It would appear she would have to remain under Charles's protection a while longer, and Henry was sure Sir Charles wouldn't mind seeing her safely to London where they would be reunited and married right away.

With a strange feeling of relief that she had been handed a reprieve, Maria folded the letter and handed it back to Charles. 'I'm sorry, Charles. It looks as if you'll have to put up with me a while longer.' She expected the news that he would have charge of her for a while yet to get a reaction, but except for a muscle that began to twitch in his jaw, there was none. She sensed a change in him. His manner and the way he was looking at her was in sharp variance to what she had become used to.

Charles thought Maria looked very small and forlorn and as he looked at her his heart softened. Absently she smoothed a lock of hair from her temple. She had twisted the heavy black tresses in a large knot at the nape of her neck, which emphasised the perfection of the delicate features and oval contours of her face. Hers was a soft and rare beauty that would remain ageless for many years to come.

He wished that he didn't feel so responsible for her. It was an absurd feeling and it irritated him, for there was no reason for it. But the truth of it was that at the very beginning he had felt obligated to protect Sir Edward's daughter, and knowing the nature of her betrothed, he had made it his duty to try to prevent her marrying Colonel Winston when the time came.

'I'm sorry, Maria. I know how bitterly disappointed you must be feeling.'

Maria looked at him. His eyes were fixed on her with a frowning intensity. Her lips curved in a cynical smile. 'If there's anything I've learnt over the years, it's that life is full of disappointments. One has to learn to bear them.'

She looked up at him, at his taut features, and it became apparent to her how Henry's tardiness affected him also. Suddenly she was overwhelmed with a loneliness that wrenched her heart. Until now she hadn't realised how much she had come to depend on Charles for both his strength and his protection. Parting from him was going to be harder than she had realised.

'It is you that concerns me, Charles. I have no doubt that you hoped to discharge your duty where I am concerned and be about your own affairs. This must have come as a blow to you. I have no wish to be a burden to you so perhaps if there is a conveyance that will take me to Gravely—'

'No,' he said sharply. 'I will not hear of it.'

'I recall you telling me that you had made your own arrangements once we reached Dover.'

He nodded. 'My home, Highgate, is in Kent. It was my intention to go there.'

'I'm so sorry. But—you don't have to change your plans. If I cannot go to Gravely, I am quite capable of going on to London alone.'

He shook his head, rejecting her suggestion. 'I will not allow it. I arranged for my own coach and driver to meet me here. As soon as they arrive, if you don't feel too bruised from your journey to Calais and in need of rest, we can leave as soon as we have eaten. Highgate is close to Canterbury. We can break our journey there.'

Still seated in the window recess, Maria raised her eyebrows, her look one of admiration as she watched a splendid coach, its body lacquered a gleaming black, drawn by four identical grey horses, the coachman turned out in formal bottle-green livery, arrive.

Charles, who had been pacing the floor impatiently, suddenly came to a halt.

'Here he is. Very soon we shall be on the road.'

Maria stared at him. 'You mean—that fine-looking carriage belongs to you?'

'It does—and I am sure you will find it a good deal more comfortable than the conveyance we travelled in to Calais.'

When the horses had been rested and fed, the coachman put up the steps and closed the door, and with scarcely any sensation of motion, the well-sprung travelling chaise glided along the road behind the four prancing greys.

Maria glanced about her, admiring the crystal lamps and the heavy silver door handles and the soft dove-grey upholstery. Luxuriating in the unexpected comfort of the spacious conveyance, she looked across at her companion, who had his legs stretched out and crossed at the ankles. He was gazing morosely out of the window. Immediately she was filled with contrition. What a nuisance all this must be for him and how he must be cursing Henry for not coming to Dover to meet her.

'I hate inconveniencing you like this, Charles,' she said softly. 'Will you stay long at Highgate?'

He flicked a glance in her direction. 'I haven't made up my mind. It depends what I find when I get there. Hopefully things will be as they were when I left for France. I have to go to London anyway. I have pressing matters and important people to see.'

'Has it anything to do with you being in France?' she dared to ask, expecting a rebuff.

She was surprised when he fixed her with a level look and said, 'To satisfy your curiosity, Maria, now it is safe to do so I can tell you that I went to France on the request of some members of the government to see and report on the general order of things in Paris. Like everyone else in England, the government is horrified about what is happening—the massacres and the burning of properties. Those with a vested interest in the social order are seriously worried that revolutionary ideas will spread to Britain.'

Maria stared at him wide-eyed in astonishment. 'Good gracious! So you are a paid spy in the employ of the British government. How exciting—though highly dangerous,' she finished on a more sombre note.

His eyes hardened and a thin, cynical smile curved his lips. 'You needn't appear so surprised, Maria. You had me cast in the role of spy from the first.'

'In all truth I didn't know what to think. I'm just relieved things have turned out the way they have—that France is behind us. What will happen in the end, do you think?'

'That depends on what you mean by the end.'

'When all the rioting and burning of noble houses and the killing has ended. Will France get her republic?'

'I believe it will.'

When he made no attempt to converse further with her, Maria sensed that he was grappling with some sort of weighty problem, and she let the silence continue, content to watch the passing scenery roll past the windows.

Arriving at Highgate they were admitted through the tall gates of the estate where Charles lived. The warm mellow brick manor house stood proudly against a backdrop of sprawling parkland as they drove up the gracefully curving drive.

Maria looked around in approval. 'What a lovely house.'

'I agree—but then I would. It's been in my family for generations.'

They stepped out of the carriage and climbed the wide flight of stone steps to the massive door. Before they reached it it was opened by a stiff-faced man dressed in dark blue and gold livery. His face relaxed with pleasure when he saw who had arrived.

'Sir Charles! It's good to see you back.'

Charles lifted a hand in an invitation for Maria to precede him. 'Thank you, Jesson,' he said, striding past him and nodding at Mrs Moor, the housekeeper at Highgate. 'It's good to be home. How is my mother?'

'Lady Osbourne left for London last month, Sir Charles. She was quite well when she left. She said she was tired of the country and was missing her friends.'

'I see. Then I shall see her there. We are on our way to London. When we have eaten and the horses have rested we'll continue with our journey. Is there anything I need to attend to while I am here?'

'I don't think so, sir. Mr Parry has everything running like clockwork. There is some private correspondence that needs attending to.'

'I'll take it with me and deal with it in London. Mark Parry is my bailiff,' Charles explained to Maria. 'He is highly competent and I don't know what I'd do without him. Have cook prepare a meal for us, Mrs Moor—and if you could, show Miss Monkton to a room. I'm sure you would like to freshen up before we eat,' he said, looking at Maria. His gaze passed over her attire and his expression became one of distaste.

'I think it's time you disposed of that dress. I'm sure Mrs Moor can find you something else to wear. My sisters both have dresses stashed somewhere. I think Georgina is more your size. There's bound to be something that will suit. For safety's sake, Miss Monkton was forced to leave everything in France in a hurry,' he explained to his housekeeper.

'Which is why I appear before you dressed as a peasant,' Maria said, looking with mock dismay at her dismal attire. 'I assure you I don't normally look like this.'

Mrs Moor faced Maria with a cheery smile. 'Come with me, Miss Monkton. I'll see what I can find.'

And she did. Attired in a delicate lemon gown, the long tresses of her hair pulled from her face and left to fall down her back beneath trails of lemon ribbon, Maria entered the drawing room like a fresh breeze, sweeping in through the door.

Seated by the window flicking through some correspondence, Charles quickly came to his feet in appreciation of her dazzling beauty. His gaze slid boldly over her, from the top of her shining head to her swelling breasts beneath the bodice of her gown and right down to her feet. Maria was accustomed to the admiring glances of gentlemen, but there was nothing gentlemanly about Charles's lazy perusal of her body.

'Are you quite finished?' she asked tersely.

His unhurried gaze lifted to her eyes and a wry smile quirked his stern lips when he heard the exasperation in her voice. Perhaps she resented him suggesting she shed her unflattering black gown that had seen better days on her maid. 'I was merely admiring the transformation, Maria. You look quite radiant.'

She had been lovely before, but he hadn't expected her to blossom into a full-fledged beauty simply by changing her gown. When she reached London she would dazzle society's gentlemen. And therein lay his problem, for she was a complete innocent, an inexperienced innocent in his charge, and for whom he was responsible. The image of himself as guardian of her virtue—not forgetting her fortune—was so ludicrous it was laughable. But that was the role he would be forced to play when Maria had sent Henry Winston packing—which she would, when she laid eyes on his gross bulk, and she was truly alone.

'Now come and eat. I would like to resume our journey as soon as possible if we are to reach London before dark.'

Feeling slightly mellow and in good spirits after partaking of a delicious meal, happy that Charles's sombre mood had lightened somewhat with the food and wine, when they had left Highgate and were settled once more in the carriage, not wishing to impose on Charles any longer and impatient to see Henry so she could take stock and do what she thought was necessary, Maria ventured to ask, 'Will you take me straight to wherever it is that Henry lives when we reach London?' She smiled, and, without giving him chance to reply, went on, 'Don't you find it strange that I have no idea where that is?' Charles merely gave her a wry smile. 'Whenever I wrote to him I always sent the letters to his address in India.' She looked at him sideways. 'Where does he live now he's left the company and is back in England, Charles?'

'He has taken a modest house in the Strand,' he answered brusquely.

'I see, although I really have no idea where that is. I'm not at all familiar with London, never having been there. Whatever the outcome of our meeting, I'm impatient to go to Gravely, to see if it's just as I remember it when my father was alive.'

Suddenly Charles shot her a glance of exasperation. He looked angry and agitated. 'Maria, I would be grateful if you would speak of something else. The last thing I wish to discuss right now is Henry Winston.'

Maria stiffened and pressed herself back against the cushions, her face blank with hurt, surprised at the coldness in his eyes.

Charles met the look squarely. 'You think that's callous and brutal of me, don't you?' he said with deliberate harshness.

'I'm sorry. I seem to have been talking a deal too much. I did not mean to bore you. But you needn't worry. We'll soon be in London and then you'll be free of me. Your obligation to me will be over. That must please you.'

'What pleases me is that I've managed to get you out of France unharmed. What doesn't please me is that you might decide to honour your father's wish and wed Henry Winston regardless,' he snapped irately.

Maria met his gaze with anguish in her eyes. 'You know how to wound, don't you, Charles? Do we have to go through this again? You have made your feelings plain where Henry is concerned. Your point is well taken.'

The lines around Charles's mouth tightened and a hard gleam shone from his eyes. 'But is it, Maria? I think I should tell you the truth about the man before you meet so you can prepare yourself.'

'Prepare myself? What on earth for?' she said, her voice quick with indignation and reproach. 'Has he sprouted two heads or something?'

'Don't be ridiculous. Initially I decided your betrothal was none of my business—'

'You were right,' Maria flared. 'It isn't. But why didn't you tell me if you had something to say?'

'I didn't tell you because I suppose I meant it for the best,' he replied, ignoring her jibe.

'And now it's too late.' With a stubborn lift of her chin she turned her head away.

His hand shot out and grasped her wrist. 'You *will* listen to what I have to say.'

Maria pulled furiously at her imprisoned wrist. 'Let me go.' When he released her, she rubbed her wrist and glowered at him. 'Very well, say what you have to say. But in the end I shall make up my own mind about him.'

Despite her determined words, Charles saw there was doubt in Maria's face, and something else. A dawning apprehension and fear.

'So, what is wrong with him?' she asked to prompt him when he delayed answering.

'What is wrong with him,' Charles said with brutal clarity, 'is that Henry Winston suffers from overindulgence of all the pleasures in life: drink, drugs, gambling—and women.'

Maria caught her breath in shock and turned quickly. 'Oh—I see.'

'You don't know him. How can you? You have not set eyes on him in six years, don't forget. He is not a fit person for you to associate yourself with—or any other woman, come to that—never mind becoming his wife. He's totally unsuitable for a decently reared young woman as yourself.'

'Please stop it. If he is as bad as you say, then I shall soon see for myself.'

'I do not know why, when he left India, and knowing what was happening in France, he did not go himself to bring you back. Nor do I know why he could not meet us at Dover. What I do know is that after attending wild, debauched parties he is frequently incapable of standing upright.'

Maria could not deny that she was deeply shocked by what he was telling her, and however much she wanted to disbelieve it, she knew Charles would not lie to her. 'Why are you trying so hard to discredit him to me?'

'Perhaps it's because I don't like to see pearls cast before swine.'

'It won't be like that,' she whispered, averting her eyes.

Charles saw she was hurt. The truth always did that. 'When you were a young girl you no doubt cherished a vision of a fine-looking soldier of the East India Company—a handsome knight in splendorous armour—and dreamt of him returning and carrying you off to a wondrous place. Am I right, Maria?'

'Perhaps…when I was thirteen, but the fantasy dimmed very quickly.'

'Strip away his rank and his uniform and you will see what is left—a blackguard, *roué,* drunkard, gamester— all in all a complete hedonist. It's impossible to respect a man like that.'

Seeing the confusion and bewilderment that filled her

eyes, aware that she had no experience of the kind of man he spoke of, once again Charles was conscious of the pain in his heart when he looked at her.

'Now you know, I would advise you to go directly to Gravely when you are rested.'

Maria didn't answer him. The moment seemed to stretch interminably. At length she managed to say, 'If he is all the terrible things you accuse him of being, why would he want to marry me?'

Charles's smile was ironic. 'Come now, Maria. Surely not even you could be that naïve. Your wealth speaks for itself.'

Maria was profoundly offended and humiliated by his remark, and ire sparked in her eyes. 'And I don't suppose you believe that Henry could possibly want to marry me for myself,' she retorted, deeply hurt and insulted that he should think this.

'You were thirteen years old. That should speak for itself.'

No, this was too much. She felt that he was laughing at her, and she could feel the red flames of outrage scorch her body. She drew herself up to her full height. 'How dare you say that? Yes, I was very young, I cannot deny that and nor can I help it, but I—I trusted him,' she finished, somewhat lamely.

'I know you did, and I also know it must be dreadful to trust someone and then find yourself totally let down.'

Angry sparks flared in her eyes. 'Until I have seen Henry I don't know that. I don't doubt there is some element of truth in what you are saying, but I shall reserve judgement until I have seen for myself.'

Charles's gaze held hers; he knew he was being brutal, but if it was the only way he could get her to listen, then so be it. 'Think about it, Maria? He has worked for the East India Company for years, enjoying his pleasures too much to be taken seriously by his superiors to be offered promotion. Instead, he was considered an embarrassment to the Company and asked to leave.'

'You—mean he didn't leave of his own volition?'

'That is precisely what I am saying.'

'Then there must have been some other reason.'

Charles uttered a curse beneath his breath at her stubborn refusal to consider, let alone believe, what he was saying to be true. 'Consider this. Winston has no wealth of his own to speak of. When he called on your father at Gravely, it was just what he needed, an ill man with a fortune, with a daughter to inherit, who would drop that same fortune at the feet of the man she married. With his knowledge of India and your father's thirst to hear all about the land he loved, a land he knew he would never set eyes on again, this was child's play for him to win your father over.'

Maria was stricken. 'No.' Her voice cracked painfully. 'I do not believe any of this—nor do I know why you should want to discredit him so.'

'Because I know him, Maria. Everything went off as Winston had hoped, better than that since your father did not live long after your betrothal, leaving everything to you. Can you not see the cynical calculation of which you have been the object, and the cold-blooded way in which Winston set about playing on your father's goodness and your innocence?'

'My father was an excellent judge of character. He trusted Henry implicitly, otherwise he would never have agreed to the betrothal.'

'He was an ill man who was desperate to settle his daughter's future. Winston appeared at Gravely like manna from heaven. Your father was hoodwinked by Winston. If you go ahead and marry him, your precious Henry will not enjoy your fortune for long.'

'Why, what are you saying?'

'In no time at all he will have got rid of it. He is head over heels in debt and disgrace. Maria, listen to me. You will be in as much danger from Henry Winston as you were from the mob in France.'

'No,' she seethed. 'I do not know how I shall feel when I meet Henry—I confess to feeling apprehensive—and more than a little afraid. Since my father consented to my marriage to Henry, then I feel I owe it to his memory to at least give Henry the benefit of the doubt. I do not know why you are saying these things, Charles, why you hate him so much, unless it's because you are jealous of him for some reason and are doing your best to blacken his name to me.'

'And why would I want to do that? What reason could I possibly have?'

'Because—because you—you might want me for yourself.'

Elevating a dark brow, he looked at her speculatively, the hint of a smile curving his lips. 'And have I given you reason to think that, Maria?' he asked softly.

'All the time—in France—and on—on the boat—something happened...but I don't see... I don't understand... Oh...' Her cheeks flamed red. She was bewildered and totally out of her depth when it came to speaking of such intimate matters.

'No—you don't, do you?' His gaze was fixed intently on her. 'You don't know and you don't see—that's one of the things which makes you so extraordinary. You're so lovely, so innocent, somehow. Something did happen between us,' he admitted, his voice softening. 'We both felt it, but I am surprised that you should mention it. It shows your inexperience and innocence, Maria—and there is nothing to be ashamed of in that.'

Maria felt her cheeks grow hotter and she lowered her head to hide her embarrassment. That exchange of incredulous glances—incredulous on her part—had lasted no more than a few seconds but had seemed absolutely right and so amazingly natural, she could feel it even now, a smoothness of something sweet like honey running through her veins.

But that incredulous feeling also brought with it a sense of fear, fear of Charles, but why this should be she did not know. She found him altogether too disturbing, and she didn't know how to deal with the strange, alien feelings he had evoked in her.

Straightening her slim shoulders, she lifted her chin and glared at him with defiance, trying to still the trembling of her body with a visible effort of will. She said, 'My inexperience is because of the sheltered life I have led at Chateau Feroc—which is the way of things in my aunt's world; no matter how disparaging you are about Henry, ultimately the decision as to whether I marry him or not is my decision.'

Charles's face stiffened into a scornful mask of stone. 'Don't be a little fool, Maria. If you go ahead with this foolishness it will not be long before you discover the misery of living from hand to mouth with a man for whom you will no longer hold any commercial value. But, as you say, that is your affair.'

Maria was angry and confused. How could Charles do this to her? How could he deliberately hurt her like this? 'I hate you for this.' Her voice was low and breathless and edged with scorn.

Charles's eyes had turned cold, cold and disdainful. One corner of his mouth lifted in a mocking smile. 'Hate me as much as you like, Maria, but you won't hate me nearly as much as you will hate Henry Winston when he has abused your body and disposed of your wealth—which, as your husband, he will have every right to do.'

Maria turned her head away and looked out of the window. Suddenly, despite the sun shining out of a clear blue sky she felt icy cold and more alone and isolated than she had ever felt in her life.

When the coach drew to a halt she peered out of the window. The light from the carriage lamps showed they were in a fashionable part of London, with fine-looking houses. It was too dark for her to see much, and there wasn't a light showing from any of the windows to suggest the house was occupied. A small *frisson* of alarm passed through her.

'Where is this? Is this where Henry lives?'

'No,' Charles answered curtly. 'This is my house— my town house, that is.'

'But—I don't understand…'

'You can't go to Winston tonight. It's far too late.'

Maria felt a perverse rush of fury at him for taking it upon himself to make a decision that concerned her without consulting her first.

'At least we have to be thankful for reaching home safely.' His tone was matter-of-fact.

Maria threw him a killing look. 'I'm glad you think so.'

Ignoring her heated remark and in no mood for further argument, Charles climbed out. 'Let's go inside.' He turned and looked back at her, still pressed in her seat. 'Maria,' he said with strained patience, 'don't make this any harder on yourself than it needs to be. If you were expecting me to take you to Winston then you were mistaken. You have your reputation to consider and it would not be right for you to stay with him. The scandal would be enormous.'

'And yet it's all right for me to stay with you. That, too, is highly irregular. Living with you, also a bachelor, will create as great a scandal as it would were I to go to Henry,' she taunted coldly.

'Before you raise any further objections you needn't worry. Your reputation will be quite safe, since you will be under the protection of my mother.'

Maria stared at him in astonishment, trying to assimilate what was happening. 'Your mother? She lives here—in this house?'

He nodded. 'So you see my home is not such a bad place for you to spend a few days.' With that he stalked off towards the door.

For a split second Maria was too furious and too miserable and tired to move, then she blinked back the tears of futility stinging her eyes and got out of the coach and followed in his wake. She knew she was being completely irrational in feeling so resentful, but she couldn't help it. Wrapping her arms around herself, she watched him tug at the bell.

'Don't tell me your servants are all abed,' she remarked with intended sarcasm when there was no response from inside.

He threw her an ironic glance. 'It looks like it. I am not expected.'

'Perhaps you could break a window,' she quipped.

'It won't come to that.' He scowled at her and said with exaggerated patience, 'Have you always been so difficult?'

'Difficult? Me? No, I have not. You seem to bring out the worst in me, that's all.'

The door opened and a manservant looked cautiously out into the gloom. Astonishment registered in his eyes and the poor man became flustered.

'Sir Charles.... Forgive me—I didn't realise...'

'It's all right, Denning. You weren't to know.' He turned to Maria, his tone authoritative when he spoke. 'We've already broken all the rules of etiquette where you are concerned, Maria, so I suggest you come inside and make yourself at home while a room is made ready.'

Realising she couldn't remain standing on the doorstep, she stepped over the threshold and without taking any notice of her surroundings, she glared at him. 'I'm not here out of choice,' she retorted irately, 'and don't you forget it.'

In answer, he gave her a long-suffering look, as if she were being impossibly difficult, so she jerked her gaze from his. 'And you will take some perverse pleasure in reminding me, I don't doubt. This is not an ideal situation for either of us, Maria, but I am determined to make the best of it. Welcome to my home,' he said drily.

Until that moment Maria wouldn't have believed she could feel more humiliated than she already did. She saw his eyes narrow and sensed his exasperation as he realised he might be stuck with her indefinitely, unless he sent her on her way and left her to whatever fate awaited her at the hands of her fiancé.

Terrified that the tears burning the backs of her eyes were going to fall, she tipped her head back and turned away, pretending to inspect her surroundings. Through the haze of her tears, as the hastily lit candles began to illuminate the hall, she noticed for the first time the splendour of Charles's house, the graceful, curving staircases that swept upwards on both sides of the large marble hall. Two huge chandeliers hung from the ceiling, and she could imagine them glittering like giant tiers of brilliant diamonds when lit.

There had been moments on the journey when she had been curious about Charles and his background, imagining him to be a man of modest means with a lifestyle to match. It was obvious she had been very wrong, for he was clearly a man of means, a man who could well afford a country residence as well as a town house.

'You must be hungry,' he said brusquely. 'I'll arrange for us to have something to eat.'

'I don't want anything to eat,' she stated ungraciously. 'I just want to go to bed. I have to get some sleep.'

Something in her pale face and heavy eyes made Charles respond without argument. He turned to Denning. 'What Miss Monkton means is that she's rather exhausted from her long journey and not very good company, Denning. She is to be my guest for an indeterminate period. How is my mother?'

'Lady Osbourne is very well.'

'Good. If she's awake, I'll go up and see her directly. Wake one of the chambermaids and have them attend Miss Monkton.'

'There's no need to do that,' Maria said quickly, hating the thought of dragging anyone from their bed at such a late hour. 'I am perfectly capable of managing by myself.'

'I insist.'

Which was precisely what he did. In no time at all a young girl called Ruby—her eyes still full of sleep and not much older than Maria—presented herself and attended to her in an enormous bedchamber every bit as comfortable and tastefully decorated and furnished as her room at the chateau. Looking at the silk-covered bed with longing, refusing the maid's offer to help her undress, Maria wearily pulled off her clothes, bade the chambermaid goodnight, climbed into bed, and fell into an exhausted slumber.

Maria woke late the following day—midday, in fact. Ruby brought her some buttered toast and muffins and tea on a tray, drawing back the curtains and filling the room with light. Climbing out of the huge four-poster bed, her feet sinking into the plush Aubusson carpet, feeling refreshed after a sound night's sleep, the strangeness of her new situation did not seem as intimidating as when Charles had brought her to his house.

She dressed quickly. Having memorised her way to her room the night before for fear of getting lost in this vast house—a showpiece of opulence designed to awe those who entered—she went downstairs. In the hall she paused and looked around her at the closed doors in confusion. Seeing her hesitation, Denning, attired in a black suit and shirt, which was more in keeping with his position as the Osbourne butler than his dishevelled appearance of last night, came towards her.

'Can I be of help, Miss Monkton?'

'I do hope so, Mr Denning,' Maria said, favouring him with a broad smile.

Denning was blown away by the beauty of it. It was so effective, so startling, that it took him a moment to realise it was the same young woman. It was such a transformation from the disgruntled young lady of the previous night.

'Where can I find Sir Charles? There are so many doors I am totally bemused.'

'I agree it is confusing. Sir Charles is in his study. I shall announce you.'

He swept the doors open in a soundless flourish and Maria found herself stepping into a room dominated by a large mahogany desk and book-lined walls and paintings in ornate frames. Maria's gaze was immediately drawn to its occupant. The man seated behind the richly carved desk bore little resemblance to the man she had travelled halfway across France with. Today, he was an aloof, icy stranger, a man who for no accountable reason she was suddenly shy of, and she felt a *frisson* of something that wasn't quite nervousness. She couldn't suppress an unruly surge of excitement at being once again in his presence. However, she was encouraged when she saw his granite features soften and his eyes warm when he looked up and his gaze rested on her, as if he understood how awkward she must be feeling.

Reassured and feeling the comfort and security of his presence, she entered the room quietly and walked towards the desk. His dark hair glinted in the bright sunlight, and she could see tiny lines around his eyes from all those times when he must have squinted into the bright sun in India.

'Good morning, Charles.'

He stood up. 'Morning? I think you will find it's well into the afternoon, Maria.'

'I know. I have no excuse other than I must have been more exhausted than I realised.' She gestured to a pile of documents and correspondence on his desk. 'I hope I'm not interrupting you.'

'You aren't,' he assured her, 'although the work has been piling up during my absence. I trust you slept well.'

'Very well, thank you,' she replied calmly, her heart beating faster than she would have wished, thinking that for a man who'd had less sleep than she had, he looked surprisingly vigorous. Clad in a tan frock coat, brown trousers and shiny black boots, there was a virile energy in his lean body, which provoked an immediate response in her own ardent nature.

'Good,' he said, relieved that she had tempered the cold animosity that had marked her mood on arriving at his home, and her tone. 'Have you eaten?'

'Yes, one of the maids brought me some food on a tray.'

The study looked out onto the square, which was surrounded by many fine residences. She moved towards the window, looking out. The sky was bright and clear blue, the branches of the trees swaying gently in the light breeze.

'You've missed the best part of the day,' said Charles quietly behind her, making her start. She hadn't realised he was so close. 'I much prefer the early mornings, which is when I usually take the opportunity to ride out in the park. If one goes early enough, there are few people about.'

Maria stood perfectly still, all coherent thought driven from her mind by his unexpected proximity. She was grateful she had her back to him and he couldn't see her confusion. It would not do to let him see he had her at a disadvantage.

'I like the early part of the day the best, too, which is when I would ride out when I lived in France. Although it is certainly a lovely day,' she murmured, turning to face him.

Immediately she realised her mistake. He really was standing too close and she had no avenue of retreat. He looked straight into her eyes for a few seconds, almost overwhelming her with the force of his personality. For a fleeting second the intensity of his light blue eyes seemed to explode. An expression she did not understand flashed through them and was gone. She felt extremely confused and vulnerable by the unexpected intimacy of that brief contact—and something else as well—a lick of desire, brief but horribly, dangerously strong. It must have showed because a glint of amusement flickered in the intelligent eyes and he suddenly smiled, a slow almost triumphant smile, almost as if he had guessed what she was thinking.

Seeing the gentle flush that mounted her cheeks and sensing her discomfort, Charles stepped away from her.

Maria relaxed slightly, only then aware that she had

been holding her breath. She began to breathe normally, chastising herself for acting so foolishly. 'Charles, I am sorry for my behaviour last night. It was unforgivable of me. I am not normally so rude. I can only put it down to exhaustion.'

'Don't worry about it,' he said. 'I'm sorry I was churlish.' Combing his fingers through his hair, he sighed. 'We were both tired. It's been a trying few days since we set out on our journey.'

Maria's throat constricted at his decency to apologise to her when she was the one who had been difficult. Charles had been a godsend to her. He deserved more from her than petty sulks, she thought fiercely, vowing in future to curb her temper and to find a way of dealing with her own irrational attraction to him.

'Yes, it has. I can't believe that just four days ago I was still at the chateau. When are we leaving?'

His eyes narrowed. 'Leaving?'

'For Henry's house.'

'Soon.' His tone was dismissive. 'We'll discuss it later.'

'When will we discuss it?' she persisted stubbornly.

'Later,' he repeated.

'I want to go, Charles. I am impatient to get my meeting with Henry behind me. Why are you being difficult about it?' He lifted his brows and regarded her in cold silence for a long moment. 'You can't stop me seeing him, you know, no matter how hard you try.'

'If it were up to me, I would see that the two of you never met.'

'It is not up to you,' Maria said quietly. 'You have no right.'

He nodded, his expression suddenly grave. 'You are

quite correct. I have no right. I promise I shall take you to see him later, but first my mother would like to meet you.'

'And I would like to meet her.'

'Unfortunately she does not enjoy the best of health—she tires easily,' he explained, 'and she spends a great deal of her time in bed.'

'I am sorry to hear that. I will try not to tire her.'

Chapter Six

Claudette Osbourne lay in a large bed. She was propped up by several thick white pillows, down which fell a thick plait of silver hair streaked with traces of gold. Her eyes were pale blue and tiny wrinkles creased her face. She was a striking-looking woman, a forceful woman secure in her own strength and will, a will, along with the dominating power of life that shone in her eyes, that filled the room with her presence.

Her shrewd eyes took in every inch of Maria before she spoke. 'I'm glad to meet you, Miss Monkton—but come closer where I can see you,' she said pleasantly.

Taking Maria's hand, Charles drew her closer to the bed. 'Maria, meet my mother.'

'I'm happy to meet you, Lady Osbourne. I apologise for imposing myself on you like this, but I assure you my stay will by of short duration.'

'My dear, you are welcome to stay just as long as you like—is that not so, Charles?' she said, with a strong trace of her French accent. 'I apologise most sincerely for not getting up to greet you. I was not expecting you, you see.'

'Please don't worry about it. We arrived very late and I was exhausted after all the travelling.'

'I hope your room is comfortable and to your satisfaction.'

'Yes, thank you.'

'I understand you've had quite a journey and I am relieved you have managed to reach England safely—you and Charles.' An odd tenderness glowed in her eyes whey they rested on her son. 'I have every confidence you would have been safe in his care. But you have left relatives there.'

'Yes, my aunt and her daughter—my cousin Constance.'

'And naturally you must be very worried about them—as I am about my own family in the south of France.'

Maria nodded. 'I pray for them and hope they are safe.'

'Then I hope your prayers are answered. My son tells me you are in London to meet your betrothed.'

'Yes.' Maria glanced pointedly at Charles, thinking how considerate he was to his mother, although his persona, that of caring, loving, sympathetic son and committed guardian of herself, disguised the fact that, where keeping her from Henry was concerned, he could have put Machiavelli in the shade.

'I hope to see Colonel Winston before the day is out, is that not so, Charles?' The light from the window illuminated her face and picked out the midnight-blue lights in her black hair. She was pale, and her expression seemed strained, but her candid green eyes met

Charles's with an almost innocent steadfastness, for she had no intention of letting him renege on his promise.

'I told you I shall arrange it,' he replied stiffly.

'And make sure you do.' Lady Osbourne laughed, surprising Maria with the youthful zest with which she dismissed her son's statement. 'It would be cruel of you to postpone their meeting any longer.'

'I have no intention of doing so,' he replied, breaking off as Denning knocked on the door to announce he had a visitor. 'Excuse me,' he said, striding to the door. 'A gentleman of some importance I've been expecting has arrived. I'll be downstairs.'

'You mustn't let Charles bully you, my dear,' Lady Osbourne said when he'd gone out, indicating with a wave of her hand that Maria should sit in the comfortable chair beside the bed. 'Pay him no attention, at least not when he's in one of his moods. He's really a very nice man, but having to leave his precious India when his father died, and with an invalid for a mother, it hasn't been easy for him.' She sighed, a softening entering her eyes as they rested on Maria's face. 'I remember your father from the brief time I spent in India. I have much to be grateful to him for—Charles's life, for one. Charles told you how your father saved his life by pulling him out of a swollen river?'

'Yes—yes, he did.'

'It was an act of immense bravery on your father's part. You resemble him very much. He was very handsome as I recall.'

Maria was unprepared for the lump that suddenly clogged her throat. 'I thought so, too. He spoke of India all the time and his life there. It saddened him to leave, but when my mother died he thought it in my best interest to be raised in England.'

'You were born in India as I recall.'

'I was, but I don't remember it. I was a baby when I left,' Maria said, finding herself responding to Lady Osbourne's warmth and friendliness.

'You must miss him dreadfully—as Charles misses his own, my dear Frederick. Frederick was so proud of Charles. After completing his training at the East India Company's military college, he went to India, where he served with distinction. He was filled with ambition in those days, and he had the ability to go far in the Company's rapidly expanding empire.'

'Will he go back to India?'

'No. Not now. He came home when Frederick died—there was so much to do at Highgate. I know he worries a great deal about me.' She smiled gently. 'I tell him there's no need, but he still does.'

Maria suspected that Lady Osbourne was stronger and had more stamina than she liked people to think. 'Do you stay in London all the time?' Maria asked.

'I do now. Until last month I spent a good deal of my time at Highgate, but I have many good friends in London—and I do not like to travel any great distance any more. But what of you, Maria—you don't mind if I call you that?'

Maria shook her head. 'I would like that.'

'I confess I am confused about the matter of your betrothal to Colonel Winston. Charles did mention it. Did your father give his blessing to it?'

'Yes. But he insisted that I must be eighteen before we could marry.'

'Very wise. And you are how old now?'

'Nineteen.'

'And you have not laid eyes on him for six years?'

'No. Father had no reservations about the betrothal. Besides, he knew he was dying and it was important to him that my future was taken care of.'

'Are you apprehensive about meeting Colonel Winston?'

'I'm afraid I am. Charles has firmly set his mind against Henry. He—must have told you.'

'He has known Colonel Winston for a good many years. Their work with the Company often brought them into contact with each other.'

'Charles's opinion of Henry is not—favourable. However I have told him I shall make up my own mind when I meet him.'

Lady Osbourne patted her hand. 'And quite right, too. Now, let's forget about Colonel Winston and be glad you're here safe in England. Have you much to do while you are in London?'

'I do have some matters to take care of. I have to speak to my lawyer and see my bankers—I've been away from England a long time and I would like a summary of my affairs. I would also like to purchase a carriage and some horses. The horses at Gravely were sold when I went to France so I must think about replenishing the stables. I also desperately need a new wardrobe. I left France with just a few necessary items I would need for the journey and nothing else. Never having been to London, I am at a loss as to where to begin.'

'I shall be delighted to advise you. I shall have Madame Cecile—my own modiste, who is one of the most fashionable in London—come here and design an extensive wardrobe for you.'

Maria smiled. 'Not too extensive. I have no intention of remaining in London for too long.'

'That shouldn't be a problem at this time. You must try to see as much of London as you can while you are here.'

And so Maria passed a pleasant hour chatting to Lady Osbourne with unbelievable swiftness, while downstairs Charles remained closeted in a meeting with two members of the government.

As night fell over the city the focus of pleasure was to be found behind the heavily curtained windows of some licentious establishments. Charles's town coach stopped before one such house sandwiched between two others on the Strand, and sounds of gaiety could be heard.

'This is it,' Charles said, grim faced as he took Maria's hand to assist her down.

The fleeting moment of contact, feeling his hand in hers, Maria found reassuring. She wanted to hold on to him and beg him not to make her go in this house, but she said nothing. She had been anxiously anticipating this moment for so long, but now it was here she was reluctant to go inside. However, whatever awaited her behind that door must be faced sooner or later. Best to get it over with.

'It sounds as if Henry is entertaining friends.'

'I told you of Winston's insatiable addiction for pleasure, but I did not think you would have to be confronted by it as soon as this.' Charles looked at her and frowned. 'You don't have to go in.'

Despite being drawn to flight and evasion, Maria stiffened her spine. 'I want to. I must.'

She smoothed her skirts and squared her shoulders and then they walked together up the steps to the house. Some of the guests in the hall dropped back as Charles pushed open the door. Tall, radiating command and authority, he stalked over the threshold, Maria following him a step behind.

The scene that met their eyes was quite shocking, lurid and bizarre and all Maria could do was stand and stare with morbid fascination. The house was full of partying people, with men and women drinking and carousing and lolling on couches. Powdered and patched and drenched with perfume, the ladies were dressed in high fashion to excite the curiosity of the males, and their unerring instinct for pleasure was freely suggested in low-cut gowns and unfastened bodices and deliberately exposed bosoms.

Charles glanced around, his face hardening, realising his mistake in bringing Maria to a place such as this. In this house the debauchery of human nature levelled all distinctions, making the gentry no better than the meanest street worker, the high-born lady no more respectable than the cheapest whore. That Henry Winston's dissolute habits were much the same as when he had been in India was blatantly obvious.

All those present were under the influence of liquor and inflamed by the time-honoured desire to have their fun, each succumbing to the compelling sensuality of lengthy foreplay that would eventually have them falling into bed with whomsoever took their fancy. The ribald laughter and conversation was crudely sexual and many a carnal encounter took place in the heated shadows of this house on the Strand.

Maria's eyes swept the hall, coming to light on a well-rounded giggling woman draped around the bulk of a large man. He wore an elaborately curled bobbed wig that failed to sit straight on his head. The woman's ample breasts almost spilled out of her tight, firmly waisted bodice. Her blonde hair was styled high and wide and frizzed to complement the width of her dress. Maria shuddered as she saw the man's fleshy fingers pawing at her body.

Suddenly the man became distracted on seeing the newcomers, all the more noticeable because of the plain black garb they wore, stark against so much garish colour. The man used his elbows and his considerable bulk to ease himself sideways through the throng.

Charles looked down at Maria. She hadn't uttered a word since entering this den of debauchery. Her face was white and drawn with shock, her eyes wide and fixed and unbelieving.

'I did warn you,' he murmured.

Maria turned her eyes up to his. His figure was tall and erect, his lean face stiffened into a mask of scorn as he looked at the man approaching them.

'I know, and I should have listened.' Her voice was stiff and expressionless.

'It's good to see you back, Osbourne, and that you've managed to escape those damned Frenchies, eh,' a deep voice boomed.

Maria's attention was drawn to the voice and she turned her head and looked directly at the man she had seen fondling the buxom blonde woman. Her feeling was one of revulsion. Instinctively she moved closer to Charles.

'As you see, Winston, I have survived unscathed.'

The man's gaze shifted to Maria. 'And who have we here, might I ask?'

'Miss Maria Monkton.' Charles took Maria's arm and drew her a step closer to her betrothed. 'Maria, this is your betrothed. Don't you recognise him?'

To Maria, there was nothing recognisable about this man. She had expected him to be changed—a little older, to have put on a little weight perhaps—but this bloated, red-faced individual reeking of spirits, with protuberant eyes and slack mouth and whose fleshy fingers were already reaching for her, she found un-expectedly shocking. She was repelled by him and drew back as if stung. She fought down a childish desire to clutch at Charles's sleeve and hold it tightly. She doubted he would have noticed had she done so, for he appeared to be singularly distracted with his own thoughts.

Henry moved closer to Maria to take stock of the woman and the fortune he expected to marry, looking her over with considerable approval. She wasn't the type he usually went for, but she was a good looker. The day he married her would be the pinnacle of triumph for him. Laughing out loud, he turned and, making a wide sweeping gesture with his arm to include those around him who were evidently finding the whole situation highly diverting, said loudly, 'Meet the lady who is to be my wife—a beauty—a rich one, too, and no mistake. I am well blessed—twice so. A toast—only the best champagne, no less.'

More loud laughter and congratulations filled the house.

'I intend for us to be married by special licence the

day after tomorrow.' He bent low, his mouth close to Maria's ear. 'Enough time for us to get to know each other, Maria, eh?' he said, chuckling low, sliding his arm around her slender waist and giving it a hard squeeze, ignoring Charles, whose face had hardened into a mask of icy wrath.

Buoyed up with the excitement of knowing he was about to become a very rich man, and congratulating himself on his successful manipulation of this girl's father, Henry released her and left them to organise the opening of more champagne.

'It's evident that you cannot remain here,' Charles murmured, drawing her aside in an attempt to shield her from the curious, appraising glances being cast their way.

Maria's eyes had turned a brilliant green in her despair. It was all happening like a crazy dream. 'I have no wish to.' Her face crumpled like a hurt child's. She turned sharply away from him and said in a suffocated whisper, 'This place is quite shocking. Please, Charles, do not leave me here alone with him…'

Her voice failed and she moved her head in a small helpless gesture that was more pitiful than words.

For a moment—for as long as it would take a tear to gather and fall—Charles hesitated. Then he reached out and grasped her shoulders and pulled her round to face him. The sight of her wet cheeks and wounded eyes sent a physical pain through his heart and made him speak with more violence than he had intended.

'I would not do that. Alone with him—do you imagine for one minute that he would keep his hands off you? Can you not see that if you were to remain here your position would be intolerable?'

She nodded. 'You have been right all along, Charles, I can see that now. I have never considered myself to be a coward. I would not shrink from my duty, no matter how unpleasant or dangerous the situation, but I cannot marry Henry—and had my father been aware of the true nature of his character, he would have shown him the door. Everything you told me about him is true. I—I am repelled by him.'

Charles placed his hands on her shoulders, looking deep into her eyes. 'Be assured, Maria, that I have no intention of leaving you here.'

Henry appeared before them, his sharp eyes flitting from one to the other with suspicion. He had appeared to be quite drunk when they had arrived, but he had sobered quickly. 'Come, I will not have you skulking in a corner. Come and meet my guests and then I'll personally show you to your quarters.'

'You must realise that Miss Monkton cannot possibly stay here,' Charles said, dropping his hands from Maria's shoulders.

'No? Where else would she stay?'

'She is a gently reared young lady, Winston. Take a look around you. That should speak for itself.'

Henry's eyes narrowed. 'I asked you where she would stay.'

'At my home, which is where she has been since last night. My mother is in residence, so it is all proper and above board.'

A slow smile curved Henry's fleshy lips and his eyes slid to Maria. 'Damn, m'dear! You've an admirer here.' Again he looked at Charles. 'I trust you kept your hands off my property and that my judgement wasn't miscast when I asked you to escort my future wife to England, Osbourne.'

'Henry, I would be obliged if we could go somewhere more private to discuss this matter of our betrothal,' Maria said, aware of Charles's anger simmering just below the surface that was in danger of erupting.

Henry looked at her hard and nodded. 'Come with me. I would like to speak with you alone.'

He led them to a small study. Surprisingly it was empty of cavorting bodies. When Charles was about to follow Maria inside, Henry barred his way with a supercilious smile. 'Not now, Osbourne. Where my future wife is concerned, your mission ends here. She belongs to me, remember.'

Maria looked at Charles. 'Please give me a moment.'

'Maria, don't—'

'I have to do this.'

Charles frowned. 'Will you be all right?'

'Yes, perfectly,' she replied. She appeared composed and the mistress of her emotions, but her heart was beating like a soldier's drum.

Charles threw Henry a warning look. 'I'll be just outside the door.'

When the door closed on Maria, Charles waited, his patience stretched, but the thought of her alone with Winston sat like a hot coal in the pit of his stomach. He knew Winston's twisted nature too well not to feel deeply anxious, for the man was not to be defeated so easily.

Alone with her betrothed, Maria looked at him, marvelling that she could achieve such cool composure when she was burning, trembling inside. His leering stare seemed to burn through her dress. She cringed. Then suddenly everything shifted and she felt strong. She looked at him in every disgusting detail and knew she couldn't stand being touched by him, being close to a man like him—and even if he were not so rotten with dissipation, her attraction to Charles was so deeply embedded in her heart that she knew that she could not marry Henry.

'You've changed, Maria—all grown up now, I see—ready for me at last.'

'Please don't speak like that. I find it most offensive.'

'You are here to marry me are you not, Maria?'

'No, Henry. I left France to escape the terror.'

'Ah, yes, that too.'

His airy tone whipped Maria to anger. She did not flinch before the barely concealed menace. Now that she had decided not to marry him, she had recovered all her poise and confidence, as she always did when a fight was in prospect. Suddenly his bloated, insolently smiling face maddened her beyond bearing.

'Are you about to tell me you are to retract your decision to marry me? If so, I would advise you to reconsider.'

Realising that Henry was determined to provoke her, Maria turned with the intention of opening the door to admit Charles. Henry stepped forwards to bar her path. Their combined movements brought them close together. He stared down at her with impudent admiration. Instinctively she stepped back, shrinking inside when he raised his hand towards her face, feeling her cheeks grow hot beneath his lecherous scrutiny.

'Be so kind as to step aside,' she said tightly.

'Not yet, m'dear. I have in my possession a contract signed by your father agreeing to our betrothal. He fully approved of a marriage between us.'

'My father is dead. He no longer has any authority over me,' she informed him sharply. 'Please don't touch me.'

His smile was slow and lascivious. 'Oh, such a proud one.' He allowed his fingers to touch her hair, aware of the moment when she shuddered, but instead of being angered by her reaction, he was excited and challenged by it. 'When we are wed I can see life will not be dull, and I was thinking it would have nothing to offer. I like my mounts to have fire in their veins, and I see you have plenty.'

Maria cut through his words. 'Henry, I think you have not understood me. Things have changed. Over the past months I have come to have many reservations about our suitability. I will not be your wife. Please let me pass.'

'You heard her, Winston,' Charles said as he entered, having heard Maria's raised voice and unable to stand outside the room any longer. Seeing Winston towering over her, crimson rage such as he had never felt rushed up from the depths of him, a sickening guilt that he'd brought her here in the first place. 'That's enough.'

'Get out of here, Osbourne,' Henry ground out, his voice hoarse with rage, his hands opening and closing convulsively.

Henry stepped back, the space he created giving Maria the opportunity to go to Charles. Her gaze became riveted on the drumming pulse in his cheek and the glittering violence in his eyes. The room was highly charged with tension and hostility.

'Please, Charles, I think we should go. I don't want

to cause a scene. I have told Henry I will not be his wife and I would like that to be an end to the matter.'

'I would advise you to reconsider,' Henry uttered furiously. 'You'll regret this, I promise you.'

'How can you possibly expect me to marry you when you openly keep a licentious house of ill repute? I will not.'

Henry's eyes blazed with fury into Charles's. 'You treacherous, backstabbing villain. I should have known you would do this. I understood you were escorting Maria to England for me, not to go sniffing after her like a dog yourself. I confess I had my doubts about you, but I listened to everyone else telling me that if anyone could smuggle Maria safely out of France it was you. You're a strange mixture of trust and suspicion, Osbourne.'

'Think what you like. It matters not one iota to me. Where Maria's safety is concerned you have nothing to complain about, since she is here now. Suffice to say I've offered Maria my protection. She has agreed and will reside at my home for the time being. That is the end of it as far as I am concerned.'

Henry's face became flushed and seemed to swell with the enormity of his fury. 'You can't do this. I will not let you take her.'

'She is not yours to withhold.'

'Yes, she damned well is,' Henry spluttered, already seeing the fortune he craved slipping away from him. 'I'll kill you for this.'

Charles watched him with amusement. 'No, you won't. You know, Winston, you really should learn to control your passions. They've got you into trouble on numerous occasions.'

'You traitor. You tricked me. You think you're smart,

don't you, and that I am a fool?' he rasped, his drink-sodden face getting redder, his eyes bulging. 'But you'll not have her. I'll see you in hell first.'

'My goodness, such venom,' Charles uttered with cold disdain. 'Be careful. It's not good for the digestion.'

'Maria Monkton is mine—mine, I tell you. I had a legitimate arrangement with her father. I have loved and waited six years to marry the girl and I'll not be cheated.'

Charles's lips twisted with derision. 'Love? Your actions towards Maria bespeak anything but love. Considering what she has witnessed tonight, is it any wonder she's changed her mind? You have done it to yourself. Accept it. The lady no longer wants to marry you—and who can blame her? Look at you, man.' His eyes passed over him with contempt. Debauchery and overindulgence in every vice and gratification had bloated his body and ravaged his face. 'You're a disgrace. Do you think you own her? She has her own wishes and her own will. She doesn't want you. She is leaving with me.'

'Like hell she is.'

'When I brought her out of France, I did not do so solely on your behalf. I did it for her father, who was a close friend of my own. The terror in France is real. It is what they would have wanted me to do. They would have expected no less.'

Henry's eyes narrowed and began to glitter dangerously. His smile was unpleasant. 'A noble and honourable act,' he sneered, 'and you should be commended, but why don't you admit that you want her for yourself?'

'I am assured you have no hope of succeeding with

her, so if I have a mind I see no reason not to pursue her for myself.' Charles's eyes narrowed. He had been keeping a firm grip on his temper, partly for Maria's sake, and partly because he didn't want to cause a scene. He moved closer to Winston. 'Whether you like it or not, she is leaving with me,' he said, an icy, dangerous edge to his soft controlled voice. 'My obligations where she is concerned are not finished. Nor will I stoop to barter insults with you. I suggest you speak to her courteously, for I will not allow you to abuse her.'

Maria stared wide-eyed at Charles in pure astonishment. He was furious, his lean dark face rigid with barely controlled anger.

'*You* won't allow it!' Henry's bloated face was scarlet with uncontrollable rage. 'Who do you think you are? I will destroy you for this—you swaggering cockscomb. How dare you interfere in what is none of your business? Maria—'

'Is no longer your betrothed. She deserves better than to be made to share the dunghill you have made of your own life.'

Henry raised his head, shocked out of his ranting fury into some deeper, darker emotion by Charles's words. He held out his hand. 'Maria, come here.'

Maria stared at his hand and shuddered. She took a step closer to Charles and looked up at him. His expression was taut.

'By God! You will pay for this,' Henry raged.

'Your threats hold no fear for me, Winston. But know this. Maria is now under my protection. You are not to try to contact her. All communications must cease. Do I make myself clear?'

Charles turned to Maria, who was looking at him stony faced. Despite the strong attraction she felt for him, she resented the way he assumed authority over her, and what he had said about pursuing her himself was not to her liking at all and she was deeply angered and disturbed by it.

'I would like to leave now,' she said through frozen lips.

Charles raised his arm to guide her to the door. Henry reached out to stop him.

'Take your hand off me before I break it,' Charles said coldly. 'Heed my warning, Winston. Keep your distance from Miss Monkton. You come near her or offend her in any way and you shall find society a very cold place to be. Remember how it was when your disgrace was made public in India.'

Henry's eyes registered the threat. His expression sobered, but he glanced at Maria, as though mulling over how to get her back.

Seeing that look, Charles moved closer and looked him straight in the eye. 'Leave it if you know what is good for you. You know what I mean.'

Henry settled his furious eyes on Maria. 'Don't think you'll get away with this,' he hissed. 'I've wasted six years waiting for you to come of age. Six years wasted. This isn't the end. I'll find you.'

'You'll have to go through me to get to Maria.' Turning on his heel, Charles took Maria's arm. 'Come. There's nothing to be gained here.'

Outside the house the silence was like a solid sheet of ice forming about them. Charles watched Maria's face become shadowed, gaunt and white as marble.

It was a difficult moment for Maria. She wanted to maintain an air of cold disdain, to face Charles in calm defiance, but her mauled pride and an aching uncertainty of her future assailed her senses. Momentarily blinded by a sudden rush of tears to her eyes, she stumbled, only to find a supportive hand coming to her aid. Long fingers grasped her elbow and held her firmly until she regained her balance.

'I'm all right,' she whispered, pushing him away.

She turned her face away and when Charles heard a sob he realised she was weeping. She swayed once more and he caught her to him, holding her body against his, his arms strong about her, his cheek resting on her hair, feeling the violent trembling of her as shock gripped her, saying nothing.

He hadn't known how she would react, but this clinging, this desolate weeping, was totally unexpected. He should not have taken her there, but he knew he must shock her, hurt her. However, he didn't want to add to her desolation by destroying her altogether.

At last she was quiet, leaning against him. After a moment she pushed herself away from him, the tracks of her tears still shining on her cheeks.

'I apologise. I did not intend crying like that. Henry's not worth it, I realise that now. I'm exhausted, that's all.' She looked at him, and Charles saw her lips become a thin and bitter line and her eyes darken and deaden. 'I suppose you're satisfied now. Everything you told me about him is true. Aren't you going to say I told you so?'

'Of course not,' he said, handing her into the carriage and instructing the driver to take them back to

Grosvenor Square. 'You were very courageous, Maria, but I should not have put you through that.'

'I'm glad you did,' she said, settling herself into the seat. 'At least I now know what Henry's like. It's over. I can't quite believe it. All these years…'

'What?'

'Wasted,' she answered, her tone flat. 'That's what Henry said. He was right.'

'In no way do I feel guilty for depriving you of your fiancé. You deserve someone better. How do you feel now you've seen him after six years?'

'I feel lots of things. Disappointed—terribly let down and betrayed. Now the truth is revealed there is no use pretending, and, if I am honest, most of all I feel relieved.'

'And I am relieved to hear it.'

Maria looked at Charles in the orange glow from the carriage lamps. 'Why did the Company dismiss him? Did he do something very bad?'

'In the Company's eyes it was unpardonable—his behaviour in India had become a scandal. Unfortunately this was the image the Company recognised, and when Winston's regiment went to settle some insurgency— an insurgency that turned out to be more serious than initially thought and resulted in many lives lost in the Company regiment—Winston was nowhere to be seen. He was found much later drunk out of his mind in a brothel. Naturally the Company took a grim view of his conduct—it was one time too many—and he was forced to leave in disgrace.'

'It was no less than what he deserved, but it doesn't seem to have affected him very much. I hope I never see him again.'

Charles gave her a dubious look, for he had no doubt that she would. 'I'm relieved you are to stay with me and I must insist that you stay there until this matter with Winston is settled and he is no longer a threat. While you are in London you will have to consult with your lawyer and bankers regarding money and business affairs—'

'I have already decided to do that,' Maria interrupted.

'Good. Then I shall arrange for them to come to the house. If you do leave the house, I must insist that you are escorted at all times.'

His tone was brusque. Maria could feel her resentment growing and with it her anger bubbling up inside her, but as yet she could not seem to find the strength to fight back. How dare he feel he had the right to order her about as if she was his to direct? How dare he assume that now she had decided not to marry Henry she would turn to him?

She sat looking at him. She could still hear Henry— *she is mine...* She was filled with a bitterness of pain that she had not allowed for a long time. It seemed to rise up in her throat. Men betrayed. Henry had betrayed her. He had wanted to manipulate her and take what he wanted, first and foremost her money, without a thought to what she might want. And then Charles had remarked how he would pursue her if he had a mind—without reference to her, without a care for her feelings.

Her expression seemed to freeze him. She did her best to hold on to the resentment she felt, to be dignified as she had been taught to be at all times, but feeling terribly let down and hurt by Henry was very difficult and her expression was icy.

'You have been very kind to me, Charles. In fact, I

can't imagine what I would have done without your help and I am grateful, but that does not mean you can take me over as you seem to be doing. I will tell you now that I deeply resent the remark you made to Henry about pursuing me yourself—if you have a mind, that is.'

'What I said was clumsy, foolish. I do admit that.'

'I am not subject to your wishes, so I suggest you do not use that particular attitude with me. It is most arbitrary, and for some reason it makes my hackles rise. I insist on speaking for myself, and I will also tell you that at the earliest opportunity I shall be going to Gravely, after I have purchased a new carriage and some horses.'

Charles turned his head to look at her in the dim light, his face working with the strength of his emotions, which had for the moment got the better of him. He could not bear to think of her where she was not under his protection. She was alone and he resolved to fulfil his role as her temporary guardian. In keeping with this, he would henceforth see that she was made to feel secure and spared any future advances from Winston.

'I shall be only too happy to look for a carriage and horses, but you must remain at my home and forget for now this nonsense of leaving for Gravely until—'

'Nonsense! What are you talking about? Of course I must go home. And who do you think you are,' she flared, 'laying down the law and telling me what I should and should not do? I am a grown woman and I am quite capable of running my own life without you. Accept it, Charles. I will be a burden to you no longer. Your obligation to me ended when we reached London.'

A gleam of anger showed in Charles's eyes. The stern features seemed to become even harder. He turned his head away abruptly, perhaps to shut out the seductive vision of the woman who had seemed so innocent, but was now exhibiting an alarming self-possession.

'That was before you told Winston you would not marry him.'

Both angry, they fell silent.

When they reached the house, Maria excused herself, pleading tiredness, and retired to her room.

Charles watched her go and, striding into the drawing room, he poured himself a large brandy. His mind busy, he settled himself in a comfortable chair near the hearth, propping his feet on a low stool. He stared at the shifting flames, but his mind was wandering far afield as an image of Maria entered his thoughts—of dark-fringed green eyes, glowing with their own light, the colour in their depths forever changing like a roughly hued gemstone. Often a frown gathered her brows in anger, and her eyes grew cold.

Casting this image aside, he brought a more favourable one to mind, of moments when they had been bright and full of laughter, expressive and alive, of a pert nose, gently curving lips—then he held the image in his mind where it burned with the memory of their incredible softness beneath his own. The rest of her crowded in—her slender limbs and the sleek, gently rounded grace of her body, which possessed a subdued strength and honesty that lent her a naïve elegance. She was unaware of how lovely she was, and she dwelt very firmly in his mind—and now his heart.

So, what was to be done now she had declared her aversion for Henry Winston? How was such a vulnerable girl to be kept safe from a man like that? The fire flamed high, then died back, the coals snapping as if with a stoic purpose. Charles stared into the softly burning embers until the clock chimed twelve.

He rose, having reached a decision.

Seated before the mirror in her room in her night attire and brushing her hair with long, steady strokes, Maria lifted her head and looked at her reflection in the mirror while a new strength, a new force, built inside her. Her head surged with terror and confusion, roaming from place to place, looking for an answer to her critical dilemma. She had to get away from London where her attraction for Charles was becoming more profound with each new day, and her shuddering aversion to Henry filled her with sick despair.

As yet she had done nothing that was inexcusable with Charles and she made up her mind that she would leave for Gravely before she did do something to betray herself. She had to get away from London before her will weakened and her fragile moral fibre crumbled in the face of his appeal.

True to her word Lady Osbourne sent for her modiste, Madame Cecile. Maria had not long been out of bed when a maid came to summon her to the sewing room, where Lady Osbourne, always an early riser, attired in a sumptuous oriental robe, her hand resting on the brass knob of her walking cane, was waiting.

Seamstresses were swirling bolts of fabric over furniture and anything else where it could be draped. The entire room was a riot of colour, with newly fashionable fabrics such as printed cotton and fine muslin, delicate lawn and silk gauze, which provided a fluttering floating look and was highly popular.

'Ah, there you are, Maria.' Lady Osbourne was in a particularly cheerful mood as Maria crossed towards her. 'As you can see, we are in for a busy morning.'

Maria smiled down at her. 'I never expected Madame Cecile to come so soon, Lady Osbourne—and with such wonderful fabrics. What fine materials.'

Lady Osbourne took her hand, her face becoming sombre. 'Once I have my mind set on something I like to get on with it. I don't believe in letting the grass grow under my feet. So, Maria, your engagement to Colonel Winston is off. I saw Charles earlier before he set off for Westminster and he told me a little of what transpired.'

'What Charles told you is true. Colonel Winston was—was much changed. I had not been in his house one minute before I realised that becoming his wife would be a huge mistake.'

'You were quite right to refuse to marry him. Your life would have been very unhappy—although I have to say that I think Madame Cecile had high hopes of making your wedding dress.'

'Then I am sorry to disappoint her. But I'm sure there will be other brides for her to accommodate.'

'Perhaps.' She looked past Maria and a dreamy look came over her face as memories assailed her. 'Charles's sisters both made such beautiful brides. My younger daughter, Georgina, lives in Surrey. She married a Member of Parliament and they have two adorable children. Mary, who is older than Charles, has been married these twelve years past—to a gentleman in the north. They live in Harrogate. Unfortunately I don't see them as often as I would like, but Mary is a prolific letter writer, so she keeps me abreast of all the news.'

'I can see how you must miss them.'

'I have high hopes that Charles will meet a suitable young woman to marry now he has come home—' her eyes twinkled mischievously '—and give me more grandchildren. Hopefully the right woman will come along soon.'

She raised her brows and Maria stirred uneasily beneath the intent gaze, wondering if Lady Osbourne could possibly be harbouring the hope that now she was no longer betrothed to Henry, she was that woman. Rather than continue with this conversation, she tactfully changed the subject and suggested that Madame Cecile took her measurements.

Maria stood patiently on a raised platform while she was measured and prodded and turned and pinned, while Lady Osbourne sat and smiled and uttered encouraging comments expressing her pleasure and her preferences. She insisted Maria was fitted for morning dresses, evening gowns, carriage and walking dresses and any other kind of dress she could think of.

Maria felt strangely light-hearted for the first time in years. 'I do not wish to be rude, Lady Osbourne,' she said, laughing lightly, 'but I will not require a quarter of the gowns when I go to Gravely.'

'Nonsense. People socialise in the country all the time. You will have a splendid time and you will come to London—often, I hope. Tell me, my dear, do you have a lady's maid?'

'No—I have to confess I haven't thought about it. I

shall have to look for one, I suppose—or wait until I reach Gravely.'

'There is no need. I might have the very girl. Ruby.'

'I know Ruby. She seems to have been assigned to me since I came here.'

'She's a competent girl—been with us two years. Her family lives in Eastbourne. Her father is not in the best of health and I know she would like to find work closer to home to be of help to her mother.'

'I see. Then if she is willing, and you don't mind losing her, I would be more than happy to take her to Gravely when I leave.'

'Good. Then that's settled. I shall speak to Ruby.'

Chapter Seven

Everyone thought it rather strange that the very next day Lady Osbourne, forsaking the confines of the Osbourne's palatial London house, was seen driving in the Ring in Hyde Park with all the fashionable folk, and the following day in the popular Vauxhall Gardens, accompanied by a beautiful young lady whose identity was a mystery to those in fashionable society, which aroused much speculation and curiosity.

When Lady Osbourne was unable to accompany her, Maria was accompanied by Ruby, who proved to be not only a competent and experienced lady's maid, but also a delightful companion. The city was a shopper's paradise, full of markets and arcades, with shops and stalls spilling over with beautiful and expensive treasures. They drank tea in the tea gardens and ate mouthwatering custard buns in Chelsea.

It was the middle of the afternoon when they visited Westminster and gazed in awe at the Houses of Parliament, the heart of the government, with its Gothic detailing and romantic towers. The traffic was heavy and there were so many people milling about. When the carriage came to a halt, Maria was absently looking towards the Parliament building when her eyes came to rest on a gentleman emerging from a side door. Suddenly her heart lifted and a smile widened her lips when she recognised Charles.

Seeing him took her wholly by surprise—although she saw no reason why it should, for since arriving in London he had spent a great deal of his time—if not all of it, for she saw very little of him—with members of the government discussing his time spent in France. Raising her hand, she was about to call his name, but when she saw a woman following close behind him, slowly she lowered her arm and watched as he assisted her into a carriage. She sat beside another woman—probably her maid, but she wasn't the one Maria was looking at.

She stared at the woman, a beautiful woman, beautifully dressed in deep rose, her dark hair beautifully coiffed beneath a small fetching hat. As though out of a fog, she watched the woman lean down and slip her hand round Charles's nape, drawing his face close and place a kiss on his cheek.

Why this woman, who had suddenly appeared out of the blue, should suddenly shatter her newfound happiness, Maria could not have said. There was no room in her heart or mind but this one vast disappointment, which little by little became an aching pain.

The lady's carriage drove on and, standing for a moment to watch it go, Charles then turned and went back inside.

Turning her eyes away, Maria looked ahead. The driver's attention was on trying to negotiate the carriage through the traffic and, having lost interest in all that was happening around her, she ordered the driver to return to the house.

What she had witnessed had a profound effect on her. How could she have been so blind to the true depth of her own feelings? And all it had taken was to see Charles with another woman in his arms for the truth to break upon her unwilling eyes, blindingly, but too late—she had fallen in love with Charles.

When she recalled their closeness in France, every instinct she had been capable of feeling had conveyed to her that he wanted her, and like a simpleton she had allowed herself to believe there existed a chance that, now Henry was out of her life, Charles might court her. And so, much to the injury of her heart, she had allowed herself to fall more deeply in love with him.

The following evening, the same young lady who had roused so much interest among London's fashionable elite made her appearance in a box at Covent Garden, this time accompanied by both Lady Osbourne and Sir Charles.

Madame Cecile had had her seamstresses working round the clock to have some gowns made ready for Miss Monkton. Tonight she was dressed in a fashionable chemis dress in a bluish-white hue with a low neck and short puffed sleeves, a style made fashionable by Marie Antoinette. Her glowing hair was upswept into a small matching headdress of feathers, close fitting around the elaboration of ringlets and the twist of corkscrew curls at the nape of her neck.

She was a superb and arresting sight, her whole appearance provocative.

Maria had seen nothing of Charles since she had returned from her unpleasant visit to Henry and the scene she had witnessed at Westminster, which she was unable to banish from her mind. However, the more she thought about it, the more she began to doubt what she had seen and that maybe she had put the wrong interpretation on the incident. If the woman meant anything at all to Charles, then surely Lady Osbourne would have mentioned it to her.

Perhaps the woman was merely a friend—but then, gentlemen did not embrace lady friends with so much affection in full view of the public eye.

When Lady Osbourne told her Charles was to accompany them to the theatre she had spent the day nervously waiting for him to appear, wondering how he would act towards her after their angry words in the carriage when they had been returning from seeing Henry. Perhaps he was still angry with her. Perhaps he thought her ungrateful and despised her for her outburst, or perhaps he hadn't meant to appear so high-handed and might want to apologise.

Most of what she had said to him had been induced by disappointment and anger, and she wanted very much to believe they could go back to the way things had been between them in France. She had come to care for him very much—to love him, and she also liked and admired him—beyond that she refused to think.

By the time he strolled into the drawing room dressed for the theatre and waiting for Lady Osbourne to come down, she was so tightly wound she nearly jumped to her feet when she saw him.

She stared at him, the rush of familiar excitement causing her to become tongue-tied, affected strongly as she was by the force of his presence. She was still profoundly disturbed by her meeting with Henry, yet she couldn't suppress a surge of excitement at being once more close to Charles.

But she wasn't entirely comfortable with this self-awareness, so she tried to direct her thoughts to more practical matters, such as how she looked and whether or not he approved. She needn't have worried, for his gaze moved over her with unhidden masculine appreciation, his eyes lingering on the ringlets on either side of her cheeks. Maria's stomach clenched nervously when she saw it. He had never looked at her like this before, as if she were a tasty morsel he was planning to devour at his pleasure.

'You look lovely, Maria—a beautiful and fashionable young lady and about to hit London by storm,' he said casually, stopping in front of her.

'I sincerely hope not. I'm merely looking forward to a quiet evening at the theatre.'

'Me also. I think there's time for a drink before we leave.'

Maria watched as he deftly poured sparkling champagne into two glasses. He handed her one and she sipped it appreciatively. When she was about to turn towards the sofa, he put a restraining hand on her bare arm and drew her back. With his other he opened the lid of a long velvet box on the table and withdrew a single strand of small creamy white pearls and matching drop earrings.

Maria gasped and reaching out she gently fingered them. 'They are so beautiful.'

'They are a gift from me to you, Maria.'

She looked up at him sharply. If there was a woman in his life, why would he be giving her pearls? None of it made sense. 'I remember what you said to me about wearing pearls when we were in France.'

'I said they would suit you, that they were soothing to the touch.'

She swallowed, suddenly uneasy. 'Yes, I—I do remember.'

'I also said I would like to attach some pearls here,' he murmured. Taking her glass he set it down before gently and quickly fastening the earrings to the lobes of her ears. He turned her towards the large gilt-framed mirror over the fireplace. 'And here.' His fingers sent tiny tremors down her spine as he laid the pearl necklace around her slim neck.

In the mirror, Maria watched his expressionless features as he fastened the diamond clasp at the back of her neck, then raised his eyes to hers.

'Charles—I cannot possibly accept such an expensive gift.'

'Why? Don't you like them?'

'Of course I like them. They really are lovely... but...'

'But nothing. It gives me pleasure to give you nice things. I shall be offended—mortally wounded, even— if you don't accept them.'

She sighed. 'Then what can I say—except thank you.'

'I'd rather be thanked with a kiss,' he commanded patiently.

At first Maria hesitated, but, seeing he would accept nothing less, she turned and obediently pressed a light kiss on his freshly shaven cheek in a lightning move.

When she stood back he gave her a frown of disapproval. 'That is not what I would call a thank-you kiss for such a beautiful gift. That was a peck on the cheek.'

'It was a kiss.'

'I say it was not. My definition of a kiss differs from yours. I believe I know more about kissing than you.' And, taking her arms, he pulled her close and took her lips with sudden, demanding insistence.

Like an alarmed rabbit, Maria jerked back, but he held her firm and his lips stunned her into immobility. And then she felt his hands stroke soothingly up and down her bare arms, while his lips moved on hers with inflaming expertise.

When Charles released her, he smiled into her apprehensive green eyes. 'There, that settles it.'

'For you, maybe, but you must forgive me if I seem somewhat confused.'

His lips quirked in a near-smile. 'I can't think why. I have kissed you before—remember?'

'I am hardly likely to forget.'

Charles looked down into her bewildered eyes and repressed the sudden urge to gather her into his arms again and devour her mouth with his. 'Maria,' he began, and for the first time Maria noticed the tension on his face. He hesitated, as if searching for the right words, then said, 'About the other night—what I said.'

'What did you say?' she asked, still reeling from his kiss.

The ghost of a smile hovered at his mouth. 'Now

don't tell me that you don't remember how angry I made you, and the dressing down you gave me. I haven't been so severely chastised since I was a boy.'

'Yes, I do remember that. And in my opinion it was well deserved.'

'And no doubt you feel I should apologise for coming over too high-handed.'

Maria gave an impudent, choking laugh. 'Well—it would be appreciated, but only if you meant it, otherwise there is no point.'

'Then I apologise.'

'Charles Osbourne,' she said, smiling broadly, 'I think you are the most exasperating man I have ever met.'

A glint of mischief sparked in his eyes. 'I couldn't agree more,' he admitted unrepentantly. 'But you do like me, don't you, Maria?' he murmured softly, sounding casual, but there was also a note of command behind it that demanded an answer.

She gasped and hot colour sprang to her cheeks. 'I am hardly likely to say anything to the contrary when you have given me the comfort of your beautiful home,' she said, thinking that he would not be speaking to her like this if he were in love with another woman. Hope began to stir in her heart.

Charles looked down at her laughing, upturned face. 'And you're not afraid of anything, are you?'

'I am not afraid of you,' she informed him blithely.

'Then perhaps you should be,' he said, and on that enigmatic remark he had turned to greet his mother as she swept in.

Now Maria looked at him. Scorning curling-tongs and powder, he wore his dark hair as she was used to seeing it, drawn from his face and secured in his nape with a narrow black ribbon. He was immaculately clad in tailored claret-velvet coat and trousers, with a cream brocade waistcoat and the rich creamy lace of his shirt and cravat spilling out at throat and wrist. Maria's heart turned over.

He was light-hearted tonight, lover-like, even, and feeling that this was the first and in all probability the last time she would find herself at the theatre with him, she was determined not to let thoughts of another woman spoil it.

The theatre was packed to capacity, the people a variety of colourful contrasts. Many of them, men and women, were foppishly overdressed, with hairstyles frizzed and curled and fluffed up ridiculously high and wide, faces rouged, powdered and painted so that the effect was almost theatrical. As Charles drew back the curtains of their reserved box, every pair of eyes seemed to be directed on them.

'Everyone watches us a great deal,' Charles commented. 'I can only surmise they are curious about you, Maria, and speculating on who you are. Curiosity is matched by envy from the ladies and open admiration from the gentlemen.' He glanced at her from beneath hooded eyes. 'And who can blame them, looking as you do?'

Maria glanced apprehensively at him. 'Do you think they assume I am your…?' Suddenly realising that she had been about to say his intended, realising how tactless she was being, the word died on her lips and she flushed hotly. However, the way he cocked his brow and the sudden gleam in his eye told her that he had read her mind and that this was exactly what everybody was thinking. Her flush deepened. 'Oh, then my coming here with you was a dreadful mistake. The last thing I want is to cause you and Lady Osbourne even the slightest embarrassment.'

He laughed, enjoying her confusion. 'Why do you say that? Where are you at fault in appearing in public escorted by a gentleman—an extremely gallant gentleman, I might add, to whom you owe your escape from France and maybe even your life?'

Their eyes met and she nodded, accepting this. Without his protection she would never have got out of France, and now, alone and friendless in England, there was no one else whom she could trust and rely on like Charles.

'You are right, Charles, and I can never express my gratitude enough. But not one of the people here tonight knows that and their speculation might be running along more unsavoury lines.'

'Never concern yourself with what other people think, Maria. You're enjoying yourself—that's the most important thing, and,' he murmured, his voice soft and seductive, his eyelids half-lowered over his eyes, 'I am enjoying watching you.'

'Then please don't,' she said, trying to ignore the surge of pleasure she felt at his easy compliment.

'Why not?'

Maria lifted her nose primly, but a sweet smile curved her soft pink lips. 'Because I have no wish to become the object of *too* much speculation, and I do not like being gossiped about.'

This was true. Almost every eye in the theatre was drawn to them, and Colonel Henry Winston was no exception. Seated in a box full of his noisy and ill-behaved friends directly across from their own, he quietly seethed.

As if she could feel his eyes on her, Maria looked directly at him. The warm and pleasant sensations Charles had stirred inside her, her surroundings and the glittering crowd of people vanished in an instant. Instinctively her fingers clenched on the fragile sticks of her costly fan and she began to ply it with quick nervous movements.

Charles gave her a quizzical glance. 'Is something wrong, Maria?'

She nodded, her face ashen. 'Henry is here, in the box opposite, watching us.'

'I know.'

'You do? Then why didn't you say something?'

'Because I didn't see the point and I had no wish to upset you. Ignore him and enjoy the music. He cannot hurt you.'

Charles leaned back in his seat, watching her rather than what was happening on the stage with a fascinated interest. Having shaken off her anxieties and not looking in Henry's direction once, she was relaxed and her face glowed happily. She had a natural sophistication and he was amazed by the gracious ease with which she received those who came to their box wanting to be introduced, and the way she so effortlessly charmed each and every one of them—and he took note and would remember the gentlemen who admired and desired her, determined to avoid them in the future when he was with Maria.

Throughout his adult life and his liaisons with women, some of them had accused him of being everything from distant and unapproachable, to cold and ruthless. He was ten years older and a thousand times harder than Maria, yet something about her softened him, and he had decided he liked being soft.

During an interlude, he leaned towards her. 'The amount of interest you have attracted is hardly surprising,' he murmured to her half-turned face. 'You look stunning. At this rate there isn't going to be a heart left intact when you're through with them. By tomorrow morning, every eligible bachelor in London will be presenting their calling card.'

Maria was astonished at his high opinion of her effect on the gentlemen. 'And what would you do, Charles? Send them all packing or choose one that you would deem suitable?' she ventured daringly, enjoying herself enormously despite Henry's glowering countenance from his box.

Charles lazed in his seat, studying her laughing face and sparkling eyes while he appeared to consider the matter. 'I think if I were to do that, you would not approve of my choice.'

Maria turned her face fully and looked at him, and the dazzling charm of his lazy white smile did odd things to her pulse. The very air felt charged and crackled with life. It was a moment she would never forget. And beside her was a man who she scarcely knew, but whose face and voice, whose being, utterly captivated her. He had got right under her skin. Perhaps she should have been worried by this, frightened even. But all she could feel was a sense of expectation as if she was fully, abundantly alive.

'I'm sure I can rely on you to defend my honour, Charles. You've done pretty well so far.'

'By protecting you from Colonel Winston?'

'Of course—and more.'

They were so engrossed in their light banter that they didn't notice the expression of pure joy on Lady Osbourne's face as she quietly observed them from behind. A tender smile curved her lips. She was already aware of the discreet interest Charles was showing in Maria. They had so much in common—their Indian backgrounds, both wealthy, their families honest and worthy. They were perfect for each other, she decided. Maria wasn't in awe of Charles. What a handsome couple they would make. Charles was a hard, experienced man and Maria had courage and gentleness. Her spirit and warmth would gentle him.

The performance over, Maria allowed Charles to place her wrap around her shoulders; then, smiling at Lady Osbourne and placing her hand on his arm, she left the box. They spent some considerable time exchanging pleasantries with friends and acquaintances, and made their way slowly down the staircase to the lobby, almost empty now except for the footmen standing rigidly on either side. Charles sent one of the attendants for his carriage.

Maria went cold and shuddered with distaste when her eyes lighted on Henry waiting to one side in the foyer. His figure appeared fatter and taller than she remembered, his clothes and his curled wig having seen better days.

Henry fixed his lowering gaze on Charles, whose hand was placed possessively on Maria's elbow. When at last he had thought he was on the brink of achieving his goal, that the fortune he'd awaited for so long was about to be his, he had found himself trembling with anticipation, certain that he would have his reward soon; now he was to be thwarted of it by Charles Osbourne.

Charles had seen him, and he was not surprised when he stepped in front of them. Thankfully his mother was engrossed in happy conversation with a couple of friends and strolled on ahead of them.

'You arrogant son of a bitch,' Henry hissed, his voice vibrating with fury. 'This is your doing, Osbourne. I blame you entirely. As to your intentions where Maria is concerned—or should I say your pretensions—she'd have to be addle headed to trust you.'

'Have a care what you say, Winston.'

'Do you expect me to ignore what you have done? Let me remind you that, where I am concerned, Maria is still my betrothed. My regret is that I did not travel to Dover and whisk her away there and then to her wedding.'

Charles gave a hard, low laugh. 'After what she witnessed at your house, Winston—sights a gently reared young lady should never have to see—she may thank heaven that you did not go to Dover. Because of it, I have been able to save her from a fate she had done nothing to deserve, while as for you, I think you are best left to a future which seems altogether too repugnant for words.'

'You have tricked me.'

Charles didn't move, holding his stare.

Henry glared at him in outrage. 'You're nothing but a thief and a liar.'

Maria moved closer to Charles, certain now of what was to happen. When a man called another a liar, there was only one possible outcome. Honour had its price.

'You've stolen her, damn you, and in doing so you have insulted me. It is too much and you will answer for it. I regret only that I am unable to kill you more than once.'

Henry's voice sounded thick with anger, his manner dramatic, and his great bulk trembling with quiet rage, but he was making a visible effort to control his temper as their altercation was attracting unwelcome attention. Those still leaving the theatre paused to look, following every moment of the quarrel with eyes agog at the prospect of a juicy scandal to relate. Charles faced him with a faint, contemptuous smile, which only added to Henry's rage.

'You may be a superb shot, Winston, but this time I think that you may well find you have met your match. Does it not occur to you that I might possibly kill you?'

'Never,' Henry said simply. 'I may be many things, Osbourne, but I am a fine marksman and a damned crack shot and you know it.'

Charles looked at him, his hard face wiped clean of all expression. Acceding to a demand for a duel, he nodded curtly. 'Then I am at your service. I have known that this was bound to happen, sooner or later. I shall have my second call on you.' Then he turned as if to leave.

Maria stepped between the two prospective adversaries in alarm. 'No,' she cried wildly, looking appealingly at Henry, unable to bear the thought that he wanted to spill Charles's blood simply because she refused to marry him. 'You cannot do this. I will not let you. This isn't Charles's fault, Henry. I made up my own mind not to marry you. I won't let you fight over me. It's madness. I do not care to have you slay one another.'

Henry glared at her. 'I appreciate the ardour with

which you spring to his defence. What better proof do I need that you and Osbourne are lovers?' He looked at Charles. 'I can tell you the time and place, Osbourne, without sending your second,' he said coldly, ignoring Maria's plea.

Charles turned to Maria. 'My mother is in the carriage. Go and get in.'

'But, Charles—you can't—' Maria tried again, but his murderous voice stopped her cold.

'I told you to go,' he said between clenched teeth, and while Maria was willing to ignore his order, the look in his eyes made her quake.

Her chest heaving, she looked at his rigid face. 'Please, Charles, promise me you won't do anything rash.' She watched him make a Herculean effort not to further frighten her and to agree with what she asked.

'I won't, Maria,' he bit out. 'Now go. I'll only be a moment,' he promised.

Maria felt physically ill when she turned away and walked to the carriage which stood in a line of others. In the cushioned darkness she abandoned herself to her anxiety, loathing herself for the trouble she had caused, and the hurt. What if Henry should wound Charles, or even…? Her mind shied away from the thought.

A short while later Charles climbed inside, his manner rigidly controlled.

'Well?' she ventured to ask in a small voice.

'The matter is settled.'

'But—what…?'

He fixed her with a hard glare. 'Enough, Maria. The matter is closed.'

As the coachman cracked his whip and the equipage

moved off, Charles did not stir, but Maria could see his eyes glittering in the dimness of the carriage, narrow silver slits, luminous as cats' eyes in the dark. In helpless misery she leaned back against the upholstery, listening to Lady Osbourne, who had been speaking to an acquaintance and had missed their altercation with Colonel Winston. But picking up on her son's black mood, curious as to the reason, but preferring to remain in ignorance, she fell silent.

In bed Maria could not sleep, tortured as she was by what was to happen the following morning and with the terror that one or both men would be wounded or killed. She pulled the covers up about her and with her chin on her knees thought of Charles and the duel. How could she save him from Henry's murderous intent? Although she did understand how humiliated Henry must feel by her rejection, along with his overriding jealousy and hatred of Charles.

She had a sudden vision of Charles's bloodied body lying inert on the ground, and she shuddered as she stared into the shadows. Her heart was heavy and aching and a lump of harsh despair was growing in her thoughts.

With her boundless generosity, her heart contracting with contrition and guilt, she blamed herself entirely for what was to happen. It appeared Henry was a deadly shot, yet Charles had refused to defend his honour when Henry had accused him of stealing her from him, which was what he should have done.

Unable to settle, she got out of bed and wandered about like a lost soul until, unable to stand it any longer, she flung on her robe and went in search of Charles. She had to speak to him, to plead with him at the cost of whatever scene might be necessary, in order to avert the duel, to stop the perilous assignation, or at best ask him to delope.

She was aware of some of the rules of duelling, and she knew that to delope meant an exchange of fire, when one or both of the participants would intentionally miss in order to fulfil the conditions of the duel without loss of life or honour.

Moving silently along the corridor, she stopped when she reached Charles's rooms. A light shone from beneath the door, indicating he wasn't in bed. Knocking softly on the door, to her surprise she heard him say enter. Slipping quickly inside his beautiful apartment, her feet sinking into the plush Flemish carpet, she quickly closed the door, for it would never do for her to be seen entering his room. Light from the candles caressed the satinwood furniture, and through open double doors on a dais was a large four-poster bed hung with rich damask drapes.

Charles was seated at a writing desk, writing intently, the long quill moving quickly over the paper. Maria looked at him, uncertain what she should do. She had come, in short, hurrying to meet the man she loved— and found a cool, impersonal stranger.

He looked up briefly, his face impassive, showing no surprise or pleasure at seeing her standing nervously across the room.

'Charles—I—I had to come.' The words came out in a faltering rush.

'I know. I was expecting you,' he said, his tone terse. 'I won't be a moment. Make yourself comfortable.'

Eyes down, he carried on writing. Maria's heart contracted as she moved to sit down on the green sofa placed at right angles to the fire. The silence was so complete that the scratching of the pen across the paper seemed to her to make a shattering noise. The light from the candles fell on his aquiline nose and firmly jutting chin while deeper shadows lurked around his firm mouth and eyes, now hidden by lowered lids.

He had discarded his coat and waistcoat and neck-cloth, and his fine linen shirt, open at the neck, revealed a firm, strongly muscled throat. She stared at him, for the moment forgetful of the reason which had brought her there, conscious of a strange rush of tenderness at the sight of a heavy lock of black hair which fell forward over his forehead. She saw the well-defined eyebrows and wanted to go and touch them as one touches a bird's feathers. She was suddenly so sharply conscious of her love that she had to make an effort not to throw her arms about his neck.

She watched him, noting the authority, the strength held in check as he wrote. So many conflicting emotions churned inside her, fighting for ascendancy. Ever since she had become conscious of the depth of her feelings, her thoughts had not gone beyond holding and caressing—not knowing much beyond that, she had felt the delight of secrecy and swirling madness at her forbidden thoughts. But now, as she watched him, he was more attractive than ever, more desirable, and the need to be closer to him was more vivid than ever.

Suddenly he threw down the quill and pushing his chair back stood up, bringing Maria down from the dreaming heights of a moment before. She stood up quickly.

'I'm sorry, Charles. I didn't mean to interrupt.'

The metallic blue of his eyes was hard as he looked at her. 'You haven't. I was writing a letter.'

'It's a strange time to do that.'

'To my mother.'

'Oh.' She understood. 'Have—you told her—about…?'

'The duel? No.'

Maria moved closer. 'Charles, please don't do this,' she pleaded, gazing at the cold, dispassionate man standing before her. He looked powerful, aloof and completely self-assured. It was impossible to believe that Henry might kill him or maim him for life.

'I have to. It is a matter of honour.'

'But—are duels not illegal?'

'Technically, yes, but people are rarely prosecuted for doing so.'

'And have you chosen your second?'

He nodded. 'Michael Mead, a close friend of mine, who also happens to be my brother-in-law.'

'And a surgeon?'

'That, too.'

'Where is the rendezvous?'

'Green Park. Don't worry, Maria. Everything—even down to the pistols that are to be used—has been taken care of.'

Her face pale and drawn with worry, Maria flinched at this brutal reminder of the deadly weapons. 'Charles, I really don't want you to do this. I beseech you. Speak to Henry?' she implored passionately. 'If—if you could settle the matter by firing into the air…'

He looked at her sharply, almost with contempt at

what she was suggesting. 'If you are asking me to delope,' he said in a low, dangerous voice, 'the answer is no. To do that could imply that a man's opponent wasn't worth shooting. It is what a man might do if he considers the duel is stupid.'

'But isn't that what it is?' she cried. 'Ever since I told Henry I wouldn't marry him things have got out of hand. This has nothing to do with you and I feel entirely to blame. I don't want anyone fighting over me—and certainly not you. Never you, Charles.'

Hearing the catch in her voice, he said nothing as his fascinated gaze moved over her, touching her everywhere. Her new pale-blue robe flowed in fluid lines about her body, moulding itself against her, showing the womanly roundness of her breasts and the graceful curve of her hips. Her shining black hair fell over her shoulders in a gloriously untidy mass, framing a face of heart-breaking beauty. Pride and courage showed in every feature, from her small nose, which was lovely and pert, to her mouth, vulnerable and soft, as soft as the breasts that swelled beneath her robe. Her eyes surrounded by dark silken lashes were like large luminous emeralds as they anxiously searched his face, looking for some sign that he would somehow find a way out of this mess.

'You shouldn't be here,' he said on a softer note, the rigid lines of his face relaxing and a smile forming on his lips. 'Young ladies who visit gentlemen in their rooms are considered—fast.'

'Proprieties are the least of my worries just now. Besides,' she murmured, tilting her head to one side, her look lingering, 'it isn't all that long ago when you came to mine.'

'Circumstances were different then and our situation was quite desperate.'

'Not as desperate as they are now. Charles, Henry might shoot you—he—he might…'

'What? Kill me?'

Her face blanched. 'Don't—don't say that. I can't bear it. Please persuade Henry to fire in the air, and if you do the same—'

'I'll be admitting my guilt.' Reaching out, he cradled her shocked face between his two hands, drawing her closer to him, and his voice dropped to a whisper. 'Now if I had done something to be guilty of, Henry would be justified in challenging me to a duel. Suddenly I feel tempted to give him just cause—although I confess that I have lusted after you in my mind ever since I first set eyes on you, so I suppose I could be guilty in that sense.'

While her heart soared at the intimacy of his words, Maria's gently naïve heart rejected his self-proclaimed guilt, knowing only that were it not for her, he would not be doing this. 'I cannot believe that,' she murmured.

'Believe it,' he countered, willing to let her cast him in the role of her knight in shining armour if it would help his cause. His eyes caressed her face and he sighed, smoothing the curve of her cheeks with his thumbs. 'Ever since we embarked on our journey you have been like a shadow by my side. Everywhere I went, whatever I was doing, I could see you. I am not made of stone, Maria, and, God help me, I cannot stop wanting you.'

'And I despaired of hearing you say those words to me. I came here because I am worried about you— naturally so.'

He smiled crookedly. 'I like it when you worry about

me. I like it very much.' He bent closer, his lips drawing perilously close. 'Now you are no longer engaged to Winston, you are allowed to kiss me. You are very beautiful.'

Her eyes widened in disbelief. He was teasing her, he had to be. The effect of his words was disconcerting, bringing a faint flush to her cheeks. 'Beautiful? No one has ever said that to me before. Constance was far prettier than me.'

'Not to me.'

'How do you know that?' she asked, feeling his warm breath fan her face. 'As I recall, the two of you never met.'

'I saw you both at the church—at the Count's funeral. Constance could not hold a candle to you.'

'Oh, I see. I didn't know.'

'You seem surprised that I say you are beautiful. Why shouldn't a man say such things to you?'

'I always dreamed someone would, but I always considered myself to be on the plain side.'

'You actually dreamed such things?'

She smiled up at him softly. 'Even plain girls have dreams.'

'Maria, take it from me that you are not plain. You are very lovely,' he murmured, more attracted to her than to any other woman and wondering about her allure. It was more than her face and body that attracted him. Maria was a glowing, soft gentleness that warmed him, a fiery spirit that challenged him, and a radiance that kept drawing him towards her with increasing power.

'Do not attempt to flatter me, Charles, because you haven't a hope of success,' Maria gently teased, enjoying the feel of his hands on her face, the strength of his long fingers. 'And please stop trying to change the conversation. We were discussing ways in which to prevent you getting shot.'

'No, Maria, you were.'

'But Henry is a crack shot.'

'Be that as it may—when he's sober, that is. I am not unskilled.'

'I don't doubt that. I just hope you know what you are doing. Little wonder you looked so tense when I came in just now.'

'Perhaps a little relaxation will settle my nerves.' His words were suggestive, his look both intimate and provocative.

'Your nerves?' The words came out in a gasp. 'Charles Osbourne, right now it is your nerve that must be reckoned with.'

He chuckled low in his throat, sliding his hands about her waist and drawing her close to his chest. 'You wrong me. I know my wants and I am only seeking them out if I am to honour the challenge. Just think, Maria, your kiss might be my last.'

'Honour? You have so little honour that you would blackmail me into succumbing to your demands,' she teased.

She saw his cheeks crease with a maddeningly slow and roguish smile. 'You are already in my arms and I do not see you struggling to be set free.'

When she opened her mouth to argue he silenced the words with a finger on her lips. 'Hush now. I don't want to lose moments in talking. They may never come again. I have prayed so hard to hold you again like this.'

Fear for him drove the joy she felt from her heart.

'What do you mean—these moments may never come again? The duel—'

'I have no illusions about that,' he said. 'Winston will not be satisfied until he has—'

'Oh, no—not…' She could not bring herself to say the word that, in the intimate setting of Charles's bedroom, had acquired a dreadful reality. But Charles nodded.

'Very possibly—even probable.'

He lightly brushed her lips with his own, tasting the sweetness of them. 'It is always best to look things in the face. Unless Winston has a change of heart and will agree to delope, without loss of honour, then it's unlikely I shall walk away from the duel unharmed. I know that.'

'This is insane. I will not let you sacrifice yourself for me. I shall go and speak to Henry myself.'

'There is only one thing you could do to stop the duel.'

'What is that?'

'Marry him as you originally intended. It is the only thing that will get him to call it off.'

'I can't do that,' she said in a small voice, 'but if I thought it would prevent anything dreadful happening to you, then I would.'

'You would do that for me?'

She nodded. 'Yes.'

'Bless you for that,' he said, his voice thick with emotion, deeply moved by the sincerity of her reply, 'but I would not let you. You would be consigning yourself to a lifetime of misery.'

His arms tightened round her and he sought her lips again. Clasped to his hardened frame, Maria could feel his heart hammering so hard that she seemed to feel it in her own breast. She was suddenly conscious of his nearness, of every detail about him once more, and the energy that radiated from him. She felt the shuddering in his whole body and she knew his desires were growing beyond his power to master them.

His mouth on hers was warm, firm and rousing, his lips searing her, possessing her. She struggled weakly, trying to summon some logic from all this, and all she could think of was that tomorrow he could die for her, for his refusal to hand her over to Henry. This touched her deeply. How she loved him in that moment. It was a feeling almost too full, too powerful to bear, as passion and a deeper longing stabbed through her like a piercing pain.

The fires within her now burned hot and bright with passion, and Charles found himself in the midst of a kiss that was becoming wildly erotic—and rapidly getting out of control.

He heard her low moan of awed pleasure, but instead of encouraging him to press her to further intimacy, the helpless sound made him tense and then gently he released her lips, reminding himself that it was his duty to protect and be responsible for her, even though that meant denying himself.

'I think you had better go back to your room, Maria, otherwise I'm in danger of taking you to bed—which is becoming more appealing by the second, but may result in me missing the duel altogether.'

She drew back in alarm and he laughed and pulled her back into his embrace. 'On the other hand, my second could stand in for me. He's not as fine a shot or as fast as I am, but it's me Winston wants to shoot so he may decide to fire in the air after all.' He saw Maria's eyes fill with hope, which he dashed with his next words. 'Of course it's out of the question. The code of honour dictates that I attend.'

'Yes, I imagine it does.' She sighed and stepped out of his arms. 'I suppose I'd better go.'

'I think you should. Love is a slow process, my love,' he murmured, 'and much as I would like you to stay so we can enjoy it to its fullest, I think you should go.'

'Do you want me to?'

'What do you think?'

She looked at him, seeing the answer in his eyes. This might be their last chance to be together, their only chance. Nervous now, she turned her gaze away, but not before he had seen the need in her eyes.

Charles placed his finger gently beneath her chin and turned her head back to his. 'Yes, Maria, I want you, but this is not the time.'

'But I want to stay with you. I don't want to lose you.'

'Not tonight. Not like this.'

'But this time may be all we have.'

'And it may not. Neither of us knows that. If you were to stay, to give me this night, it would have to be of your own accord, but I feel I must warn you now that afterwards you may find something in our loving that will bind you to me more firmly and more eternally than anything in your life.'

She nodded, thinking at first that he was implying that a child might be the outcome of their loving, but, looking into his eyes, she knew it was something deeper, something profound that would happen to her emotionally.

'So go to bed. Rest assured, it will all be over quickly. I expect to deal with Winston exactly as I think fit.'

Reluctantly Maria left him then, confused but some-how encouraged by his remark, but as he kissed her one more time, he refused to enlarge on it.

Chapter Eight

Shortly before dawn Maria fell into an uneasy slumber, only to wake what seemed like minutes later to the sound of someone moving down the landing outside her room. When she heard the front door open and close, immediately she was out of bed. Rushing to the window, in the first rosy glow of the pre-dawn light she was just in time to see a closed carriage drive away.

It was only now, facing the possibility of Charles's death, that suddenly it was important that he should know that she loved him. She had to tell him. A new sense of urgency banished the defeatist despair that had clouded her thinking. Hurriedly she dressed and dashed to the stables. She managed to wake one of the grooms and asked him to saddle her a horse.

Yawning and shaking the sleep from his head, he clearly thought she was quite mad, but in the end he did as she bade with surprising swiftness and soon had a horse saddled, and one for himself—it was more than his life was worth should Sir Charles find out he had let his guest ride out alone.

Maria was an excellent horsewoman. In the normal way, she would have enjoyed enormously the hectic ride, but today the stakes were too high and the risk of failure too great. Galloping in a desperate bid to see Charles before the duel, she knew beyond all doubt that her own life, too, hung on the outcome.

A slight mist hung in the low spots as they entered the park in the chill, brisk morning air. It was deserted at that hour. She rode in every direction, her eyes searching for the carriage she had seen drive away from the house.

And then there it was, along with two others in a grove almost concealed by trees and shrubs. She was too far away to see what was happening.

'Wait here,' she commanded the groom. 'I may have need of you. I don't know.'

Without further ado she left the bemused groom and rode towards the grove, keeping to the confines of the trees. Within sight of where the duel was to take place, she dismounted. Grateful for the camouflage of the foliage, she peered ahead. She stood for a moment listening, then her throat tightened as her gaze settled on a small gathering of people some distance away. She saw Charles and Henry, but did not recognise the other men.

The physicians and surgeons both men had obtained waited impassively by their carriages. The two seconds were in quiet discussion, making sure the bullets carried equal charges of powder. Charles and Henry had removed their coats and kept some distance apart.

Out of the corner of her eye Maria caught a movement. Directing her gaze to one of the carriages, she saw a face peering out, an attractive face, a very worried face, a face she had seen before.

It was the same woman who had embraced and kissed Charles at Westminster.

Maria clung to a low branch, feeling as if every drop of blood in her brain had left it, seeping away into other parts of her body and leaving her sick and faint. In a daze she watched the proceedings. She watched Charles and Henry take a loaded pistol each and stand back to back in the centre of the grove. Charles's second was to do the honours of dropping a small white square of silk to mark the start of the duel. Henry's second would give another signal and the two men would start walking the required twenty paces.

Then everything seemed to happen at once, but to Maria, it was as if it happened in slow motion. She watched with a mounting horror when Henry turned and fired before the call was given or the silk dropped. Charles turned just as the ball whined viciously and ripped across his upper arm.

Too far away to hear Maria's gasp from the confines of the trees, Charles's expression was incredulous. Ignoring the fiery pain in his arm and the blood that poured out and covered his fingers, he raised his dark, glittering eyes to his quivering assailant. Slowly, he raised his weapon and, taking his time, aimed directly at Henry's heart. Maria could almost smell Henry's fear and see the perspiration dripping from his forehead. Then Charles changed his aim at the last possible moment and aimed high, the crack sending birds startled from their roosts flapping into the sky.

Henry backed away as chaos broke out on the field of honour. Angry words of disgust from the two seconds, that he had broken the rules in a cowardly act, were directed at him. In the natural order of things, Maria wanted to run and fling herself thankfully into Charles's arms, but someone was there before her. The woman had left the carriage and hurried to his side, calling his name, quite distraught, and the doctor, carrying his bag, crossed towards him to tend the wound in his arm before he bled to death.

They did not see her as the slow death of Maria's heart began. She watched as, for an achingly tender moment, Charles placed his good arm about the woman and cradled her against him. He smiled, a warm, gentle smile, saying something to her, something that made her tip her head back and return his smile. The moment was very tender, very intimate. Then very deliberately he bent his head and placed a kiss on her forehead.

Maria started to tremble, cold now where not so very long ago she had been sweetly warm with the intoxicating memory of the illicit pleasure she and Charles had shared, delighting in the precious world of her new-found love—a love that was not reciprocated. Heartbroken and humiliated, she now understood that his decision to fight this duel of honour was for no other reason than to protect her.

Unable to stand it, Maria turned and stumbled towards her horse.

The jealousy she felt was a fierce, burning thing. It was a pain, a rending agony, an uncontrollable quivering at the thought of Charles and that woman together.

Who was she? What did she mean to Charles? Since coming home he spent little of his time there. Did he spend all his time discussing his time in France with those members of the government who had sent him there, or was that what he wanted them to think? And why hadn't he introduced her to his mother—unless she wasn't the type of woman a man would introduce to his mother?

That could explain everything. Yes, she could be his mistress—and besides, a lady would never have attended a duel. Nor did men marry their mistresses, but she was not so naïve as not to know they often kept them on when they married a woman according to their station.

Feeling that she had lost any chance of happiness with Charles, as she rode back to the house she resolved to leave London for Gravely at the earliest possible moment.

Inordinately pleased with the way the duel had gone, although he cursed the injury, impatient to see Maria and put her out of her agony, Charles walked swiftly down the main hall to the breakfast room. His mother was breakfasting alone.

'Ah, here you are, Charles,' she said, reaching for a small piece of freshly buttered toast.

'Good morning, Mother.' He grinned and, bending over, kissed her cheek before striding to the sideboard and helping himself to bacon and eggs, careful not to overwork his injured arm, which was sore rather than painful.

'I see your ride has given you an appetite,' Lady

Osbourne commented, biting into her toast, licking her lips delicately.

'It was most enjoyable,' he replied, wincing as he pulled out his chair.

'What is wrong with your arm? Does it pain you?' Her sharp eyes missed very little.

'I met with a mishap in the park—nothing serious.' He glanced towards the door. 'Where's Maria? Have you seen her? Has she—?'

Lady Osbourne looked across at him, her expression so foreboding that Charles stopped in mid-sentence.

'She's helping Ruby to pack.'

Unable to react, Charles stared at her in blank disbelief. 'Pack? Is she going somewhere?'

'To Gravely. She decided all at once. Of course we can't stop her going home—and it's only natural that she should, after being away for so long. She's already instructed Denning to have her carriage made ready.' She sighed, her expression one of melancholy.

Rather forcefully, Charles pushed his chair back and stood up. 'Excuse me, Mother.' He stalked to the door.

As Charles headed for Maria's room with rampaging emotions, his expression was as murderous as his feelings. What was she playing at—leaving without a by your leave or without waiting to hear the outcome of the duel? He might have been killed, for all she knew. He had returned expecting her to be confused and distraught and to fling herself into his arms and cry tears of relief at his safe deliverance, but instead he found she was preparing to leave his house.

He was so angry he entered her room without bothering to knock. Maria came out of the dressing room carrying an armful of clothes. She was not at all surprised to see him, having expected him, fully prepared for a confrontation.

'Charles! Come in—I'm sorry, I didn't hear you knock.'

Ignoring her sarcasm, his eyes slid to Ruby, who stood frozen to the spot. 'Leave us.'

Ruby seemed to wilt from the cutting tone. She looked desperately at Maria.

'It's all right, Ruby. Do as Sir Charles says. You can go and pack your own things. I'll send for you shortly.'

When the door had closed on the terrified maid, Charles strode to the window, standing with his back to Maria, trying to calm his temper before speaking. After a moment he turned, the warm daylight behind him, his shadow stretching across the room. There was a brief silence, then he was striding forwards, tousled dark hair curling into his neck and outlining his handsome face. There was that magnetism in his light blue eyes. The room seemed to jump to life about him as his presence filled it, infusing it with his own energy and vigour.

Placing the clothes into an open trunk, joining her hands in front of her, Maria calmly stood and watched him as he began to pace back and forth in feverish rapidity.

'My mother has informed me that you are leaving for Gravely this morning. I assume you have some legitimate reason for doing so.'

'As a matter of fact I have a very good reason. I want to go home. It's as simple as that. I have spent enough time replenishing my wardrobe and attending to business matters. I have my own carriage and horses—for which I have you to thank—and I am now ready to leave.'

'And the fact that I might be lying dead in some secluded grove in Green Park on your behalf does not concern you?'

She flinched. There was a fleeting spark of guilt in her eyes and then it was gone. 'Of course I was concerned. Are you hurt?'

'A flesh wound in my arm. Nothing serious.'

'I'm glad—not that you're wounded, but that it isn't serious. And Henry? Is—is he wounded?' Maria asked—even though she knew the answer she had to go through with the deception. Charles must not find out she had been there, had seen what had happened, had seen that woman.

He shook his head. 'As you now know he refused to delope. Before the duel it was agreed that we would both fire at the same time. Winston fired before the call was given. He didn't miss. It was fortunate for me that he was still drunk from the previous night and it affected his aim. The man's a coward and a disgrace—a man without honour.'

'And you?'

'I fired into the air. I could have killed him—I may live to regret not doing so.'

'So Henry walked away.'

'He didn't wait around.' Charles stopped pacing and looked at her sharply. His eyes narrowed, his forehead creasing in a familiar frown, a look so familiar to Maria she felt her heart knock agonisingly against the wall of her chest, but her face remained smooth and unconcerned, her eyes a frosted, brilliant green. 'But I didn't come here to talk about him. I came to talk about us.'

'I know. I do so hope you are not going to object to me leaving.'

'As a matter of fact, I do object and I cannot understand why you are behaving like this. Are you telling me your show of affection last night was a delusion on my part?'

'I—we—got carried away.'

He moved to stand in front of her, looking deep into her eyes, as if trying to read something in their depths that would give him some indication of what was wrong. 'What has happened, Maria?' he asked on a softer note. 'What has happened that has brought about this change in you—to make you angry? Have I done something wrong—something to offend you?'

She was not angry. She was trying to harden herself against him, but the tenderness in his voice was making her raw. She wanted nothing more than to drag him to her, for him to set her on fire as he had done last night. She looked up at him, looked away, and looked back at him again. She wanted to ask him about the woman she had seen him with, but her pride forbade her.

'You have done nothing wrong, Charles. I simply want to go home. Why can't you accept that?'

'You cannot travel alone—'

'I shall have Ruby with me.'

'You have no idea what you will find when you get there.'

'Yes, I do. The house has been in the hands of caretakers—a Mr and Mr Thomas and his wife. My solicitor, Mr Pettigrew, has assured me that things have been kept in order and are just the same as when I left for France.'

'And how would Mr Pettigrew know this? Has he visited Gravely?'

The startling eyes rested on her ironically. 'No, but

Mr Thomas sends him regular reports. Anyway, I shall see for myself very soon.'

'I take full responsibility for this,' he told her, beginning to pace the carpet again. 'I know how insecure you must be feeling, but let me assure you that you need not fear for your future.'

She stared at him in bewilderment, feeling an uneasy disquiet setting in. 'Insecure? My future?' She could feel her heart moving in slow but gigantic beats. Her mouth was dry with some inner emotion. 'What do you mean? I am a very wealthy woman, so I shall never be insecure, and surely my future is my own affair.'

Standing with his hands clasped behind his back, Charles gave her what he hoped was an enthusiastic smile and put his plan for her future into action. 'I would like to make it mine, too. Maria, I want you to marry me.'

Maria had not seen the answer coming and she gasped with the shock of it.

Charles was aware that she was looking at him as though he was speaking in Arabic or Chinese. Her mouth was open in a gape of disbelief, her eyes wide and staring and stunned.

'I'm sorry. My proposal seems to have taken you by surprise.'

That was true, and two days ago she would have said yes without hesitation. But how could he have the impudence to propose marriage to her while he was conducting an affair with another woman? She knew he wanted her—his passionate embraces last night had told her so, but she had not thought it would lead to this. Charles was offering to marry her. She could not quite believe she had heard him right. And yet she wished he hadn't sounded so dispassionate. She was not quite sure if she had received a proposal of marriage or an enquiry about her health.

'But—isn't that a bit extreme? Are you doing this to protect me from Henry? Do you think I shall feel not only secure but that I shall also be spared any future physical advances from him? If this is the case, then you need not worry. I am sure when Henry has had time to realise I will not marry him, he will adjust to it.'

'It is clear you do not know him.'

'I don't know you either, Charles,' she remarked irately. 'How do I know I won't be exchanging one reprobate for another—that I wouldn't be jumping out of the pan into the fire? After all, I have known you such a short time and already you have showered me with amorous advances.'

'I'm glad you remember.'

'It's difficult not to,' she replied with severe chastisement of herself, knowing that while ever she remained with him she would be unable to resist him.

'Maria, I am asking you to trust me.'

Slowly shaking her head as the enormity of his proposal sank in, she took several paces back. 'You don't have to marry me. Besides, I don't want to marry you. After my experience with Henry, I am not ready commit myself to anyone else for the foreseeable future. In fact, when I think of that awful scene at his house, it has set me against forming any kind or relationship.'

'Maria, you are alone and very rich, and prey to fortune hunters.'

'I suppose I am. And you? Could you not be accused of being one of them?'

'I too have enormous wealth,' he told her quietly. 'I have no need of your fortune.'

Having lived in the opulent grandeur of his home in Grosvenor Square and seen Highgate in Kent, Maria knew this to be true. She also knew that he was renowned in both the military field and government circles for his courage, high character and unyielding sense of justice. He was not merely a bachelor of immense wealth, he was a good catch, but so far no young lady had quite measured up to his exacting standards. So why he would offer for her she could not imagine.

'You would do this for me?'

He shrugged. 'I have to marry some time—Mother is always telling me.'

With anger and frustration washing over her in sickening waves, Maria felt disproportionately outraged. He was talking as if she had no say in the matter. 'Why—because it's expected of men in your position to marry and to produce an heir? I am not so naïve as to believe the reason you wish to marry me is because you have suddenly fallen in love with me.'

'You must know that I have come to have a high regard for you, and a strong and very passionate desire and affection for you.'

'Desire and affection are all very well, Charles, but wonderful as it is, it is not enough—not enough to provoke this absurd compulsion to marry me.'

'Is it a proper proposal you wish to have? Would you like it if I were to kneel?' he asked in a demanding voice, annoyed that she was being so obstinate, hostile, even.

'That won't be necessary,' she bit back.

'So? What do you say, Maria? Will you look favourably on my proposal?'

Her steady expression regarded him coolly. 'You do not speak of love, Charles.'

She waited, searching that expressionless face for some sign that he felt something, anything for her. Instead he lifted his brows and said, 'Should I?'

'Not if it's—not felt.'

'By whom?'

'Either of us, I suppose.'

Charles had never loved a woman, except in the physical sense, and his heart being as it was, he did not expect ever to experience what was called true love.

'I shall be a good husband. I protect what is mine. No one shall hurt you, I promise you that.'

Maria's heart contracted with pain, for she suspected that this was how he would conduct a business arrangement and could not, should not, be treated as something romantic.

'I'm not accepting your offer, Charles.'

'Dear God, Maria,' he said, thoroughly exasperated, his handsome face working with emotion, for he was not a man who liked to plead. His head and his heart told him this woman was the right wife for him, and there was nothing to stop her marrying him.

'I want nothing more than to look after you,' he went on, 'to see you come to no harm. I want to put Henry Winston behind us and have you safe—with me—*as my wife*. And don't look at me like that. You act as though I'd offered you some insult and not an honourable proposal of marriage. It is a sensible solution,' he argued, unable to believe all his plans were being demolished and sorely tempted to try a more persuasive method, to drag her into his arms and bring about a victory.

In his expression there was a resolute determination to have his way, an expression Maria was coming to know quite well.

'Sensible?' Anger rose up like flames licking inside her, spreading up her limbs. 'Why, you—you arrogant, overbearing…' Her eyes shot daggers into his. 'Can't you understand that I don't want to be *sensible?* I have been sensible all my life, letting others direct my every move, but no more.'

Charles turned from her. He leant his hands on the mantelpiece, his body rigid, his dark head bowed. 'What is this, Maria? Why are you fighting me like this? Can you not see that I am not your enemy? I want nothing more than to help you.'

Maria moved away from him. She did not want to hear any more for she could feel her weak woman's body straining towards him, yearning to give in, to lean against his strong lean body. He dropped his arms and he rose to his full height. Her heart contracted with pain. She loved him so much, more than anything she had known since she had been old enough to understand reason, and yet when she left, she would never see him again.

Charles turned and looked at her, an ironic twist to his finely chiselled lips in an otherwise cold face. He wanted to shake her. He knew she was playing a part— he believed that behind the bright expression and glib speech the real warm, passionate Maria was still to be found—only he had lost the key. What was it that had driven the girl he knew underground and replaced her with this correct, guarded puppet, who carefully kept him at arm's length and used her desire to go home as an excuse to avoid his company?

'Am I so unattractive a prospect, Maria, that you prefer to look elsewhere?'

His voice was so cool that she lifted her chin in hot indignation. 'It is the privilege of a woman to act as she chooses, and in this instance I have done so.'

He faced her with challenging eyes. 'You have made your feelings quite clear—blatantly so. And you are quite right. It is your privilege and prerogative to choose who you will marry and who you will not.' Even as he spoke he was bemused by the way the sunlight tangled in her dark shining hair. It curled vigorously about her head and down her back.

Maria glanced at him with two stormy eyes. 'I'm glad you understand.'

He didn't understand, but if she wanted to go home then he wouldn't stand in her way. He had watched over her since the day she had left the chateau. He was prepared to allow her her freedom, for he wanted this woman to come to him of her own volition.

'So, what will you do?'

'You talk as if I have no control over any of this. I see no reason for me to marry you. What you said to Henry about me having my own wishes and my own will was true. For the first time in my life I am independent of others and I am already beginning to enjoy the feeling.'

'Clearly,' he uttered coldly. 'Maria, I am just trying to protect you.'

Maria's voice was like splintered ice as she took up a stance in front of him. 'Protection? Is that the only reason you can come up with for asking me to marry you? Or are there other reasons—because you feel sorry for me, perhaps pity me? Do you honestly believe I am so desperate for a husband that I would say yes to an offer like that?' Pride caused her to lift her chin and calmly meet his ruthless stare. 'No, Charles. Absolutely not. I will make my own way. I don't need anyone—and I certainly don't want a husband whose sole reason for marrying me is to protect me from Henry.'

'It is protection of a different kind I speak of—the protection of a husband for his wife. Winston is no longer a threat.'

Maria stared at him. He sounded so certain. Something unpleasant began to unfold inside her. Slowly she moved closer to him. 'You know that, do you, Charles? How?'

'Because he is to return to India.'

'India? But—this is all rather sudden—and rather odd. Henry cannot go back to India. He left the Company in disgrace. He has no money—I thought he was relying on his marriage to me to secure his future…' Suddenly she froze and looked at him hard as something cold gripped her heart. 'Charles, what have you done?'

'Why should I have *done* anything?'

'I don't know, but I think you have. Charles—have you given him some money? Have you?' When he was about to turn from her, she grasped his arm. 'Tell me,' she demanded fiercely. When he didn't reply, she withdrew her hand and stepped back, glaring at him. 'If you don't tell me, I shall go and ask Henry myself. You have, haven't you?'

'Yes.'

For a long moment there was a black silence as what he told her sank in. She stood as though turned to stone, every vestige of colour having left her face. 'I knew it. Tell me how much you gave him to leave me alone.'

'Very well. Twenty thousand pounds.'

There was another deep and dreadful silence, a silence so menacing, so filled with the unwavering determination of the two people who faced each other, their eyes locked together in awful combat, that neither was about to retreat.

'You can't mean that,' Maria exploded, her body shaking with wrath, her hands clenched into fists by her sides. 'How dare you do that? How dare you, Charles?'

'There's no need to get into such a temper about it.'

'Temper?' Turning on her heel she stormed away from him. 'Has it not occurred to you that I might be against you giving him anything?' Suddenly the rage erupted inside her, and she whirled around on Charles in a frenzy of fury. 'How could you do that? You had no right.'

'That's enough, Maria,' he snapped, striding towards her. 'I gave him the money to get rid of him. Being the kind of man he is, not for one second did he consider refusing it. No doubt he will return to India and languish in his usual decadence for the rest of his miserable days.'

'I would have preferred to deal with Henry in my own way. Did you really think I would approve of such a move? And to give him twenty thousand pounds! It beggars belief, it really does.'

Charles loathed the idea of paying Winston off to get him to disappear out of Maria's life—also in return for his silence, to keep him from speaking of the duel, which would become a scandal that would explode all over London if it came out. His mother would be deeply hurt by it and that was the last thing he wanted.

'I knew he would pose a problem while ever he remained in London.'

'And when he's spent his twenty thousand pounds—as he surely will—what then? Will he be back for more?'

'There won't be any more.'

'You're right, there won't. And as for the money he has already received—you have given it to him, I presume?' He nodded. 'I shall reimburse you.'

His brows snapped together over biting light blue eyes. 'I don't want your money.'

'I insist. I will not be beholden to you, Charles—not to you, not to anyone—and certainly not for twenty thousand pounds. And now if you don't mind I have things to do. I would be obliged if you would allow me to leave without any fuss. I have no wish to upset Lady Osbourne.'

'And you refuse to consider my offer of marriage?'

'What do you think?' she retorted heatedly. 'You'd best go. It seems we cannot agree.'

'Damn it, Maria. Don't do this. Believe me, I'm not a man to beg and if—'

'Don't threaten me, Charles.'

'I'm not,' he bit back, white-lipped with anger, his eyes glittering down at her. 'To hell with it. I'll find someone more amenable to a proper offer of marriage. Someone who will—'

'I'm sure you won't have any difficulty in doing so.'

Charles's face was expressionless. His eyes were empty, a glacial blue emptiness that told her nothing of what he felt. He spoke only seven words.

'I think you have said quite enough,' he said, then turning on his heel, his composure held tightly about him, he strode from the room.

Full of anger and of a longing regret, Maria watched him leave and wanted to call him back. She felt the pressure inside her of rage and hurt and tears, which strangled the words in her throat. *I do want you—of course I do.* She lowered her head, full of panic, forcing herself to build a barricade around her. *Don't let him in. He'll hurt you—again and again.*

It was time to leave. Settled in the shining new carriage with Ruby beside her, having said her goodbyes to Lady Osbourne, she looked at Charles. He looked so handsome with the sun casting a warm halo about his dark head—and so distant, so cold when he looked at her. She wanted to tell him how sorry she was for all that had happened between them, but an image of the woman in his arms intruded into her mind and her pride came forth, forbidding her that comfort.

Maria would have been surprised to know that as Charles stood aside to watch her go, despite his impassive expression, inside him everything was breaking up, for he could not contemplate a life without her in it.

Once the carriage had pulled away, all the emotions Maria had been forced to suppress surged up inside her. An acid feeling of helplessness swirled through her. The anguish of their parting was ferocious. She, who had until recently been betrothed to one man, had rejected him—and fallen in love with Charles Osbourne. She was savage in her anger, not just with herself for allowing it to happen, but with him for encouraging it—especially at this time when she was in a precarious position, and she felt herself torn most distressfully by a raging conflict of emotions.

Had he thought of her when he held that woman in his arms? An ache so fierce and sharp that it caught her breath shot through her, a tormenting, fierce thrust of hot female need, unfamiliar to her and shocking in its intensity.

As Charles strode back into the house, his expression was as murderous as his feelings. He told himself that Maria would come back. But the one painful and irrefutable fact that he could not ignore was that she had run from him and he hadn't the faintest idea why.

His first thought was to go after her, demand an explanation for why she was behaving like this, but on second thoughts he decided it would be best to wait a while before following her to Gravely—if he could bring himself to do that—so that she could think over the situation in a calm and prudent fashion. For his part he realised his proposal had been made in a less than romantic fashion and he would have to find a way to remedy that.

The morning after Maria had left Grosvenor Square, another carriage pulled up outside the Osbourne residence. Lady Osbourne's younger daughter, Georgina, accompanied by two boisterous children, alighted. She cast a concerned glance at her handsome older brother who had come to the door to receive her.

Bending his head, he kissed her cheek affectionately. 'Good morning, Georgina. Not a word to Mother about yesterday,' he said, pulling her arm through his and walking with her into the house, the children scampering on ahead. 'I don't wish to upset her.'

Georgina gave him a conspiratorial smile. 'I

wouldn't dream of it. How is your arm, by the way? Not too painful, I hope.'

'It's just a flesh wound and should soon heal. I've suffered worse.'

'I'm sure you have, but promise me you won't make a habit of duelling, Charles. I don't think my nerves could stand it. I don't approve of grown men settling their quarrels in that way.'

'You shouldn't have been there, Georgina,' Charles rebuked. 'Little did I know when I asked your husband to be my second he would bring you along. He should have had more sense than to allow a respectable young woman to attend a duel.'

'Michael couldn't stop me. He did try, but I insisted. I wanted to be there. It wasn't a fair fight, was it—Colonel Winston firing before the call? Next time choose sabres. All it takes is a good aim and a steady eye. Now, let's forget about that wretched duel and come and introduce me to the lady whose honour you were fighting for. I'm so looking forward to meeting her.'

'I can't.'

'Oh, why not?'

'She left for Sussex—yesterday morning, as a matter of fact.'

Georgina stopped and looked at him in blank disbelief, worried by what she saw. His face looked hard and cold as granite, his attitude even to her was distant, and there were deep lines etched at his eyes and mouth. He looked as if he hadn't been to sleep in a week. Her expression was one of sympathy and disappointment.

'I'm sorry, Charles. Wasn't it rather sudden?'

'Very.'

'Did she say why?'

'Not a word.'

'But—how very odd. I thought…'

He looked at her sharply. 'What did you think, Georgina?'

'With the amount of attention you have been showing her, that at last you might have found a woman to settle down with. Clearly I was mistaken.'

He sighed. 'You weren't mistaken. I asked Maria to be my wife.'

Georgina's eyes lit up. 'You did? And?'

'She turned me down.'

'Oh.' Georgina was unable to hide her disappointment.

'She thought I was asking her out of pity and responsibility, not because I cared for her.'

'And you do care for her, don't you, Charles? After all, you would have died for her. I've heard how you speak about her. She is the one, isn't she? And you let her go.'

He nodded, his jaw tense. 'I'm a fool.'

'Go after her.'

'No.'

'Why not?'

'Because she left me. What am I supposed to do?'

'Whatever it takes,' his sister told him forcefully. 'Anything is better than losing her because of your silly male pride.'

Chapter Nine

Suspended between the North and South Downs in the high, broken patchwork of the Sussex Weald, a place of charming villages on hillsides once cloaked by the vast, prehistoric Forest of Anderida, was Gravely Manor, a splendid house, not a particularly large one, but gracious and welcoming, standing in an idyllic position among the hills.

Crossing the narrow wooden bridge that spanned a wide, slowly moving stream, when the house came into view Maria gazed at it, her eyes inspecting every aspect. Beautiful shrubs grew around the house, and sweet honeysuckle climbed in profusion up the walls. Little had changed. It was a joy to the eye, as were the horse chestnut trees, which had been a glory in the early summer with their thickly clustered brilliant cascades of pink and white flowers, and were now clothed in conkers, which would soon begin to fall.

She sighed, her lips curving in a sad smile. The years had been kind to her old home, though not so kind to her, for she could not shake off the feeling that she would be as a stranger when she walked through the door.

She was greeted by Mr and Mrs Thomas, a pleasant couple in middle age. They assured her that she would find everything in order and, abiding by her instructions, had taken on more staff. After thanking them and leaving Ruby to take charge of their baggage, she wandered listlessly through the rooms where the furniture remained much as it had been before her departure.

Like many nabobs, her father had chosen to spend some of his fortune on a country estate and, true to form, he had decorated the interior of his house with furniture, paintings and miniatures reflecting his abiding interest in Indian culture, but now he was no longer with her these things had lost their appeal to Maria.

In despair she sank to the edge of a chair, aching inside. The elusive sound of her father's voice shouting a lusty welcome whenever she sought him out drifted through her mind, while the faces of the past she had known in childhood passed wraithlike through her memory. She had been happy living in this house with her father, but nothing was left of the gaiety she had known here. Its charm, like the rest of her loved ones, was gone for ever—like Charles, for he, too, was gone.

Her heart beat agonisingly, despairingly, for she wanted Charles's arms about her, wanted his hard, protecting body against hers, his lips on hers in the way of a man who loves a woman. He did love a woman, but it wasn't her and she must find the strength to accept that.

It had been two weeks since the duel, two weeks since Maria had left his home and stormed out of his life. Charles had gone through the following days in a state of fury, regret and a fog of desolation.

His briefings with those he had worked for in France at an end, he attended an endless round of social events, going through them all with his usual aloof, cordial reserve. But everywhere he went he had the same brooding, angry feeling that nothing could dispel.

Wandering into Maria's room shortly after she'd left, he looked around, gently touching the things she had touched. Going to the dressing table, he picked up a rumpled handkerchief she had absently set down on a cut-glass tray. Picking it up, he placed it to his nose, smelling the sweet essence of her perfume. He was tempted to pocket the handkerchief, a treasured memento from a dark-haired angel with laughing green eyes.

Charles felt as if he was shattering into a thousand pieces as his fingers tightened convulsively around it, and then he forced himself to let it go. Just as he had forced himself to let Maria go. Bitter rage boiled up inside of him at her casual rejection of his proposal of marriage, and after casting the delicate fabric to the floor, his hand clenched into a fist with the savage urge to smash something, he turned on his heel and stalked out of the room.

For Maria, life slowly began to take on some normality. Picking up the threads of her life, with courage and determination she devoted herself to running Gravely. At nineteen years old she was her own mistress, and despite her loneliness and the loss of the man she loved—a painful love that blurred her mind—she had come home, where she tried to convince herself she belonged.

When news of her arrival got about the neighbourhood, people began calling and she returned their calls. As the days passed she became contented and busy, and she adamantly refused to think of Charles or the events that had driven her from London, but suddenly everything changed when she received a letter from Constance, who was a fugitive in France and begged Maria to help her.

Constance wrote how their worst fears had been realised and that the chateau had been set on fire by the mob shortly after Maria had left. Maria's aunt had died in the flames and Constance had managed to escape and hide in the woods. A groom had befriended her and taken her to the coast, to a village close to Calais, where she was in hiding and desperate to get to England.

Maria was deeply distressed by the contents of her cousin's letter and could well imagine how terrified Constance must be. She must do something, and immediately. There was no time to be lost. She could not go to France herself, but—but Charles could.

Charles. There was no one else.

Her cousin's letter was not only forcing Maria to think of Charles, but to see him. She was shocked. It was unbearable to be forced to think of him so soon after the fierce battle she had fought with herself to put him from her mind and thoughts. To have to think of him now, at a time when she was feeling so vulnerable, filled her with an intense feeling of loss and grief. But who else could she turn to for help? She knew of no one. There was nothing else for it. She would have to return to London and confront him, to throw herself on his mercy.

* * *

Darkness had settled over the afternoon and the windows of the house in Grosvenor Square were aglow with lights when the coach pulled to a stop. Only then did Maria realise that such had been her anxiety over Constance and her haste to reach London that she had given little thought to what she would do if Charles was not at home. Nor had she given any thought as to where she and Ruby were to stay. She knew no one in London and she could not impose on Charles and Lady Osbourne.

It was Denning who opened the door. He stared in amazement as the beautiful young woman wrapped in an aquamarine velvet cape lined with white ermine, swept inside. When she pushed the hood back on to her shoulders, his face broke into a smile of recognition and he favoured her with a broad, welcoming smile.

'Welcome back, Miss Monkton. You are here to see Sir Charles?'

'I am, Denning. I apologise for my untimely and unexpected arrival. I would very much like to see Lady Osbourne, too, if I may.'

'Lady Osbourne is away from home visiting friends, Miss Monkton, but Sir Charles is in the drawing room. I'm sure he'll be delighted to see you. I shall inform him you are here.'

As Denning went towards the drawing room he was uncertain how Sir Charles would react to Miss Monkton's arrival. Being a quiet observer of everything that went on in the house, nothing escaped his notice, not even the fact that relations had been extremely frosty between the young lady and his master on the day she had left for her home in Sussex. Sir Charles's mood had been black and morose ever since.

With a reassuring smile at the nervous young woman as she swept past him, Denning closed the door behind her. Charles was standing by the fireplace, drinking a glass of brandy before leaving for his club. He lifted one eyebrow.

'Well!' he exclaimed, giving no indication of how his heartbeat quickened or the astonishment he felt that Maria had sought him out. He held his body rigid, tense with conflicting emotions, as he struggled to master himself. He knew something unthinkable had happened to him. He had felt it, he supposed, at the start—when she had been feeding the hungry children and they had exchanged angry words. She had left the very essence of herself in the house when she had left, entering into that place that had been so sorely hurt when she had refused to become his wife—his heart, the flesh and bones of him, which had ached for her.

'I didn't believe Denning when he told me you were gracing us with your presence. I was under the impression,' he said in such Arctic tones that Maria felt an involuntary shiver down her spine, 'that everything had been said between us. So what brings you here with such urgency? No doubt you have excellent reasons.'

The tone, aggressive and deliberately offensive, would, in the normal way, have provoked Maria to an equally stinging reply. But she knew if she wanted to save Constance she must cast off her pride and humble herself. 'Yes.'

He looked at her, the memories of their time together, the memories he couldn't seem to stifle parading across his mind. But most of all he remembered how she felt when she melted in his arms, the sweet generosity of that soft mouth of hers.

Furious with his weakening resolve, he shoved himself away from the fireplace, put his glass down and faced her. Maria actually flinched at the coldness in his eyes as they raked over her. 'You are well?'

She swallowed convulsively. He was so stern, so rigid, so oppressive and yet so…breathtaking. She could feel his scorching gaze on her and bravely met it head-on.

'I am very well, thank you,' she replied quietly. 'And you, Charles?'

He nodded curtly. 'As you see. Forgive me, Maria, if I appear surprised to see you back in London so soon. I confess I am baffled by it. I imagined you would be fully occupied at Gravely putting your house in order.'

'I am—I was. I—I have something to ask you.' She could sense he was wary, that his guard had not dropped. There was still a distance between them that might never be closed. The startling light blue eyes rested on her ironically.

'Of what possible help could I be to you? Have you come to tell me you have considered my proposal of marriage and have decided to accept—to use all your feminine wiles to placate me? If so, you can forget it.'

'I—I haven't…' she stammered.

'Good,' he bit back, ignoring the painful twist to his heart. 'When I asked you to be my wife I did so because I wanted to give you the protection of my name, to give you a life replete with every luxury within my power to grant you—and also because I thought you cared for me as much as I have come to care for you. It was an insane idea and I curse ever having thought of it.'

Maria controlled a tremor of temper as his tall, powerful frame moved from the fireplace and he stood watching her. He had not invited her to a seat and she knew he was deliberately keeping her on tenterhooks until he found out the full reason for her visit. He was treating her as if there had been nothing between them, as if they had not shared tender moments of passion.

His eyes never left hers as she walked—at the cost of a violent effort of will towards him on legs that felt like jelly—over the miles of empty desert that the room seemed to have become. A mere step away from him she paused to still the quaking of her knees. With her head bowed, she waited a moment before lifting her head and raising her shining eyes to his.

'Charles, please listen to me,' she begged a trifle impatiently, unable to hide the desperation in her voice, keen to get down to the business in hand. 'I haven't come to speak of that.'

'Then what? Well, Maria...I am waiting,' he demanded in a lazy, sensual drawl that always made Maria's heart melt. He was leaning with one arm resting on the mantelpiece, dark and imperturbable, infuriatingly unresponsive to Maria's beseeching green eyes. 'What is it that is so important that has brought you back to this house—to see me?'

'The purpose of my visit is because I need your help quite desperately.'

He arched his brows. 'You do? And I was under the impression that you never wanted to set eyes on me again,' he retorted drily.

Maria drew a tortured breath, trying not to show

her fear. 'Please, Charles, I have not come here to argue with you.'

'No, of course you haven't. So what is it you want me to do that you cannot do yourself? Why have you come to me?'

'Because you have connections that are not available to most men—and besides, I didn't know who else to turn to.'

His eyebrows crawled slowly upwards. 'Really?' Despite his resolution not to give a damn what her problems were, he was a little unnerved by her visible anxiety. 'What is it you want?'

'I want you to rescue Constance.'

'Constance?' Whatever he had been expecting, it wasn't this.

'Something dreadful happened when we left the chateau, Charles—something frightful. It was burned and my aunt, along with many of the servants, died in the fire. According to Constance, the mob showed no mercy.'

Charles's expression softened and he nodded sombrely, studying Maria with an enigmatic expression in his eyes. 'I'm truly sorry, though it comes as no surprise. The Countess was a stubborn woman. I gave her strong warning of what might happen.'

'I know you did and if only she had heeded your warning and come to England with us she would still be alive. But there is nothing to be done now except to help Constance. She managed to escape with the help of a groom and made it to the coast. It cannot have been easy for her and she must be suffering dreadfully. She says she has been ill and is very weak from her journey and having to constantly conceal her identity. The people who are hiding her are kindly folk, but she lives in constant fear that she will be discovered.'

'So, where is she?' he asked, his expression revealing nothing of his thoughts, but he was frowning slightly and Maria at least had the satisfaction of knowing that he was giving the problem his full attention. She retained a deep conviction that, if he wanted to do something, he would find a way.

'At a village close to Calais. I—I have her letter.' Quickly she produced her cousin's crumpled letter from her reticule and handed it to him. 'As you see, there is an address.'

'How did the letter reach you?'

'It was brought to me by someone she paid to smuggle it out of France. She says she is having problems getting a boat to bring her to England—that everyone trying to cross the Channel is treated with suspicion. She has tried and failed. That is why she wrote to me in the hope that I would help her.'

'And am I to assume you want me to go to France, to return to a country that is gripped in a reign of terror, to find your cousin and bring her back?'

Maria swallowed and nodded, her anxiety and hope apparent in her eyes. 'It is a matter of life or death. Can you find a way of helping her? It will be dangerous, I know…'

His eyes flashed unexpectedly. 'I am all too aware of the perils of embarking on such a mad scheme—I have first-hand experience, remember? What you are asking is insane.'

Maria bit her lip, unable to face the expression of aloof contempt in his eyes. There was an undercurrent of fierce inflexibility in his voice, which was difficult to confront. She had inadvertently angered him, already forgetting her resolution to be humble.

'If you found yourself in my place, wouldn't you do the same?'

'Maybe, but I cannot believe you have come all this way to ask this one mad, impossible thing of me.'

Maria felt a wave of desperation as she strove for control and to calm her mounting fears. 'Mad, yes, that is true—but not impossible—surely not impossible?' she cried, gazing up at him imploringly.

'No,' he conceded. 'Perhaps not.'

Maria was conscious now that he was studying her with a different interest. She returned his look. His expression did not alter and yet she felt the air between them charged with emotion, as if he were reaching out to her, drawing her to him by some irresistible force. At last she forced herself to say, 'You have to help me, Charles, for without you Constance is doomed.' Now she felt anguished. What was she to do if he refused? 'All she needs is someone to go to her and help her get safe passage over the Channel.'

'And what happens to Constance if I am apprehended?'

'I sincerely hope you won't be.'

'And if I am arrested and detained and thrown into prison—accused of being a British agent? I could even be shot. Have you given any thought to what tragedy could ensue?'

He stared at her for a long, unyielding moment. Maria looked away, unable to meet his cold gaze. The flame of hope that had risen in her heart dwindled to a pale glimmer. She was feeling very shaken, but unable, in all honesty, to argue with him. She knew his objections were valid and she had no answer to them. Her eyes filled with tears at this cool, sardonic reference to the perils he would have to face on Constance's behalf and a lump came and went in her throat, a lump of misery and shame that she was asking him to put his life in danger. But what else could she do?

'I confess that I haven't given much thought to how it can be achieved—and I really shouldn't be asking this of you, but, as I said, I am quite desperate. I cannot simply ignore Constance and carry on with my life. If you cannot help her, then perhaps you know of someone else who can be trusted—who would do this? Naturally I would—I would reward them well—and you, too, of course—'

'Reward!' Charles's icy voice sliced through Maria's words like a knife. 'Save your money, Maria. To speak of paying me for such an undertaking—something I would like to think I was doing for a friend—I find insulting and you earn my contempt.'

The scorn in Charles's tone, even more than his words, stabbed straight at Maria's heart, striking with the freezing intensity of a winter frost, and she regretted having drawn such a strong, emotional response from him. She dragged in several painful breaths, no longer feeling the warmth of the room. She was thrown into a dark, barren world of her own, the words flung into her face with uncompromising directness by a man she could not help but love.

'I realise you must despise me,' she said tonelessly.

'No.' The word was harsh, but the fury had gone out of his voice. 'I pray God I will never have cause to do that.'

'But I can understand why I have earned your contempt. I am sorry, but ever since I received my cousin's letter, I have been shaken out of my usual reserve.' She stepped away from him and drew her cloak around her. 'I see it as my duty to help Constance, to do everything I can. It is clear to me that you feel you cannot help me—and, if I am honest, I can understand your natural apprehension. I can see I should not have come to you.'

'Did I say I wouldn't help?'

A tentative flicker of hope flared in her eyes. 'You mean you will go to France?'

'I might,' he said, more gently.

'That isn't good enough. You have to be positive.'

'There is a lot to consider. It will be complicated. It is not always easy for even the wisest man to decide on the best course of action.'

'Do you think I don't know that?'

'What will you do if I refuse to help you?'

Maria blanched and took a step back. 'Then I would have to find some other way. I am deeply suspicious of entrusting such an undertaking to a stranger—unless he is recommended by you, for I trust your judgement. If you refuse to recommend someone, then I shall go to France myself.'

His eyes were as watchful as ever, but they didn't lack warmth. 'I believe you would and I salute your courage and boldness. You are undeniably brave—and totally reckless.'

She managed a little smile. 'Goodness. Am I supposed to feel complimented or chastised?'

'Both. I compliment your commitment to your cousin, and I reproach your foolhardiness to go rushing off into a situation that could well get you into trouble.'

Maria's eyes locked on his. 'Will you help me, Charles? I shall be most grateful.'

'You should be.'

Turning from her, deep in thought, he considered Constance's predicament, for the thought of Maria's cousin at the mercy of the mob, should she be discovered, was almost more than he could bear. Doing his best to calm himself, he pulled himself together, knowing he must get over to Calais as soon as possible.

'It will be best if you leave it up to me as to how I proceed. It is unfortunate that Constance is unwell, but the good news is that we know she is close to Calais. I know the town and the surrounding villages well so I should have a better chance of getting her back than if she were in a place that is unfamiliar to me.'

'When will you go?'

'At first light I will head for Dover.'

'How will you travel?'

'On horseback. It's quicker than the carriage. Why?'

She shrugged. 'I—just thought—well, that I might go with you and wait there when you cross to Calais.'

'No, Maria. Definitely not. I absolutely forbid it,' he said, his voice harsh. 'Our days of travelling anywhere together are behind us. You can wait here—although on second thoughts, perhaps it would be advisable if you were to return to Gravely.'

He passed a hand over his hair, which immediately fell over his brow. Maria saw the movement and wanted to go to him and smooth the lock of hair back again, perhaps touch his cheek and tell him how grateful she was for his concern, for his help—for him. He had been there at exactly the right moment in all the adversities of her life since she had left the chateau. Steadfast, reliable, steadying her with his calm strength, smiling sometimes to let her know that everything would be all right—just as he would see it was for Constance. Keeping a cool head, he would be calm and in control.

Maria was suddenly overwhelmed with weariness. 'I do not wish to impose, but I didn't give any thought to where I would stay when I set out.'

Seeing the sudden droop of her shoulders, Charles wanted to go to her, take her in his arms, kiss her and soothe her and tell her he would make everything all right. And yet how could he after what had happened between them? But she was evidently much distressed, and who could blame her after what had befallen her cousin? Walking past her, he went to the door to instruct Denning to have rooms prepared for her and Ruby.

'You look exhausted,' he said, coming back to her. 'The journey has obviously tired you. A meal will be brought to you in your room and after that I suggest you go to bed. Tomorrow you must return to Gravely and wait for me there.'

'But Denning informed me that Lady Osbourne is away.'

'That can't be helped. Does it concern you that you will be in the house with me alone?'

She shook her head wearily. 'Let people say what they will. This is too important a matter to worry about protocol. And my coachman?'

'Will be taken care of.'

'Thank you, Charles. I—I don't deserve this.'

'No, you don't. As you said, Maria, your cousin needs help. It's impossible for you to go to Calais, so I must.'

His mouth, which at the moment was not smiling, was well cut, curling and sensual. He was doing his best to appear calm, but Maria could see he was only being polite. She wished she didn't have to put him through this, for though he was a basically decent person, he did not want to be involved with anything that had to do with her, but because he was the sort of man who had a tendency to rescue a defenceless creature—just like he had rescued her in France—he wouldn't let her down.

In the same room she had occupied when she had been a guest in the house before, Maria tossed and turned in her bed, too anxious to sleep and unable to still her churning thoughts. At midnight she gave up trying and got out of bed and paced the carpet, her thoughts as bleak and dismal as tomorrow promised to be.

She paused in her pacing when she heard soft footsteps outside her door. It was Charles, going to his own rooms, who had paused and stood looking at her door, seeing a light beneath and a shadow passing too and fro, which told him that she was having difficulty sleeping.

When Maria heard the soft tap on her door she was momentarily startled and didn't move. When the tap was repeated, wrapping her robe over her nightdress, she went and opened it, surprised to see Charles standing there.

'Charles!'

'I saw the light under your door. Can't you sleep?'

'You shouldn't be here—and, no, I can't seem to settle. I have too much on my mind.' She smiled wanly, pushing her hair back from her face and tucking it behind her ear. 'I can't help it. Ever since I got Constance's letter I have been so worried.'

'Care for some company?'

'Do you mean you want to come in?'

'If you like. Nothing that has happened between us—our journey across France and the times when we found ourselves in each other's arms—should make us antagonistic to each other now. Should it?'

'No, of course not. But—the times when you—when we—' colour crept into her cheeks when she recalled the intimacies they had shared '—it was nothing but a mild flirtation—wasn't it, Charles?'

His eyes met hers in mocking challenge. 'And you are sure about that, are you, Maria? That's not the way that I remember it. I think you've tried very hard to convince yourself that it was nothing more than that.' His gaze settled on her lips. 'You were something more to me than a mild flirtation.'

Beneath his penetrating gaze Maria's flush deepened and she looked a little flustered, her delicately beautiful face framed by a halo of black hair—a dainty image of fragility standing before a man who dwarfed her. They were like vulnerability and strength, stubborn pride and iron resolve—two opposites whose differences had once drawn them together and now those differences separated them.

'There is still no reason why we shouldn't be cordial to each other,' she said.

'Flirtations don't usually end in duels.'

'I know and I'm sorry Henry shot you.'

'Forget about it.' Without waiting for her to reply he stepped inside, closing the door softly behind him. Moving to stand close to her, he looked at her upturned face and smiled, his eyes warmly glowing. 'I seem to recall that we've been in a similar situation as this before, Maria—in France, when you posed as my wife. Remember?'

Hot, embarrassed colour stained Maria's smooth cheeks as they faced each other. He stood there with his dark hair tousled, his sternly handsome face stamped with nobility and pride. Having removed his jacket and loosened his neck linen, his muscular body emanated raw power, and she thought he seemed as rugged and invulnerable as the cliffs at Dover.

'I shall never forget it. I also remember how afraid I was—afraid that we wouldn't make it to Calais.'

Laughter shone in his eyes and his smile broadened. 'Afraid? You? I recall a beautiful young woman who came to my defence and bravely confronted a rampaging mob who would have torn us to pieces had you not covered your face in spots and frightened them away.'

'That wasn't bravery, it was desperation. In fact, I recall you berating me so severely for not staying in the coach that I was tempted to get out and walk to Calais.'

'I have every confidence that you would have succeeded—although I would not have taken kindly to being deprived of your charming company. So, Maria,' he said, walking slowly across the room, 'how do you like being back at Gravely? Is it as you remember?'

'Yes and no. Before I went to France my father was there, but now the house seems—empty—as though it's lost its heart.' She sighed and sat in the chair by the dying fire. 'Nothing stays the same.'

'No, it never does.'

His voice had a hint of regret and Maria looked at him curiously. 'You said that with feeling, Charles. Were you sorry to leave India?'

He nodded. 'At the time.' He grinned. 'India has a habit of getting under your skin, into your blood.' Sitting across from her, he stretched out his long legs, crossing them at the ankles, calmly watching her.

Maria lowered her gaze and idly smoothed out the creases in her robe. 'That was what my father said. He never did settle in England—well, not really—for all his wealth. I think he would rather have stayed in India a pauper than live in England a rich man.'

'It was no secret that he amassed a large fortune in India.'

'Which enabled him to buy his beautiful Gravely.' She raised her head and looked at him. Her expression was soft and her magnificent eyes suddenly glowed like bright green jewels. 'Did you know that I was born in India?'

Charles regarded her with frank curiosity. 'I recall my mother saying something of the sort. Whereabouts?'

'In Simla. To avoid the heat, Mother always went to the coolness of the hills during the summer months. She died soon after I was born and Father—who was not a well man—brought me to England to live.'

'And chose to settle in Sussex.'

'Yes. He did love living there. Leaving India was difficult for him, but he wanted me to be brought up in England.' Her expression became sad. 'Little did I know how short a time I would have with him.'

'You were close, I can see that.'

'Yes. He was all I had. Nothing was the same when he died.'

Charles leant his head against the back of the chair. Maria saw his body relax, slackening perceptibly. He was silent, but his silence was as devoid of tension as his body, and the familiar sense of safety and reassurance that his presence would bring her, gradually smoothed out the turmoil in her mind.

Charles had always been able to give her this feeling of security, and, looking at his abstracted face, she thought how strange it was that this would always be so. Now that she had discovered she loved him, she did not feel embarrassed or shy in his presence. But she was a single woman and they were no longer fleeing for their lives in France, but installed in respectable society where it was shockingly improper for her to be alone in a bedroom with a man, a man she was convinced was in love with another woman.

But the feeling of security was only temporary, for she knew when Charles had left for Dover her anxiety would return and she would know no peace until he returned with Constance. She was profoundly afraid for him.

'Charles, I'm sorry.'

'You are? For what?'

'Placing you in this situation. I—I cannot bear to think I am placing you in danger like this. If anything should happen to you, I will never forgive myself.'

'Why, what's this, Maria?' Getting up, he took her hands and drew her to her feet. 'You sound as if you care.'

'Of course I care,' she uttered passionately. 'I care that you may be hurt yet again because of me. Was it not enough that I let you fight that wretched duel…?'

She was silent for a moment or two, and Charles, watching her, said gently, 'Does that make a difference?'

Maria's gaze came back to his, and she said thoughtfully, 'Yes. But I don't know why it should.'

'Better or worse?'

'Worse.'

Noting the tension and anxiety on her face, Charles lifted a hand and brushed his fingers lightly across her forehead. 'Don't frown so, Maria,' he murmured. 'It can't matter as much as all that.'

She wanted to cry, *But it does*. It mattered more than anything else, but she could not tell him that. 'I may have refused to be your wife, Charles,' she said quietly, 'but that does not mean I wish you harm.'

'I do know that.' Charles was aware of nothing but her. The complexity of his emotions both overwhelmed and exasperated him. He was prepared to do anything if he could win her to him—even travelling to France to rescue her cousin if it would help his cause where she was concerned. When he spoke his voice was very serious. Gently cupping her chin in his hand, he turned her face up to him.

'You know, Maria, when you left for Gravely, I thought I could put you out of my mind, yet the moment I laid eyes on you again, the moment I saw your face, I was astonished by the depth of my feelings. When I asked you to be my wife it was because I wanted to look after you. I also need a lover, a friend, as my wife, to share laughter and love.'

She wanted to tell him that it was not enough, to shout that she wanted more than that, that she wanted him to say he loved her and only her, that there was no one else and never would be. Her senses swirled under the power of his proximity. How was it possible that he could dispel her resolve to stand against him just with a touch of his hand? She clenched her hands to stop them from trembling, but that only made the tremors race up her arm and through to her innermost being like molten heat. Charles was looking at her hard, and somehow she felt compelled to look back. Their gazes locked.

'Charles,' she whispered, her voice heavy with objection and longing. 'What do you think I am? Do you presume that because I am in your house alone with you, I'm fair sport to be ravished in my bed?'

His light blue eyes were sharp, speculative, darker now as they looked into her face. 'I do not, Maria. If I had wished it, it would already have happened. There have been many opportunities for me to seduce you, but I respected your naïvety and your innocence. Now it is different.'

She gasped at his arrogance. But the potency of his desire couldn't be denied, and she knew his words were true. She returned his look and a sudden tension in his tall figure woke her senses, her female senses, to the danger—not danger from Charles, for he would never do anything to hurt her, but the hazards she was allowing herself to be led into by this familiar and fascinating man.

'The hour is late,' she whispered, not wanting to make it too easy for him, nor of letting him think she was almost drowning in her own pleasure as the wanton sensations ran through her body at his very touch. 'I— I think you should go. Tomorrow—'

'What we do now will not interfere with what I have to do tomorrow, Maria. At first light I shall be on the Dover road, so don't fret. I do not know what it was that turned you away from me—fear, maybe, of committing yourself to another man so soon after Winston. But whatever it was, you cannot deny your feelings. Your eyes give you away.'

Maria stared at him, beginning to panic. She had to make him leave while she was capable of letting him go. Her heart was racing now, and instead of obeying the frantic urgency of her thoughts, her fingers were curling round his wrist as his hand still held her chin instead of thrusting him away. She drew a deep breath, unaware that she had been holding herself stiffly, her shoulders slightly hunched as though to defend something vulnerable inside her that exposed the slender column of her throat and lifted her breasts beneath her robe.

From beneath hooded lids Charles smiled down at her. 'You see, Maria, you do want me, and I will show you how much.'

She made one last effort to draw back from this perilous moment, for she finally knew this should not be happening, but when he started to draw her into his arms and his mouth found hers, she felt her lips parting.

Their bodies pressed together, breast to breast, thigh to thigh, their mouths fused, caressing, their tongues touching. Maria gave herself up to the magic of his kiss. Charles put his hand to the back of her head, entwining his fingers in her hair until it fell about her, a tangled mane of blackness. She lifted her chin and his lips slid along it and along her jaw, taking her earlobe gently between his teeth, and with a groan they both fell to their knees, as though the strength had left them.

Maria held his head as his mouth slid down her neck, his hands tearing open the front of her robe, the fullness of her breasts outlined beneath her nightdress, the hardness of her nipples clearly defined, the dark flush a tormenting shadow just discernible beneath the fine fabric. He slipped her arms out of her robe and slid the shoulders of her nightdress down, easing her breasts free so that he could feast his eyes on them—his eyes, his lips, his tongue savouring their texture, their responsiveness to him as he slowly sucked them into his mouth.

Maria gasped when she felt her nipples swell and ache with longing, a longing that shocked her. It was as though she had taken on the identity of a wanton, the sensations he was arousing in her lapping at the most sensitive part of her. When he took her mouth in a deep, devouring kiss once more, reality faded, and exciting, dangerous intimacy followed the discovery of her womanhood and the sharing of their feelings for one another.

Despite her reasons for refusing to become his wife, she was a woman who had senses and emotions, whose body wanted fulfilment, to meet a need so strongly rooted within her and so fiercely suppressed that now it turned against her and overwhelmed her with its intensity, and his scent, the reality of the man, was all the more dangerous because of her own denial. She recognised with all her youthful passion that she wanted him with the hungry intensity of the woman she had become, awakening sensations so unexpected and unknown to her that she moaned and recoiled from him.

When Charles swung her up into his arms and carried her to the bed, where he laid her down on the covers, soft and ready for them, she was made to realise that there was no going back, no escaping what was to happen.

'Charles!'

When she spoke his name he raised his head to look into her eyes, his darkening as he recognised the desire in hers. He wanted her so much. Her mouth was soft, her lips parted, moist and inviting.

'What is it you want, Maria? For me to stop?' He gave a small sensual laugh. 'Or is it more of this you want?' And he again took her mouth in a savage kiss.

Maria shuddered, her senses whipped by pleasure and pain, her body so acutely sensitised that the sweet ferocity of his kiss sent darts of aching heat through her body.

When he pulled back from her and said, 'Is it, Maria? Tell me?' she reached out to draw him back to her, her lips finding his, seemingly mesmerised by his seduction.

'Yes,' she told him fiercely, her awakening needs dictating all thoughts of common sense or decorum. 'Kiss me again,' she pleaded softly against his mouth.

Charles paused. Now was the time to reject her as she had rejected him, but instead he lowered himself on to her, his hands thrusting into the thickness of her hair so she could not escape. Opening his mouth on hers, he explored its softness, revelling in the taste of her, until Maria moaned and clutched at him with pleasure.

For a second a small lance of sanity seemed to make her pull back and question her behaviour. She was like a demented woman, lying on the bed with a man who was not her husband. She was shocked, but only for a moment.

Thinking she was about to wriggle free, Charles raised his head. 'What is it?' he demanded. 'You said you wanted me to kiss you.'

'I do, Charles. I do.'

'Maria, you know what will happen if we continue.'

'Yes,' she gasped, knowing what he was saying and accepting it.

Maria watched him pull off his clothes, admiring the breadth of his shoulders, the solid muscles of his thighs, the strength of his arms and held out her arms to him.

He came to her and lay beside her, removing her night-dress, pausing for a moment to stare, absorbed, at the naked beauty of her body, the flush of her skin, its warmth, its softness, its responsiveness, before drawing her against him, his arms tight about her, her full breasts against his furred chest. His kisses trailed over her body, slowly and lingeringly, as if he had all the time in the world. She became helpless with desire, allowing it all to happen, wanting it with primitive ferocity.

There was no gentleness in him, nor in her when he entered her. She was almost delirious with the new sensations and by the powerful response of her own body, exquisitely pulsating and seeming to have a will of its own.

Afterwards they lay together, not speaking, her face buried in his neck and shoulder, his against her tangled hair, both replete. Maria knew nothing would ever be the same again. Charles had put his masculine mark on her, discovered the woman in her, the latent desire of which she had never known. The little green devil of jealousy of the other woman pushed its way into her consciousness just when she least expected it. She lay in the bed with them, a drifting, dangerous ghost.

In the cradle of Charles's arms, Maria bit her lips hard. She was aware that he had not said he loved her in the heat of passion, but not for the world would she spoil these moments by questioning this, for they would never come again. Nothing could be so sweet, so perfect, as this first time that she lay with a man, a man she loved so desperately.

Charles said nothing for a long time, content to simply hold her to him, and then slowly he disentangled himself and reached for his clothes. Bending down, he touched his lips to hers, and whispered against her mouth, 'You and I are as good as married now, Maria.'

Maria watched him from her love-drugged eyes as he covered her nakedness with the covers, her body still warm from its contact with that magnificent, virile body of his. Blankly she focused on him, his words bringing her back from that dangerous bewitchment. 'Marry? Charles—I don't understand…?'

'You might be carrying my child,' he told her.

She opened her mouth to deny the assertion and then discovered that she could not.

'So, my love, you will have to reconsider my proposal. We shall be married, and as soon as possible.' He spoke with the arrogance and certainty that said it would do her no good to argue.

Charles frowned as he heard his own declaration. That wasn't what he had intended to say. It was as if he had contrived what had happened between them to persuade her to reconsider his proposal. But it was far from the truth. He had wanted her like hell and been unable to resist her. But now the words had been said, he had no intention of calling them back. In fact, he discovered that he was glad that he had said them. A cavalier attitude of reckless determination filled him with a sense of hope, of his life suddenly taking an unexpectedly enticing and longed-for turn.

He kissed her again with all the possessive pride of a man who had taken his woman to enchantment and would do so again at the earliest opportunity.

'I am going to leave you now, though I would dearly like to stay.' He smiled. 'My mother would be scandalised, and I dare not risk gossip among the early-rising maids. You have a reputation to maintain. I'll see you at Gravely when I get back from France—with Constance. Hopefully we will only be parted for a little while.'

Maria was not to be so easily won over. Immediately her body tensed in defiant pride and she propped herself on her elbow. 'Nothing is changed, Charles. Did you really think that after making love I would accept your suit?'

'Yes,' he admitted. 'I am determined you will be my wife. I hoped at this point I would have persuaded you to say yes.'

'I will not marry you, Charles. I have told you.'

'And if you are with child?'

'If I am, I will consider what to do then. This changes nothing. Why will you not accept that?'

'Because I cannot stop thinking of you. Of the time we spent together. I cannot stop thinking of the times when I have held you and kissed you,' he said, his voice low and fierce and wrenching to hear. 'I remember many things, Maria—how soft your lips were—reluctant at first, and how quickly they responded to my own. When you were in my arms I remember how you filled my senses until I could not think.'

'Please don't say these things,' she whispered.

'Why? Because you felt the same and for some insane reason you don't want to be reminded in case it weakens your resolve to stand against me for God knows what reason? If you felt this way, then why didn't you stop me?'

'I couldn't,' she confessed. 'We both lost control so neither of us can be blamed for what we have done. I knew what the result would be, yet I could not stop myself from doing it anyway.'

'You want me, Maria, admit it, and when I get back I will make you see it. I am determined I will.' He kissed her once more and reluctantly left her.

Only then did Maria begin to feel as if she was coming back down to earth again. Quieter and colder without his presence, the slow reaction to all that had happened began to sink in.

She struggled to forget about the other woman, to let her body lead her back to pleasurable thoughts of Charles and what he had done to her, and found herself wondering if he compared this with what he had done with *her*. And so she was very unhappy and she just didn't know what to do about it.

Chapter Ten

In a state of frenetic restlessness, Charles went to his room, and, unable to think of going to bed, paced the carpet in an attempt to ease his frustration, trying to make some sense of why Maria was being so unreasonable. He was completely baffled by her behaviour. What had happened between the time when she had left his room on the night before the duel until he had returned from Green Park? It didn't make sense.

Something elusive nagged at the back of his mind. He thought back to the duel, going over every detail, everything that had been said, missing nothing. When Charles had left the grove he had returned to the house in the carriage, nursing his injured arm, preferring to leave the carriage at the stables to avoid being seen from the house by his mother, who would be sure to ask awkward questions.

He remembered the grooms had been getting ready to start the day—in fact, one of them had been rubbing down one of the horses. He frowned. Rubbing it down?

A horse wasn't rubbed down unless it had been ridden. But who, at that time in the morning, had been riding out? The thought bothered him.

The following morning when he was setting out for Dover he sought out the groom and questioned him, stunned when he was told it had been Miss Monkton who had ridden out, and that this same groom had accompanied her.

'Where? Where did she ride?' Charles demanded.

'The Park, Sir Charles. Green Park.'

'And did you stay with her?'

The groom shifted uneasily, thinking he was about to get a ticking off for neglecting Miss Monkton. 'No. She told me to wait and rode off.'

'Did you see anything—anyone else?'

He shook his head. 'But I heard a couple of shots. I was just about to go looking for her when she came back.'

'I see.'

Not wishing to waste any more time, Charles mounted his horse and rode out of the yard to begin his journey, as confused as ever. If Maria had witnessed the duel, why the hell hadn't she shown herself, or told him? Why the secrecy? Thinking back to their bitter confrontation, when he had told her he would find someone else, someone more amenable to a proper offer of marriage, she had replied that she was sure he wouldn't have any difficulty in doing so. Recalling how forcefully she had spoken, he frowned.

That was the moment he remembered Georgina, how his sister had run to him when he had been shot, and how intimate that scene must have looked to someone looking on, who didn't know that the woman in his arms was his own sister.

Suddenly every piece of the bizarre puzzle began to slot into place. If Maria believed Georgina was his mistress, if she actually believed that, it explained why she had behaved as she had. Naked pain flashed across his handsome features as he rode his horse hard. When she had refused his proposal, it had been her pride she had been trying to save, for Maria wasn't the kind of woman who would share her husband with a mistress.

Maria left for Gravely after an early breakfast. Rain was falling out of a leaden sky as it had been doing for the past week, turning the roads into quagmires of mud and making the journey extremely hazardous at times. She was relieved when the coach turned down the road to Gravely, although she looked in alarm at the sight of the narrow wooden bridge spanning the stream.

For three days as the rain continued to fall, she was on tenterhooks as she waited for Charles. She was unable to think of anything other than the night she had spent in his arms, one minute thinking of the joy she had felt, and the next filled with recriminations at what she had done.

She should not have let him into her room, into her bed, but he had put his hands on her, allowed her to feel the warmth and masculine vigour of him. His lean dark face with its oddly slanting smile had bewitched her and she had felt her flesh warm with what could only be called desire as her hands had felt the ripple of muscles on his chest, lean and yet strong. She had wanted the night to go on for ever, for she had experienced a strange languor, warm and sweet and deep, holding her in a most unusual need to be carried wherever he fancied taking her. From that moment she had gloried in it, in him, despaired over it, and known it was too late to draw back.

It was noon on the fourth day when a mud-spattered coach came up the drive and drew to a halt in front of the house. Maria saw it arrive from an upstairs window. Her heart leapt. She descended the stairs in a rush, smoothing her hair and arranging her skirts in place. Crossing the hall, she flung open the door. It was Charles, it had to be—and, please God, Constance.

When the occupant heaved his corpulent body out of the coach her heart missed a beat. The cause was not surprise, but an unpleasant sensation more akin to revulsion.

It was Henry.

Maria saw the bloated features set in an expression of boredom, the heavy chin supported by the folds of the high muslin cravat. Her proud, disdainful green eyes met and held those of the man she had once thought she would marry without flinching. She was discovering agreeably that now she was face to face with him, the vague fear that had haunted her ever since their encounter at his house, and again at the theatre, had melted away.

Considering the turmoil within her, she managed to retain her poise. 'Henry. This is a surprise. I did not expect to see you here.'

'I am on my way to Portsmouth to visit friends and from where I intend to take ship for India.'

'Gravely is a long way from Portsmouth,' she said, her tone telling him he was not welcome. 'I think you must have lost your way.'

Her sarcasm was not lost on Henry, but, having come with a purpose and not wishing to rouse her antagonism, he chose to ignore it. 'I came to pay my respects—and perhaps to talk a little, if you please.' Taking out his handkerchief, he dabbed the rain from his florid face peering out from beneath his elaborately curled wig, which was getting wetter by the second.

'I don't please, Henry, and I wonder at your audacity in coming to my home after what you have done,' Maria replied disdainfully, reluctant to ask him inside the house. 'You fought a duel with Sir Charles with no honour in it, thinking you were man enough to take him on.'

Henry smiled, not in the least ashamed of his cowardly conduct when he had fired before the call. 'A man must survive by whatever means he can.'

'By cheating?'

'I have proven myself to many gentlemen in my time, Maria—and ladies,' he added casually. 'I have no doubt as to my abilities. I can be most caring to one with your charm and grace.'

'Spare me your flattery, Henry. I congratulate myself on having made a lucky escape. I would prefer it if you left. We have nothing to say to each other.'

'And I was looking forward to a delightful *tête-à-tête,*' he countered sardonically.

'Then I must disappoint you.'

He laughed softly, breathing heavily. 'I see you cherish some prejudice against me, Maria. I can only suppose Osbourne must have put them into your head. I do believe he takes me for some kind of criminal.'

'What I think is neither here nor there. However, I may say that I have seen nothing in your behaviour to cause me to change my mind.'

'As you rightly say,' Henry agreed smoothly, 'that is neither here nor there.'

'I suppose that since you seem to have something to say to me, you may come inside out of the rain. But then you must go. I have no wish to prolong this interview.'

Henry followed her inside. Maria's nerves had suffered so much as she awaited Charles that the sight of Henry awakened no other feeling in her than one of profound irritation. However dangerous he might be, she had reached a degree of indifference where she was wholly beyond fear.

When they reached the drawing room she stood and assessed him closely. Too many years of dinner-table excesses had increased his girth to considerable dimensions. Being also a pompous, rather grandiose character, he was an impressive figure in his sky-blue knee breeches, fancy waistcoat and buckled shoes, high stiff collar and folds and flounces of his neck linen. He reminded Maria of a portly—if somewhat grotesque—colourful bird of paradise.

'I understand you are to return to India.'

'I am. My departure from the Company was somewhat—unfortunate, you understand—my finances embarrassed.' As he moved about the room his eyes took in his surroundings, appreciatively lingering over the Indian artefacts. 'You have some interesting things, I see. Your father was obviously a connoisseur.'

Maria faced him squarely. 'That will do, Henry! You did not come here for idle chit-chat. Say what you have to say and go. What do you want? Money?'

Henry smiled at her under drooping eyelids. 'Of course I want some money. Why not? I know you have plenty—too much for you to spend. For me, matters are a little different.' He gestured to the room about them. 'You've got all this. Such a grand place. 'Tis a pity you have so much and I so little, and I can't help thinking if it weren't for Charles Osbourne, the two of us would be together now.'

'My change of heart had nothing to do with Charles. Having met you again, I would not have married you— never in a thousand years.'

Henry's protruding eyes were cold and unemotional, his smile sardonic. Looking at him, Maria saw everything that Charles had said of him was true, and she felt the soul that animated this man was a chilling quagmire of selfishness, cruelty, deceit and wickedness. It was a soul its owner would sell to the devil without a qualm for a handful of gold. She no longer had any illusions about his character and it was not surprising that he should stoop to such depths as to try to extricate money out of her when they were no longer betrothed.

'You are despicable, Henry. To think that my father believed you to be worthy to be my husband.' Her expression was one of disgust. 'You sicken me and you won't get another penny out of me.'

He stiffened, watching her warily. 'Another penny?'

She nodded. 'Twenty thousand pounds, to be precise.' She was conscious of a certain satisfaction as she observed that Henry seemed disappointed. No doubt he had expected her to recoil. This cold indifference must be disconcerting for him. She smiled. 'Yes, Henry. Charles told me he gave you twenty thousand pounds to get rid of you, and now you have the audacity to come to me asking for more.'

He shrugged nonchalantly. 'What of it?'

'He should never have given you the money in the first place. Naturally I reimbursed him. I pay my own dues, but had it been up to me you would not have got a penny piece. The duel was not fought in the spirit of gentlemen. I know you fired before the call, intending to kill Charles. Where was your honour then, Henry?' she sneered. 'Thank God you missed and he didn't die. You, alas, are still alive.'

'True, but one cannot live without money, Maria, and money is important to me.'

'I have already gathered that. I think twenty thousand pounds is enough for you to live the life of a lord in India for a long time.'

'You think so? To finance a lifestyle to which I have become accustomed and lacking the pedigree and status of a nobleman, I have learned to recognise the value of impressive packaging.'

'Then earn it, Henry.'

'You owe me. Are you not forgetting something, Maria? If my memory serves me correctly, we were to be married. We had an arrangement—a contract was signed by both me and your father.'

Maria's eyes glittered with a coldness that should have chilled him to the bone. 'I released myself from it, if you remember.'

'I didn't. Another twenty thousand pounds would be

compensation enough for the time I've spent waiting to marry you. There have been many women I could have made my wife while I have been waiting for you to come of age.'

'I don't doubt that, and I am certain that if one had been as wealthy as me, Henry, you would have cast me off without a thought and married her.'

'You have vast sums at your disposal. It is true I wanted to marry you for the wealth that would be yours on your father's demise. Unfortunately, things went bad for me in India and I find it quite natural to turn to you for money. Give me what I want and I guarantee that in your turn you will be left undisturbed.'

Incensed by his gall, Maria did not flinch before the barely concealed menace. She permitted herself a small, contemptuous smile. 'For how long? Until it runs out?' Henry's eyes narrowed to thin slits and began to glitter dangerously. His face was flushed and she knew the greed of money was paramount to all else. 'The idea that you can try to gain a reward for all the years you have been betrothed to me is despicable. You are only concerned about what you can reap from this affair. I will have none of it.' She moved a little closer, looking him squarely in the eye. 'You won't get anything from me.'

Henry wondered at the spine of steel the wench had found. His own was pricked by little barbs of apprehension, for he was convinced she meant every word she said. Determined to batter down her bravado, his smile was unpleasant. 'You've a hard heart, Maria, but I know you will. You know, you make me almost sorry for my conduct in the past. You've turned out to be a comely wench. No man could help but desire you.' He let his eyes dwell appreciatively on her face and caress her long, graceful throat, the proud curves swelling beneath the low-cut bodice of her gown and the tiny waist. There was no softness in his gaze, only the calculating greed of a horse dealer looking over a filly he wished to purchase.

Maria's eyes blazed with outrage at the naked lust in his face, his eyes undressing her as he lumbered across the carpet to where she stood. He leaned close. She shrank back and spoke through clenched teeth. 'Don't touch me. Don't come near me—you are disgusting.'

As he looked at her, the rage that had been gathering since she had told him their betrothal was off boiled up in him like a volcano. The fumes of it rose to his brain so that he saw her through a red mist of rage as the sole architect of all his misfortunes.

'Disgusting, you say. I'll show you just how disgusting I can be.'

Maria backed away, suddenly fearful of what he might do. 'If you lay one finger on me, I'll scream. The servants will hear me.'

Henry leapt at her and, before she could utter a sound, caught her by the throat, shouting a torrent of accusations and obscenities, shaking her like a rag doll as his hands choked the breath from her in a strangling, frenzied grip.

Neither of them heard the door being flung open, or the shout of rage as booted feet pounded across the carpet towards them.

Charles managed to drag Maria free and hit Henry on the side of the face, felling him to the carpet with one blow—he toppled over like a stout tree and fell with a heavy thud, momentarily dazed.

Charles scooped Maria up into his arms and laid her on the sofa. Hearing the commotion, one of the servants came rushing in, paying no attention to the young woman hovering nervously on the edge of the room as her eyes were drawn to her young mistress. Charles ordered her to fetch cold compresses for Maria's bruised throat, all the while looking worriedly at the inert young woman, glad he'd risked the bridge despite his misgivings on seeing the torrent of water rushing underneath and being afraid they might all be plunged into the swollen water, and that he'd had the sense to come straight in when he'd seen and recognised Winston's coach in the drive.

Charles's face was white and the lines cut deep about his mouth as he looked down at Maria, the woman he loved more than life itself. When he had seen Winston with his hands around her throat, his mood was murderous; he would have killed him if he could, and even now, as he watched the grotesque figure struggle to his feet, shaking his head like a great bear, his wig awry and the makings of a bruise already marking his face, he could not trust himself within range of the man.

Breathing heavily, Maria was just rousing from her stupor. The thickly lashed eyelids fluttered open slowly, and for a moment she stared about her in confusion, then, as Charles leaned over her, her gaze turned to find him. 'Charles?' she murmured, her voice hoarse. His face swam before her eyes as though in a mist, one dark eyebrow raised, his light blue eyes smiling and the pain in her chest and throat eased. 'You…'

'Feeling better now?' he murmured with a tender smile.

'Charles—it was Henry,' she whispered brokenly.

Seeing a movement out of the corner of her eye, she looked towards it, panicking when she saw her attacker. 'He's still here…'

Charles stared down at her, his gaze probing hers and finding fear and distress within the translucent depths. 'I came in time. He can no longer harm you, Maria. Try to calm yourself.'

'No, I won't calm down,' she cried, the pain in her throat a horrible reminder that Henry had tried to strangle her. 'I won't rest until this—this beast has gone from my home.' She never took her slitted, catlike green eyes from Henry, who was now upright, his face crimson with anger. He was regarding Charles with active hatred and corroding resentment, looking ready to swing his fists at him in his frustrated rage.

His jaw set, his brow furrowed, Charles glared at him. 'How dare you contaminate this house with your presence, and how dare you attack Maria?' he snarled. 'You want horse whipping. Attempt to touch her again and, by God, I'll kill you. Now get out before I have the law on you or before I throw down a challenge to you. And be assured, Winston, that this time I shall not delope.'

Breathing heavily, Henry took a step towards him, his eyes bulging in their sockets. 'I'm going, damn your eyes, Osbourne. I'll leave you to enjoy each other— although considering the time you've spent together, I suspect you've done so many times.'

With a cry of rage, Charles hurtled across the space that separated them, knocking Henry to the floor, going with him and taking a small table as well. He was too refined in his habits to be a brawler, but his fists were loaded with his male hatred of the man who had hurt Maria.

'Charles!' Maria shrieked, seemingly unaware of the woman who cowered across the room as she dragged herself off the sofa in a desperate attempt to separate the two men, but they were like a couple of snarling dogs, teeth bared, eyes glaring, fighting over the same bitch, oblivious to everything but the need to kill.

'Charles!' she repeated, not knowing what to do. 'Please stop it.'

Servants burst into the room, and in a moment the two men were dragged apart. Henry had blood streaming across his face from a wound that was not yet discernible. Shrugging himself free of the man that held him, he backed to the door, glowering at Charles, ready to lash out again if required, but Charles, his madness dissipating, stepped back.

'Get out,' he said flatly, 'and don't you ever come here or attempt to approach Maria again.'

Without further ado and not wishing to stay and have the law brought down on him for attempted murder, Henry hurried out of the room and across the hall. Blindly he stumbled down the steps and across the drive to his waiting coach. A cold wind was blowing, mingled with rain, which struck him with full force. Cursing loudly and ordering the driver to drive on and to be quick about it, ignoring the warning shouts of one of the gardeners who was running towards the coach yelling something about the bridge, he hoisted himself inside. He was flung against the upholstery as the driver did exactly as he was bade, the wheels sending up gravel in their wake.

On reaching the bridge, where the stream was now a brown, turgid torrent swirling and thundering beneath its timbers, the driver pulled on the reins in an attempt to slow down the racing horses, but too late. The structure, already weakened by the force of the water, creaked and swayed precariously.

Inside the coach, a sense of fear seized Henry as the coach lurched and seemed to tip on to its side. Looking out of the window, he was suddenly slammed against the door with the point of his shoulder. It swung open and he was thrown out, and in a fractional second before his head struck against the boulder on the bank, he heard his collar bone snap as he went down into the murky darkness.

Inside the room everyone stood rooted to the floor. Instinctively, knowing their place, the servants left. Charles was still seething. He was striding about the room, smacking his right fist into the palm of his left hand. He could not bear the images that formed in his mind, violent and sickening, of Maria being attacked by that brute, but he could not seem to blot them out and it appalled him, as did his own reaction to it. He would be appalled by any attack on any woman by any man, but this, what Winston had almost succeeded in doing to Maria, filled him with a savagery that would not be appeased until he had ground the perpetrator down.

Maria looked at Charles and went to him and gripped his arm, her face stricken by what had happened.

'It's all right now, Charles. Henry won't come back.'

Only then did she become aware of the black-clad woman standing across the room like a frozen pillar of ice, her bowed head covered by a woollen shawl. She stared, recognition slow to register, and then she found her feet going slowly towards her, her arms outstretched.

'Constance? Oh, Constance! It is you.' Slowly the

woman's head came up and Maria saw that it was indeed her cousin. Uttering a cry of thankfulness and relief, she went and gathered her into her arms, holding her tight.

Constance didn't say a word until Maria held her at arm's length, and then she smiled. It was not one of the sneering, supercilious smiles Maria had become accustomed to when she had lived at the chateau, but a sad, almost despairing smile, her eyes full of the tortures she had suffered since the mob had stormed the Chateau Feroc. What she had been through had almost changed her beyond all recognition. She was much thinner than she had been, her face pale and gaunt, and she was desperately in need of a bath and a change of clothes.

Tearfully Maria turned to Charles. 'Thank you, Charles. You have indeed done Constance a great service. How can I ever repay you for what you have done?'

His eyes narrowed and he threw her a roguish grin, rubbing his sore knuckles. 'Be assured, Maria, that I'll think of something.'

'But—how did you get here?'

'I had my coachman travel to Dover.' His gaze settled on Constance. 'Look after your cousin, Maria. She's had a hard time of it. In fact, she was lucky to escape what happened at the Chateau Feroc with her life.'

'I will.' Taking Constance's hand, she led her to the sofa, where she drew her down beside her, taking her in her arms once more.

She didn't notice when an anguished servant appeared in the doorway and Charles left.

'I'm so glad you're here at last,' Maria said. 'Ever since I got your letter I've been so worried about you.'

'Sir Charles found me easily enough. I can't tell you

how relieved I was to know that you had received my letter—how relieved I was to leave France. The mob—those people—many of them known to us, were like crazed beasts. I saw some terrible things I will never forget. But…' Her eyes filled with tears and she said brokenly, 'Poor Mama. If—if only we had left the chateau with you she—she would still be here.' Her expression was bleak. 'I've lost everything, Maria. Everything I had went in the fire. Not only that, I am homeless.'

'No, you are not,' Maria uttered firmly. 'You still have me. My home is your home for as long as you want it to be. It's the least I can do. I shall never forget that your mother took me in when my father died.'

Constance's tears overflowed at her cousin's kindness. 'You're too good to me, Maria. I don't deserve it.'

Maria gripped Constance's hand. 'Stop it, Constance. There's no need for any of this.'

'Yes, there is. You can't gain someone's trust unless you are prepared to be perfectly honest.'

'You are my family, the only family I have. I'm glad you're going to stay with me because now I won't feel so alone.'

Constance took her hand and squeezed it affectionately. 'You are the only family I have, too, Maria, so I suppose we shall have to make the best of it. Charles told me a little of what has happened between you and Colonel Winston. Was—was that him I saw…?'

'With his hands round my throat? Yes. Henry—he was only marrying me for my money, Constance. Charles tried telling me what a terrible person Henry is. I didn't believe him—I didn't want to believe him, but on meeting Henry I soon saw Charles had been telling the truth. He came here to try to extract some money out of me. When I refused, he attacked me. Thank goodness Charles arrived when he did.'

'Yes, thank goodness, and I only hope Colonel Winston doesn't bother you again.' Constance smiled, beginning to look more like her old self. 'Now, are you going to feed me or must I starve to death?'

Already several horrified watchers had gathered at the shattered bridge. The horses and the driver with the broken coach had managed to reach secure ground on the other side, but there was no sign of Colonel Winston. The driver and terrified animals were led away to be taken care of. Charles joined others walking up and the bank, littered with debris, searching for any sign of the missing man, but to no avail. After two hours, soaked to the skin and with the light fading, they gave up, intending to resume their search at first light.

Maria was curled up in an overstuffed armchair before the fire when Charles entered. Having been informed about what had happened at the bridge and that Henry was missing, presumed drowned, she had no wish to go and see. Instead she ministered to her cousin, installing her in the guest room that had been prepared, where she was bathed and put to bed.

Now, looking at Charles, she saw with a pang of remorse how tired he looked. The lines around his mouth and at the corners of his eyes seemed deeper, his face leaner. His journey to France at her request had clearly taken its toll.

Charles went to stand in front of the fire, placing

more logs on it before spreading his hands before its warmth. 'I was told I would find you in here.'

'This was my father's study,' Maria told him. 'I like to come and sit in here where he spent so much of his time.' She sat up, absently rubbing her bruised neck. 'Is there any sign of Henry?'

He shook his head. 'It's too dark to go on searching. We'll begin again at first light—but it's not looking good.' He turned his head and looked at her. 'How are you, Maria? Does your neck pain you?'

'A little. It could have been worse.'

'Thank God I came when I did. How is Constance?'

'Sleeping. She was exhausted. She's been through a terrible ordeal I know, but she's strong and healthy and I am sure that given time she will recover. But what of you, Charles? How was your journey?'

'There were moments that were difficult, when I was unable to locate Jaques, but for a tidy sum I managed to secure passage across the Channel on a fishing boat.'

'I'm so glad you're back. I—I was worried about you.'

He turned his head and looked at her. 'I'm glad to hear your concern wasn't all for Constance.'

'I've instructed the housekeeper to have a room prepared for you, Charles. I hope you have no objections to that?'

'Why should I? A night in the comfort of your home is preferable to being relegated to the village inn.' Folding his hands behind his back, he stared thoughtfully into the flames. His deep voice seemed to fill the corners of the room as he said, 'Why didn't you tell me you were in the park when I fought the duel, Maria?'

Maria stared at his back, surprised by his question.

When he turned she instantly noticed the altering of his expression and watched nervously as he crossed his arms over his chest, watching her, his face inscrutable.

'Well, Maria?'

'H—how do you know I was?'

'Afterwards several things—your odd behaviour, for one—didn't make sense. When I got back to the house I recall seeing a horse being rubbed down. I didn't think much of it at the time—it didn't seem to be important— but then I got to wondering who could have left the house at such an early hour to go riding. For obvious reasons it could not have been my mother or me. That left just you. The groom who accompanied you confirmed my suspicions.'

'I see. Then what can I say?'

'So you were there that morning? You did witness the duel?'

'Yes,' she answered tightly.

'When are you going to tell me the reason why you turned down my offer of marriage, Maria?'

'I—I did so because of what I saw that day. I will not marry a man who keeps a mistress,' she replied, surprised now she had said it how calm she felt. 'Although I can see the attraction. She—the lady I saw—is very lovely.'

'I have to agree with you—she is very beautiful—exceptionally so.'

Maria felt a pain like a knife thrust to her heart. 'When I marry I will hold the vows I make as sacred, and I shall expect my husband to do the same. I would not take kindly to him committing adultery when he is not with me.'

'And you have it firmly fixed in your mind that I keep a mistress?'

Maria was not so ready to soften to him—not when the memory of that woman she had seen him embracing was still harsh in her mind. 'Yes—and with good reason. Does your mother know about her?'

'No,' he replied flatly. 'And neither do you.'

Maria got to her feet, ready to attack, her tone bitter. 'I know what I saw. I saw how she fell into your arms after the duel—and I saw the two of you together before that—at Westminster—saying your farewells so very tenderly—before you came to me with your proposal of marriage.'

'That's true.'

'You—admit it?'

He shrugged casually. 'Why should I deny it, when you say you saw everything with your own eyes? What you don't know is that the lady you saw—the lady you were so ready to assume was my mistress—is, in fact, my younger sister, Georgina—her husband Michael was acting as my second.'

'Your sister?' Maria stared at him. Never had she felt so foolish in her life.

'Yes, Maria, my sister.' Humour glinted in his eyes. Clearly he was enjoying her discomfiture. 'Georgina is headstrong and strong willed with a mind of her own. When she got wind of the duel nothing would keep her away. On the day you saw us together at Westminster, she had been to listen to her husband—who is a Member of Parliament for the constituency in which they live—speak in the House.'

'Oh.' Maria felt deflated, as if the wind had been knocked out of her.

'So now what do you have to say?'

Charles waited, not making an effort to touch her

or to make it easy for her. She remained silent, as sweet warmth washed through her. Unbearable relief stirred inside her, seeping over the terrible mortification. What a fool she had been, a silly, ignorant fool. She wanted to say all this, but the words stuck in her throat. She continued to stare at the face, the face she loved so much.

'Well,' he said, reading her mind, 'is there something you wish to say to me?'

After a moment, in the quietness of the room, with a raw ache in her voice, she said, 'I'm sorry. I have been unbelievably stupid. Please say that you forgive me. I could not bear it if you don't.' She turned her face away to hide her growing embarrassment and distress. She could feel her heart beating in slow but gigantic leaps. Her mouth was dry with some inner emotion. Struggling for words to adequately smooth a situation of her making, she suddenly felt inept, and turned back to him.

'If you can find it in your heart to forgive me, I—I will marry you, Charles. Happily.'

Charles laughed softly and, taking her hands, drew her to her feet. He leaned forwards to lift her chin so that he could look into her eyes. 'I can't believe that you actually thought I meant to make you my wife while I had a mistress. Dear God, Maria Monkton, don't you know me better than that? You are the most stubborn woman I have ever met and I am sure I shall have a good deal of trouble with you, but it seems, Maria, that I love you and I know you love me.'

Indignation sparked in her eyes. 'You know no such thing.'

He grinned delightedly. 'See what I mean? Stubborn

to the hilt. The truth is that I want you. I have always wanted you, and I know you want me.'

'I do?'

'Yes. You say it every time you are in my arms, which was why I couldn't understand why you rejected my proposal of marriage so adamantly.'

Still cupping her chin, he bent his head and took her soft mouth in a slow, compelling kiss, sensually moulding and shaping her lips to his. As soon as he felt her begin to respond, his arms went around her, crushing her to him, his mouth moving against hers with hungry urgency, his hands shifting possessively over her spine and hips. Dragging his mouth from hers, he drew an unsteady breath. Gazing down at her, he noted the telltale flush on her cheeks, the soft confusion in her searching green gaze.

'I want you very badly, Maria,' he said quietly with a tender smile at her upturned face. 'So what do you say? Are you sure you are prepared to marry me? Say yes, for even though I accept that the decision is yours, I have no intention of letting you get away from me again. And before you start pestering me on the subject of keeping Gravely, you can do as you wish with it or I would never hear the end of it.'

'You've obviously thought it all out, haven't you, Charles? I've a good mind to say no—' But his mouth claimed hers once more and, like the one before, his kiss was long and deep.

Maria leaned into him, fitting her body into the shape of him, luxuriating in the moment, but she also knew that despite their love they were both strong willed and there would be many times when they would not see eye to eye.

Releasing her lips, but continuing to hold her within the circle of his arms, Charles sighed and looked down at her upturned face, her eyes dark with love. 'I have been drawn to you ever since the day I saw you handing out bread to starving children and on every other occasion since,' he said in a low voice. 'I have been in love with you for some time now. Even before we reached England. I think I realised it on the boat. I tried to discount it and lay it down to lust and infatuation, but I had to finally face the truth—although when I did I found it difficult finding the right moment to tell you.'

'And Henry didn't help matters—always lurking in the shadows. Did I make it very difficult for you?' she enquired softly.

'You did put down my overtures rather firmly when I finally proposed.'

'You really did want to marry me?'

'Maria, I wanted you any way I could get you, and that's no lie.'

Tears filled her eyes, and a softening warmth mellowed her emotions. After all her arguments, implying that she did not care for him in a romantic sense, she could not believe that he really did care for her and that he still wanted to marry her after all she had put him through.

'I love you very much, Charles. You cannot imagine what torment I went through when I thought you had a mistress.'

'I think I can.'

'There is something I must say to you, something I had already decided before all this. I intend to sell Gravely.'

Charles frowned at the seriousness of what she was

saying. Dropping his arms, he took a step back. 'You can't mean that, Maria. You love this house.'

'I did. All those years when I was at the chateau I yearned to be back, always imagining it would be as it was when I left. But it isn't. It feels empty—full of ghosts. I feel like a stranger—an intruder.'

'So you have decided to sell it.'

She nodded. 'I thought of buying a house closer to London—or in London.'

'And Constance?'

'Will come with me. My aunt gave me a home when I needed one, it is the least I can do for Constance. She has nothing.'

'She has you, Maria,' he said softly. 'However, since you have agreed to be my wife, it rather changes things.'

Maria looked at him in alarm. 'I will not abandon Constance. After all she has suffered, she needs me. She has no one else.'

'I agree, which is why she will always have a home with us—either in London or at Highgate. I am sure my mother will like having her around.'

Maria's heart swelled with so much love for this man that she thought it would burst. She looked up at him and smiled, and Charles smiled back. Suddenly she felt in complete harmony with the world. 'Thank you, Charles. I don't deserve you—not after treating you so abominably.'

'Let's leave the past in the past. The only thing that's important is what's between us, you and me.'

His eyes blazed suddenly with their own vivid light. Maria breathed deeply as feelings rushed to her in a flood. She loved him so much. He was her destiny, her future and she had to make that clear to him now. Reaching for him, she pulled him to her, locking her arms about him fiercely.

'I love you so much. Believe it, for it is true. It's good to have you back with me, safe, to feel you and hold you. I missed you when I left you in London—which was the most senseless thing I have ever done—and again when you went to France. You see, Charles, after the closeness we shared in France, I've got so used to having you near me. You have given a meaning to my life—to everything I do. Always, inside of me, I have had a kind of loneliness, but with you there has always been something private—a special kind of sharing. Not only do I love you, but you have become—in a manner of speaking, a special friend, a best friend.'

Moved by her words, Charles looked at her with admiration and respect, and when he spoke his voice was husky. 'Then I am indeed honoured, Maria.'

'I have never shared so much with anyone as I have with you. I was afraid to try.' A lump constricted her throat so that she could not speak. Taking his face between her hands, loving the feel of his skin, lovingly she traced the lines around his mouth with her finger. Then she pressed herself close to him, as close as she could with a fierce new protectiveness, her eyes large and tear-bright.

Charles seemed poignantly touched by the warm spontaneity of her actions, for he said, in the gentlest of voices, 'I am indeed blessed.' He kissed her then, with all the old possessiveness she knew so well. She slid her arms around his neck, and sifted her fingers through his thick hair. How she had longed to do that again.

Drawing away from him and taking his hand, she led him to the door, an adorable twinkle in her eyes.

'We'll forget that room, shall we? You can share mine.'

Henry's body was recovered the next day further down stream, lodged against a tree trunk on the bank. Maria was sorry that his end had come about in such a tragic way, but apart from that she felt nothing. She knew he had no one, no family, and because of their past association, she felt she owed it to him to see he had a decent burial in the village churchyard, close to Gravely, where he had aspired to live.

Maria and Charles were married at Highgate six weeks later. Neither of them wanted to wait any longer. It was a quiet affair, with none of the pageantry that would have accompanied the wedding had it been in London. Constance, Maria's matron of honour, had recovered from her terrible ordeal in France, although she still mourned her mother and had nightmares over the brutal manner of her death. She was to return to London with Lady Osbourne after the wedding, and Maria was confident she would delight in the society events Lady Osbourne had planned for her.

Lady Osbourne was well pleased with Charles's choice of bride. Right from the start she had thought that Maria was just the sort of beautiful and brave young woman she would have picked for her son, and she let every one of her friends know it.

Nervous and happy, resplendent in her wedding finery of ivory silk, Maria stood beside Charles as the festivities were about to begin. They devoted themselves to smiling at the wedding guests who passed by to wish them happiness—exchanging meaningful glances when Georgina kissed them both—before Charles took her in his arms and they led the dancing in the ballroom.

'Do you mind not getting married in London, Maria?'

'You know I don't,' she returned as he whirled her round. 'I love Highgate. It's perfect for a wedding. And I love you, Charles, more than anything. I have never met anyone like you, ever.'

His eyes fastened on her lips. 'Do you know what I'm thinking?'

She smiled up at him, her eyes telling him she did. 'I think I do. What can we do about it?'

Immediately he danced her on to the terrace and caught her to him, and Maria soared with a sense of overwhelming elation as his arms went round her with a strength that wrapped her with a satisfying reassurance. As he kissed her all she was aware of was heat, the pressure of hard muscles in a strong body, a complete blending of passion and tenderness, then he smiled and put her from him.

'There's time for this later, my love. All the time in the world.' And, taking her hand, he led her back to their guests.

* * * * *

Beauty in Breeches

Helen Dickson

Chapter One

Beatrice halted her horse beneath the spreading canopy of a great beech tree. The scene was like a little tableau to be viewed by any who passed by. The summertime smells of Larkhill wafted around her. She knew every tree, every meadow and bridal way and rutted track, and every stream where trout could be found. Everything around her was pulsating with life, except the beautiful old house where the squire, her father, had once ruled. The house sat like a queen in the centre of her domain. It faced due south so the sun, before it sank over the gently rolling hills in the west, shone on the mellow stone walls all day, making them warm to the touch.

From her vantage point she watched a happy group of fashionable society people stroll along the paths in the long-neglected gardens. The beautiful ladies wore high-waisted dresses, their fair complexions protected from the sun by delicate parasols, the gentlemen attired in the pinnacle of fashion. Her eyes were drawn to one of the gentlemen like metal filings to a magnet. He stood out from the others by his admirable bearing and heightened stature. She had never seen him before, but by instinct she knew who he was.

Lord Julius Chadwick—the Marquess of Maitland.

Her heart tightened with a long-held hatred and resentment. He was walking at a leisurely pace with his hands clasped behind his back. Making no attempt to hide herself from view, she continued to watch him as he strolled closer to the house. The sun's rays caught his hair. It was thick and dark and curled into his nape.

As if he could feel her eyes on him he paused and waited a moment before he turned and looked directly at her. Surprised to see her there, he broke away from the party. His handsome face was set in lines which were quite unreadable, but his amber eyes danced as though he found their meeting and the manner of her dress vastly entertaining. Below a white silk shirt, skin-tight breeches clung to her long, shapely legs above black riding boots. Being buff in colour, from a distance the breeches gave the impression that she was naked from the waist down. She had tied back her abundant gold-and-copper curls with a bright emerald-green ribbon.

Beatrice sat on her horse unmoving, as if she were some stone goddess, insensate but powerful. She gripped the reins in her slender fingers and stared back at him, defiance in every line of her young body. She was seeing this man in the flesh for the first time in her life, but she had thought of him often over the years. He had appeared in her mind like some sinister spectre, a malevolent giant, with the power to do as he liked—as he had when he'd blotted all happiness from her future.

Her head lifted and there was no softness in her eyes, which had turned to flint. Her mouth hardened to an unsmiling resentment. She had no doubt that he was curious and wondering who she was and what she was doing trespassing on his land so close to the house. He made no attempt to approach her or speak to her. Neither of them moving, over the twenty yards or so that separated them they continued to watch each other until, with a casual toss of her lovely head, Beatrice turned her horse and disappeared as silently as she had come amongst the tall, shadowy trees.

At Standish House, just two miles from Larkhill, Lady Moira Standish was taking tea in the drawing room. She was a striking woman, tall and robust with iron-grey hair, good cheekbones and a square jaw. Her husband had killed himself when he had taken a tumble from his horse during a hunt three years ago, leaving her a very wealthy widow. With a twenty-five-year-old son and a nineteen-year-old daughter, she had much on her plate if she was to see them affianced before the year was out. Her son, George, had inherited Standish House on his father's demise. The dowager Lady Standish continued to act as mistress. When George took a wife she would move into the dower house.

She had returned from London that very day, where

she had been on a short visit with her daughter, Astrid. She sat stiffly upright on the green-and-gold brocaded couch. With a firm hand she fluttered a delicate ivory-and-lace fan before her heated face. Her grey eyes were narrowed with annoyance as she darted sharp disapproving glances at her niece, who had just burst into the room, shattering the peace. Beatrice presented a frightful vision in her breeches, stained from her ride. Shoving her untidy mop of hair back from her face, the girl sank into a chair in a most unladylike pose and yawned, doing little to hide her boredom.

As she looked at her, Lady Standish wondered if this niece of hers would ever grow up. She was clever, intelligent, quick-thinking and sharp witted. She was also problematical and a constant headache. Beatrice was little more than an impoverished orphan, but she still walked about with her head high, just like her arrogant, reckless father before her. She was more beautiful than Astrid would ever be, but she lived for the moment and noticed nothing that was not to do with outdoor pursuits and horses.

'Really, Beatrice,' Lady Standish exclaimed sharply, wrinkling her nose as the smell of horses wafted in her direction. 'I have told you time and again not to appear before me dressed in those outrageous breeches. They smell of the stables and that is where I wish they would remain. It's high time you stopped gallivanting about the district and occupied yourself with something useful. I swear one would think the expensive governesses we provided for you would have taught you about behaviour and comportment. Do you forget that you are quality born with bloodlines, breeding and ancestry? And don't slouch. It's bad for the posture.'

Beatrice sat up straight and obediently squared her shoulders and raised her chin, though she continued to fidget in her chair. Her aunt rarely spoke to her, except to lecture, criticise, instruct or command. 'It is certainly desirable to be well bred,' she remarked calmly, 'but the glory belongs to my father and his father, not to me.'

Lady Standish rolled her eyes upwards and worked her fan harder, the corkscrew curls on either side of her face almost springing to life. 'That is rubbish, Beatrice, and just another one of your absurdities. Glory? See what good his *glory* has done you—having to live off your only kin. Your father was a fool, throwing his money away without a care to anyone but himself.'

Beatrice looked at her wearily. She had heard the argument so often she knew it by heart—it failed to shake her kinder memories of her father. 'I loved him dearly,' she said simply. 'He was a good father.'

'That's a matter of opinion. The devil did his work when he made you just like him, you ungrateful girl.'

Beatrice flinched, but her aunt ranted on, turning her narrowed eyes upon her and shaking a bejewelled, damning finger. 'He left you in a fix—no dowry and now you're eighteen years old with not a penny to your name. There isn't a man that will marry you without one. The Lord knows what a task you are for me.' Lady Standish sighed heavily, as if tired of her burden. 'It's better that you were married and off my hands—and I know I shall have to provide your dowry to bring that about, but I pity the man who would wed you. I swear you will be the death of me—I know you will. And do wear a bonnet when you are out. Your face is much too brown and freckles are most unbecoming on a young lady.'

'Yes, Aunt Moira.'

Beatrice knew she was a disappointment to her aunt, that she had never considered her anything but an irksome responsibility. Lady Standish tried to instil discipline in her and to make her into an obedient, biddable young woman like Astrid—Astrid had exquisite manners, was skilled in everything a young woman of quality should be, would sit still and work her sampler, would stay clean and tidy—and she failed miserably.

Beatrice tried not to fidget for fear that if she moved it would draw her aunt's attention again, but she was weary of tiptoeing about the house and doubted her ability to last much longer. Life was hard for her at Standish House, but she wearily accepted the way her aunt treated her without complaint. She had been out since dawn, for the countryside was the only place she could seek succour from her aunt's angry, cruel taunts.

Beatrice glanced at her cousin Astrid, whose face was alight with intense excitement over her forthcoming birthday party in two weeks. It was to be an afternoon of enjoyment at Standish House, which was more appealing to Astrid than a grand ball. Bright sunlight on the windows streamed through her light brown ringlets shot through with chestnut glints. She was pouting prettily and sitting poised and straight backed, her hands folded in her lap. She was small and slender, with china-blue eyes and rosy dimpled cheeks. She bore only the faintest resemblance to her cousin Beatrice and was cast in a sweeter, gentler mould than Beatrice's nature could ever imitate with success. The apple of her mother's eye, Astrid was in the ascendant.

'I have returned to organise Astrid's birthday party,' Lady Standish said. 'It is to be a large affair, with only the finest society people invited. You should have seen her in London, Beatrice. I think Lord Chadwick was most struck.'

Beatrice was all attention. 'Lord Chadwick? The Marquess of Maitland?' she said mechanically. She realised her aunt was watching her intently and that her face was unguarded before her.

'Of course. There could scarcely be a better match.' Lady Standish paused to take a sip of tea. 'There is no need to look so incredulous. It is quite natural. Did you not think Astrid was to marry some time?'

Beatrice gaped at her. If she had not been so taken aback by her aunt's pronouncement that made her want to shriek, she would have laughed aloud. She had given little thought to the matter of Astrid's future. She never thought beyond her own life, what *she* wanted—of returning to Larkhill, which was so very dear to her.

'Lord Chadwick—he has been abroad for several months on one of his ships and only recently returned—showed great interest in Astrid. Indeed, the attention he showed her was commented upon by several; I am hoping he will approach me to offer for her. He is of excellent family, of sound character, sharp wits, intelligence and his fortune is quite remarkable.

Through his own endeavours there is a fleet of ships flying his flag and carrying his cargo. He has mines of gold and silver that bought those ships, and his ownership of land is so vast no one knows how much. Astrid will indeed be a fortunate young woman if she manages to secure him.'

'He sounds an impressive figure, Aunt Moira, but a grand title, wealth and happiness don't always come hand in glove,' Beatrice retorted tersely.

Lady Standish gave her a sour, disapproving look. 'Any woman would be a fool to turn away from it. Astrid is certainly willing to entertain Lord Chadwick. The wedding will be a truly grand affair, with one of those new-fangled wedding tours to France and Italy, before they settle down to married life at Highfield Manor in Kent. It is an estate of some significance.'

While her aunt twittered on, Beatrice kept her face lowered, feigning interest in a magazine so Lady Standish could not see her, would not see that her face was white. She blindly turned a page so that her aunt would not be able to tell she could not control a grimace of anger and the tears stinging hot. She felt murderous. She wanted to leap to her feet and remind her aunt of the harm Lord Chadwick had done her family, harm she seemed to have forgotten, or considered unimportant when it came to choosing a husband for her darling Astrid. But Beatrice had not forgotten.

Beatrice wanted Lord Chadwick to suffer all the torments of the damned and crawl to her for forgiveness for being the architect of all her misery. She simply could not bear the thought of Astrid being the Marchioness of Maitland, Lady Chadwick, living her life in grand style, while Aunt Moira would have Beatrice married off to the first suitor who chanced her way.

'Of course, should Astrid marry Lord Chadwick it will be a perfect match. If he offers for her now, they can be betrothed before the little Season starts in the autumn.'

Astrid had come out the year before and had been the toast of the Season. She had received several offers of marriage, but Lady Standish had considered the young men who made them too low down the social ladder and not rich enough for her daughter and had declined their offers, hoping for better things, a brilliant match, and to that end she had in mind Lord Chadwick.

'If he does indeed offer for Astrid, it will be a spring wedding.'

Beatrice was unable to keep quiet a moment longer. Blinking back angry tears, she looked at her aunt. 'But, Aunt Moira, how can you let such a thing happen? He alone is responsible for all the misfortunes that have befallen me. I shall neither forget nor forgive what he did to Father. Would you not feel as I do?'

'That is in the past and you would do well to put it behind you since nothing can be done about it now.' She gave her niece a watery smile. 'If you think of your scriptures, Beatrice, you will remember being taught that Jesus told us to love our enemies?'

'Jesus hadn't met Lord Chadwick,' Beatrice retorted bitterly. She glanced at Astrid's crestfallen face and dared to ask, 'And is this what Astrid wants—marriage to a total stranger?'

'He will not be a stranger to her by the time they are married. The marriage of my only daughter is of great importance.' Her aunt's face was stern, her eyes as hard as steel. 'This is family business, not sentiment.'

'But—Lord Chadwick has not offered for me and he might not,' Astrid said quietly, hesitantly—the old habit of obedience and deference to her mother had a strong hold on her. 'He has shown kindness towards me and nothing more. I—think you read too much into it, Mama.'

'Nonsense.' Lady Standish waved the objection aside. 'It's early days, I agree, but he did pay you a good deal of attention. It shows real promise. He saw what a gem you are. The party must be a success. It is a perfect opportunity to demonstrate to Lord Chadwick that you are, at county level, well qualified to be his bride. We must ensure that you spend as much time in each other's company as possible at the party.'

'But—Mama, he may not want to.'

Her mother shot her a dark look. 'Don't argue, Astrid. I do know what I am talking about. Marriage is not something you can settle for yourself. You are young, you can't decide these things. You have to be guided. In the end it will be down to me. I will decide where you wed.'

'But Lord Chadwick is hardly a suitable candidate,' Beatrice dared to voice. In this instant she refused to sit with her head bowed as Astrid always did. She sat with her head high, one dark eyebrow slightly raised, and she met her aunt's level gaze as if she were her equal. 'Do you forget what that man did to my father—and that my mother was so ill and distressed by the whole sorry affair that she died of a broken heart? The man should have been horse-whipped for taking advantage of a man in a weakened state.'

Lady Standish looked at her coldly. 'How dare you speak to me in that tone, Beatrice. Know your place. But since you are so eager to have your say, I will tell you that I do not forget and I do not like it that you feel you must remind me. But I do not hold it against Lord Chadwick. Your father—my own dear husband's brother-in-law—was lamentably weak. His weakened state, as you put it, was brought about by an over-indulgence in alcoholic spirits. It was his fault that he lost Larkhill and shot himself. It cannot be blamed on anyone else.'

Her aunt's cruel words cut Beatrice to the heart. 'I blame Lord Chadwick absolutely,' she persisted firmly. 'I always will. Anyway, what is he like, this noble lord? Does he have any afflictions?'

'Not unless one considers shocking arrogance an affliction,' Lady Standish answered sharply. 'Of course he has every right to be so, with friends constantly following in his wake. Why, if it were up to females to do the asking, Lord Chadwick would have had more offers of marriage than all the ladies in London combined.'

'I can't see why,' Beatrice remarked in a low, cold voice. 'He is absolutely loathsome to me.'

'Oh, no, Beatrice,' Astrid said breathlessly, rising quickly to his defence. 'You do not know him. He is handsome and charming; I know you will think so too when you meet him.'

Only the prospect of another dressing down from her aunt prevented Beatrice from saying that she had already encountered the odious Lord Chadwick at Larkhill and was not hankering after an introduction.

From the open window of her bedroom, with her shoulder propped against the frame and her arms folded across her chest, Beatrice gazed dispassionately as the titled, wealthy and influential guests gathered on the extensive lawns of Standish House to celebrate Astrid's nineteenth birthday, which was to go on into the night. The terraces all around were ablaze with blossoms, magnolias and sweet-scented azaleas.

Guests continued to roll up the drive in chaises and carriages, many open so the occupants could bask in the sun's warmth. A full staff of footmen were on hand to assist them from their carriages and a full army of servants ready to dance attendance on them as they wined and dined. Trestle tables decorated with summer flowers had been set up in the shade of the terrace where only the finest food was served and bowls of punch and chilled lemonade. Tables and chairs were scattered about the lawns, and, for anyone overcome by the heat, ice-cold drinks had been laid out in the drawing room.

Standish House was no more than two hours' drive from London. It was a fascinating, gorgeous paradise populated by beautiful, carefree people in all their sumptuous finery. Several of the gentlemen sported military uniforms, a reminder to everyone of the battle they had fought at Waterloo a year ago. To Beatrice, the scene held little interest and no beauty, but there was something morbidly compelling about observing from a distance how people interacted with each other. At eighteen years old, restrained and guarded, she did not believe in the inherent goodness in anyone.

George and Lady Standish received the guests— Lady Standish, in her element, looking as if she would burst with her own importance. She presented an imposing figure in a high-necked gown of lavender-grey shot silk, with a matching turban trimmed with large purple plumes. A picture of sweet perfection, Astrid, looking like an angel in her high-waisted cream gown and perfectly coiffed hair, a bunch of fat ringlets trailing over one shoulder, was surrounded by fawning fops. Against a fabulous colourful backdrop of banks of rhododendrons, azaleas and a small lake, she was seated beneath a white gazebo. Her face was pink and rosy and glowing with happiness, the very picture of a demure young lady on her birthday as she raised her head and laughed delightedly at something that was said.

Voices and laughter and the clink of champagne glasses drifted up to Beatrice. One newly arrived guest caught her attention as soon as he alighted from a splendid midnight-blue open carriage, the Chadwick coat of arms emblazoned on the door. He was accompanied by two gentlemen and two ladies.

Julius Chadwick was as handsome as any man present, wickedly so, with his superb build and panther-like black hair. As he strolled the lawns with a smooth, elegant stride, every movement polished and assured, he was a natural target for the sighing host of young girls making sheep's eyes at him.

Through narrowed eyes Beatrice watched him. Conversations among the guests had broken off; even the servants passing among them with trays of food and drink almost bumped into each other as they paused to look at him. He was tall, rugged and muscular, with dark good looks and an aquiline nose; despite the way he casually moved among the guests, looking completely relaxed, he seemed to radiate barely leashed, ruthless power.

In contrast to the pale complexions and bored languor of the other gentlemen present, his skin was deeply tanned by a tropical sun. He exuded charm, yet there was an aura about him of a man who had seen and done all sorts of things—terrible things, dangerous things, forbidden things—and enjoyed it, and Beatrice could not deny that if she had not already determined that he was her enemy, she would have liked to get to know him.

He was elegantly attired in a beautifully tailored dark-green jacket that clung to his wide shoulders. His pristine white cravat was folded precisely and secured by a winking gold pin, and dove-grey tight breeches outlined his long, muscular legs above highly polished Hessians—the perfect outfit for a wealthy gentleman meeting his neighbours for the first time.

Beatrice was distracted when Lizzie, one of the

chambermaids, came in bearing an armload of freshly laundered linen.

'Great heavens! Miss Beatrice! Why aren't you at Miss Astrid's party? Why, it's a grand affair and it's high time you went out and enjoyed yourself.'

Beatrice shrugged and turned to survey the scene once more with little interest, her arms folded across her chest. 'You know I'm not one for parties, Lizzie. Besides, I doubt my presence will be missed. And why Astrid insisted on Aunt Moira inviting half of London society to Standish House I cannot imagine. It's such an extravagance.'

'Is it, now?' Lizzie said, in total disagreement. 'Your cousin is a young lady of considerable beauty and consequence. Her mama will be hoping she will attract the attention of one of the wealthy young men she has invited.' Placing her burden on the bed, Lizzie raised her brows and stared disapprovingly at Beatrice's breeches. 'Perhaps if you took more care in your appearance, you, too, would attract the same kind of attention. You are a very beautiful young woman, Miss Beatrice, and you should socialise more.'

Beatrice accepted Lizzie's well-intentioned rebuke with cheerful philosophical indifference. 'I'm not so vain that I allow my looks to concern me. It would take more than silks and satins and powder and paint to make me into a proper lady, Lizzie.'

All Beatrice's hopes of becoming a lady had been dashed when she had been thirteen years old. She was an only child, the daughter of Sir James Fanshaw. She'd been raised at Larkhill. Apart from visits to Standish

House when she was allowed to play with Astrid, her parents had kept her isolated in protective gentility, hidden behind the high stone walls of Larkhill like an enchanted child, waiting for the magic of a prince charming to set her free.

And then one day her prince did come, but not in any magical way like the one she had read about in her story books, on a white steed and as handsome as a Greek god, but in the dark forbidding form of a thief of the highest order. Her papa had lost Larkhill to that man in a game of cards; afterwards, unable to live with the shame of what he had done, he'd shot himself.

The humiliation, shame and heartbreak of it all and being forced to live in shabby, penny-pinching gentility on the charity of her mother's brother, Lord Standish, was too much for her mama. Unable to come to terms with her husband's suicide, ill and distressed she had taken to her bed and retreated into herself and did not speak to anyone. Just six months after coming to live at Standish House, she had followed her husband to the grave. Even now Beatrice felt the wrenching loss of her parents.

Aunt Moira was a woman of strong personality who had despised Beatrice's father's weakness and despised even more her mother's inability to come to terms with her loss. Unable to turn Beatrice out since her husband would not allow it—and if she did it would reflect badly on her—she had grudgingly endured her impoverished niece living at Standish House with the intention of finding her a husband and getting her off her hands as soon as possible. But her strong-willed niece had other ideas and they did not involve a husband.

Beatrice had a mop of unruly chestnut-and-copper curls, a small, stubborn chin, pert nose, and a pair of sooty-lashed, slanting sea-green eyes that completely dominated her face. Her face was lightly tanned from being outdoors riding Major, her precious horse given to her by her uncle before his tragic accident, or fishing and shooting with her feckless and charming, though eternally loyal, rogue of a cousin called George. Even though she lived in a house full of people, Beatrice was her own person and as isolated as she had been as a child at Larkhill.

'Do you know that man, Lizzie—the one with black hair and wearing a dark-green coat—the arrogant one? Who are those with him?'

Lizzie, a young woman who always knew everything, came and peered over her shoulder, her eyes settling on the object of Miss Beatrice's interest. The gentleman in question was conversing with others close to the house. 'Why, that's the Marquess of Maitland, Lord Julius Chadwick—and as handsome as a man can be, don't you think?' she uttered on a sigh, as struck as all the other females drooling over him. 'According to Miss Astrid, he's been off on one of his sailing ships to some far-off foreign place I've never heard of. Came back last month—much to the delight of the ladies of the *ton*. He's staying at Larkhill and has brought a small party with him. That's Lord Roderick Caruthers he's talking to, and his wife, Miranda. Sir James Sedbury and his sister Josephine are also in his party. I heard Lord Chadwick is extremely rich.'

'Apparently so,' Beatrice said with derision. 'Most of his wealth has come from what he can attain from others. He's a gambler—and good at it. I know that for a fact.'

Hatred and an odd sense of excitement stirred in her heart as her interest in Lord Chadwick deepened. Of course she'd already known he was at Larkhill with guests, but she could not seem to check her desire to find out as much as possible about him. As if he could sense her eyes on him, he paused his conversation with Lord Caruthers and looked up and Beatrice was caught in the act of staring at him. His light amber eyes captured hers and Beatrice raised her chin, looking at him coldly, trying to stare him out of countenance. A strange, unfathomable smile curved his lips before he looked away and carried on his conversation. She might as well have been invisible for all the notice he took.

'It would be a feather in your aunt's cap if Miss Astrid managed to capture that particular gentleman. She's counting on it and has made no secret of it either,' Lizzie prattled on as she busied herself storing away the linen. 'What a match that would be—to have her only daughter a marchioness and married to a man of such wealth.'

'I'm sure you're right, Lizzie,' Beatrice murmured drily. What Lizzie said was true, but Beatrice knew they were ill matched and that marriage to a man of such strong character would terrify her gentle cousin when the time came for her to walk down the aisle.

'Now he's back and being a man still in his prime, I imagine he will be looking for a wife.' Having finished packing away the linen, Lizzie came and peered over her shoulder. 'Look at Miss Astrid. How beautiful she is—and enjoying herself. Whereas you, Miss Beatrice—volatile and moody, that's what your aunt says you are. Now why don't you put on something nice and get along down there and join in the celebrations?'

Deep in thought, Beatrice continued to lean against the window frame as she watched the man she truly believed to be the architect of all her misery. A man in his prime, Lizzie had said, and probably looking for a wife. But who said that wife had to be Astrid? Beatrice had dreamed of Larkhill, of one day returning to live there. She did not dream now. She started to think. In the back of her mind a plan was forming to give her back her home and to forge out some stability for her future.

Suddenly she was presented with an idea that brought her up straight—an idea that was as preposterous as it was splendid and she congratulated herself on having thought of it. Her mind was racing like a ferret in a cage to find the spring on the trap that would catch Lord Chadwick. She let the silence ride and watched him with renewed interest, her green eyes as inscrutable as a snake's. So, they thought she was moody and volatile. Well, let them. After today they would know just how moody and volatile she could be.

As the afternoon wore on, the more liquor the guests consumed and the more boisterous they became.

Beatrice observed Lord Chadwick's popularity as people rushed to speak to him. He talked and joked, speaking to those around him with lazy good humour. He threw back his head and laughed loud at something her aunt said to him, his even white teeth gleaming between his lips, causing everyone within close proximity to turn their heads in his direction, such was the effect this handsome, most popular bachelor of London society had on others.

She particularly watched him when he conversed with Astrid, noting that he never betrayed any emotion other than polite interest, and there were moments when he observed the festivities that his expression slipped and he looked bored, as if he would prefer to be elsewhere.

Beatrice folded her arms across her chest. Already she had decided to use this handsome lord in her desire to return to Larkhill. She could not help her aunt's dreams. She had her own dreams. Someone had to be disappointed. However, she did consider what Astrid's feeling might be on the matter and she would speak to her first, but an opportunity had presented itself that she did not intend letting slip away. This was the time and the place. The way to capture Lord Chadwick was to surprise him before his conscience was awake, not to let him prepare and consider and reject her in advance.

With Henry Talbot, the son of a close neighbour by her side, Astrid wandered away from Lord Chadwick and Beatrice saw her aunt's bright, demanding stare, prompting her daughter to make herself available to Lord Chadwick once more. Beatrice saw Astrid's shoulders slump and watched her walk back to him. Her cream parasol trembled over her fair head as he stepped forwards to meet her. He bowed low and took her gloved hand, but Beatrice knew, with keen insight, that it was not the heat of passion Lord Chadwick felt for Astrid. And what was her silly cousin blushing for? Why was she trembling?

'What's happening now?' she asked Lizzie when the maid returned to the room. 'It looks as if some kind of debate is taking place at the far end of the garden.'

'And so it is. One of the footmen told me in the kitchen that the main topic of conversation just now is the racing at Goodwood and about Lord Chadwick's acquisition of a horse he purchased recently at Newmarket. Apparently he's challenged anyone to a race who thinks they have a mount that can beat his. As yet no one's been brave enough to take him up on his challenge, but it still stands.'

A slow smile curved Beatrice's mouth and her eyes lit. 'Well now, that is most interesting.' At last she'd heard something that caused her to turn from the window. Despite the impropriety of what she was about to do and her aunt's wrath when she found out, she would seize this God-given opportunity before it slipped away. 'You're right, Lizzie,' she said, with more enthusiasm than she'd shown all day. 'Perhaps I should go down. Help me dress, will you? My green, I think. I must look my best for Astrid's party.'

Assured of her beauty, the green of her gown making her hair glow more golden and her eyes to shine brighter, she was endowed with a boldness second to none. The beautiful setting, the laughter and the warmth of the day spurred Beatrice on through a sea of nameless faces to carry out her scheme to its limit. She was quite mad, of course, but that neither concerned nor deterred her from her purpose. She was not about to act like a rider who falls from their horse before the race was done.

With a false smile pinned to her face, she followed the pretty path that wound its way through the attractive garden drenched in warm sunshine, her eyes on the large group of people at the other end. Some of the fashionable, overdressed gentlemen were sprawled out on the lawn, drinking champagne and talking and laughing much too loudly as the liquor loosened their inhibitions. Beatrice was confidently aware of the gleam of her silk dress hinting at the contours of her long shapely legs as she walked. Long gloves encased her arms and her shining hair was caught up at the crown in a mass of thick, glossy curls.

She was surrounded by other ladies, beautiful ladies, but when Beatrice put her mind to it only she had that perfect self-conscious way of walking. She moved as if every man present was watching her. She walked as if she were irresistible, such was the power of her conviction that she would achieve her goal in what she had set out to do. Even the diamonds adorning the throats of the ladies winked at her like bright-eyed conspirators as they caught the sun. A certainty stronger than anything else assured her that her hour of triumph was near.

She was aware of the stir she created as she

continued to advance, with a strange sensation of fatality and enjoying a kind of immunity. A lightning bolt of anticipation seemed to shoot through the crowd, breaking off conversation and choking off laughter as some two hundred guests turned in near unison to see where she was heading.

In the surrounding haze Beatrice no longer saw anyone but him. Her attention was focused entirely on him. She looked at him fixedly. Had she wanted to look away, she could not have done. She was not even conscious that people were watching her, feeling they were about to witness something surprising.

Never had Beatrice seen such a figure of masculine elegance. Lord Julius Chadwick looked so poised, so debonair. His movements, his habitual air of languid indolence, hung about him like a cloak. With his dark hair tousled by the breeze, he looked every inch the well-heeled businessman and landowner—and a great deal more dangerous than the average country gentleman.

The perfect fit of his coat and the tapering trousers accentuated the long lines of his body. It was impossible not to respond to this man as his masculine magnetism dominated the scene. A slow half-smile curved his lips and she saw him give a careless shrug. He raised his fine, dark eyebrows at some remark. She completely ignored the young women in the knot eyeing him with encouraging, flirtatious glances over their fans, tittering and giggling. Where other women might have succumbed to the irresistible pull to see behind the cool façade and start uncovering the man beneath, Beatrice could feel the palpable danger around him. She was never a rational person, but this time she knew she should have the good sense to heed the warning and turn and walk away. But her mind was made up. Too much was at stake.

Lord Chadwick cast a pair of laughing eyes over those around him; his gaze came to rest on a pair of jade-green eyes in which gold-and-brown flecks blazed, a sure sign that their owner was under some urgent compulsion, staring at him with a fixed intensity. He stood watching her in silent fascination, then he smiled slowly. Julius was easily moved by the beauty of a woman and the calm boldness with which this one was looking at him intrigued him.

He saw a sculpted face of unforgettable beauty, with high, delicately moulded cheekbones, a perfect nose and generous lips. It was a strong face, but essentially feminine. Her hair was burnished gold by the sun. Bright curls clustered in artful disarray on the top of her head, a few gilded wisps wreathed about her delicate ears and nape, drawing attention to her slender neck. There was something unusual in her attitude. A strange sense of shock quivered through him when he recognised her as the woman he had seen at Larkhill some days past, and again today when instinct had drawn his gaze to an upstairs window of the house. Who was she and why did she watch him so intently?

Beatrice faced him with outward calm. She looked at him for a long, thoughtful moment, as though estimating her chances. The corner of her mouth rose insensibly as her eyes narrowed. Now that the moment of confrontation had arrived she was strangely relieved.

'I hear you have offered a wager to anyone who believes their horse can beat yours. I will accept your challenge,' she announced clearly. A loud gasp ran through the guests as they gathered about, parting for her to pass through. At the sight of Beatrice Fanshaw the frosty eyes of the hopeful young ladies pierced her back with a thousand darts; those young ladies fanned themselves with growing annoyance.

Lord Chadwick excused himself and came forwards to meet her. Her face was uptilted; as he looked at her, deep inside, he felt something tighten, harden, clarifying and coalescing into one crystal-clear emotion. Taking her gloved hand, he gallantly bowed over it. As she lightly rested her fingers in his, he brushed them with a kiss.

'Whoever you are, you look extremely beautiful, a rare jewel adorning the garden.'

How dashing he is, Beatrice thought, smiling triumphantly at him as he looked at her searchingly. The warm liquid of his amber gaze missed nothing as he became caught up in the excitement of her presence. She totally ignored the other women struggling to maintain their composure as they tried to hide their hostility towards her.

'What it is to be so popular, sir. I thank you for the compliment,' she said coolly, lightly, withdrawing her hand, as if his compliment meant nothing to her at all while secretly feeling a trifle flattered that a man should find her attractive, 'but I have an aversion to flattery.'

His eyebrows lifted at her forthright remark. 'Really? I am surprised to hear that since every female of my acquaintance welcomes adulation from the opposite sex.'

'Do they?' she replied airily. 'Flattery and false praise are much the same in my book.'

Curious about her casual, cool manner, yet undaunted, his smile was humorous. 'I assure you that my flattery was genuine and well meant. It is not flattery to tell the truth.'

Beatrice glanced around. 'You appear to have attracted a great deal of attention yourself. Why, ladies surround you like moths around a candle.'

He tilted his eyebrows with amusement and leaned forwards so that only she might hear his words. 'Many moths, but only one rare butterfly. Besides, I have never been partial to moths,' he murmured, and Beatrice read in his face such evident desire that heat flamed for a moment in her cheeks. A curious sharp thrill ran through her as the force between them seemed to explode wordlessly, but she did not forget who he was or why she was here.

He took a step back from her. 'So, who have we here?' he asked, regarding her down the length of his aristocratic nose. Her body was slender but rounded in all the right places and disturbing in its femininity. The swell of her hips was outlined softly beneath the soft folds of her gown and her breasts, exposed just enough above the low neckline, hinted at their firm shapeliness. He had not been so intrigued by a woman in a long time. 'Will someone not introduce us?'

Beatrice stiffened as his challenging and impertinent eyes sharpened and narrowed in amusement. And did his gaze actually linger on her breasts pushing their way up out of her bodice, or was it only her confused imagination that made it seem that way?

With Henry Talbot by her side, Astrid glanced up at him shyly and said breathlessly, 'Oh, this is Beatrice, my cousin, Lord Chadwick. She is quite mad about horses. Indeed, she can think and talk of nothing else from morning till night. It comes as no surprise that she is interested in taking you up on your wager.'

Julius arched a brow, smiling. 'Beatrice?'

'I am Beatrice Fanshaw,' Beatrice provided, lifting her chin proudly and looking directly into his narrowed amber eyes. Her own were glowing with brilliance and fire, her gaze never wavering from his face as she awaited his reaction to her announcement.

In a split second his smile was wiped clean from his face and his eyes were now sharp and penetrating with interest and something that resembled shock. The young lady who had so intrigued him a moment before had suddenly taken on a whole new identity. 'Ah! Fanshaw! Of course. How very interesting. I do recall the name.'

'You should. My father was Sir James Fanshaw.'

'I remember your father. However, I was not aware that he had a daughter.' Already nettled by her cool attitude, Julius delivered his reply with a small bow and an exaggerated show of disdain. 'It is obvious you know who I am, Miss Fanshaw.'

'You are Julius Chadwick.' Her words were firm and measured as she failed to address him with the courtesy of his title. 'The same man who ruined my father.'

'And is that what all this is about? You are here to beg me to retrieve all that he lost?'

Something welled up in Beatrice, a powerful surge of emotion to which she had no alternative but to give full rein. It was as if she had suddenly become someone else, someone bigger and much stronger than the woman who had joined the party. Her eyes flashed as cold fury drained her face of colour and added a steely edge to her voice.

'Those who know me know that I never beg, Lord Chadwick, and by my oath I intend to take more from you than an old man's loss.' Her promise was made with an icy, threatening calmness.

Julius looked at her, his face a mask of indignation, but then he was so taken aback by her outburst that his superiority evaporated. He stared down at the lovely young woman whose fury turned her eyes to a darker green.

'Dear me, Miss Fanshaw. I can see I will have to watch my step.'

'More than that, my lord. You are the man directly responsible for my father's death.'

Her attack took him so completely by surprise that he looked startled for a moment and more than a little uneasy, then a hard gleam entered his eyes, for his conscience was sore with the irony of trying to protect the reputation of his own undeserving father while—at least where Miss Fanshaw was concerned—damaging his own. 'I don't think so,' he replied, aware that those around them had fallen silent and were watching and listening with an uneasy, open curiosity. 'Your father brought about his own death.' He smiled. 'It was easy to beat him. He had no skill when it came to cards.'

'Then why did you allow him to stake Larkhill? You certainly didn't want it—indeed, you have not spent a penny piece on it since, for it is crumbling with neglect. Do you enjoy taking things from people who are weaker than you—humbling people? In my opinion that is the mark of a coward.' She took a step towards him and was pleased to see him take a step back.

Not discouraged and ignoring the gasp that went up from the crowd, he gave a bark of laughter. 'You call me a coward?'

She smiled. 'Only a coward would do what you did. You knew he couldn't win. You knew his loss would destroy him. Didn't that worry you?'

He shook his head slowly. 'Not unduly. He was a grown man. He knew perfectly well what he was doing when he staked a house and estate that was already mortgaged up to the hilt.'

Beatrice stared at him in disbelief. 'I might have known you would say something like that to discredit my father, but I do not believe you.'

He shrugged. 'You may believe what you like, but it is true. I do not lie. I did not find out myself until later—when I had to find the finance to pay off the mortgage.'

Beatrice looked at him directly, finding what he said hard to believe and wondering what sort of man this Julius Chadwick actually was. 'My father was a man without deceit, a man you could trust, who had fallen on hard times. And you, Lord Chadwick, took advantage of his weakened state. Larkhill meant more to me and my mother than to be put on a gambling table in a seedy gentleman's club.'

'It was a private gentleman's club,' he countered, needlessly provocative. 'There was nothing seedy about it.'

'A gambler would say that. So now you have two homes.'

'Three, actually.'

Momentarily thrown, she stared at him in amazement. 'Three? How can one person live in three places at once?'

'I don't. I travel a lot,' he stated by way of explanation. 'Miss Fanshaw, must I remind you that we have an audience. Might I suggest that you lower your tone? You embarrass us both with your show of emotion. I understand your antagonism towards me, which must have increased a thousandfold as you have allowed it to fester over the years. Indeed, I would feel very much the same were the situation reversed.'

'I'm glad you understand,' she uttered scathingly, 'although it doesn't alter the way I feel. I am not like my father. If you are a courageous man, you will allow me to accept your wager.'

'If nothing else, you are forward and recklessly bold, Miss Fanshaw.'

'I always believe in being direct and I enjoy walking on the wild side. I am sure you find it shocking and unfeminine that I have interest in things beyond *petit point* and fashion, but that's the way I am.'

'I do, but in your case I will overlook your unfeminine interests—but will your aunt, Lady Standish?'

'I don't doubt she will flay me alive for daring to intimate that I am anything less than a perfect lady. But a perfect lady I am not and never will be. You are staying at Larkhill?'

'I am. I've been out of the country for several months; now I'm back I intend spending more time in London. I found the time was ripe to visit Larkhill, to look over the property and decide what is to be done.' A subtle smile curved his lips. 'There are many factors which might influence how long I stay.'

'Then I hope you enjoy your stay. So, Lord Chadwick, what do you say? Will you accept my challenge?'

'I am a huntsman, Miss Fanshaw. I enjoy the chase.'

'Aye, and once the prey is caught, the sport is over. You should know better than to gamble against my good friend Julius at any game of skill,' Lord Roderick Caruthers warned. Like everyone else he had been listening to the interesting altercation between these two.

Beatrice looked at Lord Caruthers coolly. 'Lord Chadwick and I are not acquainted, sir, so how could

I possibly know that? But I am sure that if he is as skilled as you say he is, then he will have no qualms about me taking him up on his challenge.'

Chapter Two

Julius smiled at her words. His smile was the same smile that caused Astrid to flush and tremble—but it would take more than a smile from Julius Chadwick to have the same effect on Beatrice.

'So, Miss Fanshaw, are you really serious about taking me up on my wager?'

'I would not have put myself forward if I wasn't—unless you have an aversion to accepting a challenge from a woman, afraid of how it will look should I win.'

'Win?' His lips curved in mockery. 'Do you seriously think you can beat me?'

'I stand as good a chance as anyone else.'

'I see. Then the answer is, no, I do not have an aversion to a race between us.'

Common sense told Julius not to encourage her, and yet, confronted by her challenge, he was intrigued and was unable to resist the temptation. He was compelled to take her on, merely to see how well she could ride. He stared at her profile as she turned her head slightly, tracing with his gaze the beautiful lines of her face, the curved brush of her lustrous dark eyelashes. Yes, Miss Fanshaw was quite extraordinarily lovely. She had an untamed quality running in dangerous undercurrents just below the surface and a wild freedom of spirit that found its counterpart in his own hot-blooded, temperamental nature.

'The place and the distance will be of your choosing and we shall meet at eight o'clock tomorrow morning.' He turned to George. 'Arrange it, will you, George? Who will you place your bets on?'

George laughed. 'Now there's a challenge in itself. Were it anyone else, Julius, I would certainly back you, but be warned. My cousin has a special affinity with the equine species, preferring them to people. She would rather throw a saddle over a horse than attend a ball. She'll do anything for a dare and is a demon on a horse. Her own is no dainty mare, but a brute of an animal—a gelding. On such an impressive mount she stands to win.'

Beatrice threw Lord Chadwick a challenging look. 'Perhaps Lord Chadwick considers it most improper for a young lady to ride a gelding.'

An eyebrow jutted upwards. 'Young lady? My dear Miss Fanshaw, you are the most controversial and exciting woman I have ever met in my life; I suspect that your vitality is such that you are a menace to everyone you meet. It does not surprise me in the least that you ride a gelding.' A roguish grin tugged at his lips. 'If you told me you rode an elephant, I would believe you. As it is I shall take my chance.'

The wager had attracted a good deal of attention and others began to place their bets.

'I'll back you, Chadwick,' someone shouted. 'Fifty guineas you win.'

Julius turned and grinned as interest in the race began to mount. 'See what is happening, Miss Fanshaw. You have fallen among desperate gamblers.'

'I already knew that before I accepted your challenge,' she uttered, not bothering to hide her sarcasm. He gave her a cold look, but chose not to comment on her provocative remark.

'Seventy-five guineas,' another voice shouted.

'A hundred.'

'My diamond necklace,' a lady from the back of the crowd piped up.

And so it went on until the stakes reached heady proportions. But neither participant was listening as they continued to watch each other warily. Beatrice's gaze was ensnared by the glittering sheen of the amber eyes.

'And us, Miss Fanshaw?' Julius murmured. 'What will we forfeit?'

There was a deathly hush. From beneath the gazebo Lady Standish watched what was happening in appalled, stony silence, unable to believe her niece's shocking behaviour. The look in her eyes was as potent as a spoken curse.

'I say the winner names the forfeit,' Beatrice suggested.

Julius nodded. 'I think you have planned this, Miss Fanshaw.'

Beatrice raised her chin a notch. 'You don't *have* to agree to race against me, Lord Chadwick. Indeed, I don't know why I entertained such a notion.'

He looked at her directly and she felt her breath come a little short. 'Oh, I think you do,' he said quietly. 'I think you know *exactly* what you want and you will stop at nothing to get it. I read people well, Miss Fanshaw, and I think you have the ability to be absolutely single minded. You know very well why you entertained this notion.'

Her smile was one of thin sarcasm. 'You do a lot of thinking, Lord Chadwick.'

'All the time.'

'If I am as you say, then indirectly it is your doing.'

'I am sorry to find that after all these years you still carry a grudge. And now all I need to do is discover what forfeit you will ask of me, and the only way I can do that is to race against you—unless you will indulge me and tell me now.'

She tossed her head haughtily. To forgo propriety and do what one wished was quite liberating. 'No, not before the end of the race.'

'Very well. Until after the race.'

There were loud guffaws from the crowd. 'Careful, Julius,' Roderick Caruthers shouted. 'Be careful what you commit yourself to. You are a gentleman, remember, and gentlemen never renege on their word.'

He grinned. 'I'd better win, then.'

'And should I win, you will give me your word to honour the forfeit?' Beatrice asked, holding his gaze.

'I do.'

Her expression was innocent, but her eyes were hard to read. She raised her brows slightly, and said, 'I intend to hold you to that.'

'So the wager is made—but your forfeit? I think I have guessed, which wasn't too difficult considering the circumstances. Though it is immaterial since you cannot win.' Julius's grin broadened and he looked at her knowingly, holding up one hand. 'Don't tell me. Larkhill.'

Beatrice gave him a level look. 'Oh, no. Believe me, Lord Chadwick, nothing I could ask from you would be as fine or as grand as Larkhill.'

His eyes narrowed. 'I am intrigued. Tell me.'

'Like I said, not until after the race—although if your horse is as splendid as you would have everyone believe, then I might well be tempted to take it from you.'

'Oh, no, lady—my horse is an exception. I have waited too long to get a horse by its sire—a winner of some top races—and I am not about to lose him now. But why are we discussing this? I shall win.'

Beatrice smiled almost sweetly. 'Then you have nothing to worry about, have you, Lord Chadwick?'

'You must be confident, to accept my challenge.'

'I would not be doing this if I wasn't confident that I could beat you.'

Beatrice would make sure that Lord Chadwick could not refuse the forfeit she would ask of him if she won the race, even while telling herself that what she was doing was foolish. Her eyes held his and she knew he would read her absolute determination to go ahead with this wager—foolish or not.

'Cousin Beatrice is no docile, ordinary young lady,' George laughingly told Lord Chadwick. 'She is a mannerless hoyden—a dark horse if ever there was is how I would describe her.' He paused with a small private smile and a playful wink at Beatrice. 'Dark horse, maybe, but she is also clever and cunning and always dangerous.'

'Really,' Julius uttered quietly. 'A woman after my own heart.'

Beatrice was so close, she had to tilt her head up to meet his eyes. 'Oh, no, Lord Chadwick,' she countered coldly. 'You can keep your heart. That is the last thing I want from you.'

He regarded her long and hard before replying. 'I shall. My heart has always been in my own safe keeping, and there it will remain. Safe. But you intrigue me, Miss Fanshaw. Already I am wondering what I have let myself in for. And I was beginning to imagine you would become unseated at the first hurdle.'

'Don't you believe it,' George told him. 'Beatrice has the best pair of hands I've ever seen. She knows horses—could whisper a horse out of a field. But should you win, Julius, what forfeit will you ask of her?'

Lord Chadwick looked at George as he considered his question, but his penetrating gaze returned to Beatrice.

Curious as to what his reply would be, Beatrice waited expectantly. The glow in her face now faded. She straightened her back.

At length he said, 'As to that, I have not yet decided. But I will, and she may not like it when I have.' He bowed his head ever so slightly. 'Until tomorrow, Miss Fanshaw. I look forward to our race.'

Beatrice had not imagined confronting Lord Chadwick would require such an effort. On reaching the house her stomach was still tied in knots and her heart had yet to find its customary rhythm. Nervousness was not a reaction to which she was normally susceptible. There was no place in her scheme of things for faint heartedness, and this afternoon she had taken the first step to reclaiming Larkhill. Recalling how Lord Chadwick had looked at her with open admiration, her lips quirked. In the circumstances, it was a definitely heartening thought.

She was about to cross the hall to the stairs when a voice rang out, halting her.

'A word, Beatrice.'

She turned to face her aunt, her brow furrowed with a twinge of premonition. She got the familiar feeling that trouble was afoot, and as she noted her aunt's sharp look, that piercing glance told her plainly that some kind of storm was brewing. It was plain that Lady Standish was both appalled and incensed over her niece's conduct.

'Beatrice! How dare you conduct yourself in this manner? How dare you? And to publicly take Lord

Chadwick to task over past grievances was outrageous—an absolute disgrace.'

Beatrice's green eyes flashed, but when she spoke she managed to moderate her tone. 'I meant no offence, Aunt Moira. Truly.'

'I know about the wager between the two of you and you forget yourself. Not only do you shame yourself, but me and our good name. I will not have it. You make yourself a disgrace. Such freakish sports are not fitting for a young lady of quality. I will not have the reputation of this family jeopardised by your folly.'

'I'm sorry if I have upset you, Aunt Moira, but I never could resist a challenge.'

'A challenge? Beatrice, this is *me* you are talking to, not a fool. You haven't the first inkling of social graces. In that I have tried and failed, for you were determined not to learn. By your activities you encourage Lord Chadwick. I see that. Why do you always take such delight in being disobedient?'

Tired of being told what to do, Beatrice averted her eyes, trying to keep her anger and frustration at bay, but rebellion was bubbling away inside her. 'Because I am old enough to look after myself.'

Lady Moira appeared undaunted. 'In society no woman is old enough to look after herself in certain circumstances—and you are just eighteen years old.'

'I am old enough and can look after myself. There's not one weak bone in my body.' Her fingers curled tightly into her palm as she tried to remain calm. 'I have enough good sense in my head to know what I am doing.'

'That is where we differ, Beatrice. Had you any sense at all, you would not have entered into this disgraceful wager with Lord Chadwick.' Her eyes narrowing, she thrust her head forwards and glared knowingly at this disappointing niece of hers. 'What do you hope for? To push Astrid out of her place? To supplant her in Lord Chadwick's attention? Though this was supposed to be Astrid's birthday party, you have stolen her attention. In fact, you have eclipsed Astrid in success. There is some doubt that Lord Chadwick will offer for her now. Are you jealous of your cousin, Beatrice? Is that it?'

A frown crossed Beatrice's beautiful face, then her anger fled and she knew a moment of shame. 'I am not jealous of Astrid. Please do not think that. I love Astrid as a sister and I would never do anything that would cause her pain. Astrid doesn't have a place in Lord Chadwick's affections, Aunt Moira, that is plain to see. You wanted him to notice her. He was polite. You saw what you wanted to see.'

'And you hate him—remember?' she pointed out coldly.

'Yes, I do.'

'Then I would have thought you would have wanted to steer well clear of him. And the wager? I do not believe in flouting propriety in this way. It is the most disgraceful thing I have ever heard in my life.'

'I am sorry if it has caused you distress, Aunt, but the wager is made. I cannot go back on my word.'

'And what do you hope to get out of it—if you win, that is,' she sneered, 'which I very much doubt, since by all accounts no one handles a horse quite like Lord Chadwick?'

'Then perhaps he has met his match. I accept that what I am doing is a risk.'

'Risk?' Lady Standish gave her a thin, sarcastic smile. 'I think that is putting it mildly, Beatrice.'

Beatrice lifted her head and looked squarely into her aunt's eyes. 'If I win and Lord Chadwick agrees to my forfeit, not only will I be able to return to Larkhill, I will also have the means to make it one of the finest houses in the county. You will also have me off your hands for good, which I know you will look on as a blessing.'

'That is the most foolish thing I have ever heard. This time you have gone too far. You will not do it. Do you hear me? Don't you dare disobey me. I will not have it. I will not be accused of being unable to keep my niece in check and made a laughing stock. Now go to your room and think good and hard about what I have said.'

'I will, Aunt Moira.' On that note Beatrice excused herself, leaving a thoroughly shocked Aunt Moira staring after her.

Beatrice returned to the party as dusk was beginning to fall. After an hour spent talking to friends and acquaintances, she went in search of Astrid. She found her listening to the musicians. They were all dressed alike in crimson coats and white trousers, seated on a rostrum hung with coloured lanterns. Astrid turned her head when Beatrice stood beside her and smiled. Her eyes sparkled and a pretty flush coloured her cheeks as she sipped a glass of lemonade cooled with crushed ice.

'There you are, Beatrice. I thought you had disappeared for good.'

'Are you enjoying your party, Astrid?'

'Oh, yes. Mama has gone to a lot of trouble and expense to make it right. Although I do find it all rather awe-inspiring,' she admitted, envious of her cousin's self-assurance.

Beatrice nodded in agreement. Looking around, she saw couples wandering away to indulge in a little starlit privacy. Lord Chadwick was watching her from across the stretch of lawn that lay like a rich velvet carpet between them. He raised his glass and bowed briefly, his smile both approving and challenging as his gaze from beneath hooded lids swept over her with practised scrutiny. She turned away to listen to what Astrid was saying.

'George is paying a good deal of attention to Leonora Fenton, Sir Philip Fenton's daughter. He always does. He's never said anything, but I think he's quite taken with her. What do you think, Beatrice?'

Beatrice glanced towards where George conversed with a slender, extremely attractive young woman in a yellow high-waisted gown. 'She's very pretty. But I wonder if your mother would agree to a match between them.'

'I don't see why not. George is of an age to choose his own wife. Miss Fenton has all the required requisites—title and money—so I don't see why Mama should have any objections. But come, Beatrice,' she said, linking her arm through her cousin's, 'I care nothing to standing still. Let's circulate. I want to have a word with you about this wager you have made with Lord Chadwick. It is quite insane—you know that, don't you? Mama is furious.'

'She's already spoken to me about it, but I know what I am doing. I will not be bullied out of it. I have no intention of backing out.'

'But—you could get hurt. Lord Chadwick is not the sort of man to take kindly to being bested by a woman.'

Beatrice stared at her. 'Bested? Yes, I might well beat him. I certainly intend to try. But does the forfeit I will demand of him not concern you?'

'No. When you accepted his wager I heard you tell him that you will not ask him to return Larkhill to you, but I suspect it features somewhere in the forfeit.'

'Yes it does. I wanted to speak to you about the race, Astrid. Your opinion matters to me very much. Aunt Moira has her sights set on Lord Chadwick as a serious contender for your hand in marriage. Will it upset you very much to see us together, racing hell for leather against each other?'

Astrid paused and turned to her cousin, her attitude one of calm resolve. 'Be assured, Beatrice, that whatever aspirations Mama has of my future husband, it will definitely not be Lord Chadwick. I will not marry him, not even to appease Mama.'

They carried on walking. Astrid said nothing else. Beatrice had expected something—a word of blame, of disappointment, of condemnation for the manner in which she had asserted herself in Lord Chadwick's eyes, but she had nothing from Astrid but a calm look which was somehow full of relief…and gratitude.

Why, Beatrice thought, seeing her gentle cousin truly, as if for the first time, *I have done her a favour.* Astrid really didn't want to marry Lord Chadwick. She never did. She was being pushed into it by her forceful mama, and she, Beatrice, was giving her a way out.

Astrid glanced across at a young man sitting on a bench in the shadow of a spouting fountain. 'Will you excuse me?' she said a little breathlessly, excitement leaping to her eyes and brightness lighting her face as she spoke. 'I can see Henry and I simply must speak to him.'

Beatrice watched her hurry away. Normally Astrid was always far too timid and serious to be giddy. And yet when Henry Talbot was near it was like the sun coming out after a dark period and she suddenly became light-hearted, foolish and gay. With a smile Beatrice turned and sauntered in the direction of the house. Her step was light as she walked slowly along a walkway lined with a profusion of fragrant pink roses that clambered all over trellising. It was a tunnel of shadow, broken at intervals by warm squares of light from lanterns hanging in the trees. With a contented sigh she closed her eyes and listened to the murmur of distant voices, a wistful expression on her lovely face. It was a warm night, heavy and sweet with summer scents.

She intended to find a quiet shady place on the terrace to sit a while before going to her room. The warmth of the evening caressed her bare shoulders and a light breeze stirred the skirts of her gown.

'Well, well, Miss Fanshaw! So we meet again.' Julius was ahead of her and, seeing her walking alone along the privacy of the arched walkway, he had paused to watch her, completely captivated by the look on her face. This was not the face of the young woman who had boldly challenged him to race his horse against hers earlier. Then her haughty manner had marked her as strong of character whereas now, with her eyes closed and a gentle smile on her lips, there was a softness about her, an elusive gentleness that declared her to be as fragile and vulnerable as the roses that clambered about them.

Clearly she was a woman of ever-changing moods and subtle contradictions, and while her physical beauty first arrested the attention, it was this spectrum, this bewildering, indefinable quality that held him captive. A strange sweet melting feeling softened his innermost core without warning, the place in him that he usually kept as hard as steel.

His appearance pulled Beatrice from the strange spell that had seemed to enclose her. She started, alarmed by the unexpected greeting, and opened her eyes. He appeared too suddenly for her to prepare herself, so the heady surge of pleasure she experienced on seeing him again was clearly evident, stamped like an unbidden confession on her lovely face.

Stepping in front of her, he towered above her. His smile was full of gentle mockery when he said, 'Are you about to retire, Miss Fanshaw?'

Beneath his impassive gaze Beatrice stood perfectly still, refusing to blush or look away, her delicately beautiful face framed by a halo of golden hair—a dainty image of fragility standing before a man who dwarfed her.

'I thought I might.'

'A sensible move, I would say. I fear if you party too long into the night you will not do full justice to the race tomorrow.'

'Your concern—if that is what it is—for my state of health is quite touching, Lord Chadwick. But worry not. If I were to party till dawn, I would still beat you hands down.'

'Your courage and confidence are to be admired, but you are going to be disappointed. I'm afraid the outcome is inevitable.'

'I don't think so,' she remarked.

'And here was I thinking you might wish to retract your challenge.' He stared at her with impudent admiration, letting his gaze travel from her eyes to her mouth, then down to the swell of her breasts. Beatrice wished she had a shawl to cover herself, as she felt her cheeks grow hot beneath his scrutiny.

'My challenge stands. Now be so kind as to step aside.'

He did as she bade, but she was not to be rid of him. As she continued to walk on he fell into step beside her.

'Will you return to the party?' he asked.

They had reached the terrace and she stopped and turned to him. 'I might, but then I might not.' Taking a deep breath, she looked up into the night sky and saw the moon, a new moon, a thin sickle of a moon. Seeing it for the first time, she closed her eyes.

Beside her Julius followed her gaze, his eyes on the slender sickle. 'Have you made a wish?' he asked.

Opening her eyes, she nodded.

'Then I hope the new moon brings you luck.'

'So do I, but I believe you make your own luck in this world.'

'That is a very cynical view, Miss Fanshaw.'

'I have a cynical outlook on life, Lord Chadwick.' She gazed up at the stars beginning to twinkle. 'I love looking at the sky at night,' she murmured. 'There are so many stars up there. To some people all the constellations just look like a jumble of stars, but they're not. See that bright one over there?'

Julius continued to look up, as if he, too, found something of interest there.

'That's Jupiter.'

'So it is—and over there is the Great Bear—and you see that faint smudge,' he said, pointing at the sky, 'that is the Andromeda constellation, which is the nearest galaxy to our own Milky Way and was named after the mythological princess Andromeda. The seven stars of the Plough are the easiest to make out, which is of the constellation Ursa Major.'

Beatrice laughed. 'You are very knowledgeable about the stars, Lord Chadwick. Do you make a study of the galaxies yourself?'

'I spend a lot of my time travelling. On board ship the nights are long and one spends many hours on deck, looking at the sky. The northern sky—which you are looking at—is very different from the southern sky and so is the sky around the equatorial zone. I'm sure you would find it interesting.'

'I'm sure I would—if I ever get the opportunity to travel. It never occurred to me that the sky would look different in other parts of the world. Do you think anyone lives up there, that any of those stars are inhabited with people like us?'

'I don't know. What do you think?'

'I don't—not really. But then, it would be arrogant of us to assume that out of all those thousands and millions of stars the Earth is the only planet where life exists. It's like saying the Earth is the centre of the universe and everything revolves around it.' She dragged her gaze from the sky and looked at him when she heard him chuckle. Her lips broke into a smile. 'What is it? Why do you laugh?'

'I am astonished. Since when did young ladies begin studying astronomy?'

'I don't know about the others, but this particular young lady began as soon as she learnt to read.' He was smiling, a smile she found almost endearing. He did seem to have a way about him and she could not fault any woman for falling under his spell, for she found to her amazement that her heart was not so distantly detached as she might have imagined it to be. Even his deep mellow voice seemed like a warm caress over her senses. For all the animosity she felt for him, she could not deny what a fine specimen of a man he was.

He took her hand to kiss it. He looked so relaxed

that she found herself responding to him. Then a glint of mischief in his eyes reminded her of who he was. Shaking off the effects of his winning smile, she took herself mentally in hand and snatched her hand free. She tossed her head proudly, but Julius Chadwick was undaunted by her show of indignation. He touched her arm very gently and reached so close that she could smell the sharp scent of his cologne.

'Please forgive me,' he murmured, softly and with disconcerting sincerity. 'I was boorish in my behaviour to you earlier when you accepted my wager. It was never my intention and now I heartily beg your pardon.'

Beatrice was astonished. She stared into his deep amber eyes, looking for the mockery, the veiled contempt. She found neither. 'No more than I was,' she conceded.

'You were angry and I understand the reason and you intend to punish me for it. Will you not tell me that I am forgiven?'

Beatrice found herself weakening before his smile. Her own smile came slowly. 'Very well. You are forgiven.'

'Then I am once more a happy man and I look forward to seeing you tomorrow.' He raised her fingers to his lips and pressed a light kiss on them. As he did so he surreptitiously pressed a small object into the palm of her hand. 'I would like you to have this. It is just a small token of my respect and admiration,' he said. 'May it serve to remind you of happier times and of the value I place on your forgiveness.'

Beatrice uttered her thanks and watched him turn

and stride away. When he was out of sight she opened her hand and looked down at the small object he had placed there. Only then did her brief softening turn to humiliation. The colour drained from her face. Damn him, she thought. He had used subtle trickery and flattery on her and she had fallen for it and allowed herself to become as stupid and gullible as all those silly girls who simpered and followed him around like sheep.

What he had given her was a gold signet ring she had last seen on her father's finger. She had not given it a thought during all the years she had been without him, and now she knew that this, too, must have been among the things he had taken from her father. It did remind her of happier times, but it also reminded her of how those times had cruelly ended. With the death of her mother following so soon on her father's suicide, the deep, dark void of hollowness and sorrow was complete.

Wounded and angry, she could not even begin to imagine the desperation that had driven her father to part with his ring, but as she stared down at it she swore she would make Lord Chadwick pay most dearly for what he had done to her. She would not rest until she had retrieved everything her father had lost to Julius Chadwick. Nothing would stand in her way after she had come this far.

The dew was still on the grass when Beatrice headed for the stables the next morning with her riding crop tucked underneath her arm. She arrived to a great fuss of excitement. She had done as her aunt had said and thought good and hard about the wager, but it had made no difference. Her mind was made up. Respect was everything to her aunt and what her niece was doing would have a damaging effect on her own standing in society, but in the end nothing was changed. Beatrice would not back out now.

Everyone had heard about the race and had come to watch. Major had been brought out of his stable and tacked up. The stable lad was giving his powerful haunches and glossy neck one last polish. He was by the mounting block, arching his neck and pawing the ground, waiting for his mistress.

The groom knew of her aversion to the side saddle and that she preferred the masculine way of riding astride, so Major had been tacked up appropriately. No one was surprised to see Beatrice wearing her breeches, for it was a familiar sight.

As spry as a young athlete, she swung herself up on to Major's back as George rode towards her.

'Is it all arranged?' she asked him as they rode together out of the stable yard, her horse so fresh and eager that she had to hold him in check.

'I have planned the route to your satisfaction, I hope.' Of an understanding nature, George glanced sideways at her, his brow creased with a worried frown. 'I'm sorry Astrid cannot watch the race. I know how much she wanted to, but I'm afraid Mama is incensed by your acceptance of Lord Chadwick's wager and has forbidden her to attend.'

Unmoved, Beatrice looked straight ahead. With his shock of fair hair and bright blue eyes, many were the times when she had thanked God for her fun-loving, easy-mannered, handsome cousin. He had been her friend for as long as she could remember, and she really didn't know how she would have coped without him. She would never forget the lack of welcome at Standish House from Aunt Moira, and things had not improved. She had soon learned that her aunt's love was reserved solely for her own children and that there was none for her.

'I am sorry that Astrid cannot watch the race, George—I know how much she wanted to. I am also sorry about the way Aunt Moira feels about me, but I cannot change that.' At these words George glanced at her. How typical of him to be concerned for her, she thought. She smiled to reassure him and said, 'Don't worry, George, I've grown used to it. As for the wager, it is done and too much is at stake for me to pull out now. Besides, I would not give Lord Chadwick the satisfaction. How much do you know about him?'

'Not much, as it happens. I only met him myself when he arrived back in London—from India, I believe. He is very rich, but there was a time when his family were destitute. Equipped with a clever mind, through his own endeavours and gambling everything on a series of investments, which paid off for him again and again, he brought his family out of penury.'

'If he used the same gambling methods he used on my father, then I do not care for them. It does him no credit,' Beatrice retorted bitterly, at the same time grudgingly impressed by his success. 'I suppose if he's as rich as all that, then there's little wonder people court his favour.'

'They do, but his success has come at a price. Some years ago tragedy hit his family—I'm not sure of the details. Because of it and to guard his privacy, he spends most of his time abroad.'

'I see. Tell me about the circuit.'

'It will start and end at the gate in the lower meadow. You will both do a full circuit of Larkhill, riding over the common and open ground past the village, up to the woods and through the park, where you will pick up the trail back to the meadow. It's punishing and steep in places. The full circuit will take an hour or more, but it shouldn't be difficult since you have ridden it almost every day. The hardest part will be the steep ride up the woods.'

'Have you familiarised Lord Chadwick with the route?'

'Yes. He rode it earlier and he's up for it if you are.'

'Of course. I can trust Major to handle it.'

'Lord Chadwick is already at the starting point— along with a hundred others from the house party who have come to watch and to collect their winnings.'

'No doubt everyone is expecting him to win.'

'Absolutely—although there are several who have laid bets on you.'

Beatrice looked sideways at her cousin. 'Where is your bet placed, George? I trust you remember that I am family and that you owe your loyalty to me. Were you brave enough to risk your money on me?'

Kicking his horse into a gallop, he went ahead. 'That

is for me to know and for you to find out,' he shouted laughingly over his shoulder.

The reception party was larger than Beatrice had anticipated. The entire meadow was filled with all types of people from house guests to grooms, footmen and stable hands and locals from the nearby village. The sun shone down on fashionable ladies beneath bobbing parasols, feathered hats and a colourful array of silk turbans. Curricles and chases were everywhere and those who wished to follow the race were on horseback. Everyone jockeyed for the best position, all animatedly discussing the forthcoming race.

Atop her spirited mount, Beatrice looked radiant, undeniably beautiful, as only she could do when there was something she wanted badly enough and had set her mind to getting it. She slanted an admiring look at her opponent as he approached leading his mount. He wore a tanned riding coat, a pair of buckskin breeches and highly polished brown boots.

Julius also wore a look of unconcealed appreciation on his handsome face as he surveyed her perched atop a raw-boned gelding, a giant of a horse, a glossy chestnut, its coat gleaming almost red. She presented a slender figure and it seemed incomprehensible that she could control the great beast. She met his gaze squarely, her face bright with invitation and challenge.

'Good morning,' he greeted politely. 'It's a good turnout. All it's short of to make it a fair are the acrobats and tents. Are you still up for this, Miss Fanshaw—or perhaps you would prefer pistols at twenty paces?' he teased as he leapt on to his mount with the physical prowess of an athlete.

Beatrice lifted her head, intending to treat him with cool formality, but he looked so relaxed atop his powerful horse and his smile was so disarming that she almost smiled. Confident, her expression open and her green eyes direct, she said, 'Of course I am up to it, Lord Chadwick—we can try pistols at twenty paces if I lose, which I have no intention of doing.'

'Then if a duel to the death is to follow, you'd better win if you value your life.'

She laughed lightly. 'Not only am I a competent horsewoman, I am also a crack shot, so whichever method we use, you stand to lose.'

His horse drew Beatrice's eye. It was a beautiful dappled grey gelding, its coat as smooth as silk. With sharp features, bright, intelligent eyes and a perfectly arched neck, it really was a beautiful animal, with powerful legs and shoulders. Her opponent was watching her closely and he saw her eyes gleam with appreciation.

'He is a splendid animal, is he not, Miss Fanshaw?'

'He certainly is,' she agreed longingly. 'As I told you yesterday, had I not already decided on the forfeit, I would be more than happy to take that horse from you.'

'Never. I will never part with him,' he laughingly declared.

They rode towards the open gate to the meadow where George was waiting to get the race under way. It was a bright day, but not too hot. The haymakers in the field next to the meadow leaned on their scythes and watched them pass side by side, doffing their caps as they saw the noble bearing of the Marquess, their hearts warming at the sight of their own Miss Fanshaw.

Julius slanted her a look. 'It's still not too late to pull out.'

Without looking at him, Beatrice beamed upon the crowd. 'Of course I'm not going to pull out. Indeed, I couldn't disappoint so many earnest cavaliers who have placed their bets on me.'

'Don't let that put you off. They'll get their money back.'

Now she did look at him. 'That's not the point. I am honour bound to take your wager. Besides I can think of nothing that would please me more than to beat you.' She shot him a suspicious, mischievous glance. 'Unless you have cold feet, my lord, and *you* would like to pull out?'

Julius trapped her gaze in his. 'Not a bit of it. I'm looking forward to it, though the course has many pitfalls.'

Beatrice took in the hard planes of his face, the subtle aggression in the line of his jaw, and the clear intent that stared at her from the depths of his amber eyes. A slight trembling sensation skittered over her skin. Ignoring it, she smiled. 'I dare say there will be many distractions along the way, but I am familiar with every one of them.'

'Then the fight is on. I promise you a hard race,' Julius called over his shoulder as he trotted ahead.

Maybe so, Beatrice thought, eyeing his back through

narrowed eyes. But with everything to play for, she would win.

At the drop of George's handkerchief and with the roar of the crowd, the two horses lunged forwards. The two riders were galloping at full speed, crouched low over the horses' necks. Neck and neck they left the meadow and thundered across the common to open spaces and up the steep track towards the woods. One glance as they cleared a fence assured Julius that Beatrice Fanshaw was indeed a skilled horsewoman.

Both horses held their paces well up the long, punishing slope, then raced across the rough ground at the edge of the woods, where the undergrowth was home to badgers and foxes. Her head down to avoid low branches that might sweep her out of the saddle, Beatrice kept a careful lookout for loose rocks, dangerous, treacherous roots and slippery puddles which the sun was unable to reach and dry out. Major fell behind Lord Chadwick's horse. Both horses were blowing foam as they crested the hill. The track now lead down to circle Larkhill.

Leaning forwards like a jockey to get every inch of speed from Major, urging him on harder and harder, Beatrice was after Lord Chadwick in a mad, downward dash. The hooves pounded, sending divots of earth up behind. She urged Major onwards, then there was a giant hedge before her, white with summer blossom. His body flowing easily with his horse's stride, Lord Chadwick held the advantage and cleared it first. Beatrice felt Major's hind quarters bunching up beneath her and with one giant leap she cleared it with an effortless, breezy unconcern and hit the ground on the other side. Lord Chadwick glanced around and waved his hand, laughing jubilantly on seeing her several lengths behind. With a laugh in her own throat, Beatrice recovered and was off again, pounding into her fastest gallop once more.

Racing across the soft parkland grass, Lord Chadwick was just ahead of her, his attention fixed on winning the race. But Beatrice was gaining on him. She could feel the ripple of her hair as it loosed its pins and laughed recklessly to feel the wind in her face. Major's ears were back to hear her laugh, then forward as they came to another hedge with a ditch before it. She checked only for a moment and then they soared over it as one. She could smell the scent of summer flowers and crushed woodbine as Major's hooves clipped the top of the hedge and then they were moving on, even faster.

With the meadow and the finishing post within sight, there were only two lengths between them now and with a surge of energy, knowing exactly what his mistress wanted, Major, confident, trusting and elated, sailed past Lord Chadwick's beautiful grey, the crowd shouting, 'Go on, Miss Beatrice!' They flew past the winning post, at the point where they had started.

The crowd erupted, everyone laughing and cheering. Julius pulled his sweating horse to a halt and took in Beatrice's mud-spattered face and tumbling, tangled hair. Her golden skin was flushed with heat and excitement and her eyes—winner's eyes—were a sparkling, brilliant green. Dragging in a deep breath, exhilaration coursing through their veins, their wide smiles were mirror images. Julius couldn't help thinking that it was worth losing the race to see her laughing with such unfeigned delight. It was a warm, husky, rippling sound. His eyes locked on her lips, on the column of her slender throat. Instinctively his hands tightened on the reins.

He dismounted and went to her, placing his hand on her horse's foam-flecked neck. 'It was a good race. Quite splendid. You win. You rode well,' he conceded. 'Congratulations.'

She sprang from the saddle and stood close to him, her smile shamelessly triumphant. She was able to feel the heat of his body as he could feel hers. Fuelled by the breathless excitement of the race and her win, and the pleasure of standing so close to his strong manly body, she was aware that she was trembling.

It was a long time since Julius had enjoyed a ride as much, or as fast and unrestrained, with company that could handle the going as well as he. 'George was right. You're an intrepid horsewoman.'

Tossing her head, she laughed happily. 'I couldn't let you have the advantage of me now, could I?'

'I suppose not. So, Miss Fanshaw—the forfeit? What is it to be?' He stood without moving, awaiting her pleasure.

Unsmiling, she met his gaze and held it. He was looking at her with quiet patience—like a cat before a mousehole. Having puzzled on how to approach him, she chose directness, calming herself and saying, 'By his own actions my father gambled away everything he owned to you, causing him to lose his self-respect and his sanity. Now you are the only person I can think of who can help me.' She could sense he was wary, that his guard was up. There was a distance between her and this man which might never be closed. The startling amber eyes rested on her ironically.

'Of what help could I possibly be to you? What is it that I can do? My curiosity is aroused as to why you should go to all this trouble to take me up on my wager. I detect a certain recklessness in you, and if I know anything of feminine vanity it will be something of value that you think only I can give you. Will you please put us all out of our misery and tell us what it is?'

Beatrice drew a deep breath, then fired her salvo. 'That you marry me.'

Chapter Three

Julius was deaf to the collective gasps that followed this statement. Suddenly his entire body tensed. His fists clenched on his riding crop and then convulsively tightened. His features, about to relax into lines of arrogant satisfaction, froze and his face became a hard, cynical mask.

'Either you are carrying pity for me in losing the race to an unbelievable extreme, or else you're not playing with a full deck.'

'I am neither dim-witted nor crazy,' Beatrice stated, 'and pity has nothing to do with my reasons for wanting this marriage.'

'Marriage? Come, Miss Fanshaw. Think about it,' Lord Chadwick intoned in silken menace, as though his brooding eyes and smooth voice and his slight, dark smile could mesmerise any unsuspecting female. 'Admit it. You were having a lark.'

'Oh, no, Lord Chadwick. I never lark about, as those who know me will tell you.'

Gazing at her directly, Julius searched her face for some indication that she was joking, but her expression was completely unemotional. The soft pink lips were tantalising and gracefully curved, vaguely smiling. It stirred his imagination no small amount.

'Despite what you say, I think this really must be some kind of charade you play. You are asking me to do the impossible.' She remained silent, holding his gaze, and the fire that had sprung in her eyes convinced him that this was no charade and that she was deadly serious. 'Good God!' The words were exhaled slowly, but otherwise he simply stared at her. Then the corner of his mouth twisted wryly in a gesture that was not quite a smile. 'I suppose I left myself wide open for that.'

As everyone looked on with shocked, incredulous expressions, he smiled coolly. 'You must forgive me if I appear shocked. Naturally I am flattered by your proposal, Miss Fanshaw—in fact, I am quite blown away by it. Well—if this isn't the most peculiar marriage proposal I have ever heard. You are without doubt a most shameless, impulsive creature.' He was now amused. 'You expressed admiration for my horse earlier. Will you not take him instead?'

Beatrice shot him an indignant look, straightening her back. She recognised that her impromptu proposal had taken him completely unawares, but she played the game on. She shook her head, tossing the curling tresses that had become loosened by the race enticingly.

'Please have the good sense to take me seriously. Am I so ugly, sir, that you would prefer to rid yourself of your precious horse than to be wed to me?' His bold gaze stirred something deep within her and the sensation was not unpleasant.

'On the contrary,' he answered with an apparent ease he was far from feeling, 'your beauty so blinds me, I fear I must be led to the altar by the hand—should I accept your proposal. Now, about my horse. What do you say?'

Disregarding the sarcasm in his tone, Beatrice pinned a brilliant smile on her face. 'But I couldn't possibly take your horse. I recall you saying that you could not possibly part with him, in which case I would not dream of taking him from you. So I will settle for you instead. Come, Lord Chadwick? What do you say?' She flicked a glance around the bystanders within earshot. They were waiting to hear what he had to say with baited breath.

Julius let them wait a while longer as he faced the open challenge and measured the power of her will in her green gaze. There was plenty that he wanted to say, but not here, not now. In her resentment, if this young hellion thought to make a fool of him and believed she had him cornered, then she didn't know who she was dealing with. She would find out, but in the meantime he would play along with her game—for knowing how she held him in absolute contempt, that's all it could be. However, he was intrigued, all his senses completely involved with her. There could be worse things than being married to this beautiful, feisty firecracker.

'Then what can I say except that I consider myself fortunate to find myself betrothed to the most beautiful young lady in Essex.' Taking her hand, he raised it to his lips, and in so doing played the forfeit, as if young ladies proposed to gentlemen in this way every day of the week.

After a good deal of laughter, disbelief and hesitant congratulations, Julius and Beatrice, accompanied by a thoroughly bemused George, rode back to Standish House.

Clattering into the stable yard, the two men swung from their saddles and Julius tossed the reins to George, who led both horses away. Beatrice turned in the saddle, but before she had a chance to dismount, Julius's hands closed, strong and sure, about her waist. He lifted her as if she weighed no more than a child, lowering her slowly until her feet touched the ground.

Beatrice felt a blush tinge her cheeks—it was all she could do to meet his gaze fleetingly. It was the first time a man had touched her, had dared take such liberties.

'Thank you, my lord,' she said tightly, 'but the time has not yet come when I cannot get off a horse without assistance.'

Julius looked down at her, his tone slightly acid. 'The pleasure is all mine,' he said in clipped tones. 'Would you deprive me of that?' He stepped away from her. 'We need to talk.'

'Yes, we do.'

'Now would be as good a time as any.' His eyes

held hers. His face was a taut mask of controlled anger. For an instant he thought she would argue—he was relieved when she tightened her lips and inclined her head in apparent acquiescence. 'Come, let's take a walk.'

With studied calm Beatrice allowed him to place his hand on her elbow and escort her out of the stable yard and into a quiet part of the gardens. There was a controlled alertness in his manner, like that of a large cat, its strength ready to explode, but for the present docile. She was reminded of a large black panther she had seen on her visit to the zoo at the Tower of London with Astrid. In repose the panther's sinews had flexed and stretched in a fantastic rhythm of life that mesmerised. Julius Chadwick was slim, yet sturdy, and moved with almost sensuous grace. There was a sureness in his stride as if he carefully planned where to place each foot. At the moment he appeared relaxed, but Beatrice knew that he was aware of her and everything around him.

His grip felt strong and steely. A host of unfamiliar sensations passed along her nerves and her heart turned over distractingly. Such unexpected susceptibility was not, to her mind, a helpful development. She had never before been so afflicted—she hoped the effect would fade quickly. To her chagrin it did not go away when he removed his hand.

'I don't think we'll be disturbed here.'

His tone, clipped and dry, had Beatrice shifting her gaze to his face. He was a towering masculine presence in this quiet corner of the garden. 'What is it you want to say?' she asked, beginning to feel the first pangs of discomfort with the dark way he was regarding her, his gaze narrowed and assessing.

The corner of his mouth twisted wryly. 'Don't look so worried. I don't intend to harm you.' Looking down into her wide eyes, Julius saw speculation leap in their depths only to be replaced by wariness. His gaze locked on hers. 'I believe it's time for a little plain speaking.'

Beatrice stiffened. 'On what subject?'

'On the subject of your ridiculous forfeit—our future.' In an endeavour to disguise the tension that had gripped him and the way her nearness was affecting him, how he found it nigh impossible to look away from her golden hair lightened by the sun, her unfathomable green eyes and beckoning fragrance, he took a couple of steps away from her and gazed over the gardens. 'Am I *honestly* supposed to take you—I mean, this proposal—seriously?'

'I assure you, I am completely serious.'

'Then do you mind if I ask you a few questions?'

'Ask me anything you like.'

He tilted his head to one side, his face a mirror of bewilderment and disbelief. 'Are you, by any chance, under the influence of drink, Miss Fanshaw?'

'Absolutely not. I rarely drink anything stronger than watered-down wine.'

'Then am I supposed to believe that at some point you might have fallen in love with my larger-than-life reputation? That is what it would have to be since, to my knowledge, we have never met.'

'That scenario is as ludicrous as the one before it.'

'Then it can hardly come as a surprise to you to learn that I might have some objections to the proposal.'

'It wasn't a proposal.'

Julius's contemplation was steady. 'What was it, then? An order?'

'No.' The word was out before Beatrice had considered it. She tried to erase the admission with a casual wave of her hand. 'That is…'

'*Plain* speaking I believe I said. I *don't* like being forced. It goes against my grain. It is a most unwise thing for you to do. Most unwise. How dare you compromise me in this manner?'

Beatrice lifted her chin. 'I had hoped you were too much of a gentleman to renege on your word.'

'I don't have to be a genius to work out that you *planned* this. What concerns me now, what we need to discuss, is what comes next.' Leaning against a low stone wall and resting his arm on the top, letting his hand dangle limply, he caught her glittering gaze and held it. 'Tell me. When do you want the wedding to take place?'

'Why, I…' Feeling heat wash over her face, she faltered, taken off guard.

'Come now,' he pressed. 'Don't tell me you haven't thought it out. One day? Two days? A week—a month? How long?'

'As soon as possible was what I imagined.'

'Well, imagine again. If you *imagined* I'd meekly consent to this madness, you were far off track.'

'If you recall, my lord, you did consent to it. Very well, we will wed at your convenience, I suppose.'

'And *I* suppose that would be never.'

'You mean you *will* go back on your word?'

'You can bet your damned life there is nothing that would please me more. But were I to do that, I would blacken my reputation. The short of it is, Miss Fanshaw, I don't want to marry you—and if you know what is good for you, *you* wouldn't want to marry me either. Which is why I am leaving it up to you to cry off.'

She gaped at him. It was her turn to be nervous. 'Cry off?'

His eyes mocked her. 'That's what I said. It's very simple. You can let it be known that your forfeit was a joke, that you did it for a laugh, that you had no intention of holding me to my word. *You* will have to be the one to say it. Everyone must hear it from your own lips.'

'But I can't do that.'

'No? Pray tell me why not?'

'Because it would be a lie.'

'You mean you actually do want to marry me?'

She looked at him surreptitiously. 'Yes,' she replied—not that she had any idea what marriage to him would entail once she had caught him. 'I will not withdraw the forfeit.'

She would not beg him to wed her. Nor would she back down. But what a disaster she had made of it. She must have been out of her mind to think she could manage this. With that characteristic recklessness with which she tackled everything in her life, she had rushed to accept his wager without much thought to how he would react should she win the race and request his forfeit. But it was too late now. She had set the ball rolling, so to speak, and she would not back out now.

'When I named the forfeit, why did you concede by going so far as to announce our engagement?'

'Because at the time I did not take your proposal seriously. I thought you were playing some kind of mischievous game—that it was some light-hearted jest, that in some twisted way you were trying to get back at me for what you accuse me of doing to your father. I merely entered into the spirit of things. Naturally I believed you would withdraw your ridiculous proposal and it could be laughed off with no ill feeling.'

Beatrice met his look squarely. 'You do not know me. You were wrong to think that.' She glared at him. 'It was no twisted, mischievous game, Lord Chadwick. I have thought long and hard about this. Perhaps now you will realise that I was being deadly serious. Besides, after asking you to marry me in front of an audience, the scandal will be being broadcast throughout London as we speak. If you refuse to marry me, I will have ruined any chance I might have had of making a suitable marriage.'

'That is unfortunate for you, but it is entirely your own doing. It does not concern me.'

'I accept that, but you could do a lot worse than marry me. I have nothing of my own to bring to a marriage, but both my parents were well connected. I meet a gentleman's criteria of youth, good health, breeding,

I am reasonably pretty, or so I've been told, and I have an unblemished reputation.'

Julius raised a sardonic brow at her self-praise and contemplated her wickedly gleaming green eyes. 'I am impressed, but you failed to mention problematical, as bold as brass and as determined as they come.'

She smiled. 'I admit that I can be troublesome on occasion, but on the whole, you can have no objections to my suitability.'

Julius's expression was one of disbelief. He looked her over carefully, as if to judge her for her worth, and appeared dubious as he crinkled his brows. 'No objections—' he retorted sharply, then bit back the rest of his words, clenching his jaw so tightly a muscle jerked in the side of his cheek. 'I have plenty, Miss Fanshaw, and I can imagine Lady Standish will have some of her own to add. How will your esteemed aunt receive your outlandish proposal to me?'

'She will be livid, I expect. You see, where my aunt is concerned, as an impoverished orphan she has never had any regard for me. I am a duty she is forced to endure. In her world, marriages are arranged for consequence and money. She has you in her sights for Astrid. Not only are you outrageously wealthy, but you are also a marquess and we haven't had one of those in the family before, so she sees it as advancing the family cause.' She cocked her head on one side and looked at him steadily. 'Would you have offered for Astrid? Did my aunt read your attentions toward Astrid correctly?'

'Good Lord, no. Miss Standish is exquisite and quite charming, but she is not to my taste.' Julius meant it. To anyone with experience, Astrid Standish's mere prettiness could not hold a candle to Beatrice Fanshaw's raw kind of beauty. Miss Standish could prove troublesome in her own way, but she was very definitely not the same sort of trouble Miss Fanshaw would be. He would never be bored with her, that was for sure. 'In any case, you have spiked your aunt's ambitions well and truly with this outrageous escapade.' Suddenly curious to know more about this self-contained young woman, although he couldn't for the life of him think why, he said, 'Why does she resent you?'

'I think she sees me as some kind of threat to Astrid. Against her wishes, my uncle took us in when my mother and I had nowhere else to go. To add to our difficulties my mother was very ill. Her illness began immediately after my father died. Aunt Moira didn't go out of her way to make us welcome. When my mother died she would have turned me out were it not for my uncle.'

'I'm sorry,' Julius said, his tone suddenly sympathetic. 'That must have been an awful time for you when you lost your mother. I am not unacquainted with death and loss,' he said, thinking of the loss of his own mother. 'I have not forgotten the pain of it. How was your relationship with your uncle?'

'He always treated me kindly. Before he died he made Aunt Moira promise to do right by me: to maintain me as one of her own children, to bring me out into society and to ensure that the man I married was suitable. I suppose she considers she has kept this promise as well as her nature will permit, but as soon as my uncle died she made it plain that I should not think myself on an equal footing with my cousins. How could she like or accept an irksome alien, someone inferior and unconnected to her by any tie, an intruder on her own family?'

The softening of her manner enhanced her beauty and Julius boldly and appreciatively stared at her hard for several moments. There was a forlorn, lost look about her and he sensed she bore a deep inner pain and bitterness that had driven her to where she was now. In fact, he saw in her that which was in himself, and *that* something stirred, something moved that had not moved in a long time. It came unbidden, unexpected, born of the bleakness of his own life. Over the years he'd stifled that feeling as best he could, but it had been there just the same, telling him how he felt, and it was ridiculous, totally ridiculous, for with so much to do his life was full. But always there was something not quite right, something missing from his life.

'I can see your life at Standish House has not been easy and that you do indeed need rescuing,' he said softly.

'I have become accustomed to it.' She gave him a sideways, almost coy look. 'Will you be my rescuer, Lord Chadwick?'

He considered her remark in silence. Perhaps he should rescue her from her predicament. After all, if it wasn't for his father, she wouldn't be in this position, so maybe he should accept her marriage proposal. 'Tell me. Why do you want to marry me so badly?'

'You know why. Because you own Larkhill.'

'Yes, I thought that might have something to do with it,' he remarked drily.

'But I have no money. I can't afford Larkhill. I have nothing save what my aunt chooses to give me, which is very little, therefore it is up to me to provide for myself. I will no longer be a burden to my aunt. I can no longer submit to her opinion as a matter of course. In short, Lord Chadwick, I have decided to be my own advocate and make my own case.'

'Will that be such a hardship for you?'

Beatrice detected a mild concern in his voice. 'I hope not. I am indeed at your mercy. After this I cannot stay here. My aunt will cut me off from all connection with her family because I dared ask you to marry me. If you refuse to do this, I shall have to find somewhere else to live and an occupation to support myself.'

His eyes held hers in an enquiring glance. 'What you really mean is that your pride won't let you show defeat.'

She bristled at his light, mocking tone. 'After this I shall be regarded as low as a fallen woman—a helpless and defenceless female.'

Her words were so inappropriate he laughed out loud. 'Helpless and defenceless be damned. A woman who can ride as you do and beat me at my own challenge, a woman who can ask a man to marry her and when he rejects her can still lift her head with fire in her eyes, is not what I would call helpless or defenceless. I salute your courage and your boldness, Miss Fanshaw. You are undeniably brave—and reckless. But you are being selfish in throwing your desirable self at me, daring me to take advantage of you because you want something badly enough. You are playing with fire and it is inevitable that at some time you will be burned. I am unwilling to satisfy your wicked schemes and am most reluctant to take advantage of you—though God knows I would like to and you fully deserve it.'

'I don't know if I should be flattered or insulted by that remark, Lord Chadwick,' Beatrice retorted, her cheeks flushed with indignation.

'Take it either way. It is immaterial to me. So, it all boils down to the fact that you want to marry me for my money.'

'Your wealth does make marriage to you more palatable.'

'You don't have to go to such lengths as to tie yourself to me for life to return to your former home. When I asked you if you would demand Larkhill as the forfeit I recall you saying it would be nothing as fine or as grand as that—which makes me feel decidedly inferior that you consider me less important than a house.' He gave her a steady look. 'Why settle for me?'

'Because I need you—your money—to restore Larkhill to what it was. You have neglected the property sorely since you took it from my father.'

Shrugging himself away from the wall and thrusting his hands deep into his pockets, he began to pace. 'I understand your resentment. It can't be a comfortable situation for a woman like you, a young woman robbed of her own family, yet with your whole life ahead of you. While ever you live with your aunt you are in

Astrid's shadow—you, who are the more beautiful of the two.'

Beatrice was so humiliated by his reference to her plight that her heart clenched with the truth of it. It was such a bleak and accurate summary of her life that she almost choked at the future that opened up before her. 'That's how it is for a lot of women,' she said, stung into honesty, 'especially when a woman finds herself without a family of her own. It's not what one would choose. I don't like it and I decided long ago to find my own way out—hence the wager. Do you have family, Lord Chadwick?'

He shook his head. Pain and desolation entered his eyes, but it quickly disappeared and his expression was suddenly guarded. 'No, Miss Fanshaw, I do not. From the moment I saw you I realised that we might have something in common. Like me, you like to make your own choices. I owe no man a living and I owe no woman a duty. In short, I am my own man, free to do as I choose. That's the way I like it and how I want it to remain.'

'It's different for a woman.'

'I know. But if all you want is to return to Larkhill, you don't have to marry me.'

'No?' She looked at him warily. 'It seems to me, Lord Chadwick, that you are trying to wriggle out of your promise. You really are going to renege on your word, aren't you?' She took a deep breath, her eyes flashing daggers. 'Very well. I can't force you to marry me. Now, I think you'd better leave.'

When she tried to sweep past him, his strong hand

gripped her arm and spun her around. He hadn't known her twenty-four hours and yet somehow she already showed a talent for clouding his cool calculation. He shouldn't be angry with her—not when he was the one hiding too many dark and brooding secrets. It was himself he should be angry with.

'Devil take it, woman, I don't want to marry you! I'm not the marrying kind. I'm no good for you. Can't you get that through that beautiful head of yours?'

Suddenly he seemed enormous and very close to Beatrice. His powerful body emanated heat, matching the heat that was rising in her cheeks. 'I don't want to marry you, either. You are nothing but a—a barbarian. But I will not withdraw the forfeit. I will not make it easy for you. It is up to you to extricate yourself in whichever way you see fit.'

His eyes blazed. 'Barbarian? Lady,' he warned, his voice hoarse with fury above her, 'as yet I haven't even begun to act the barbarian. If you insist on marrying me, then let me warn you in advance that I have learned from an expert how to make a wife's life a living hell.'

His hold on her arm tightened and he looked at her for a long moment. She was so lovely, cool, virginal and stunningly arousing—and the most hair-raising woman he had ever met. He could feel himself responding, a fact that only inflamed his anger. Slowly, with menacing deliberation, he backed her against the shadowy garden wall. His grip wasn't painful, but the casual strength in his fingers was unyielding and made it impossible for her to escape his grip despite her struggle.

'Take your hands off me,' she snapped to cover her growing alarm. Giving up her futile struggle, she glared murderously at the angry light glinting in his eyes. 'How dare you call yourself a gentleman when you go around molesting women?'

'Only those who stupidly believe they can get the better of me,' he said between his teeth. 'I'm merely trying to assure you that you don't want to be my wife—to give you a taste of what you will be up against if you continue with this farce.'

One hand rose to grasp her chin, but Beatrice turned her face away, eluding capture. When his hard fingers at last closed over her jaw, she gasped with fury. 'Stop it. Do you hear me? Don't you dare hurt me! Kindly take your hands off me!'

Julius stared down at her. He hadn't missed the flare of temper in her eyes, or the fright. 'I've never hurt a woman in my life. But I mean to convince you to reconsider the forfeit you demand from me.' His gaze dropped to her soft lips, then slid lower, following the line of her throat down to the tantalising mounds beneath the soft fabric of her shirt. With her head thrown back, they quivered and thrust forwards invitingly, emphasising the undeniable fact that she was an alluring woman.

As he released her chin, his fingers unintentionally brushed her breast. He was instantly aware of the contact. So was she—he could tell by the furious blush that rose to her cheeks.

Beatrice tried to ignore the effect of his touch.

'Release me this instant,' she demanded heatedly. 'Kindly remove your hands.'

It was a supremely proper response—prim, restrained, ladylike, just the kind he would expect from a woman of her social standing, who had been taught to hold the physical side of marriage in aversion. 'Why? Don't you want me to touch you?' he murmured, deliberately running his fingers along the line of her jaw. She was so close that he could smell the fragrance of violets in her hair. 'Don't you know that as my wife I shall be able to touch you where I like and when I like, that you must accept my attentions no matter how repugnant you find them to be? Shall I give you a taste of what to expect when I exert my husbandly rights?'

Drawing her rigid body closer, he pressed it against his, and the sensation of her soft body and her slender legs encased in breeches moulded to his own acted on him like a powerful aphrodisiac. Desire surged through him, heating his blood, sending it singing through his veins, and then his mouth crushed hers with a controlled expertise that left her gasping, shocking her with his arousing warmth.

Julius finally raised his head. 'Consider it, Miss Fanshaw. You will have to learn to enjoy my lovemaking,' he warned, 'to be available to me whenever I want you, so if you still insist on being my wife, perhaps you should start enjoying it now.'

Still reeling from his devastating kiss, Beatrice stared up at him, two bright spots of colour highlighting her cheeks. His voice had suddenly grown husky with sensuality.

Julius's smouldering eyes stared back at her. She knew what he was doing and why he was doing it. If he was trying to destroy her resistance, he was succeeding. When he fitted his body to hers, she tensed with a mingling of dread and wanton longing. She hardly had time to catch her breath before his mouth descended on hers once more and his tongue plundered the inner softness in a fierce, brutal kiss that was meant to punish and humiliate her.

Rigid with fury, she clawed and squirmed against him, trying to break his hold and to drag her mouth away from the fierce possession of his lips. Her struggle only seemed to encourage him on his course of persuasion and he deepened the kiss. His arm went around her, his hand cupping her buttocks to bring her hips even closer to his. Raising his head a fraction, he murmured, 'I would take my pleasure of you any time, at my leisure, any time I choose. I would make you moan for me,' he rasped against her lips, 'moan with pleasure.'

Beatrice shuddered, seeing something primitive and terrifying flare in his eyes as his arms tightened. She jerked back, a protest rising in her throat, but his lips stifled her voice with a demanding insistence that stunned her into immobility. She had never even imagined what it would be like to be kissed—at least not in the way Julius Chadwick was kissing her, with his mouth moist and parted, warmly tasting hers, his tongue parting her lips to probe and explore with a hungry ardour and an inflaming expertise that rendered her weak.

Mindlessly she slid her hands up his chest, trying to cling for support to the very object that was destroying her balance. Confused and lost in a haze of nameless yearnings, she raised herself up on her toes, responding to the forceful pressure of his arms.

Julius groaned in response, deepening his kiss as she moulded her body against his. Her breath was so sweet, the feel of her so good he felt himself respond with that part of him that didn't give a damn about his mind, which was telling him to tread with care. In his mind he knew that what he had intended wasn't working. He was driving himself insane and losing the battle for control.

Recollecting herself when a small lance of sanity entered her mind and made her wonder at her behaviour, Beatrice tore her mouth free. She was horrified by what was happening, what he was doing to her. She should have found his kiss repulsive, but in truth she found it wildly exciting and found it hard to keep her world together. It was as if she had drunk too much wine and was giddy from it. What was the matter with her? She was neither a tippler nor a woman of easy virtue. She was a virgin, for heaven's sake. In her fury she pushed against him with all her strength. She must be out of her mind to think she could do this, could manage this charade—and him. Julius Chadwick was more than she'd bargained for.

'You beast,' she hissed. 'You filthy beast.' As she wiped the moisture from her mouth with the back of her hand, sparks of indignation flashed in her eyes. 'How dare you lay your hands on me?'

Julius stared at her as if seeing her for the first time. She was wide eyed and vulnerable and trembling. And lovely. Dear Lord, she was so damned lovely. He wanted her with a fierceness that took his breath away. His strategy to make her change her mind had backfired with a vengeance. He had begun by trying to frighten and threaten her and had ended up with his own resolutions threatened instead.

'Come now, Miss Fanshaw,' he managed to say mockingly, laughing lightly, though he himself was shaken by the moment. 'You needn't be so indignant or feel insulted.' A smile twitched at the corner of his mouth. 'It was only a kiss. You must have been kissed before. I told you, if you really do want to be my wife, that is something you will have to get used to. It's as well you know that I'm an amorous man. I would not take kindly to having a cold and unwilling partner in my bed.'

He still had his arms about her and he could feel contempt written in her straight back and imperious head. At that moment she was feeling insulted and degraded and her posture was implying that if he knew what was good for him he would go away and never come back. But no matter how much she wanted to utter the words, too much was at stake for her to utter them.

Julius let her go so abruptly that she staggered back a step, then he drew a long, audible breath. She glared at him. 'How dare you do that to me? No doubt you will say I was asking for such treatment.'

His mobile mouth twisted into a grim smile and

Beatrice had the fleeting impression that he was struggling for composure, as she was. Before this he had been a man unknown to her. She had not thought of him as anything but the man who had ruined her father and taken Larkhill and how she could use him to get it back. She'd had no reason to think of him in intimate terms. Now she saw him as a strong, attractive man who was unsettling her. For the first time in her life she felt unsure of herself.

Julius studied her, grudgingly thinking how magnificent she was. Her mouth had been sweet, warm and moist, and he was impatient to repeat the kiss. In her madness she had fought him like a lioness, and yet there had been a moment in that frenzied kiss when she had leaned against him as though the strength had gone from her and he had felt her hands, instead of clawing at him, hesitate and then slide up his chest and cling to his shoulders as though to steady herself in the havoc that washed over them both. He felt slightly bewildered by her now, almost bewitched.

'You made a grave mistake when you asked for my forfeit,' he said finally. 'However, after saying that, I don't think either of us can deny that we are *drawn* to each other.' Forcing himself to remain calm, he caught her glittering gaze and held it. 'I think we both know what we want, don't we?'

Beatrice scrutinised his expression warily. Her feelings were nebulous, chaotic, yet one stood out clearly— frustrated desire. She hadn't wanted him to stop kissing her. But she would not give him the satisfaction of letting him know that. Holding his gaze, she drew in a slow breath, then shook her head. 'No.'

'Liar,' he uttered quietly. 'Your eyes tell a different story.' Turning from her, he took a moment to reflect on her strong will, a quality he admired. He could not escape the fact that Beatrice Fanshaw had intrigued him from the moment he had laid eyes on her. She had no artificial airs and graces and possessed a kind of courage about her that was unusual in a woman. She was also proud and independent, with bold, forthright ways, but he considered that in the matter of the forfeit she had acted foolishly. Looking at her now, Julius felt her breathtaking beauty quicken his very soul, stirring his mind with imaginings of what life married to her would be like. He was fiercely attracted to her, yet because of the secrets he was carrying he would have to try to fight the attraction.

'There is another alternative to you becoming my wife. I have an offer to make to you.' He saw her eyes cloud with wariness and distrust at the word 'offer'. 'It is a proposition of a different kind. Once you've considered it, I think you will agree that it would be a sensible arrangement for us both.'

'What sort of proposition?' she asked with clinical, cautious calm.

'That you become my mistress.'

Beatrice was so surprised that all she could do was stare at him. After several moments of digesting what being his mistress would involve, she fixed him with indignant, angry eyes. 'You want me to become your mistress?'

'Good Lord, no!' Julius took a deep breath, trying to keep his calm. 'I don't need a mistress any more than I need a wife. But I feel obliged to offer a solution to the dilemma you have so foolishly created for us both. Do you think I consider this lightly?'

His contemplation was steady. He remained silent when she moved away from him, giving his proposal careful thought. She moved with the natural grace of one who led an active life and bore nothing of the affected daintiness and fragility so often displayed by beauties of the *ton*. There was a sureness in her stride that lent smooth, fluid grace to her every movement. Julius admired everything about her; he had already set a price in his mind and only waited the moment.

At length she turned back to him and scowled. 'So I was right. You *are* trying to wriggle out of it,' she accused sharply.

'I am merely suggesting another option, one in which neither of us has to commit ourselves. I am sure that despite our many differences we would be compatible sexually. You share my bed and in return for that you will have your own house and carriage and horses. You will have your own maid, a butler and servants, gowns and expensive baubles by the dozen. In short, I will be most generous. While you remain my mistress, you will have enough money to live like a queen—providing no other man gets to share what I am paying for.'

'I don't care for baubles,' she said at length, 'although a house of my own appeals to me. Kindly enlarge on that?'

His eyes were intent. 'I would give you your heart's desire: Larkhill. Mistress or wife, you could live there—if that is what you want. What's the difference?'

Her smile was cynical. 'You may have lost the wager, Lord Chadwick, but you still have a winning way with words. There is a vast difference. As your mistress you could kick me out on a whim. My answer is no. You insult me. My aunt would be scandalised and would never allow it. And I could never accept being any man's mistress.'

He lifted his broad shoulders in a slight shrug and said in an indifferent voice, 'That is your prerogative.'

'Exactly. Lord Chadwick, are you or are you not going to honour your word given to me in the presence of others?'

His eyes boldly roamed over her body from head to toe and back to her face. 'I'm beginning to warm to the idea. Married to you, life would never be dull. When you are near me I feel there is but one thought on my mind.'

In that moment her thoughts were far from Larkhill and how her aunt would react to what she was doing; instead, they centred on the turmoil within herself. A strong feeling of doubt blasted her confidence and she was suddenly unsure of her ability to deal with Julius Chadwick.

Julius moved to stand close to her. 'Do you mean to bait me? Do you seek to punish me and, in so doing, extract your revenge for my past sins? If that is your game, then lead on. I will welcome your attention and the challenge.'

After a moment, Beatrice realised he was looking at her with a strange and tender smile on his lips. Her curiosity was piqued at his apparent ability to turn circumstances to his benefit.

'There is one thing I would like to know. What forfeit would you have asked of me had you won?'

'That was it.'

'What?'

'That you become my mistress.'

Beatrice was about to vent her indignation in his face, but suddenly his laughter rang out once more and brought quick death to her words. Strolling away from her, clasping his hands behind his back, he was as relaxed as if he were drinking with his friends in a gentleman's club. Still chuckling derisively, he turned and strolled back to her.

'I thought that might make you see the real price of your predicament. What would you have done? Would you have honoured your forfeit and become my mistress had you lost the race?'

Beatrice was surprised and shocked and intensely relieved that she had escaped such a fate, but did not show it. Taking a deep breath she nodded. 'Yes. I may be many things, Lord Chadwick, but I always abide by my word. I can only thank God and my own skill that I beat you.'

'No man or woman will ever master me, Miss Fanshaw.'

He stood gazing down, holding her eyes in a wilful use of power. Unable to look at him any longer, Beatrice averted her gaze.

'Look at me.'

Unwillingly she turned her cool, questioning eyes to his once more and found a slow lazy smile that seemed to mock her. Leisurely he passed a knuckle along the fragile bone of her cheeks. His voice was soft as he continued, but it held a note of determination which in an odd way both frightened and angered her.

'Whatever madness has driven you to this, one thing I can promise you is that the misery you have endured since your father lost Larkhill will be as nothing compared to what your life will be like married to me. Consider it and think on it carefully. As my wife you will be at my beck and call night and day—in my bed and out of it. You will be my wife not only in the eyes of the law, but in every other way as well. So between now and the day when we say our vows, ask yourself if that damned house is worth it.'

Beatrice watched him walk away. Slowly, a warm flush of triumph permeated her being. She had achieved her object, and however Julius Chadwick viewed her, he was not a willing suitor. But as she walked back to the house her thoughts were jumbled, for despite his role in her misfortunes, she had a grudging admiration for him. He was not a man to flinch from duty and that was why he had achieved so much in his life.

Despite her anger and resentment she had to concede that courage and strength ran through his veins, a strength that was in his character as well as his body. She had come away from their encounter with a feeling that he was an isolated, lonely figure without a family of his own. Surely such a handsome man should not be alone. Well, maybe it was high time he had a wife, and, with that thought and a reputation for walking on the wild side, she fully intended to turn his life upside down. If this was how she would get her revenge, then there could be worse things.

But, she reflected, despite their unsatisfactory exchange, she owned he had many good qualities, and deep down she was quite excited at the prospect of being his wife.

George told Astrid about the outcome of the race and the forfeit Beatrice had asked of Lord Chadwick. Appalled and deeply concerned by what her cousin was doing, Astrid went in search of her. Not until the salon door had closed behind them did she speak.

'I know what happened. George told me. But—Lord Chadwick? How can you possibly marry him after the harm he has done you in the past?'

'I know, but I am going to marry him, Astrid. He agreed to the forfeit.'

Astrid frowned as she tried to comprehend Beatrice and her actions. 'But—you could make Larkhill your forfeit without going to such lengths as to marry him to get it.'

Beatrice looked at Astrid with something like pity. 'No, Astrid. What good would that be? Unlike you I have no dowry and am loathe to let your mother pay for one. She is determined to make me see my place. To obtain Larkhill I must first make myself Lord Chadwick's wife. Without wealth of my own, in no time at all I would be forced to sell it. This way I can have it all: money and Larkhill.'

'And Lord Chadwick? You speak as if he has nothing to do with it, yet he will be your husband—a man who will be hard to ignore.'

'You should look on it as a favour, Astrid. With Lord Chadwick out of the way, you mother will cease pressurising you on the matter. Although if she had succeeded in pulling off the match, he would have soon seen through you,' Beatrice said gently.

Astrid's head shot up. 'Why, what do you mean by that?'

'I don't think he is the kind of man to marry a woman who is in love with someone else.' Astrid blushed a deep scarlet. Beatrice smiled. 'I thought as much. Anyone can see—and I know I am not wrong. You are glowing like a maid in springtime; every time Henry Talbot looks at you he looks as if he wants to eat you alive. I would put a fortune on you being in love with him. I am not wrong, am I, Astrid?'

She shook her head. 'No. Henry and I have known one another all our lives, yet it is only recently that we have become close and acknowledged the depth of our feelings for each other. But with Mama being like she is, we have had to be careful not to show it.'

'You're to be congratulated, Astrid. Even I did not suspect—until your birthday party.'

'That's because your head is always filled with other things and you walk about in blinkers, seeing nothing but what is ahead of you.'

Beatrice lowered her head. 'I'm sorry, Astrid. I don't

mean to. And please don't be ashamed of me for what I am about to do. Where Larkhill is concerned, I am prepared to throw everything—even my immortal soul—into the battle to get it back.'

'Your desire to have your home returned to you must be very powerful indeed if you will go to such lengths as to marry the man who took it away from you in the first place.'

'You will never know how powerful. And as for you, you must talk to your mama. When she realises how things really are between you and Henry, perhaps she will relent.'

'Thank you, Beatrice, but somehow I don't believe Mama will consent to a marriage between us.'

'Get George on side. He might be able to talk her round.'

At that moment the door opened and Aunt Moira came in. Her face was like a stone. Beatrice breathed in deeply. Best get this over with, she thought.

Chapter Four

'Well?' Lady Standish demanded. 'What have you got to say for yourself, Beatrice? Too ashamed, are you? I am simply astounded that not only did you ask Lord Chadwick to marry you, but you practically demanded that he do so. You have behaved in a thoroughly deceitful manner and I will not have it. In one fell swoop you have broken all the rules.' Beatrice raised her head and looked at her aunt defiantly, which increased her wrath. 'How dare you humiliate me and make me look foolish in society? How dare you?' She was puce with anger and her voice rose until she was almost screeching.

'I understand that your feelings are hurt and I am sorry to have caused you so much distress, Aunt Moira,' Beatrice uttered stiffly.

'Distress? That is putting it mildly,' Lady Standish said, her aristocratic voice dripping with disdain. 'Of course as your guardian I can stop this. You do realise that, don't you?'

'But why would you want to?'

'To stop you making a fool of yourself and this family. What will you do if I don't allow it?'

Both women were facing each other. Beatrice refused to be bowed. Her sense of outrage kept her anchored to the floor.

'I'll do as I wish. You cannot stand in my way. Of late I've done a lot of thinking. I am eighteen years old—a woman—and I shall decide my own destiny. Ever since I came to live here you have wanted me off your hands. I am happy to oblige you.'

'Enough,' Lady Standish ordered. 'I am your aunt! How dare you speak to me in this disgraceful manner? I have indulged you overmuch. What other reason can there be for such behaviour? You owe me your respect. For shame! Must you always think of yourself, you insolent, ungrateful girl? You have planned this from the start. Oh, I am not deceived by you, Beatrice. You have wanted him for yourself ever since we returned from London. You seek to deny Astrid the privilege of winning his favour.'

'Lord Chadwick never had any intention of offering for Astrid. And Astrid would not favour a proposal from him anyway, feeling as she does about Henry Talbot.' She looked to where her cousin sat shrinking in a chair, watching and listening to the heated words between her mother and her cousin. 'Is that not so, Astrid?'

'I—I do have feelings for Henry,' she confessed,

which was a brave thing for her to say, for, like all young ladies of her social class, Astrid had been taught since childhood that her duty as a daughter was to marry in accordance with her parents' wishes. 'I don't want anyone else, Mama,' she said in a tear-clogged voice. 'I want Henry.'

The admission was made with such humble, hopeless misery that anyone but the hard-hearted Lady Standish would have been moved by it. Instead she glared at her. 'I think Henry Talbot presumed on your friendship and the freedom his parents have allowed him to dally at Standish House in the hope that something would come of his association with you. He is naïve to think so. That will never happen. You would be marrying beneath you.'

'I do not think Squire Talbot would care to have his son regarded as just anyone,' Beatrice dared to say. 'Henry is a fine man. He may look naïve, but I'll wager he'll make the best husband for Astrid.'

Lady Standish fixed her ice-cold eyes on her niece, her mouth twisting with derision. 'A farmer? I don't think so.'

'There is nothing to be ashamed of in that,' Beatrice argued. 'Henry loves the land and farms his father's acres tirelessly.'

'But as a younger son it will never be his. I do not like speaking ill of Squire Talbot for we have been friends and neighbours for more years than I can remember, but you deviate, Beatrice. This is not about Astrid, but about you.' Beatrice moved towards the door, but Lady Standish barred her way. 'Where are you going?'

'To my room.' With defiance Beatrice walked round her.

'And Lord Chadwick? I warn you, Beatrice. You go to him with nothing. I will not provide you with a dowry. You are a nobody and as such he will regard you like a plaything and soon tire of you and marry someone else.'

Beatrice turned from the doorway and looked back at her aunt, her brows raised in questioning sarcasm. 'Will he? And you are sure of that, are you, Aunt Moira? And this is the man you wanted for Astrid, is it—for your own daughter? Then consider yourself fortunate that he is marrying me instead.'

Beatrice was in the hall when Lord Chadwick was admitted the following morning. Their eyes met. His mood was again mocking, his eyes devouring, hers nervous and uncertain. Under his openly admiring regard, she flushed crimson. She heard his soft laugh, then he turned and went into the drawing room for his meeting with her aunt. As she followed him she noted that he was completely at ease and terribly confident of himself.

Lady Standish was seated in her usual chair by the hearth and did not trouble herself to rise when he entered. The turn of her head and the coldness of her smile conveyed very clearly that she did not approve of this marriage and that he should refuse to have any part of it.

'I think you are expecting me, Lady Standish,' Julius said in crisp tones, seeing Beatrice take a position away from her aunt.

'I am. Please be seated.'

'No, thank you,' his hard, confident voice replied. 'I am content to stand.'

'As you wish. I am interested to know your opinion about this outrageous situation concerning my niece. I am sure you will agree that her conduct is shocking.'

'I do agree, Lady Standish.' He glanced at the young woman in question with a mocking smile lightly curving his lips, wondering how she would react if he were to tell her how he had been unable to wipe her from his mind. Memories of the way she had felt in his arms, the heady sweetness of her kiss, had kept him awake all night. What a proud, spirited beauty she was. She excited him, she shocked him, and while he did not consider himself remotely in love with her, he was in her thrall.

He was aware of what she wanted and was tempted to refuse her, but the prospect of his safe, orderly life without her horrified him. It was as if she'd bewitched him, this wicked, beautiful creature, and he could not break away.

Julius had suffered hardship and tragedy throughout his life and his emotions had been stunted, which was why he had never married. His relationships with women were about sex. Just the same, he mused as he looked at Beatrice Fanshaw, life could still deliver surprises.

It was a difficult moment for Beatrice, who did not

know what to expect. She wanted to maintain an air
of cool disdain, to face Lord Chadwick in calm defiance, but her mauled pride and an aching distrust of
the future assailed her senses. Momentarily blinded by
a rush of tears, she lowered her head, but, furious with
herself that she should display such weakness, lifted
it again and found his amber eyes resting on her with
something akin to compassion or pity. It was almost
too much for her to bear.

'Beatrice always was an underhand, quarrelsome
girl,' Lady Standish went on coldly. 'She has a tendency
to deceit and does not have the character and disposi-
tion of my own dear daughter, Astrid. You have given
some thought to her—her idea,' she said, for want of
a better word.

Beatrice knew then why she disliked her aunt so
much, for it was in her nature to wound her cruelly. No
matter how she had tried to please and obey her when
she had come to Standish House, all her efforts were
repulsed and repaid by such words as Lady Standish
had just uttered. The accusation cut her to the heart,
especially as her aunt had voiced it before Lord Chadwick. The unkindness painted her as some kind of
artful, obnoxious creature, tainting any future happiness she hoped for.

Julius considered Beatrice a moment before replying
to Lady Standish's question. 'As a matter of fact I have
given it considerable thought.'

He stared rigidly at Beatrice, his profile harsh and
forbidding. With a sinking heart she knew he was
thinking hard for some way out of marrying her; she

also knew that behind that tautly controlled façade was a terrible volcanic rage. With the silence grating on her nerves, she held herself still and waited for him to speak, his expression becoming darker and more ominous by the second.

When Julius saw her putting up a valiant fight for control, a fight she won, his temper softened. Standing before him, she looked like a proud young queen, her eyes sparkling like twin jewels.

'And have you come to the sensible conclusion that you don't suit?' Lady Standish remarked coldly.

'On the contrary,' he replied, bringing his gaze back to her, 'I think we might suit very well. In the beginning I confess to being shocked by the forfeit your niece asked of me and I did not consider it lightly. I am not usually a man of hasty decision when it concerns a lasting relationship, but I suppose you could say that Miss Fanshaw forced my hand.'

'Then you are quite mad, sir. Beatrice is no relation of mine, but you do realise that I could prevent this if I so wished?' Lady Standish rushed in, her temper getting the better of her, pushed beyond the bounds of reason by her niece's unacceptable behaviour and the scandal that would ensue. 'Beatrice is eighteen. I am her guardian until she comes of age or I consider it time that she marries.'

The room was as cold as winter in January. Julius stared at the almost demented woman, her eyes feverishly bright, her hands clenched so tightly into fists that her blue veins bulged out. She meant it, he realised. She was evidently so consumed with loathing for her niece that she would subject her to a lifetime of misery for daring to defy her by taking away the man she had selected for her own daughter.

'Why would you want to do that, Lady Standish? Because you care so much for your niece that you put her happiness first—or for spite?' he said, overstepping the bounds of politeness. 'It is obvious to me that she is no favourite of yours.' He turned his head sharply to Beatrice and studied her face as if he'd never seen her before. His granite features softened and his eyes warmed, as if he understood how humiliated she felt. 'Do you still want to go through with this?'

Beatrice gazed up into his inscrutable amber eyes and nodded. 'Yes.'

'That's all I wish to know.'

Lady Standish's face whitened at his words. 'You cannot seriously mean to go through with this—this farce of a marriage!'

A muscle twitched furiously in Julius's cheek as his angry glare took in the older woman. He loathed her at that moment. The injustice of an innocent being so harshly maligned gnawed at every chivalrous inch of his body, although he did wonder what he was getting into. 'I intend to do exactly that. From now on Beatrice will be *my* responsibility.'

'Then good luck to you is what I say, for you will need it. The girl's a liar and an ambitious schemer. She's trouble, a hellion, and you will live to regret taking her on. I will not pretend that I am happy about this ill-conceived marriage. However much it galls me, however much it denigrates my family's good name,

I must accept it. But you'll get no blessing from me,' she said, her voice tight with fury and bitterness.'

Julius's voice was scathing. 'I think we can manage to live without it.'

Lady Standish glared at her niece, noting the familiar jut of defiance in her chin. 'I cannot stop you doing this foolish thing, Beatrice. But if you do you will not get my acceptance. I will be forced to cut you off from your family and our connections. You will not get a penny from me. You will be cut off from everything you have known.'

Beatrice managed to raise her head and meet her aunt's gaze unflinching. 'I am sorry you feel that way, Aunt Moira, but I do have a right to choose my own life.'

'Choice you have, girl,' her aunt replied contemptuously. 'You have always had it, but the choice to do the right thing. If you leave this house now, you will never return. I will have nothing more to do with you. You have made your bed so you must lie in it. You will not speak with Astrid or George again. You will have no communication with them. Is that clear?'

Beatrice almost choked on the hurt this caused her, but she managed to utter, 'Yes.'

Julius's eyes had turned positively glacial during this short exchange. 'You have my guarantee that as my wife Beatrice will be supported in a manner suitable to her upbringing. It is certain she must no longer live here where she will continue to be subjected to the malice of a woman who calls herself an aunt.' These words were delivered in a cold, lethal voice, his eyes gleaming with a deadly purpose. 'Having seen for myself your unfair treatment of your niece, I suspect that, failing to get what you want, you will not hesitate to stoop to slander to soothe your wounded pride. I trust you will think twice before you resort to such vile practice. Beatrice is under *my* protection now, and believe me, you don't want to have me for an enemy.'

Lady Standish drew herself up with dignified hauteur, but exposed her fury by the way her hand gripping the arm of her chair trembled. 'Please do not threaten me in my own house, Lord Chadwick. Beatrice has only a little knowledge of the kind of man that you are, having stolen her birthright, but I have more. In time she will come to know you, to know how you treat those who dare to cross you, and then she will hate you.'

Observing the puzzled look that crossed Lord Chadwick's face, she smiled a chilling, satisfied smile, but she would not enlighten him as to what she was referring. She would save that for a later date and enjoy flinging it in his face.

'Now I would appreciate it if you would leave this instant and take Beatrice with you. Indeed, the more I look at her, the more relieved I shall feel to be rid of a responsibility that is becoming too irksome.' Seeing how Beatrice flinched under the biting remark, she was glad to know it had hit its mark. 'I can't say that she has been a pleasure to have around.'

Bemused by what she had said, Julius was pushed to ask her to explain what she had meant by it, but, impatient to leave, he turned his gaze directly to Beatrice.

Only then did he realise the gamble she had taken by taking up his wager, which, once accepted, had started off a chain of events from which there was no going back on.

By asking him to marry her she had risked throwing away not only her reputation, but her family and her home. If he refused to marry her, with no one in the world to lighten her cares, penniless, she would have to leave this bizarre household and fend for herself. As a result of that wretched game of cards, inadvertently, but effectively, her future, like his own, had been destroyed. And yet, as he looked at her, he reluctantly faced the fact that she was a far cry from a pitiable homeless waif.

His mind made up, he said with implacable finality that warned further argument would be futile, 'It is settled, then.' Looking at Beatrice, he raised a finely arched brow. 'If you have anything more to say to your aunt, please do so, then get together whatever you wish to take with you. I will wait in my carriage until you have concluded your business.'

With that he strode to the door, and Beatrice caught a glimpse of his angry, aristocratic profile, then he was gone. Having nothing else to say to her aunt, she followed him. After going to her room and gathering the few possessions that belonged to her, she left Standish House for the last time.

'Now, then,' said Julius, lounging against the rich upholstery in his elegant open carriage and crossing his long legs in front of him, 'now we can relax.' He smiled at the alarm which entered his companion's eyes when his driver proceeded to travel along the London road. 'Why, what is it?' he asked blandly. 'Is there something you have forgotten? Do you have something to say? By the look on your face I would wager that you have. Please don't disappoint me by holding it in. I would hate to see you explode with frustration.'

Perched stiffly on the cushioned seat across from him, and having spent a moment to adjust her skirts in an effort to avoid meeting his gaze, Beatrice now shot him a mutinous, measuring look. 'Believe me, Lord Chadwick, you wouldn't want to see me explode. And, yes, there is something I wish to say. I thought…'

Seeming to find amusement in her confusion, he laughed lightly. 'What? That I was taking you to Larkhill? Surely you didn't think we would live there. I'm sorry to disappoint you, but I'm afraid not. My companions left Larkhill for London earlier. I have pressing matters of business to attend to and I am in a hurry to get there myself. But take heart. I am sure you will find my country residence in Kent every bit as pleasant as Larkhill.'

Beatrice's fury, combined with her disappointment, was immense. 'I doubt it,' she snapped ungraciously, leaning back in her seat and glowering at the passing scenery. 'Larkhill was my home.'

'When we are married you will look on Highfield Manor as your home.' Withdrawing a thin cheroot from his jacket pocket, he lit it, bending his dark head and cupping his hands over the flame. Unconcernedly he blew smoke into the air.

Beatrice expelled an angry breath she hadn't realised she'd been holding and the sound made him glance at her sharply. His dark brows lifted a fraction in bland enquiry.

'Do you mind?'

'I've never seen a man smoke a cigar before,' she said. 'They—always smoke in another room.'

'May I offer you one?' He grinned at her sudden start of surprise. 'Why not? A number of ladies that I know are not averse to the odd cigar. I already know that you will dare anything. With your flair for doing the unconventional, you might acquire a taste for them.'

'I don't think I would and would be obliged if you would confine your smoking to when I am not present.'

'You may have failed to notice, but we are in an open carriage, so the smoke should not bother you. I enjoy a cigar—often—and I'm afraid that if you are to be my wife, you'll just have to get used to it.' Through narrowed eyes he looked at her appraisingly, the smoke from his cigar drifting slowly over his head. 'You already know the other things you will have to get accustomed to—you will recall the demonstration I gave you. Just look on this as another.'

'You can please yourself,' Beatrice told him loftily.

'Careful. Your temper is showing.'

She swallowed hard as his eyes bored into hers. It had not taken her long to throw good judgement aside and flare up at him. She must learn to control her temper and her feelings better. Setting her jaw, she glared at him, unconcerned, it seemed, with anything else he might have to say. Her eyes sparkled like diamonds and she was flushed and could barely speak through her tightly clenched teeth.

Her hair fell about her shoulders in a tangle of glossy waves and her anger had given her eyes a luminous quality. With the cigar clamped between teeth as white as his shirt, Julius watched her from beneath hooded lids; her closeness and the mere sight of her made him desire her, but he controlled the urge to drag her on to his side of the carriage and into his arms.

She was furious with him, he knew, for not taking her directly to Larkhill, and she was dying to loose a tirade at his head—he could see it in those glorious flashing green eyes of hers. The truth was that he really did have pressing business matters to attend to in London. He had delayed his departure and sent his valet on ahead to cancel some of his appointments so he could meet with Lady Standish.

'Really, Beatrice—I may call you Beatrice? And please, do feel free to call me Julius—must you look as if you want to run me through?' There was a cynical edge to his voice and a coldness in his eyes as he regarded her. 'I am about to deliver you from a barren future at Standish House, to give you what you want, and you are staring at me as though you wish to commit murder.'

'As long as I continue to stare at you as though I could murder you and not enact the deed, then you have nothing to worry about.'

Heading towards London, the greys paced in prime style. The drive through leafy lanes and picturesque villages in the lazy warmth of bright sunshine was uneventful. The journey dragged on in painful, unbroken silence. Beatrice could not trust herself to speak for fear she would give way to her angry emotions. She was utterly devastated that he had not taken her to Larkhill. Strongly suspecting that he had done it deliberately and was clearly amused by her disappointment increased her anger. And so he sat watching her like a hungry hawk, that having been snared by his sharp talons once, was tender bait for the second tasting.

Directing her gaze to the passing scenery, she let her mind wander over all that had occurred since the morning of Astrid's birthday party—the kiss Julius had given her being paramount. Her cheeks reddened with embarrassed heat at the memory of her own wanton response, when pleasure had seeped through the barrier of her own will.

From that moment nothing was the same. Her mind was unsettled, and for the first time in years, it had nothing to do with Larkhill. Mentally flaying her thoughts into obedience, she glanced across at the man who occupied them. His eyes were closed and his handsome face with a dark lock of hair falling on to his brow looked boyish and unguarded in repose. She wanted to reach out and touch him, to run her fingers through his thick hair, to have him kiss her as he had done yesterday.

A heaviness centred in her chest when she considered her future with Julius. Her aunt's remark about how, in time, she would come to hate him still rang in her ears. She was unsettled by it and couldn't begin to understand what she had meant by it. She already knew theirs would be a marriage unlike any other—without love or even liking for one another. And yet she had discovered what it was like to be kissed by a man and her discovery had marked her physically. What would he say, she wondered, if she were to ask him to repeat his actions of yesterday? Would he be shocked? Would he mock her? Or would he be willing to oblige?

She didn't know what sort of wife she would make and had given it no thought whatsoever, but strangely, she was now looking forward to it. Although perhaps Julius would spend much of his time on one of his ships and when he was home she would be a hostess and companion in his house, but she would never be able to touch his heart—and nor did she aspire to. A brief image of cosy marital bliss faded from her mind.

And yet, battle hardened though he might be by life—toughened and with an aura of hard-bitten strength—beneath it all Julius Chadwick had exposed a streak of kindness. Today he had been kind enough to rescue her and quick enough to act immediately and whisk her away from Standish House.

When they entered the outskirts of London, to Beatrice the world suddenly became an unreal place to be. It was a blur of noise and confusion. She had only ever been to London twice in her life, once with her parents and again with Aunt Moira and Astrid. With all the attention centred on Astrid, her visit had been an unpleasant experience and she had been glad to return to the country. Now she didn't know where she was going. She knew Julius had a house in Kent, so what were they doing in London?

As if Julius could read her mind, he said, 'I should tell you that you are to reside with Lord and Lady Merrick on Upper Brook Street for the time being.'

Beatrice looked at him with alarm. So, she thought, feeling as if something were shattering inside, already he wanted rid of her. 'But why? What on earth for?'

'Because you cannot possibly stay with me, alone and unchaperoned. It will be a miracle if gossip about your behaviour over the horse race hasn't already spread; if so, it will have done you immense harm. You must be prepared for that. By the time the *on dit* have circulated, your reputation will have been shredded, and if you were to live with me everyone would assume you have become my paramour. We cannot risk that sort of gossip.'

'So you mean to place me into unfamiliar surroundings with people I don't know.'

'My dear Beatrice, you have no choice.'

The casual, empty endearment made her cheeks flame with ire. 'Please don't call me "your dear". I am not that. And I do have a choice,' she said on the spur of the moment. 'I—I could go into lodgings or something like that.'

'And just how,' he asked drily, 'do you intend to pay for lodgings? You have no money.' This was the truth and she knew it, and, short of asking him for the money, there was nothing she could do but to fall in with his plans. 'Better for you to reside with Lord and

Lady Merrick for the present than risk the social stigma of living with me.'

'And that matters to you—what people will think?'

'Personally I don't give a damn what anyone thinks about me, but I am adamant that the name that I have worked so hard to repair will not be tarnished by this.' Seeing how she was looking at him with bewildered curiosity, he went on to inform her of some basic facts.

'You may be surprised to learn that our backgrounds are not dissimilar. It is no secret that the reputation of the Chadwick family has been blackened by several in recent generations. After years of declining fortunes and a few Chadwick ne'er-do-wells—the last of them being my father—the once-proud lineage became sunk into a state of genteel poverty.'

Unaccustomed to being so open with anyone, he paused and eyed his companion, searching for signs of contempt, but read none. 'To restore the family fortunes became my goal in life. With a head for business I gambled everything in a series of investments, spotting opportunities others had missed. Fortunately they paid off—and the wars with Bonaparte brought many rich pickings for investments throughout Europe. So you see, it was my own hard work and determination that has made me what I am today.'

He had failed to mention his other gambling and Beatrice wondered how much of his wealth had been acquired in the gambling haunts of Europe.

'And are you like your father?'

'No, I am not,' he replied quickly, avoiding her gaze,

his expression grim. 'He was a blackguard along with his forebears.'

Taken aback by the steely undertone in his quiet reply, she stared at him in question. When he ignored her, she decided not to press him, but his apparent bitterness about his father puzzled her.

'Thank you for telling me of your achievements,' she said. 'I am impressed—who would not be—but apart from your name, that you are a marquess, extremely wealthy and have a house in Kent, I know nothing about you.'

'Then allow me to enlighten you. I have three middle names and several lesser titles I rarely use,' he told her. 'No doubt Constance—Lady Merrick—will give you a rundown of my character. I have a great deal of business to attend to so I shall not be able to give you my full attention—and I shudder to think what you might get up to left to your own devices. You really do not have the slightest concept of the importance of appropriate behaviour, do you, Beatrice? Didn't you learn anything under your aunt's tutelage?'

'Yes, but with all her attention fixed on Astrid and knowing it wasn't important how I turned out since finding me a suitable husband was not on my aunt's agenda, I could never see the point of it.'

Julius stared into her stormy green eyes and flushed face, wondering why, from the very first, she had been able to affect him like no other woman in a long time, wondering why he felt this consuming, unquenchable need to possess and gentle her without breaking her spirit.

'James and Constance Merrick are old friends of mine and very close to me,' he told her quietly. 'Don't worry. They will like you when they recover from their surprise that you are to be my wife. Constance is a woman of enormous consequence; she shamelessly adores forcing society to bend to her will. She will not permit anyone to say an unkind word to you or about you in her presence. She is an excellent example of how you ought to conduct yourself in society. You would be wise to observe her behaviour and emulate her.'

Beatrice felt like a naughty child who had just been told it must follow someone else's example. 'How long will it be before the wedding?'

'Three weeks—enough time for the banns to be read—unless you are so impatient to become my wife you would like me to apply for a special licence,' he said with a mocking twist to his lips.

'No,' she said tightly. 'Three weeks will be fine. Where will it be?'

'It will be a quiet affair, the venue of my choosing.'

'Isn't that supposed to be the bride's prerogative?'

'Not in this case. I shall let you know when it is arranged.'

He continued to converse, questioning her about herself, about her life at Standish House, her interest in horses and her relationship with George and Astrid. What he didn't do was talk any more about himself, which, in Beatrice's experience, was what most people did best, or at least most frequently, but apart from what he had told her about his father and how he had restored the Chadwick fortunes, his private life remained exactly that.

Beatrice found herself in some kind of indeterminate state, suspended not only in time but in emotion. Julius had been right about Lord and Lady Merrick. A middle-aged couple who had not been blessed with offspring, they were warm and friendly and went out of their way to make her feel welcome. Lord Merrick was a gentle, delightful soul, very much under his wife's dominance. Lady Merrick was quite tall with a majestic bearing and almost as formidable looking as Aunt Moira. She had a pair of penetrating hazel eyes and an imperious expression and always believed in speaking her mind, but Beatrice soon discovered that beneath it all she was very thoughtful, kind and warm and was genuinely pleased to have her stay with them.

'There is no need to describe to me what happened when Julius visited Standish House, Beatrice. I am well aware of it as is nearly everyone else in society. For a young lady to ask a man to marry her is not a civilised thing for her to do. But however it came about, I cannot suppress my exultation that, by your actions, it has prompted Julius to take a more serious interest in marriage. He needs my help in assisting him to introduce you into society. I have no control over wagging tongues, but I will do my very best.'

Beatrice was grateful for the time Lady Merrick took arranging her wardrobe. Julius had insisted that she be fitted out for every occasion and that no expense was to be spared, and Beatrice was shocked to find that

Lady Merrick took him at his word and visited some of the most fashionable modistes in London. She took her on shopping expeditions to Bruton Street and Bond Street and the larger warehouses of Covent Garden and the Strand.

'I am putting you to so much trouble,' Beatrice said, feeling some expression of gratitude was due after one particular heavy shopping trip. 'I realise my wardrobe was hardly up to town standards and it is indeed kind of you to give up so much of your time for me.'

'Nonsense. I enjoy doing it, so indulge me, Beatrice. Julius is the son of my dearest friend—tragically she is no longer with us. Indeed, I will even go so far as to say he is the son I never had. His happiness is paramount.'

The word 'tragic' and the sudden pain that she saw in Lady Merrick's eyes stuck in Beatrice's mind and she wondered why. Not wishing to pry, she dismissed the thought.

The society columns were full of her impending marriage to Julius and the nuptial date. News of the race had already been splashed across the front pages of the *Times* and the *Gazette* and the journalists were having a field day with the lurid gossip surrounding this very unconventional marriage.

For two weeks Beatrice saw nothing of Julius. She was afraid to think about him—certainly to feel more for him that she could possibly help. Each day she became more settled in the Merrick household—she would be loath to leave when the time came for her to go and live with Julius as his wife and in his house, wherever that may be. The more she got to know about him from Lady Merrick, the more she began to realise the enormity of what she had done. Hidden away in the country it hadn't mattered, but here in London everything was different.

Apparently women had been throwing themselves at Julius for years, all of them eager to trade themselves for his title and his wealth. When he wasn't sailing on one of his ships to some far-off location, he was sought after by every hostess in town and every ambitious mama, and treated with the deferential respect that his immense wealth and his title commanded amongst the *ton*. He abhorred the attention he drew and rarely attended any of the major social functions, for he understood and despised the reasons why he was coveted. As a result his attitude towards any respectable female of his own class was cynical and jaded, and when he had time to relax away from his offices in Lombard Street, he preferred to spend it at his club in St James's with friends, or at the theatre.

'The longer he's remained unattached, the more of a challenge he's become to all unmarried females,' Lady Merrick told Beatrice as they sat nibbling buttered scones and sipping tea in the morning room, taking a well-earned break from the seamstresses, who had been stitching Beatrice into the taffetas, silks and gauzes that would equip her to be Lady Chadwick, the Marchioness of Maitland. 'Failing to find a woman who can see beyond his wealth and his title and his estates, Julius is convinced she doesn't exist. He merely tolerates those who trail after him and treats them with amused condescension; if one irritates him, he is capable of delivering a crushing set down that is guaranteed to reduce the unfortunate young woman to tears.'

'Oh dear. He is that bad? Well...' Beatrice sighed '...I am not intimidated by him and nor am I in awe of him, and I am certainly not dazzled by his rank, his wealth or his power—although I admit that his wealth was a deciding factor when I decided to ask him to marry me, since it will go some way to renovating Larkhill. I suppose you could also say that I did make it difficult for him to back out of marrying me.'

Constance Merrick believed her. Even though she had known her for such a short time, she had become very fond of Beatrice. Her husband and the servants were completely enchanted by her friendly, unaffected cordiality towards everyone.

'I knew your father, my dear, and from what I know, no doubt part of Julius's decision to accept your proposal owed itself to the fact that in some way he felt responsible for your plight.'

'Which he is,' Beatrice was quick to point out.

'Not...necessarily,' Lady Merrick said hesitantly, averting her eyes. She would have liked to defend Julius, but to do so she would have to divulge the truth about what really happened on the day Beatrice's father lost Larkhill in a game of cards—and the terrible events that had ensued. Julius had asked both her and her husband not to speak of it to Beatrice and Constance would abide by that. Three people were bound by a guilty secret, but it hurt her terribly to hear Julius wrongly maligned.

'Your father was not blameless in all of this. He was a compulsive gambler—but I am sure you know that. But that doesn't mean that things won't turn out for the best. You are a young lady of excellent character and breeding and considerable pluck. There is also a gentle strength about you, a compassion and understanding that I believe will make you the perfect wife for Julius. I know him well. I have seen the way he looks at you. He already cares for you a great deal—though he may not know it yet.'

'That is something I would question, Lady Merrick,' Beatrice murmured sadly.

'Nevertheless I suspect you will be good for him and that the two of you will pull off the best match in years.'

Beatrice gave her a truly dubious look. 'If our relationship so far is anything to go by, I very much doubt it. I think you are being too optimistic, Lady Merrick. Even Julius would challenge that statement.'

Lady Merrick chuckled softly, her eyes dancing with mischief as she enfolded Beatrice in a brief, almost protective hug. 'I have not always lived a life that was beyond reproach, Beatrice. Far from it. No matter what people are saying about you, I think that you are very brave. You, my dear, as young as you are, have managed to achieve that which all the other women can only dream about. To secure Julius.'

'Does he not have any family?'

Pain slashed Lady Merrick's features and she sat

back from her. 'He has no family, Beatrice—no one close.'

There was something in her voice that made Beatrice look sharply at her. 'No one?'

'There…was a tragedy—some years ago now—when he lost both his parents,' Lady Merrick told her hesitantly. 'There was a fire. Julius has never got over it. I do not believe he ever will.'

'But—that's truly awful. Will you not tell me what happened?'

'I think Julius must do that. But it may help you to understand what drives him. His life has not been easy. As a boy he was bright, with a thirst for knowledge that put others to shame. Even though his family was financially destitute—which was down to his father, who was a wastrel and a spendthrift—he had a good education thanks to his maternal grandmother. At the end of it he'd learned all he could about the world of business and finance, and, with a small sum of money his grandmother had given him on his eighteenth birthday, he left home for the Continent to seek his fortune and to bring some pride and honour back to the Chadwick name.

'He lost himself in his work with a blind, instinctive faith as his only hope for survival. His skills were quite extraordinary. Julius has the ability to calculate huge columns of figures in his mind in moments. His achievements are quite remarkable. Yes, he gambles—it is the challenge he loves best, of selecting exactly the right venture and wagering a fortune on it, not, as you believe, at the tables. His wealth has brought him many luxuries, but little joy. That is something I would like you to remember, Beatrice, in the days ahead.'

With her mind on what Lady Merrick had told her, knowing she had given her much to think about, Beatrice's heart gradually began to fill with warmth for the man whose name she was soon to bear. True, he was guarded and frequently distant and unapproachable, but the more she contemplated the matter, the more convinced she became that Lady Merrick was right—Julius must care for her a little, or he'd never have succumbed to her forfeit. But in the light of all this, the one thing that didn't make sense was his reputation as a gambler. None of what she had been told fitted with the man who had gambled and won Larkhill from her father.

'He never speaks of his past,' Lady Merrick went on. 'He is a private person. He refuses to discuss his personal life—not even with me and my husband, even though we are the closest he has to a family of his own. Julius is a man of impeccable integrity, honour, dignity and respect. His mother meant everything to him. He has been much affected by her death and by the world in such ways as few others are. He is a clever man and true to what he believes. You could not be marrying a finer man.'

Chapter Five

Julius called the next day as Beatrice was leaving the drawing room to go up to her room.

'I do hope you're not leaving on my account,' said a deep unperturbed voice behind her.

Beatrice whirled in surprise. The pleasure at seeing him again after so long and being able to speak to him was eclipsed by her growing panic about the forthcoming nuptials, a panic she'd been trying unsuccessfully to stifle for days. He stood in the centre of the hall, a tall, slender-hipped, broad-shouldered man. Attired in a tan jacket, buff-coloured breeches and Hessian boots, Julius Chadwick was as handsome of physique as he was of face. His chiselled features were touched by the light, and a gentle ache in her bosom that grew and grew attested to the degree of his attractiveness.

'I wasn't—I mean, I'm not,' she said falteringly, walking towards him.

Shoving his hands into his pockets, he regarded her with mild curiosity. 'I apologise for not calling on you before now, but I had several pressing matters of business to attend to. Since I have no engagements this morning, I thought I would come and see how you are bearing up.'

His tone was impeccably polite, impersonal and businesslike. Relieved but wary, Beatrice's reply was coolly polite, but when she raked her copper curls back from her face, her hand was shaking. 'Perfectly well, as you see.'

Watching her unconscious gesture, Julius did see and he studied her. Sunlight slanting through the windows glinted on her hair, gilding it with a golden sheen, and turned her magnificent eyes luminous bright green. The deep yellow of her gown flattered her creamy complexion and the peach tint glowing in her cheeks.

In a long-suffering voice, Beatrice said, 'Will you please not look at me like that?'

'Like what?'

'As if you're searching for all my flaws.'

'Was I doing that?' he asked absently, noting her high cheekbones, the delicately arched brows, thick sooty lashes and the fullness of her soft lips.

'Yes, you were and it makes me feel uncomfortable.'

His eyes took on a sudden gleam of suppressed laughter and Beatrice assumed, mistakenly, that he was laughing at her. She lifted her chin to its haughtiest and most obstinate angle. 'Don't do it and will you please take me seriously.'

Julius sobered immediately at her imperious tone. 'I'm going to marry you. That's serious enough— although it's hardly the most auspicious start to a marriage and don't imagine for one minute that it will be smooth sailing.'

Lady Merrick appeared and fussed over his arrival and ushered them into the drawing room while she went to supervise the unpacking of some of Beatrice's gowns that had just arrived.

Closing the double doors behind them, Julius waited for Beatrice to be seated. Instead of sitting down, he perched a hip on the arm of a chair opposite, crossed his arms over his chest and studied her impassively.

'You are comfortable here, I hope.'

'Yes, thank you. Lord and Lady Merrick have made me feel very welcome.'

'I knew they would, but if you are to be my wife you have to face society some time. Since you have a scandal hanging over your head I suggest the sooner we are seen together the better. For your first public appearance I have accepted an invitation for us to attend the Earl and Countess of Newland's ball in St James's at the end of the week.'

Beatrice paled at the mention of the scandal. 'I can't. I have no desire whatever to enter society. I can't face everyone just yet.'

'You can and you will,' he said in his determination to convince her of the feasibility and the necessity of the plan.

Unable to endure his close scrutiny, Beatrice shot out of the chair and, ramrod straight, stood apart from him. With a superhuman effort, she took control of her rampaging ire. She looked straight into his enigmatic eyes. 'A ball is not a solution. It—it's a nightmare. I really don't think I can do that—not with everyone talking about me. I shall encounter curious strangers who will watch my every move, searching for something else to gossip about. I can't do it.'

'Yes, you can.' He spoke in a tone that brooked no argument.

'And it doesn't concern you that I shall be flayed alive by wagging tongues?'

Unbelievably, he laughed outright at that. 'Not a bit. You deserve it.'

His remark made her cheeks flame. It was exactly the sort of thing she would have expected him to say as an act of revenge. 'And I have no doubt that you will enjoy every minute of my suffering.'

Relinquishing his perch on the chair arm, he stood up straight and captured her gaze. 'I may be many things, Beatrice, but I am neither cruel nor sadistic. Of course, you don't have to go through with any of this. You could bring it to an end right now and simply walk away. It's not too late to cry off.'

'No.' She was adamant. 'How pathetic and desperate I must seem to you if, after all I have put myself through, you could even suggest such a thing and believe I would go along with it. I told you, Julius, if you want to back out of our agreement then you have to do it yourself, for I have no intention of walking away now I have come this far.'

Julius shrugged. 'Then it looks like we're stuck with each other—for better or worse.'

'That's *exactly* what it looks like. But do not forget that in the eyes of the *ton* I am a shameless wanton and unfit to mingle in polite society. I have broken all the rules governing moral conduct, so if you still insist on parading me in front of everyone like some—some performing puppet, then go ahead.'

Julius gazed at the tempestuous young woman standing before him, her breasts rising and falling with suppressed fury, and his ire gave way to reluctant admiration for her honesty and courage in admitting her fear over the coming event.

'Perhaps now you will realise what you have done. Your case is extreme. Normally social prejudices exclude young women like you from the *ton*—not that you cared much about that or about what they would think of you when you connived to trap me. But as my wife these are the people you will have to associate with and it is absolutely imperative to me that you learn to get on with them. The object is to brave it out. You have spirit enough to endure what they will put you through. As my betrothed, no one will dare disrespect you—though Lord knows you deserve it.'

She glared at him. 'Why are you doing this? For what reason do you wish to put me on display? To further humiliate me?'

'I do not make sport of you, Beatrice. As I said, I want us to be seen together. It is important that we put the right face on our relationship. I don't normally attend these affairs, but I have no intention of my wife being a social outcast. Constance and James are also invited. The three of us will support you. No one will dare give you the cut direct in front of Constance and I will terrify everyone into accepting you.'

'But what to wear,' Lady Merrick said, sweeping into the room like a restless wind, suddenly thoughtful as her eyes moved over Beatrice from head to toe, her mind absorbed with dressing her in such a way that she would outshine all the rest. 'I would normally opt for glamour rather than subdued elegance, but since it's your first outing we don't want to go over the top. The lime-green tulle will be just the thing.'

Julius smiled his agreement, his eyes appraising his future wife. 'I agree absolutely. With that hair and those eyes, it cannot fail.'

In the carriage taking him back to his house, Julius leaned back against the upholstery, thinking over his meeting with Beatrice with fascinated interest. He was amazed by the gracious ease with which she had fitted into the Merrick household and the way she had effortlessly charmed James Merrick, bringing the house to life with her presence and her smile. She was fresh and unspoiled and, despite her youth and inexperience, there was a natural sophistication about her that came from an active mind. He remembered her shy responsiveness to his kiss in the garden at Standish House and the incredible surge of desire she had ignited in his body.

Beatrice was full of surprises and full of promise, he thought, with beauty moulded into every flawless feature of her face, but her allure went deeper than that. There was something within her that made her sparkle and glow like a rare jewel.

It seemed as if everyone in London was at the Newlands' ball. When Julius arrived at the Merrick house, Beatrice was just coming down the stairs. She paused and looked down at him. With a stunned smile of admiration, he took in the full impact of her ravishing lime-green gown. High waisted, it fell from beneath her breasts into panels that clung gently to her graceful hips and ended in a swirl just above her toes. Her hair was drawn back in a sleek chignon, its lustrous simplicity providing an enticing contrast to the sophistication of the gown.

Moving towards her, he took her hand to help her down the last steps. 'You look positively enchanting. After tonight, you'll take the shine out of all the London belles.'

Buoyed by confidence stemming from wearing her first London gown, Beatrice returned his smile, while deep inside she felt something tighten and harden, clarifying and coalescing into one crystal-clear emotion. Her cheeks were delicately flushed, her eyes alight, her parted lips moist and rose tinted. She thought Julius looked incredibly handsome in his evening attire. It made him look elegantly powerful. He had a certain flair in his mode of dress—a bold splash of claret in his waistcoat beneath the black coat, an artful twist to his pristine white cravat and a flourish to the ruffle at his sleeve. It was impossible to believe he would be her husband in just a few days.

When his shrewdly judging gaze swept over her once more, with a little laugh she obligingly performed a twirl, her skirts flaring.

His eyes warmed appreciatively. 'The gown is beautiful, Beatrice. But perfection can only be attained when one works with the best of raw materials.'

Beatrice's heart skittered. She lowered her gaze. 'I appreciate your compliments, Julius. It gives me confidence for what is to come. I think I shall need it.'

'I truly expected you to send me a note informing me you had taken to your bed with a headache and a dose of salts.'

Despite her dread of the evening before her, Beatrice had to bite back a guilty smile over that remark. 'I did consider it,' she confessed, smiling reassuringly at Lady Merrick who stood looking on, immensely proud of her handiwork. 'Lady Merrick talked me out of it.'

Julius nodded his approval. This young woman who was to be his wife was brave, immensely so. It was a slightly dangerous bravery that she possessed, but it was a quality in her that he admired. 'Everyone of importance will be at the ball and it will be a complete crush—which will work to your advantage. Hopefully, afterwards, when everyone has seen you with me, the gossip will die a death and you can get on with the business of being my wife.'

The four of them travelled in Julius's long black town coach drawn by four fiercely black horses. Less than half an hour later they arrived at the Earl and Countess of Newland's mansion, which was an outstanding example of opulence on a grand scale. They stepped into the brilliance of the interior. It was lit by a multitude of candles in countless chandeliers and crystal sconces that made the marble pillars gleam.

A grand staircase swept upwards to the first floor where the ballroom was located. Gaming tables had been set up in reception rooms for those who preferred to pass the evening in dice and cards, and another two large reception rooms had tables arranged for the customary light supper served at midnight.

Beatrice could feel the stares and whispers as she stood in the receiving line, but she was pleasantly surprised when their host and hostess greeted her warmly. As they advanced up the low, wide staircase, she had the strange sensation of helplessness and fatality that one sometimes has in a dream. In the surrounding haze she was aware of no one but Julius by her side, offering her his undeserved support. She was crushed by the weight of responsibility, for her stupidity, her gullibility, and all that those two traits had brought down on her. Almost all the unattached beautiful women she saw had probably aspired to be the next Marchioness of Maitland, but not one of them had behaved with wanton indiscretion as she had. She deserved to be ostracised.

Julius looked at Beatrice, noting her pallor. 'You look terrified,' he murmured. 'Feel like running away? I couldn't blame you.'

Beatrice took a deep breath and squared her

shoulders, knowing that if she turned back now, she would cover herself in further ridicule. 'Yes, but I won't. I've never run away from anything in my life. As a result of what I've done my dignity has taken a public flogging. But if I have nothing else, I still have my pride.'

Yes, Julius thought, pride was all she had left right now, and he hoped she would face them all down with her head held high. Taking her gloved hand, he tucked it through the crook of his arm. The flesh above the edge of her glove was cold. 'Your arm is like ice. Beatrice, I could never let anybody insult you in my presence. Rest assured of that.'

Touched by his chivalrous vow and the depth of his concern, Beatrice pinned a bright smile on her face. 'Thank you. I'll be all right,' she assured him. 'After all, I faced worse than this when I confronted you to take you up on your challenge.'

He watched her rally and manufacture a smile as she lifted her head and met his gaze. She meant it, he realised with surprise. 'Is that so?' he said with an assessing smile as he studied her upturned face. 'At least the memory of your brazen challenge has put some sparkle back into your eyes. It's unfortunate that my kiss didn't have the same effect.'

Beatrice made the mistake of looking at his mouth. She studied those lips for a second, then shook off the awareness that suddenly gripped her. She had to look away because she couldn't concentrate on what was happening around her. 'I wish you wouldn't refer to that. I'm not accustomed to having men I hardly know kiss me.'

Leaning towards her so that his mouth was only inches from her ear, he whispered, 'When you are my wife you will get to know me better. That I promise you.'

As they entered the ballroom where weaving lines of dancers were progressing in a hectic country dance, Beatrice's restless glance skimmed about her, taking stock of her first Grand Ball. A multitude of voices were raised in avid chatter. Silks and satins in bright and subdued colours paraded before her. Perfumes drifted and mingled into a heady haze as bejewelled ladies nodded and curtsied, while elegant gentlemen in superbly cut evening clothes inclined their heads.

Julius escorted her forwards. A huge sea of people seemed to press towards them and voices erupted as heads turned and fans fluttered and people craned their necks to observe the new arrivals. Although they wouldn't dream of giving Julius the cut, they looked at Beatrice with raised brows and severe disapproval. Knowing how conscious she was of the spectacle she offered, Julius lifted a couple of glasses of blood-red wine from the tray of a liveried footman and handed one to her.

'Drink this. It will put some colour into your cheeks and give you a little courage.'

Beatrice accepted the glass and took a sip.

They heard whispers from those around them. A stout, elderly woman, wearing a red-satin turban and standing close enough for them to overhear, joyfully remarked behind a beringed hand to her companion that Miss Fanshaw was so desperate to find a husband that she'd had to do the proposing herself. Another was heard to say that she remembered her when she had come to London with her cousin Astrid. Astrid was a sweet young thing, whereas Miss Fanshaw had such a high opinion of herself.

Julius knew the instant he looked at Beatrice that she'd heard the malicious remarks; because he couldn't offer her any comfort, he slid his arm about her waist and moved towards the dance floor where couples were whirling about to the lilting strains of a waltz. He felt anger and protectiveness begin to simmer inside him, emotions that leapt into steady flame as other venomous remarks reached his ears. He was unable to understand why women were driven to such heartless, vengeful jealousy.

'This is worse than I imagined,' he said, silencing one malicious female with a slicing look.

He understood why she would naturally dread being the focal point of so many fascinated gossips, but not until she actually lowered her head and bit her trembling lip did he realise that her embarrassment was going to be compounded a hundred times now she was thrust into the limelight.

He was right. Beatrice turned away from him as if she couldn't bear to be there any longer, but Julius caught her arm in a gentle but unbreakable grip. Instinct and experience told him that a little tender persuasion could vastly further her cause and he was prepared to resort to that, only if logic and honesty weren't enough to persuade her.

'Don't give them anything more to talk about and condemn you for.'

Beatrice stared at him dubiously. 'How can I possibly do that? I've done all I can to ruin my reputation before I even started and heaped more embarrassment on you,' she said, realising he was a person with feelings that could be hurt. 'I am being ridiculed, scorned and snubbed—and even pitied by some, which is the worst thing of all. I wouldn't blame you if you were to drag me out of here and take me back to Standish House—except that I can't go back there. Aunt Moira would take one look at me and laugh, say I told you so and close the door in my face.'

Julius hid his amusement behind a mask of genteel imperturbability. 'Dear me. This isn't like the reckless, devil-may-care young lady I have come to know. Am I to assume you've had a change of heart, and would like to be free of me?' he taunted gently.

She scowled up at him. 'The idea is beginning to have a certain appeal, but don't get your hopes up, Julius,' she replied stonily. 'I am fully committed.'

He laughed lightly. 'I thought you might say that.'

On the sidelines where she was conversing with an acquaintance, Lady Merrick, seeing what was happening, excused herself and marched towards Beatrice like a protective mother hen guarding her chick. She collected Lord Caruthers and his wife on her way to add to the ranks. Her back was ramrod straight and her jaw thrust forwards in an aggressive stance that dared anyone to question her judgement in lending her enormous consequence to Beatrice.

Julius shot the three of them a grateful look. Right now Beatrice was vulnerable and he didn't want to do or say anything that would make things worse. So, he ignored the instinct to reach up and brush back a wayward tress of shiny hair from her cheek and squelched the temptation to tell her that he had no intention of dragging her anywhere unless it was into his bed. He was not, however, morally opposed to diverting her resistance with as much alcohol as he could pour down her.

'Drink your wine and then we'll dance—and smile, for God's sake. If we are to beat the critics and quell the gossip, it is imperative that we put up a united front— in public at least,' he said in a steely voice that was in vivid contrast to the expression of bland courtesy he was wearing for the sake of their fascinated audience. His eyes shot to hers as an absolutely ridiculous thought suddenly occurred to him. 'You can dance, I hope?'

Beatrice wondered how he would react if she were to tell him that she hadn't danced since the dancing master Aunt Moira had employed to teach her and Astrid had left Standish House two years ago. Instead, with a sparkle in her eyes and a tilt to her head, the smile she gave him was quite sublime.

'Like a fairy,' she quipped.

Eventually, to Beatrice's relief, the flurry created by their conspicuous arrival died down. But when

Julius led her on to the dance floor and gathered her into his arms for a waltz, she wasn't at all sure she could do it, but the challenge in his amber eyes made demurring unthinkable. Giddiness threatened to take hold of her.

'Relax.' Julius looked down at her. She almost missed her step, but his arm tightened, holding her steady. 'Focus your eyes on me and follow my lead,' he said, steering her into the first gliding steps as the graceful music washed over them.

Of their own volition Beatrice's feet followed where he led and her mind opened to the sensations of the dance. She was aware of the subtle play of her skirts about her legs and the hardness of her companion's thighs against hers. The closeness of his body lent to her nostrils a scent of his cologne, fleeting, inoffensive, a clean masculine smell. The seductive notes of the music were mirrored in their movements and the sway was a sensual delight. Julius's hand at her waist was firm, his touch confident as he whisked her smoothly around the ballroom.

After looking at them attentively, the couples on the dance floor renewed their interest in the music. Conversations were resumed and everyone got on with enjoying themselves.

Julius stared down at the lovely young woman in the provocative green gown, her eyes as they observed the other dancers both wary and stormy. In the three weeks since he'd kissed her in the garden at Standish House, he'd made no further attempts to kiss her or embrace her. In his opinion he'd been a perfect gentleman—considerate, courteous, even casual—and the energy of a sexually aroused male, the need in him to make this woman totally his, went by her like the dancers whirling around.

Determined to have the lead in how their marriage was conducted, he said, 'There is something you should understand, Beatrice.'

She tilted her head to his. 'What is it?'

'When you are my wife, I expect you to behave as if you married me because we are in accord—that you care for me more than my title and my money, that you will never discredit my name or your own. What transpires between us in private is our affair. I will conduct myself publicly as if I were the most devoted and faithful of husbands. I will not knowingly do anything to cause you even a moment of humiliation, even though there will be times when you may have cause to regret our bargain.'

Beatrice stared up at him. Bargain? What bargain? her mind warned her in a quiet voice. The silent argument was overturned by the effect of a sombre, handsome face, a deep hypnotic voice and the powerful, tall and strong male body that loomed over her. Here was a man who, to her surprise, was offering to shield her from the world and shoulder her burdens. The combination of that and his good looks was becoming dangerously appealing, particularly because he wasn't offering love or even affection.

'In the eyes of the world,' he went on, 'you will be my cherished wife.'

Cherished! Beatrice couldn't believe what he'd

said. It was a word that was sensitive and sentimental. It didn't apply to what was between them and it was totally unlike anything she'd expected him to say.

'Of course,' he continued, 'it works both ways. I shall expect the same promises from you. Is that agreeable?'

His future wife bit her lip, considered for a moment, then nodded and with a winsome smile gazed up at him. This was better and much more than she could have hoped for, although she couldn't understand why there was a *frisson* of disappointment underlying her relief. 'If you are asking me to give a convincing performance for all the world to see that we are a truly happily married couple while continuing as we are now, then I will do my best.'

He looked irritated by her reply, but said, 'I'm glad we are in accord on that, but as my wife you will find that things will not be the same as they are now. Marriage will change everything.'

Beatrice gazed into his unfathomable eyes, seeing the cynicism lurking in the depths. 'I don't mean to pry—what you do has nothing to do with me—but I have learned from living in the Merrick household for the past weeks that you are disenchanted with life. I know I shall be marrying a man I don't love—a man who doesn't love me. That's what makes it so perfect. Our marriage won't be complicated by messy emotions. We're the perfect solution for each other. You could say this was fate—if you were superstitious, that is.'

'Which I'm not,' Julius said with a bite in his voice. 'I don't believe in fate.'

* * *

When the dance ended, he put his hand under her elbow and guided her towards the supper room where they were joined by a jolly group of Julius's friends. Over food and wine and easy, lighthearted conversation, they both relaxed. Confident that the firestorm of gossip surrounding Beatrice and Julius had subsided, Lord and Lady Merrick left the ball early with friends to attend a quieter function in Mayfair.

In no mood for dancing and suspecting that in her nervousness, to boost her confidence, Beatrice had drunk too much wine over supper, Julius suggested they get some air on the terrace.

Beatrice glanced at him in mock horror. 'The terrace? But is that proper? Should I not have a chaperon?'

'It doesn't matter,' he murmured softly, staring at her with a half-intimate smile. 'We are already betrothed—and after the amount of wine you consumed over supper, I think some fresh air would not go amiss.'

He flashed her a smile that made her heart rebel against all the strictures she had placed on herself.

'Ah,' he said in amusement when he saw her eyes darken with warmth. 'I think you're beginning to like me in spite of yourself.'

'That is merely a delusion,' she replied, fighting back her laughter.

He knew better, said his eyes.

'And don't look at me like that,' she reproached lightly. 'You can't read my mind.'

'I am older and more experienced than you, Beatrice. I see what is written on your face.'

She laughed. 'Then I shall have to learn to school it better.'

'An impossibility for you,' he said in a husky murmur.

Taking her gloved hand, he tucked it into the crook of his arm and led her towards the French doors that opened on to the moonlit terrace. They went down some steps into the lantern-lit gardens. Strolling along the paths, they nodded politely to other couples they passed. At the end of the garden they turned off the path and stepped into a shaded arbour. Beatrice stood and looked at Julius, suffused with trepidation and a tingling excitement that was the result of being alone with him in such a dark, intimate setting. The voices of others died away, leaving only distant strains of soothing music.

'Dance with me, Beatrice,' he said suddenly, his voice like rough velvet.

Beatrice stared at him, the lilting notes of the waltz floating around her. When he opened his arms, feeling as if she were in a dream, she walked into them and felt his right arm slide around her waist, bringing her close against his solid strength. His left hand closed around her fingers and suddenly she was being whirled gently about the arbour in the arms of a man who danced the waltz with the relaxed grace of one who has danced it countless times. She should have felt overpowered— threatened—but surprisingly she felt protected instead.

Suddenly his arm tightened around her waist, forcing her into closer proximity with his powerful body. 'You are very quiet, Beatrice. Have you nothing to say?

It is customary to engage in some form of conversation with your partner.'

Tilting her head back, she smiled teasingly up at him. 'What am I to say? That you dance divinely?'

Julius smiled down at her. 'That is what I'm supposed to say to you. We could engage in some kind of harmless flirtation. It is quite acceptable for couples to do that when they are dancing.'

'Why? Is it because otherwise onlookers will perceive they don't like each other? Well, don't expect me to do that because I haven't any experience with flirting—unlike you.'

'Would you like some lessons?'

'Are you offering to show me how it's done?'

Julius stared down into her dark-green eyes and momentarily lost himself in them. Desire surged through his body and he pulled her closer still. 'I'd like to try—although you're doing very well at it right now.'

'Julius, will you kindly take me seriously!'

'I'm going to marry you,' he said coolly, loosening his hold on her as the music ended. 'That's serious enough.'

'Do you realise,' she said with a winsome smile as she tilted her head to the side, 'that you become positively grim when you speak of our marriage? Are you happy—with your life, I mean? Has the breach with your father affected you very badly?'

He looked irritated by her question, but he answered it. 'Why this curiosity to know? I've already told you that the Chadwick history is nothing to be proud of.'

'That's it. I'm curious. You told me you come from a long line of gamblers. Is that what you do when you want to replenish your coffers?'

He looked at her steadily. 'You really think I make my money at the gaming tables, don't you?'

'You didn't answer my question.'

'No, I didn't.' He stepped closer, his gaze on her mouth.

Beatrice frowned, trying to ignore the tug of his eyes and his voice. 'Why is it that when you don't wish to answer a question, you divert the conversation to something else and...' Her words died as he placed his hands gently on both sides of her face, his fingers sliding into her hair, grateful she didn't favour the fashion for silk flowers and silly ribbons so many other women seemed fond of.

'Stop talking,' he whispered, then lowered his head and kissed her.

Her lips were soft and they parted slightly to receive his. Accepting her invitation, Julius deepened the kiss with ease. She was happy to submit, even though she had the feeling she was getting in over her head. She closed her eyes, exploring the sensations of delight that flooded through her. The beauty of the setting, the romantic sense of the evening and the intoxicating nearness of this man overpowered her judgement. His kiss was exquisite, transporting her to further delights.

Lost in pure sensations of wanton yearnings, warm, strong and exciting, when his mouth left hers and trailed to her neck, she melted against him, her palms sliding up over his chest. He moved against her in the most intoxicating way that sent a shiver up her spine. Lifting his head from devouring her neck, Julius let his gaze settle on her lips. Beatrice considered him the most handsome man she had ever seen; when she thought how he had manoeuvred her into the kiss, with all his worldly elegance and experience that could instruct her in every pleasure that a woman could discover with a man, she accepted he was also a silver-tongued charmer.

'Well, I'll be blowed,' a man's voice intruded. 'If it isn't the Marquess of Maitland.'

At once Julius stiffened and released Beatrice, then turned to face an old acquaintance. It was Lord Percival Canning, a ponderous, mincing fop who was dressed like a peacock in yellow coat, red-satin waistcoat and yellow-satin breeches that swelled over his protruding midsection. Two of his friends hovered behind him.

'I'm happy to see you back among us, Chadwick.' Lord Canning's eyes shifted to Beatrice. 'By all accounts we have the lovely Miss Fanshaw to thank for bringing you out of isolation.'

'Not really,' Julius replied drily. 'I've only recently returned from one of my trips abroad. It's impossible to be in two places at once.'

'So it is. Then you won't have been down to High-field. Pity.'

'Why?'

Lord Canning shrugged. 'I hoped to discuss that little business matter with you I mentioned when you were last down there. Maybe we could meet up while you are in London.'

Julius stared at him icily. 'I don't think so, Canning. The matter you speak of is not open for negotiation.'

Anger briefly flashed into Canning's eyes and Julius's steely body tensed as the dandy drew close, striking an arrogant pose.

'Think about it. I would give you a fair price.' He turned his attention to Beatrice, his fleshy lips opening in a salacious, gargoyle-like grin from ear to ear as he ran his eyes over her in an insulting manner. 'I regret that I did not see the race at Standish House. Everyone's talking about it, Chadwick—of how the high and mighty Marquess of Maitland has been caught like a fish on a hook by a mere slip of a girl! How could you have let that happen—you of all people?' he taunted. 'I hear Miss Fanshaw beat you on a high-spirited brute of a horse. Why, I'd have put money on her myself had I been there.'

'Indeed,' Julius replied blandly. The men— Canning's companions snickering foolishly behind him—would have been dumbfounded to know that as he languidly listened to Canning, he was seething inside.

'Yes, indeed—and she's a beauty all right. Ye Gods, had she challenged me I'd have willingly thrown the race for the pleasure of paying her forfeit.'

Insulted and outraged to the core of her being by this obnoxious fop, Beatrice was furious, but, seeing the rigidity in Julius's back and knowing how he was struggling to hold his temper, she did not retaliate. But she could not bear the way he was being mocked.

'You're being very stupid, Canning—and as immature as I remember,' Julius said. 'You should know better than to bait me.'

Unperturbed and emboldened by the backup of his two friends, Canning laughed inanely and continued. 'Get the bit between her teeth, tighten her rein a bit and she'll be as docile as a lamb. I don't think you've introduced us, Chadwick.'

Julius's brows lifted. 'No.'

'It's not very sociable.'

Julius answered by slamming a fist in Canning's face that knocked him to the ground. 'I don't feel like being sociable, Canning,' he uttered icily, looking down at him with utter contempt, seeing the blood from his burst nose staining his yellow coat to match the colour of his waistcoat. His eyes sliced a warning to the stunned friends not to interfere. 'That was for insulting my future wife. Insult her again at your peril, Canning. Excuse us.' Taking Beatrice's elbow, without looking back, he strode towards the house.

Shocked by what had just happened and hoping that Canning wasn't badly hurt—although she had to admit that he deserved the punch in the nose—Beatrice was almost running to keep up with Julius's long strides. 'Julius, please slow down. Who was that man?'

'Lord Percival Canning, a neighbour of mine with an axe to grind to do with some lands he wants to buy off me. I've no intention of selling to him, but he never gives up. He never fails to take the opportunity to put my back up.'

If Julius's black scowl and rigid jaw was anything to go by, Lord Canning had succeeded admirably, Beatrice thought. But the meeting with the aforesaid gentleman made her realise for the first time what a laugh Julius's friends must be having at his expense. In the eyes of everyone who'd followed the stories in the newspapers, she had manipulated him into marrying her. She was filled with guilt and remorse over what she was asking—no, demanding—of him.

'Julius—I had no idea… I'm sorry,' she said with quiet desperation.

At those words Julius's gaze jerked to her and he stopped dead. Beatrice almost cried out at the blistering contempt blazing in his eyes.

'Julius, I—I can imagine what you must be think-ing—'

He interrupted sarcastically, 'Oh, I don't think you can. If you could, you'd be quite horrified at this moment.'

'I—I didn't think—'

'What you think is not my primary concern at this moment,' he bit back coldly.

'But…I never realised people would react this way—truly. Your friends… They are laughing at you. I will call an end to it…'

'What? And shame me more than you already have? Don't even think of quitting now, lady,' he hissed. 'We play this damned charade out to the bitter end.'

'But I…'

'Shut up,' he ground out, without relinquishing his hold on her elbow. 'Let's get out of here.'

Not until they were in the coach and Julius had regained a modicum of self-control and his hard face was wiped clean of all expression did he speak.

'So, Beatrice, what have you to say about your first London ball?'

'Until our encounter with the obnoxious Lord Canning, it went better than I thought it would, although I confess I'm glad it's over. It will be a relief to be back at the house.'

Julius nodded and not by the flicker of an eye did he betray his admiration for way she had conducted herself in the face of so much condemnation. It was a pity his admiration did not extend to himself, he thought bitterly. He should have known better than to retaliate with his fists to Canning's baiting.

'Very soon you will be coming home with me.'

Looking at him, Beatrice wondered at her sudden weakness in the garden. She really had intended backing out of their arrangement if that was what he wanted. But she could see that to walk away from him now would be tantamount to jilting him and would be a slight to him and to his rank, and she could not do such a thing to him.

'When will you be taking me to Highfield?' she asked. 'Lady Merrick has told me how splendid it is.'

'My ancestors would be pleased to hear it,' he remarked drily, feeling no pride or any warm sensation in the palatial splendour that was Highfield Manor.

'You don't like it?'

'I find it oppressive. I don't often go down there—not since the demise of my parents—and, as you have just witnessed, the neighbours leave a lot to be desired.'

'You must miss them—your parents.'

'My mother, yes. As far as my father was concerned, no. We were not close.'

He turned his head and looked out of the window, but the tension pulsating from him began to play on Beatrice's nerves. She wished that he would open up to her and tell her more about his family and why he felt such antipathy for his father. She felt sure it went beyond his father's weakness for gambling and drink. Julius was locked behind a barrier and she was on the other side. It troubled her that he seemed to know a great deal about her, then shut her out when she asked for answers in return.

'Did your father hurt you?' His expression turned glacial. She knew she should heed the warning in her head, but ploughed on regardless. 'Why do you hate him?'

'Hate? Yes, I hated him.' That was his only response, but his eyes were full of secrets, as unyielding as cold, hard steel.

'Why won't you tell me what he did that makes you feel like this?' Beatrice persisted. He gave her an impatient look, a warning look, and did not reply. She knew he was getting angry with her, but she was not ready to give up yet. 'Why do you find it so painful to speak of him? It might relieve your feelings if you were to confide—'

'Beatrice, do me a favour,' he interrupted acidly. 'Do not tell me how to deal with my feelings and I won't tell you how to deal with yours. Agreed?'

She flinched at his hard tone, but she detected a turbulent pain beneath his cold veneer.

'You are such an innocent still, Beatrice, a naïve child in many ways.'

'At least I'm not heartless,' she retorted.

For the rest of the journey back to Upper Brook Street nothing more was said. Julius had his gaze fixed out of the window, aware of Beatrice glowering at him in the light from the carriage lamps. When anyone tried to get too close or attempted to pry into his past life, resentment surfaced towards his father and the terrible crime he had committed towards Beatrice's father. May God help her—and him—should she ever discover the truth.

He shoved the painful memory away, reminding himself that his father was dead. What mattered now was getting on with his life and his future with Beatrice. And yet the old barbs stuck in his flesh and posed problems, threatened what happiness he hoped for.

Beatrice wanted answers, but her questions awoke years of anger and hurt and deception and lies. To protect his father—a father unworthy of a son's loyalty—and to prevent an almighty scandal, Julius had allowed himself to be unfairly maligned. He never realised he would meet a beautiful girl who, completely innocent about her own connection to the night that had ruined his own life, would probe into his mind in her curiosity to know him better.

And now, whatever the cost, to protect his future with Beatrice and Beatrice herself, this terrible secret must remain hidden. He would carry it to the grave.

But secrets had a way of slipping out.

Chapter Six

Despite her determination to get through it without a hitch, Beatrice's wedding to Julius had a distinct aura of unreality and strain about it. At the outset, Julius had said he did not care to surround the ceremony with any pomp. This suited Beatrice perfectly, for she did not want to attract further attention to herself.

She was numb to the world about her as she stepped through the high, main portal of St George's Church in Hanover Square, Mayfair's most fashionable church. The aisle was illuminated by candles and it seemed a long walk down on Lord Merrick's arm. She had no bridesmaids, not even a matron of honour, the only guests being a handful of Julius's close friends and Lord and Lady Merrick, for which Beatrice was thankful. Never had she felt so alone. This was supposed to be the most important and happiest day of her life, yet she had no family or friends to bear witness to her marriage.

Two men rose to their feet as she approached the pews at the front of the church. One of them, his tall, powerful frame garmented regally in midnight-blue velvet and flawless white cravat, moved forwards and half-turned so that he might watch her progress. His face was stark and serious, almost harsh, and Beatrice was not to know that Julius Chadwick was fighting to control the strong rush of emotion that went through him at the sight of her in her heavy ivory-satin wedding gown.

For a moment Beatrice was tempted to turn before the vows were spoken and fly from the insanity of what she was doing. But even as she argued with herself she took her place beside Julius, to join her life with his. The amber eyes of her husband-to-be held hers, narrowing, assessing, as though he were studying the woman who had manoeuvred him into marriage.

The vision Julius saw walking towards him bathed in candlelight snatched his breath away and pride exploded throughout his entire body until he ached with it, for no bride had ever looked as lovely. He stretched out a strong, brown, well-manicured hand and offered it to her. She lifted her own and placed it in his much larger, much warmer one. Julius felt the trembling of her fingers and saw the anxiety in her large eyes. Immensely relieved that she hadn't decided to pull out of marrying him, he gave her hand a little squeeze in an attempt to reassure her. He drew her the remainder of the way to the altar steps, where he would make her his for all eternity.

Time stood still as they were swept into the marriage ceremony. Beatrice felt as if she existed in a glass bubble as she spoke the words. She could see all that went on in a kind of mist and what she said was loud enough to be heard, but the words indistinct.

It seemed only a moment before Julius was sliding a gold band upon her finger and then it was over. Not about to forgo the custom of kissing his young bride, Julius placed his long fingers beneath the delicate bones of her jaw and tilted her face to his. His head lowered and his parted lips moved gently over hers. At last he slackened his grip and stepped back and, offering her his arm through which she slipped her hand, he led her back down the aisle.

As Julius handed her up into his shiny black coach emblazoned with the Maitland coat of arms, Beatrice thought she was being handed up into the midst of paradise, for only then did she realise fully that she had succeeded in what she had set out to do. Leaving the church for Julius's town house in Piccadilly ahead of the rest, she was conscious of the man seated across from her, watching her intently. Her heart started to beat a wild tattoo and her lips curved in a small triumphant smile. She could have floated, she felt so light.

The future—a future that involved Larkhill—was as blue as the horizon. Having seen a different side to him as she got to know him a little better over the last few days, and unable to deny her growing attraction for him, she was surprised by how much she looked forward to her new life with Julius with more than a little excitement.

Only one cloud darkened her happiness—she was deeply concerned that she might not be able to live up to his expectations and would be a disappointment to him. For days now she had been apprehensive as her wedding day approached—in particular the wedding night—and she told herself that if other women could endure what their husbands did to them, then so could she. She also told herself that perhaps the marital act wouldn't be as painful as she imagined, and, since she had been the instigator of this marriage, she would bear the pain.

But as the hour when she must submit to her husband drew ever nearer, her philosophical attitude deserted her and her dread was steadily mounting. True, she had coerced Julius into marrying her, but when she'd done so, she'd been half-delirious with winning the race. Now, however, she saw with cold clarity what the results of her coercing would be.

From beneath hooded lids, Julius watched her with brooding attentiveness. The sun shining in through the windows spread a halo around her and the diamond necklace he had given her as a wedding gift shone like droplets of dew against her flesh. At that moment he thought she was the most magnificent creature he had ever seen—and she belonged to him. This delectable, golden-haired girl was his wife, to preside at his table and bear his children. She would never bore him, this he knew.

'How does it feel to be my wife—Lady Chadwick, the Marchioness of Maitland—Beatrice?'

As Beatrice met his gaze, her lips curved in a little smile. 'If you must know, I don't feel anything at the moment. It's difficult to take it all in. I feel no different to what I did before the ceremony.' She arched her brows in question. 'Should I?'

'I can think of plenty of females who would.'

'I'm sure you can, but I am not one of them. Titles are meaningless to me.'

He nodded slowly. 'That's right. Titles don't enter into your scheme of things, do they? Only a certain property.'

'You knew that from the start. I made no secret of what I wanted.'

'No, you didn't. But now I think it's about time you realised what it is that *I* want.'

To Beatrice's absolute disbelief, he leaned forwards and stretched his hand to her. Completely unnerved, she jerked back, not knowing what he intended. Annoyed because she didn't fall into his lap, he yanked her off her seat before she knew what he was about, his long fingers curled around her wrist in a painful vice. She muffled a cry as she landed in a sprawling, uncomfortable heap on the seat beside him.

'What are you doing?' she panted, unable to hide her displeasure as she squirmed against him, his glittering eyes and his mouth only inches from hers as he leaned over her, his arms holding her fast.

'This,' he said hoarsely and his mouth swooped down, seizing hers in a ruthless kiss. For several moments Beatrice was so confounded she made no attempt to stop him. His lips moved over hers, gently, smoothing, his mouth open a fraction. Within moments her tension began to melt in the heat of his kiss and her senses swam dizzily. In a kind of sensual haze, she was aware of his hand roaming possessively over the sensitive flesh above her bodice. Then she came to life, tearing her lips from his, struggling and pushing herself back from his arms.

'Please, Julius, stop it. Don't do this. I may be your wife, but that does not give you leave to manhandle me whenever you wish. I will not be forced.'

When Julius tried to reach for her again she flinched, slapping his arm hard and pushing him away with both hands, then returning to the opposite seat. For a second as he looked at his indignant, spluttering wife, he remained dazed. In what she thought was self-defence she had used the very movements of a tavern wench accustomed to dealing with drunks. He had never seen a lady defend herself in this way before. It struck him as both funny and exasperating. Did she really imagine that he was going to leave her alone? Did she really imagine he would force her?

Frowning with concern over the anxiety and tension he saw on her face, leaning forward and resting his forearms on his knees, he said, 'I am not a monster, Beatrice. I will not force you to do anything you do not want to do. You have my word on that.'

'Thank you,' she said, her tension easing a little on hearing this.

As Julius looked at her, the sight of her stormy,

brilliant green eyes, her white shoulders and that fragile neck and soft lips aroused in him a violent but unfamiliar desire, such as no woman had ever aroused in him. It was not just blind lust. There was about it a somewhat mysterious, almost sweet and gentle allure.

Something sprang into jubilant life within him and soared. Thank God, he thought, she was not going to be a submissive wife, docile and totally insensate and frozen inside, a woman who would endure his embraces with a sigh and accept that it was her wifely duty to submit to him with compliance. He sensed Beatrice was like a cat, a tigress, ready to fight like one, to match him in strength, to be his equal both in bed and out of it.

At this moment she was openly defying him, yet he was the offended one. In the beginning she had forced his hand, humiliated him as no man can bear to be humiliated without wishing the other into purgatory, so first he must show her that she was his wife, and then he would make her realise that their marriage would be conducted on equal terms, and that what they did together could be pleasing for them both.

And yet Julius would have been most surprised at his wife's thoughts hidden behind her façade of defiance and indignation. Her emotions were all over the place following his kiss. It had left her so confused she could hardly think. Why did she feel like this? she thought wonderingly. A slow realisation of what was happening, born of the moment when he had dragged her into his arms, was moving through her, making its way to her slowly thawing heart, which had been frozen for so long.

She swallowed and turned her head so she didn't have to look at the man opposite. He was so formidable, so stern, so oppressive and yet so...so what? Breathtakingly handsome? Strong, compelling and completely masculine? Yes, she thought, he was all those things. A man lean, muscular, with wide shoulders, narrow hips and trim waist, she could not help but admire the fine figure he made—near, if not, perfection. Heat suffused her cheeks and her heart was beating hard against her ribcage, as though it were trying to get out to escape the bewildering pain it felt.

Dear Lord, what was happening to her—and in such a short space of time? Why had fate turned her feelings, in the blink of an eye, from absolute indifference to this man who was her husband of mere minutes to something so painful she could not understand it? It was blurring her mind. She could feel herself shaking inside, for she was afraid of his passion, afraid of how much it would hurt in the future if she let herself weaken now.

'Fight me if you must, Beatrice,' he said softly, 'but I promise you that we will share the more tender moments of our marriage. You say you dislike force. I, too, loathe it, but I could do nothing to get out of paying your forfeit. I did not choose *you* for a wife, *you* chose me,' he reminded her, his words dripping with disdain. 'But however it came about, I do not intend to take advantage of you. Now you're angry because you will have to pay the piper, but you do not think what it has cost me to make you my wife.'

The sound of his voice brought her back to the present. Deeply troubled and confused by her feelings, furious at her sudden weakening and hurt by what he had said, she took refuge in anger. Turning her head back to him, she laughed ungraciously.

'You didn't *have* to marry me. You could have walked away.'

'So could you. I recall telling you that as my mistress you would have been treated as a queen,'

'Whereas what I have now is a master,' she retorted irately, using her anger to fortify her against her nervousness at what was to come later. 'Is that what you are telling me, Julius?'

He smiled thinly, his amber eyes nailed to hers. 'I would never be that, Beatrice. What I will say is that if you consider refusing me your bed, remember that you are only one woman among many. For a man it is easy to find relief for his baser needs.'

'And I imagine you are low enough to do that,' she said, still wondering and bewildered at the hurt and disappointment that stirred her heart.

His jaw tightened and his eyes grew cold. Did she really think she could flout him so soon into their marriage? 'There's no need to distress yourself, my love,' he said mockingly. 'You are quite safe from me for the present.'

'I sincerely hope so,' she replied, moving as far from him as was possible within the confines of the coach.

'You cannot escape me, Beatrice,' he said easily,

concerned by her distress and attempting to lighten the moment by injecting a teasing note into his voice. 'You are now and for ever mine. Marriage with me is what you wanted and that is what you shall have for the rest of your life—or mine. But fear not. You are a beauty, my sweet. I shall not grow tired of you and have no desire to leave you too soon.' He chuckled softly, reaching out and touching her cheek, relieved that she did not pull away. 'You will find I am temperamental and that I may not be termed a pleasant man to live with—but you have my word that I shall strive to be amenable at all times when we are together.'

Beatrice managed to smile and turned her head away, looking out of the window as the coach finally drew up before the house—a splendid mansion of which Beatrice would now be mistress. Julius climbed out and turned to assist her.

'Can you manage, my love, or shall I lift you down?' he asked, a smile twisting his handsome mouth.

For the sake of appearances and because the nervous fluttering in her stomach was increasing with each passing minute, she allowed him to assist her out of the coach, placing her hand on his arm for him to escort her into the house.

'Smile,' Julius said in a quiet voice while managing to smile charmingly himself for the benefit of those who had gathered to see the return of the bride and groom and to wish them well. 'Must I remind you that this is your wedding day, which is supposed to be the happiest day of your life, whereas you, my love, look as if you are going to your execution.'

Feeling that the quiet reprimand was deserved, Beatrice did as he bade and composed her features into a more agreeable expression as he escorted her inside the house.

Beatrice was introduced to the curious but welcoming servants, who bobbed their curtsies or respectfully bent their heads, though she felt such an intruder, an interloper, not one face or one name was retained in her memory.

Julius led her into a green-and-gold salon, where a long table had been prepared for the wedding feast. It gleamed with silver cutlery and crystal glasses and was festooned with flowers. Standing in the centre of the salon, a smile pinned to her lips and a glass of champagne in her hand, the bride received the well wishes of all those present. The meal went quickly—too quickly for Beatrice—who wanted to delay the time when she would find herself alone with Julius.

Seated beside her, Julius lounged back in his chair, his arm stretched possessively across the back of hers, his expression thoughtful as he watched her smile and laugh when glasses were raised in toast to the bride and groom. It wasn't surprising that everyone was in her thrall, for she looked ravishing. She was also lively and amiable in a way that not even he had seen before. She had deliberately set herself out to charm; as he toyed with the stem of his wine glass, it was that effort which both amused and exasperated him.

If she hadn't decided to make herself so delightful, everyone would have eaten their fill and gone home earlier—which was, Julius knew, exactly what she didn't want, for their presence delayed the moment when she would have to go upstairs with him and they would be alone.

Because this was her wedding day and because he knew she was probably anxious about what was to happen later, for the last hour he had been willing to indulge her, using the time to enjoy her company and to savour the anticipation of what was to come. Now, however, he was growing tired of the wait.

Leaning close to her, he said, 'I'm sorry to put an end to your day, Beatrice, but I think it's time you and I left.'

As he stood up and held his hand out to her, Beatrice realised the moment she had dreaded all day had arrived. A delicate flush spread over her features as she rose and placed her trembling hand in his. It was growing dark and, not wishing to linger without the bride and groom, the guests began to leave. Beatrice looked pleadingly at Lady Merrick when she came up to her.

'Must you go now?' she asked in a quavering voice.

The kindly woman nodded her head and gave her a motherly kiss upon the brow. 'Yes, my dear. It's time the two of you were alone. We cannot stay any longer. Be happy, Beatrice,' she said, glancing up at Julius who stood beside her. 'I know you will be well cared for.'

Beatrice watched her go. She looked at Julius. 'If you don't mind, I would like to go to my room now.'

'It's been a long day and I'm sure you must be feeling tired. I shall escort you there myself. I hope you will find it—comfortable. And there is a connecting door to my room.'

When her eyes snapped to his he straightened, his face set in lines of challenge. His lips curled over his white teeth. 'There is nothing wrong with that, Beatrice. It is perfectly natural for a husband and wife to have connecting rooms.' As he came to stand beside her, he murmured just loud enough for her to hear, 'I trust you have no objections to the sleeping arrangements. Are you afraid of being alone with me, my love, of fulfilling your part of the bargain we made?'

Beatrice coloured hotly and turned away in sudden confusion. His hand slid about her waist and she started slightly as his hard chest pressed against her back.

His deep voice seemed to reverberate within her as he announced softly, 'I think it is time for bed.'

In that moment her mind flew from all rational thought. A bolt of doubt blasted her confidence. She turned to face him.

'You—you spoke of a bargain. What bargain might that be? I do not recall having made any bargain with you.'

He raised a sardonic brow. 'Ah, but you did. Think about it, Beatrice. When you asked me to be your husband and again when you spoke your vows.' Seeing her uncertainty, he chuckled softly. 'Did you think I would have entered into this if I had nothing to gain?' He laid a hand against her cheek in a tender caress. 'I have fulfilled my part of the bargain. It is time for you to fulfil yours. It is the price you have to pay. You belong to me until death.'

Fully realising the truth of what he said, Beatrice shrank away from him in disbelief, aware of the trap that slowly closed around her—a trap of her own making.

'Tonight you will see the real price of your predicament.' His voice became gentle, almost a whisper. His eyes were hungry with yearning and touched her everywhere. 'You sought me out for a cause dear to you and I have given you my name—a high price for me to pay. Now I ask the same of you. Do you find the price too dear that you suddenly want to reject it—to deny the bargain?'

'No,' she replied stiffly. 'Of course not.'

'I am happy to hear that, Beatrice. Come, we shall go up together', and without further ado, in silence he began to lead the new Marchioness of Maitland up the stairs, along the landing in the direction of their chambers. Not until they were inside Beatrice's room and the door closed against the world did he release her, relieved to have her alone at last.

As his bride she was certainly lovely to look at. Golden strands shimmered among the carefree copper curls, crackling and alive in the light from the candles. The soft brows arched away from eyes that were clear and green—sea green in this light, brilliant against the thick fringe of jet-black lashes and as unfathomable as any sea he had ever gazed into. The soft pink lips were tantalising and gracefully curved. Under his penetrating gaze the golden skin flushed slightly.

Feeling desire stir in his loins, with a will of iron Julius clamped a grip upon himself.

With tension twisting within her, Beatrice rubbed her arm and warily considered her husband. His face was extremely handsome above a froth of white lace, his dark hair smoothly brushed and his white teeth shining in his gypsy-brown face. With a surge of admiration, she thought how ruggedly virile he looked. He also looked relaxed as he stood watching her, his amber eyes warm and intense, a spark flaring in their depths.

She felt the bold touch of his hungry gaze and inwardly shivered. Her knees quaking violently, she walked slowly around the room that was to be hers. It was a tastefully furnished, elegant room, the bed large and canopied in the same mulberry and gold as the rest of the room. There was no sign of a maid to assist her out of her wedding finery, but the bedcovers had been turned down and the lacy white jasmine-scented sheets.

Seeing her stiffen and stare with stricken paralysis at the bed and noting how her fingers that flew to her mouth trembled, with long, easy strides that always looked both certain and relaxed, Julius walked towards her.

'Come, Beatrice, there's nothing to fear, so why are you trembling?'

She turned and looked at him, unable to tear her gaze from his, unable to hide her fear. 'I don't know,' she admitted with a tremor in her voice.

'Don't you?' he asked softly, one eyebrow raised in question. 'You do realise what is to happen between us, don't you?'

She nodded. 'Yes.'

'And is it now your hope to avoid keeping the bargain we made?'

Lifting her head, Beatrice faced him, trying to tell herself that the act she was about to commit wasn't sinful or anything like that, that in submitting herself to her husband she was actually doing something noble. But confronted with his size, his strength and his indomitable will, Beatrice found her reasoning did nothing to quell her fear.

Instead of lying to him, which Julius half-expected her to do, she surprised him by saying instead, 'It is my hope, but I am prepared to become your wife in every sense. I will not deny you the rights of my own vows. You will have what I promised you.'

'Yet you fear it.'

'Yes.'

'Do you fear me?'

'No—only what will happen. But I will submit—if that is what you want.'

'Submit?' Julius repeated, annoyed by her choice of word. 'The marital act is not some kind of punishment to which you should *submit*. Don't fear it,' he ordered softly as his fingers caressed her cheek. 'And for God's sake, don't fear me. You've never feared me before. Don't begin now.'

The deep, husky timbre of his voice, combined with the tantalising exploration of his skilful fingers caressing her face and neck, was already working its magic on Beatrice.

Julius considered his wife, seeing the set of her chin that brought a smile to his lips. 'I hope there isn't going to be a battle, my love. I wouldn't like to have a fight on my hands—not tonight. In order to make you understand that we are husband and wife, that from this night on we will share a bed, share our bodies, there is no other way.'

Beatrice started to protest, but his finger came across her lips and shushed her. Bending his head, he placed his lips close to her ear.

'I want you to relax, my love. There will be a drifting of the senses, soft kisses, an initiation into the art of love, moving towards a climax that will please us both, which is what I want,' he murmured, taking her face between his hands and kissing her sweet lips, lightly to begin with, offering her love, then deeply and tenderly. After a few moments of tense passivity, she placed her hand on his chest and began to kiss him back.

Raising his head a fraction, he asked, 'Did it concern you that our wedding was not the grand affair most young ladies dream of?'

'I didn't want a grand affair. I was perfectly satisfied the way it was.'

'You made a beautiful bride. You are so lovely your beauty blinds me. But that is not what this is about.'

Tilting her head to one side, relaxed by his kiss, she managed a teasing smile. 'No? Is it not more important to have a wife who is pleasing to look at than an ugly one?' she provoked.

'Ah—but it is not the face that is important, Beatrice.' Very slowly he walked round her, deliberately, examining her as she stood rooted to the floor, not touching her with anything but those amber eyes—and they were enough, boldly evaluating her assets. He halted and, bending his head close to her ear so that the warm breath caressed the back of her neck, said softly, 'When I was a youth, I was given some sound advice from a very wise man.'

Unable to move, Beatrice swallowed audibly, nervously, her heart beating wildly. 'What was that?'

'Never to buy a mare with a blanket on.'

'And—who was this wise man?'

'My father.'

Beatrice shivered under Julius's unrelenting gaze. He watched her with such a slow, unhurried regard that her skin burned from its intensity. 'It's a little late for that, don't you think? Perhaps you should have taken his advice.'

'I'm sure you're right, but, as you say, it's too late for that. You belong to me now. You are my wife and a husband may do as he pleases with his wife.' His voice softened until it was almost a whisper. 'Anything he likes. Now—shall we take off those clothes and see what we have?'

For a moment Beatrice shrank back, her green eyes darkening in fear, and Julius almost turned away, for before God he would not force her. Then, as he had hoped she would, her chin came up, her soft lips tightened and her eyes blazed her defiance, but she turned and presented her back for him to unbutton her wedding gown.

He worked downwards until the garment hung open. She shrugged and it fell to her feet, revealing a sheer, shimmering white-silk petticoat, the shoulders temptingly bare. The petticoat hid nothing from him and Beatrice saw the hard glint of passion strike sparks in his eyes as they moved over her. Her full, ripe breasts swelled against the silk that moulded itself to her bosom and the delicate peaks thrust forward impudently. He saw the inward curve of her waist, amazingly small without any tight lacings, the trim and seductive roundness of her hips and the lithe grace of her limbs.

Julius's breath caught in his throat. He had already realised that beneath all her clothes Beatrice was what every man dreamed of: a vision of incomparable beauty. His long fingers freed her body from the rest of her flimsy garments until she stood naked to his gaze.

The hardest thing Beatrice had ever had to do in her life was to stand calmly before him and let him look at her as he was doing now, when, feeling like a caged animal newly caught, she wanted nothing more than to find a way out. He stepped back, still smiling, but with a new fire kindled in his eyes. His gaze was direct, challenging, sweeping from her trim and shapely ankles, passing over her slender legs, and then more leisurely over her magnificent body, which was lustrous shades of honey and amber in the flickering flames of the candles and the fire. The triangle of curling fair hair at the base of her belly was now a mysterious dark enticing shadow, her breasts rose tipped and exuberant. His gaze passed on to her face. She had not flinched as she submitted herself for his perusal, but her eyes were large and hot and expectant, and a flush swept up her long shapely legs, her slender curves, staining the glowing flesh right up to her face.

Julius's lips spoke no word, but his eyes clearly expressed his wants. The bold stare touched a quickness in Beatrice that made her feel as if she were on fire. It flamed in her cheeks and set her hands to trembling as she stared back at him. Out of consideration for her obvious embarrassment, Julius extinguished the candles burning close to her, before taking his time in stripping himself naked. He unbuttoned and removed his shirt and laid it over a chair with his cravat and slipped out of his breeches and undergarments, tossing them atop the shirt.

When he was totally naked Beatrice stared at a certain part of his anatomy in horror, her face as white as the cravat he had just removed. She had always known men were different, but this was the first time she had seen one naked. Appalled by the size and colour of what she was seeing, she wanted to turn her head away, but found that she could not. Raising her eyes, she gazed at the rest of him. He was bathed in a light cast by the remaining candles and was aglow with deep golden shades that rippled along his hard, lean frame. His body was strong, proud, savage, determined and eternally masculine. Beatrice was no less shaken by the sight of him than by his slow perusal of her a few moments before. They weren't touching, but they generated enough heat between them to light a fire.

As Beatrice dragged her gaze towards the bed, her eyes lit on her nightdress where the maid had left it draped over the quilt. She made a move to get it, but Julius stepped in front of her.

'Please allow me to cover myself,' she said, unable to keep the desperation out of her voice.

'Now why would you want to do that?'

'Because I never go to bed without wearing my nightdress. As for you—you seem to have an aversion for wearing clothes which I consider to be most indecent,' she uttered with quiet reproach.

Julius chuckled softly, delighting in her innocence. 'There are times, Beatrice, when clothing can be a hindrance. One's wedding night is one of them.' His eyes again caressed her from top to toe, touching her everywhere. 'A man finds them troublesome when a wife wears them to bed.' He held his arms out wide, his lips smiling about his white pirate's teeth, proud of his nakedness. 'This is what it's about. A man and a woman alone. No maidenly blushes, no resistance, no fumbling with nightgowns.'

The colour deepened in Beatrice's cheeks and she tried to quell the trepidation that had arisen. When she met his eyes the shock was sharp, for she suddenly realised the moment had arrived when she must pay her dues. Would he seek vengeance cruelly and cause her pain? How could she have cast herself into his grasp so recklessly? She made a move towards the door, but his hand shot out, his fingers fastened about her wrist.

'Oh, no, my pet, there is no way out. Besides, you cannot leave the room undressed. You'll likely set the servants all agog. It's time for bed.'

'But I'm not in the least tired.'

'Good,' he said, his whipcord arms coming slowly around her. 'Neither am I,' he murmured thickly against her throat.

The warmth of his body pressed full against the coolness of Beatrice's own. The jolt of surprise she experienced had nothing to do with revulsion, but rather with the bold, manly feel of him. The alien hardness was a hot brand against her thighs. His face lowered. His mouth was scalding upon her breast and she was devoured in a searing, scorching flame that shot through her like a flaring rocket.

'Oh, Julius,' she panted in a whisper. 'Please— don't…' She could not draw breath. 'Please—stop…'

Leaning down, he swung her up into his arms and carried her to the bed, promising himself every step of the way that their loving would be so perfect for her that she would never fear it again.

His strength was unexpected. He carried her easily, turning her and taking her down with him. His lips caressed her neck and ventured downwards until they were warm and moist upon her breast, rousing her to a heat she had not thought possible. She told herself she should resist what he was doing, that she didn't want this, but she knew it would be useless, for she was no match against the power of his arms and shoulders, imbued with even greater strength by his charged emotional state.

The body that Julius's own so fiercely desired lay beneath him and his uncontrollable hunger for her took command. He managed to free one hand and cup her breast. Her hair was spread out on the sheets, adding to her wild beauty. Her lips responded to his. While he held her firm so that their bodies were touching, his experienced mouth parted hers and flirted with her lips, her tongue, his hands caressing her body, her breasts, circling the rosy crests with his thumb until they stood proud and firm. Beatrice shivered with delight and clung to him—but suddenly, feeling her modesty about to be invaded when his hand slid boldly up the inside of her thigh, her wakened senses alarmed, she gasped and began to pull away as if she had been scorched.

'Please—stop it. I can't do this. I don't want to do it.'

Blindly, the tears sprang from her eyes. His hard thighs were between her own, bringing his virile organ inexorably closer to the gateway of his desire.

Julius immediately knew how apprehensive she was and, although she resisted, he held her hips against his. Such was his desire, he was tempted to mount her and seek his release, but he fought it, determined to take her slowly, to cause her as little pain as possible.

'No,' he said gently as she tried to wriggle from beneath him. 'Don't pull away and I'll do my best not to hurt you.'

But he did hurt her when his manhood, swollen and hard, touched her in brief dalliance, then pressed into the delicate softness of her. A quicksilver pain shot through her and Beatrice bit her lips to keep from crying out, hiding her face against the base of his throat. Her nails dug into the soft flesh of his back, but he seemed not to notice as his mouth touched her ear and with utmost care he began to move.

For a while the pain was fierce, but like the most violent of storms this passed, all the more quickly for its furious nature, and afterwards, as she lay against her husband, she could not understand why her breasts and her belly quivered in hot anticipation for the moment when he would reach for her again.

Their second union was so very different. Even as she tried to turn from him, Beatrice felt the betraying moisture from her loins and she could resist no longer. This time there was no pain. It was forgotten in the heat of motion and the sensation of Julius filling her, thrusting, touching all of her. Surprised, she felt herself respond to him and swell against him in pulsating waves of pleasure as he brought her body to life. And then bliss as a wonderful aura burst around them. Deep inside the sensations started to build and expand through her as his life-giving seed erupted and spilled into her, warming her, combining their minds and souls in physical release and the act of love.

She knew then what it was to be a woman, the hard, powerful body of a man pressed against her, his manhood still swollen and warm, still moving, but gently now. The pulsating contractions continued to build until the heat slowly subsided and left her body quivering with the after-effects. The parting of their bodies was jarring, like a bereavement from which she could not imagine recovery. Unbidden tears came to her eyes and she turned away, burying her face in the pillow, weeping silently so he would not see. How could she explain to him how she felt? Everything was changed now. Nothing was the same—she wasn't the same. She wanted nothing more than to revel in this new discovery of herself and the fullness of the moment. Wanted desperately…what? What did she want? If only she could understand what had happened to her. What had she done? What had *he* done to her? Suddenly she knew a feeling of loneliness, for she had found such pleasure—a pagan pleasure in his arms—and something else, something dangerous to her, a feeling that shouldn't exist, but it did. For what she wanted more than anything else at that moment was for him to speak her name in that tender tone—and to say *I love you*.

No matter how hard she tried to conceal her tears, Julius heard her muffled sobs. As if her need to hear him speak communicated itself to him, he spoke, but not with the tone or the words her heart yearned for. He spoke quietly and without emotion.

'I apologise if I hurt you. I tried very hard not to. It would have hurt no matter who took you the first time.'

She shook her head and drew an unsteady breath. 'No, you didn't hurt me.' Misery engulfed her. The words he uttered were a long way from saying *I love you*, which was what she wanted him to say. At that moment she sorely wished he would go away, for his presence wreaked havoc on the serenity she so desperately sought.

Julius reached out his hand to draw her back into his arms, but when he heard her say, 'I would like to sleep now', he hesitated, then withdrew it, sensing she wished to be left alone, yet reluctant to do so. He wanted to test her honesty and ask her again, for her to reassure him that he hadn't hurt her, but he did not want her to tell him that she hadn't felt all the things he had when he'd taken her. He lay still, listening as her breathing slowed and she drifted into a deep sleep.

Hearing some imperceptible movement coming from his own chambers, he was wide awake at once. In one fluid, easy motion he got out of bed. The sight of the rumpled sheets so like a battleground brought back the sensuous memories of their lovemaking. All the emotions, the crashing waves of a tortured sea, surged and eddied in his mind. His gaze lingered on his wife a moment, thinking she was asleep. He felt a great wave of surprising tenderness wash over him. How vulnerable and utterly lovely she looked—how incredibly beautiful she was with her hair spilling over the pillows and gleaming in the pale dawn light.

He had done his level best to hurt her as little as possible. He was tempted to lean over and lay a hand on her naked shoulder before thinking better. Remembering her tears, he backed away from the bed, telling himself she would not miss him and would be simply relieved that he had spared her the unwanted task of another nocturnal pursuit.

In his own room Julius heard a controlled knock on the door. Opening it, he was presented with a footman holding a small silver tray with a letter on it.

'A message has arrived for you, sir. The courier

said it was urgent, otherwise I would have waited until morning to give it to you.'

'Here, I will take it.' Julius tore open the letter and read it quickly. The news was bad. Cursing silently, he strode to the door to issue orders to have his valet wakened to pack his bags.

Feeling the man beside her stir, through half-closed eyes feigning sleep, Beatrice heard the bed creak as Julius moved away from her and returned to his own chambers. She opened her mouth to call him back, but the thought that he might not want to strangled the words in her throat.

Drawing the sheet over her nakedness, she rolled on to her back. The movement caused her some annoyance, for in certain parts of her body she was sore and bruised, yet at the same time that small electrifying pulse, which surged just at that part of her that ached the most, flared in the most amazing way.

Immersed in her reflections, feeling languid yet clear headed, she stared up at the canopy. What Julius had done to her had left her bemused and possessed by him. She had not expected her body to respond to his in such an overwhelming way. He had done things to her that should have disgusted her; instead she had clung to him, encouraged him, even, her treacherous body glorying in it, the evidence being the red-black smears of her blood on the sheets—a sign of his entry—his gain, and her loss.

Chapter Seven

Beatrice was unable to quell the anxiety she felt as she left her room after breakfasting in bed. She did not relish the idea of confronting Julius again right now, when her emotions were still so raw and all over the place. But that was not to be. He was in the morning room waiting for her. He was dressed immaculately, fastidiously even, the cut of his expensive jacket setting off the powerful width of his shoulders, his legs smooth and shapely in the well-tailored perfection of his dove-grey breeches. His dark hair was smoothly brushed, his handsome face drawn.

This man she had married was compelling, resolute and complex, for would she ever know what he was thinking unless he told her? He was also arrogant and proud, and she believed he would fight for what he wanted, for what he believed in, and she had no doubt that he believed that he could master her, subjugate her, turn her into the wife he wanted.

With what she incorrectly imagined was his supreme indifference to her, he lounged against the fireplace, his hands in his pockets, his face carefully blank, his eyes directed away from her, as if he couldn't be bothered to look at her face.

Beatrice stared at him, her mind screaming for him to look at her. Her heart beat agonisingly with yearning, despairingly. She could not help but admire the fine shape of him, how she had come to know and like the male beauty of his naked body which overwhelmed her. She liked the hardness, the darkness of him, the width of his shoulders, the narrow grace of his hips, his flat, taut stomach, the long shapeliness of his legs. Yes, she loved all this—though it also disturbed her that she should want to see him like that again. She wanted to feel his arms about her body, his lips on hers, kissing her the way a man does when he loves a woman. But Julius had been unable to wait to leave their bed. In short, he didn't love her. He never would and she must accept that and learn to live with it, no matter how hard that would be.

Closing the door, she moved to stand in the centre of the room with more confidence than she was feeling. 'Good morning, Julius,' she said stiffly.

He glanced at her and nodded. 'Good morning, Beatrice.' His voice was clipped. 'I trust you slept well after I left.'

'Yes—perfectly,' she replied, thinking this man bore no resemblance to the one who had made love to her with such passion. This man was a stranger to her, a cold, forbidding man who looked at her with cold blatant uninterest. How could he be so nonchalant after the night they had spent together? At that moment all she could remember was her husband making love to her in a thousand tiny ways. Now his detached tone caught her off guard; his expression was as if he were studying an interesting document instead of his own wife.

Julius straightened and, with his hands behind his back, turned and strolled to the window, where he stood looking out. 'I have to go away for a while.'

Beatrice stared at him in surprise. She hadn't known what to expect when she had entered the room, but it certainly wasn't this. Had she been such a disappointment to him, then? She felt her cheeks burn. He might as well have torn her heart out, but even worse, he dashed all her hopes, her romantic dreams.

'Oh? Am I allowed to ask where you are going?'

'Portsmouth. I received a message earlier. It appears that two of my vessels returning from India were badly damaged in a storm coming through the Bay of Biscay. One of the vessels is missing. Several of the crew on the surviving vessel lost their lives and there has been considerable damage to the cargo.'

'I see—and—you have to go yourself?'

'I have agents capable of assessing the damage, but I would like to see it for myself. There's a loyal crew and thousands of pounds worth of cargo on the missing vessel, so it is imperative that I locate it.'

'And do you expect to be gone long?' she enquired, staring at his stiff back.

'No longer than necessary—two weeks at the most. Meanwhile you are to remain here—where Lady Merrick can keep an eye on you.'

'I don't need to be kept an eye on, Julius,' Beatrice replied, unable to hide her resentment. 'I am quite capable of looking after myself.'

He spun round and looked at her. 'I am sure you are, but Lady Merrick will be company for you in my absence. Were I to send you to Highfield you wouldn't know anyone. I intend to take you down there on my return. Here you will find plenty to occupy your time. I want you to familiarise yourself with the house and the servants. Hayes, the butler, and Mrs Keeble, the housekeeper, will be on hand to answer your questions. I'd prefer it if you didn't ride out just yet. None of the horses here are suitable.'

Beatrice bristled. 'I'm sure there must be one. Your horse would suit me perfectly. As you know to your cost I am an accomplished horsewoman—and it will need to be exercised in your absence.'

'No, Beatrice. Absolutely not.' He was adamant. 'You possess abundant courage, that I know—the kind of courage needed to fearlessly manage high-spirited horses—but apart from the grooms exercising my horse, he remains in the stable. Understand that. Besides, I shudder to think of the form of dress you would choose to wear. You would scandalise society if you rode through Hyde Park as you do in the country, astride in your breeches.'

'It is much more natural and comfortable to ride that way. I see nothing wrong with it,' she argued.

'You wouldn't, but ladies don't ride astride. It isn't done. Aside from any other consideration, just think of the damage it would do to my reputation if I were to allow my wife to ride in such a manner.'

'I'm fast coming to think,' Beatrice returned, 'that this reputation of yours is invented by you as a convenient excuse to prevent me riding out in public.' That riposte earned her a distinctly steely glare. Before he could think of a comment to go with it, she said, 'As you know, my own horse is still at Standish House. Could I not arrange for it to be sent here?'

'I don't see why not,' he said, having seen for himself how devoted she was to that horse of hers. 'I'll instruct the head groom to take care of it. Perhaps you should write a brief note to Lady Standish for her to authorise its removal from her stable. If she refuses to comply with your request, I shall take care of it myself on my return.'

'Thank you, Julius. I would appreciate that.'

'As my wife, I have no doubt people will want to make your acquaintance. Constance will be happy to assist you in the making and receiving of calls, and the ordering of more new gowns from your dressmaker will keep you busy.'

'Yes, although I have enough dresses and fripperies to last me a lifetime. I suppose it will be pleasant to have Lady Merrick's company on occasion—even when you return. Normal married couples cannot exist on a diet of love alone. And that description can hardly apply to us, can it, Julius?' she remarked, unable to conceal the hurt she still felt when he had left her bed so soon after making love to her.

Julius looked at her steadily. His face was expressionless, his eyes hard and empty, an emptiness that told Beatrice nothing of what he felt, then he said, 'It doesn't become you to be sarcastic, Beatrice. And as far I am concerned, you will hardly find me lacking in husbandly duties—as it will be my pleasure and yours to discover when I return.'

Duties, Beatrice thought bleakly. Was that really all their marriage meant to him—all the passion, the sensations he awoke in her that made her almost delirious when he made love to her? Despite the distant attitude she had adopted afterwards, which had been a form of self-defence, last night she had become aware that something was happening. Something awe-inspiring and frightening had happened to her in that split second it had taken her heart to acknowledge it. And she could do nothing about it.

Julius certainly didn't care for her and she had no intention of making a fool of herself by telling him she was beginning to care for him. He didn't give a damn and, in truth, she could hardly blame him. He would more than likely find it highly amusing and tell her it was unfortunate for her. So though it cost her every bit of her strength and will-power, and her own bloody-minded pride, she would keep her feelings to herself.

'When do you leave?'

'As soon as the horses have been hitched to the coach.'

'I see.'

At that moment there was a rap on the door. Julius crossed the room and opened it, speaking quietly to whoever it was before closing it.

'It is ready. I must go.'

Suddenly Beatrice wanted to cry and she didn't know why. Was it because she would miss him, would miss their sparring and the time when they would be alone in her room? How she longed for it now. He must never know how she felt. How he would laugh if he knew. She swallowed her tears and rallied.

'Then what can I say other than to wish you a safe journey, Julius.' Her voice was low, husky with an inner emotion she did her best to keep under control. Looking at him quickly, she caught a puzzling, watchful glint in his eyes—keen, eager, as though he hung on her next words, hoping she would say—what? She didn't know. 'I hope things are not as bad as you imagine when you reach Portsmouth.'

Her husband looked at her. Wearing a new morning dress, a creation of apple-green twill that emphasised her slender shape and set off the copper and gold of her hair, she looked like an alluring, enchanting temptress. He looked into her green eyes and his hands clenched at his sides as he fought the impulse to rebuke her for holding herself from him after their lovemaking, as though she could not bear for him to touch her again. And yet there had been moments in their second union when he had heard her sigh and her lips had been soft and she had returned his kisses, her hands caressing and clinging instead of clawing as though to steady herself as the climax washed over her. At that moment she had been totally his, dazed and submissive, a woman—his wife.

The urge to go to her, to take her in his arms and wrap her around him like a blanket and lose himself in her, to kiss her and tell her that he needn't leave her, that all she had to do was tell him she didn't want him to go, that she wanted him to stay with her, was strong, but, knowing the chances of her doing so was remote, without another word he turned on his heel.

His composure held tightly about him, raking his fingers through his hair and Beatrice's heart, he went out.

Restless in spite of the desultory mood which had gripped her ever since Julius's departure, over the following days Beatrice wandered about the house. It was the most opulent she had ever seen. Julius had bought it ten years ago with his newly acquired fortune. No expense had been spared. It had been decorated and furnished to his taste with every kind of luxury.

She did her best to acquaint herself with the servants and to familiarise herself with the running of the house, and the sphinxlike butler and Mrs Keeble were patience personified in telling her all she needed to know. Never having involved herself in domestic matters at Standish House, which she had considered tiresome and of little consequence anyway, and having no idea of what overseeing a large house and servants entailed, Beatrice was quite out of her depth.

She worked harder than she had ever worked before, but the multitude of responsibilities and tasks that confronted her daily as mistress of the house, rather than wearing her down, left her pleasantly exhausted and satisfied. She could not help, however, thinking of Julius, and missing him, very much aware how much he had got under her skin. Lady Merrick, who called on her most days, assured her that time would soon pass and he would return, but the confidence with which she spoke, while comforting, also left Beatrice more than a little fearful.

What would happen when he came back? Would the emotional chasm between them become an insurmountable obstacle? Was it possible that they could find a way of living together, or was there nothing there on which to build? There was little time for such thoughts until the day was done. But then, in the solitude of her bed, in the quiet of the night, her thoughts turned on themselves in a confusing mix. At these times she could stand the constriction of her room no longer and walked through the connecting door to pass a lonely vigil lying on his bed, wishing desperately for his return and the touch of his hands.

When she was not involving herself with household matters, Lady Merrick would whisk her away on excursions to the popular tea gardens of Vauxhall across the river and Pancras Wells. Beatrice went on her first river boat and went to admire the flowers at Kew and visited the museums and art galleries. In the afternoons they sometimes took advantage of the clement weather and drove in Hyde Park in the Merrick barouche to see and to be seen, often descending to join the numerous people fashionably strolling the lawns.

Shortly before her husband was expected to arrive home, a letter arrived addressed to her. It was from Julius. She stared at the bold handwriting in surprise, wondering what he could have to say to her that was so important he had to write to her. The letter was brief and to the point, its content making her heart plummet. Circumstances had arisen that meant he had to leave for Portugal on a matter of urgent business. He had no idea how long he would be gone—possibly weeks—and she was to remain in London until such time as he returned.

Beatrice was unprepared for the desolation that overwhelmed her, but she refused to be downhearted. And if Julius thought she was calmly to remain in his house doing whatever wives were supposed to do, then he could think again. Already she was tired of London and longed for the freedoms of the country where she could lose herself in the joy of riding a decent mount— and Larkhill wasn't all that far away. Suddenly elation swelled inside her and she smiled audaciously as she was presented with a new objective. Half of her was glad Julius wasn't here so that she could claim back her old home, and that half was starting to enjoy her new status and married life.

And so, the day after she had received her husband's letter, with a small contingent of servants and having sent a note to Lady Merrick informing her of what she intended, she left for Larkhill.

The days Beatrice spent in her old home were like the golden days of her childhood. The main rooms were furnished with pieces Julius had had sent down from London. She was like a child as she wandered from room to room, beset by so many wonderful memories. The house was filled with shadows, all hazy, dream-like as she moved about. How wonderful it would be, she thought, if she could remain at Larkhill for ever, but realistically she knew this was not possible. When Julius returned he would take her to Highfield, which was to be her home, but as long as she could visit Larkhill she would be content.

On her third morning while the dew was still on the ground and brilliant rays of early morning sunlight spilled across the lawn, she was pleasantly surprised when George paid her a visit. She met him on the drive, delirious with joy when she saw he had her precious Major in tow. After she had reacquainted herself with her mount, she turned her attention to her handsome cousin.

'Aunt Moira forbade me to have any further contact with either you or Astrid, George. I shudder to think of her displeasure should she discover you have been here.'

George shrugged, unconcerned. 'It was most unfair of her to do that. And anyway, I came to see you, not the other way round. We've missed you at the house. It isn't the same without you. You really did put Mama's nose out of joint when you up and married Chadwick. She accuses you of stealing him away from Astrid.'

'I suppose it must look like that to her, but in real-ity it wasn't. The whole Lord Chadwick affair was your mother's scheme from the start, a brazen bit of matchmaking in her eagerness to secure for Astrid only the best. It was unfortunate for her that Julius never had any intention of offering for Astrid, so I cannot be accused of stealing him away.'

George frowned, his expression anxious as he studied his cousin's face. 'You are happy, aren't you, Beatrice? You've no regrets about what you did?'

'No, none, George, truly. How can I not be happy when I have all this?' She opened her arms wide to embrace her beloved Larkhill, laughing joyously. 'I may not live here since Julius's home is in Kent, but I can still visit.'

'You do look radiant, Beatrice,' George said on a serious note. 'Chadwick must be doing something right.'

She flushed prettily, remembering her wedding night and all that had transpired. She was impatient for Julius to return so they could live like a properly married couple. 'Julius is a most attentive husband,' she said softly. 'He is away just now—searching for one of his ships that disappeared during a storm in the Bay of Biscay, which is the reason why I'm here now. How is Astrid? Well, I hope?'

'You will be surprised to learn that my dear sister is soon to follow you up the aisle.'

Beatrice stared at him. 'You mean Aunt Moira is to allow her to marry Henry Talbot after all?'

George wasn't smiling anymore. His concern for his sister was plain. 'Don't you believe it—no one so lowly. She's to wed Lord Alden of Alden Hall in Essex— before Christmas, if Mama has anything to do with it.

She's determined not to let him slip through the net. You must have heard of him since he was a friend of Father's.'

'Lord Alden? But—he's an old man—an extremely stout, lecherous old man as I recall.' Beatrice remembered how Lord Alden had a tendency to grope the female servants if they ventured too close. 'He's old enough to be Astrid's father.'

'Exactly. Fifty-five, to be precise—and far too old for Astrid. Naturally she is averse to the marriage and spends most of her time weeping in her room.'

'Poor Astrid. Then she mustn't marry him. She's in love with Henry—and he with her. As head of the family, it is within your power to stop her marrying Lord Alden.'

George shook his head. 'I've tried, but you know Mama. Since you left her temper has become much worse. She will not be crossed or argued with and refuses to listen to reason. She's determined to do this, Beatrice.'

'But she cannot force Astrid to marry him.'

'You're wrong there. When Mama has a bee in her bonnet about something, she's as immovable as the Rock of Gibraltar. She won't pass up the chance of Astrid being a countess. Losing her game with you has increased her determination.'

And her spite, Beatrice thought crossly. She sighed deeply and linked her arm through George's, in perfect, amiable harmony with each other as usual. 'Yes, I imagine she has. Come inside and have some breakfast with me—bacon and eggs are on the menu, and kippers, too—and if we put our heads together we'll try to work out what is to be done. Astrid cannot marry that man.'

Julius looked out of the carriage window, wishing the driver would go faster. He'd left Portsmouth at first light and now the sights and sounds of London were all around him. It had taken him two months to track down his stricken ship, which had managed to limp into a small port in Portugal, and a further two to have the cargo transferred to another vessel and to oversee the repairs before it was deemed seaworthy enough to embark for England.

Now he was impatient to be home and considered the shock his sudden arrival would cause to Beatrice. Had she changed in his absence? he wondered. Had she been lonely? Had she missed him? More than once it had occurred to him that she might resent having him return, that she might be enjoying the single life to the hilt, but that idea was nearly as repugnant as the idea that she might have found another on whom to bestow her affections.

What surprised him most was how much he had missed her. In his mind's eye she glowed like a light. Every day and night he thought of her, conjured up her image in his mind, trying to imagine what she was doing, how she looked, tracing every curve of her face in his mind, remembering her magnificent green eyes and the soft sweetness of her lips. He relived every minute he had spent with her, recalling every word, every inflection, how it had felt to hold her, to make love to her.

They would not remain in London. He would take her to Highfield. He was eager to show Beatrice her new home. She would be happy there—they would be happy together. They would make their marriage work. They had to. If he wanted his family name and the title to continue, he must start providing heirs. He wanted his life to have meaning, to have a real marriage—meaningful and lasting, a wife and children and love—not the empty relationships that passed for marriage in society.

He wanted Beatrice more than he'd wanted anyone in his life. At thirty-one years of age and after more affairs than he cared to remember, he had fallen victim to an outrageously spirited, beautiful girl who blithely incurred his displeasure, amused and infuriated him as no other woman had ever done. He had started off determined to gain the upper hand, but somehow she had managed to get him by the throat.

He was driven by a ridiculous eagerness to see her, as if his life depended on it. At last the carriage pulled up outside his house and he got out, smiling to himself when he saw the Merrick carriage in front. No doubt Constance was calling on Beatrice. He was glad his young wife had had company in his absence.

He let himself in as Constance was on the point of leaving. In the process of pulling on her gloves, she stopped and stared at him in shocked amazement.

'Why—Julius! You're back! Why didn't you let us know you were arriving today?'

He grinned, embracing her warmly. 'I thought I'd surprise you. It's taken me longer than I expected tracking down that damned ship. How is Beatrice? She is well, I hope?'

Lady Merrick became flustered as she considered how best to explain Beatrice's absence. 'I—I expect she is—but...'

He was no longer smiling as servants began moving quickly in all directions to inform those who didn't know that the master was home. 'Expect? What are you saying, Constance?'

'Beatrice isn't here, Julius. She's—at Larkhill.'

For a moment Julius was unable to absorb the full shock of what she said. In a low, deadly voice, he said, 'What did you say?'

'That Beatrice is at Larkhill.'

'But I specifically told her I wanted her to remain here in London until my return. I was under the impression that she would do just that.'

'Oh but she did—at first,' Lady Merrick said defensively.

'When did she leave?'

'Shortly after she received your letter telling her you would be away for some time.'

'And have you heard from her since she left?'

Lady Merrick shook her head. 'No, but then I didn't expect to. I called today on the off chance, thinking she might have returned.'

Furious with Beatrice for refusing to yield to his authority, Julius strode into the drawing room and poured himself a large brandy. Sinking into a chair, he drank deep, but the fiery liquid did nothing to soothe his raw nerves.

Having followed him, Lady Merrick saw the harshness in his taut features and sighed with helpless understanding. 'I know how displeased you must be about this, but can you really blame her? London is all very well, but Beatrice is a country girl at heart. Be honest with yourself, Julius. It must have crossed your mind that she would go to Larkhill.'

'As a matter of fact it didn't. When I told her to remain here I expected her to abide by my wishes. How dare she even consider disobeying me? How dare she? The conniving little… I should have realised it was no small task expecting her to remain in London when that damned house beckoned.'

In dumbfounded amazement, Lady Merrick stared at him, beginning to understand the reason why he was so furious with Beatrice. It was unbelievable that Julius, who had always treated women with a combination of easy indulgence and amused tolerance, could have fallen victim to the same kind of feelings that affected the rest of the human race. Apparently this self-confident, invulnerable man had lost his heart to his own wife.

She suppressed the urge to smile. 'Did you not realise that with Beatrice's need for control, such an order would only make her feel pressured into defying you? What do you intend to do about it?'

'Right now I can think of several things that are appealing—one of them being to wring her neck and another to go after her and drag her off to Highfield and put her under lock and key.'

Lady Merrick sighed and shook her head. 'I can imagine what society would make of that—more grist for the mill.'

'I don't give a damn what society thinks,' Julius said curtly, which was not the truth. In this case he did care; he was furious at being made to look a laughing stock by being unable to keep his wife under control. 'I know just how to handle my errant wife, believe me.'

Leaning back in his chair, he closed his eyes and took a long, harsh breath, trying to bring his temper under control. Beatrice would either bend to his will or he would break her to it, but either way she would learn to behave herself, he decided with cold resolve. For a few minutes he considered going down to Larkhill and confronting her openly with the ruthlessness that she deserved, then discarded the idea. He would make her come to him and he knew exactly how to do it.

Beatrice and George trotted into the stable yard at Larkhill, having spent a wonderful morning riding in the crisp November air over grassy tops of hills, meadows and shallow valleys. George was the first to notice the small elderly man walking about the yard, a younger man in tow, notebook in hand. In dark, sober suits they seemed to be inspecting the buildings. On seeing them they stopped what they were doing and began walking in their direction.

'I say, Beatrice, it looks as if you have visitors.'

Beatrice held her horse in check and watched

the strangers approach. 'Who are you, sir,' she said, addressing the older of the two, 'and what are you doing here?' She was somewhat bemused by their presence.

'I am Mr Sinclair of Sinclair and Lawson, estate agents, and this is my clerk, Robert Denham. I believe you must be Lady Chadwick, Marchioness of Maitland.'

Without taking her eyes off him Beatrice nodded. 'An estate agent? Forgive me, Mr Sinclair, but I have made no arrangements for an estate agent to view Larkhill. I think you must have made a mistake. Perhaps it is some other property you wish to see in the area. If so, I am sure I can direct you to it.'

'Oh, no, my lady. It is Larkhill I have been instructed to view.'

'On whose instruction?'

'Lord Chadwick—your husband, Lady Chadwick.'

Beatrice froze. A premonition of dread gripped her heart. Perfect months of dreaming away the days at Larkhill—golden days, happy days, days filled with joy and contentment, of riding with George and basking in the memories of her childhood—turned into panicked confusion.

Julius was back.

She stared at Mr Sinclair in utter disbelief, her mouth agape. A wave of dizziness rushed over her. She gripped her riding crop and for a moment could not speak at all. She was utterly stunned, crazed confusion charging through her veins.

'But there has to be some mistake. There must be.'

'There is no mistake, Lady Chadwick. Your husband

has instructed me to do a valuation on the estate with a view to selling. I hope you don't mind that I have made a start, but with such a large property to inspect it will take up most of the day. I did call at the house and was told you were not at home.'

The yard seemed to spin and Beatrice began to panic. She felt powerless, completely overwhelmed, thwarted, cornered. What a fool she had been. Why hadn't she foreseen that the blackguard would do something like this? Jolting herself out of her shock, Beatrice dismounted, handing the reins to a groom.

'Then please do continue, Mr Sinclair,' she said tightly, knowing better than to countermand her husband's instructions. 'Please excuse me.' Walking quickly towards the house, Beatrice could feel her face harden with anger. She knew why Julius was doing this. It was a means of gaining power over her. But it wasn't going to work. She glanced at George as he tried to keep up with her. 'I must leave for London at once. Julius cannot do this. To sell Larkhill—why, it's unthinkable.'

'He has every right,' George said gently. 'In truth, Beatrice, I'm surprised he hasn't done so before now.'

'But he can't,' Beatrice cried. 'He can't. Otherwise what was the point of it all?'

'Did it never occur to you that he would do it?'

'No—no, it didn't. Oh, George, what a stupid, blind fool I've been. But all is not lost. I'll go to him, speak to him. I have to make him see that he cannot do this.'

'Of course you must, but—you won't forget about Astrid, will you, Beatrice?'

She paused, looked at him and, seeing his worried look, her expression softened. 'How could I? Astrid is always in my thoughts. I am so concerned about her. I'll speak to Julius. I am sure he will know what to do.'

Beatrice's disbelieving dread increased with every mile that took her to her husband. She suddenly found herself at war with herself. Half of her was besieged by the wild joy at the thought that the man who had obsessed her thoughts since she had first laid eyes on him was home at last, and the other half was indignant and furious that he intended to take from her the very thing that had brought them together in the first place, without any discussion on the matter.

Oh, but Julius Chadwick was a sly one. By blatantly ignoring her feelings, without so much as a by your leave, like some wicked puppet master it was his way of telling her that he had taken control of her life and there was nothing she could do about it.

On reaching the house she hurried inside. She was met by Hayes in the hall. In stentorian tones he welcomed her home and informed her that her husband was in his study, working.

'Oh. Well, that's too bad. Tell him I'm here, will you, Hayes, and that I want to see him.'

'As you wish, my lady.'

Hayes crossed the hall to do her bidding. Breathing rapidly, Beatrice waited, her hands on her waist, the toe of her foot tapping impatiently, her eyes glued to the study door, behind which lurked the man responsible for her fury. She heard Hayes clear his throat and then proceed to tell Julius that his wife had arrived home and wished to speak to him.

Julius's low voice vibrated with annoyance. 'Tell my wife to go to her room. I will be up to see her shortly. In the meantime I have important work to attend to.'

Furious at being ordered to her room like a mindless piece of chattel, without further ado Beatrice marched to the wood-panelled study and pushed her way past Hayes. Julius was sitting at his desk, dictating a letter to his secretary. His head snapped up, his gaze riveting on her, and his expression went from shock to relief to cold anger.

'Beatrice!'

Putting a tight rein on her temper as she walked across the carpet, Beatrice could not take her eyes off him. He looked just as handsome as ever, just as ruggedly virile and formidably large. She refused to admit, however, that his chiselled male perfection had any effect on her. With unarguable logic, she said, 'I apologise for disturbing you, Julius. Obviously you consider me of less importance than your business concerns, but after an absence of four months, I'm sure you can spare a few minutes to speak to your wife.'

With deadly calm, Julius laid down his quill and turned his gaze on his secretary. 'Leave us, will you, Harry?' he said curtly. 'We'll finish this later.'

When Harry and Hayes had left the room Julius turned his attention on his wife. He took one look at her face and knew that his ruse to bring her back to London had worked. What he read in her face was a mixture of fury and dread. Little did she know that he had been waiting for her, that he knew that when Mr Sinclair introduced himself and informed her of his reason for being at Larkhill, it wouldn't take long for her to come hurtling back to London. He was not disappointed. In fact, she had made it faster than he'd imagined.

There was an air of barely controlled impatience about her that fairly crackled. Her hair hung in a tangled pennant of glossy waves. She was flushed. Her eyes had a luminous quality, green and dazzling, of a woman who had spent weeks in a state of bliss and contentment and with no wish to have it spoiled by a returning husband. It maddened him and fascinated him and made him desire her all at the same time, but he controlled the urge to drag her off to bed and looked at her in chilly, fierce reproach.

'Since you're here, I suppose we'd better get this over with now rather than later.'

Beatrice's head was whirling as she cast about for words. Until then she had thought she remembered exactly how he looked, but she was mistaken. His tan jacket clung to his wide shoulders and his thick hair was brushed back from his wide forehead. His face was one of arrogant handsomeness, with its sculptured mouth and striking amber eyes. But now she noticed the cynicism in those eyes and a ruthless set to his jaw. She searched his features, but found no sign that this forbidding man had held her and made love to her with seductive sensuality on their wedding night. Now everything about him exuded ruthlessness and brute strength.

She moved to stand directly in front of him, her hands clenched into fists. 'You know why I have come back to London, so don't pretend you are surprised to see me. How could you do this?' she cried in brazen confrontation. 'I find it contemptible and completely underhand.'

Julius loomed over her, holding himself completely still, his eyes boring into hers. When he spoke his voice was icier than an ice floe, and his words chilled Beatrice more than that. 'What I find underhand is for you to disobey me. It was foolish of me to expect to find my wife waiting for me to return home, to fling herself into my arms and shed tears of joy at my safe return. And if you're about to tell me how sorely you've missed me, the fact that you left for Larkhill as soon as my back was turned is a little incongruous. If you want to soften my attitude towards you and win my forgiveness for disobeying me, then you will have to think of something else.'

The sweet drift of happiness Beatrice had felt on waking at Larkhill that morning shattered away and her heart hardened and her face turned mutinous. 'Win your forgiveness?' she exploded, her colour rising with indignation, anger and confusion warring inside her head. Julius had never cared about her and he had no right to act like a self-righteous, outraged husband. 'And why, pray, should I want your forgiveness? I don't want it.'

'Oh, yes, lady, you do.' His voice was soft, mild

even, but there was a core of iron in it which told Beatrice to beware. His face was like granite, his mouth stern and his eyes had darkened in their fury.

'The way I see it, I have done nothing wrong,' she persisted. 'Your forgiveness is the *last* thing I care about.'

Julius caught his breath and his jaw clamped with the grinding resolution which had kept him always in control of those with whom he dealt. Show no one your thoughts, had always been his rule, but this rebellious wife of his had a habit of pushing his temper beyond his control.

'Beatrice,' he said, 'if you're wondering how far you can push me, you've just reached your limit. I expect you to understand the rules.' His eyes challenged her dangerously. 'The idea of being defied by my own wife is unthinkable. As long as you behave yourself I am willing to let you enjoy the full benefits of your position as the Marchioness of Maitland. So think very carefully before you make the mistake of defying my orders in the future. You'll regret it, I promise you. I can be ugly when I am crossed. You would do well to remember it.'

Anger at being spoken to like a recalcitrant child poured through Beatrice. She could not believe that this was her husband speaking to her, that he was worse than she remembered—more arrogant, more dictatorial and completely heartless. Despite the cold tingle of alarm his silken voice caused in her, stripping away some of her confidence, she lifted her chin.

'You cannot bully me into compliance, Julius. I can

see that my removing myself to the country has upset you, though I cannot for the life of me see why. What did you expect me to do—sit about all day and slowly go out of my mind?'

'Other wives seem to find plenty to fill their days.'

'Ha,' she scoffed. 'Running their husband's house— in the kitchen and the pantry, discussing menus and counting linen, and when all that is done sitting by the fireside embroidering samplers and darning socks. When you left I did all that and found it tedious.'

'For two weeks, Beatrice. You did that for two weeks, before you went haring off to Larkhill.'

'And why not?' she persisted. 'I miss the freedom of the country—my horse. London is horrid in the summer. Most people take themselves off to the country.'

'The Merricks don't. They reside in London all the year round.'

'Only because Lady Merrick likes London and likes being around people. Besides, they don't have a country residence to retire to.'

Julius stared down at the tempestuous young woman, her face both delicate and vivid with her stormy eyes and soft lips, and he suddenly saw her as she'd looked in the garden at Standish House, her enchanting face turned up to the night sky. As they'd discussed the stars there had been a softness about her, an elusive gentleness that was as fragile and vulnerable as the delicate flowers that surrounded her. She was still that same young woman, completely female, sensual and she was his wife. He had made love to her, but he did not possess her, for the sweet, wild essence of her still belonged to her.

She was not a conventional woman. She was young, naïve and vulnerable and could not be blamed for rebelling against the restrictions which held her. She was not submissive or pliant and was unwilling to be moulded to the whims of others. The fury within him lessened and, as he looked down into her glorious eyes, his stomach clenched at the thought of hurting her.

'For the time I have been away you have had more freedom than most, Beatrice, and now I have returned I would like to see your defiant heart more involved with household affairs.'

She accepted his words coldly, her head high, her cheeks flushed. 'Anyone would think you married me for my domestic accomplishments, when we both know different. It may have escaped your notice, but I haven't had a great deal of experience with being a wife. So if you have finished reprimanding me, *my lord*, I have a matter of my own to raise with you.'

'I know.' Satisfied that she was adequately chastened, Julius perched his hip on the edge of the desk and folded his arms across his chest.

'You cannot mean to sell Larkhill,' she said, unable to keep the desperation from her voice. 'Julius, you can't.'

'I don't need Larkhill. It means nothing to me.'

'But it does to me,' she flared with a sudden impassioned flourish, her eyes blurred with tears. 'It means *everything* to me. You know that. Why do you have to change things? Why are you doing this? Why do you have to hurt me? Is it to punish me for manipulating you into marriage? If so, then would you please find some other way of doing it instead of selling Larkhill.'

'I have already decided,' he said firmly. 'The matter is settled. As soon as I have a copy of Mr Sinclair's valuation, the Larkhill estate will be put on the market. I am hoping for a quick sale.'

For a moment Beatrice's mind could not adjust itself to the fact that he really was going to go through with it. How could he do that? How could she live and never see Larkhill again? At least at Standish House she had still been able to see the fields, the tall trees, the low, wet meadows, the quiet places only she knew about. Resentment of Julius burned in her heart.

When she spoke her voice was low and trembling with contempt. 'What a cold, unfeeling blackguard you are, Julius Chadwick. This is nothing short of tyranny. You are enjoying every minute of what I am going through. Because of what I did, you will naturally want to torment me as much as possible to pay me back. Little did I think when I named the forfeit after beating you in that race that you would do this to me.'

'Then you should have had more sense. You should have foreseen that I might call your bluff.'

'Well, I didn't. Why didn't you tell me at the start you might do this? Why let it go so far? Don't you see it was a way out for you? When you asked me to back down I would have done so at once and disappeared out of your life for ever.'

'Perhaps I didn't want you to disappear, Beatrice. You intrigued me. I had just returned to England after a long absence and I realised that to continue the line I must have heirs, and to have heirs I needed a wife. I was considering searching for some high-bred débutante. I hadn't started looking and then you came along with your outrageous challenge. The moment I laid eyes on you I knew you were different. I am not just referring to your beauty—I've known beautiful women before and quite frankly they bored me to tears. I had no intention of selling Larkhill when I met you. It is a valuable property. The land yields well. I would have been a fool to get rid of it then.'

'It still is. I may have made it difficult for you to refuse to honour the forfeit, but I did not believe you would be so petty or mean spirited as to retaliate and sell a property that is still viable merely to punish me.'

'And if I had told you I meant to sell it, would you really have backed down?'

'Of course I would. Without Larkhill there was no point in any of it.'

Relinquishing his perch Julius stood up and moved closer, a cynical twist curling his lips. 'You never fail to amaze me, Beatrice. You are the only woman who has not been drawn to me by my title or my gold. All you care about is that damned house. Well, all your scheming has come to nothing. No matter how much money it brings in every year from the rents and the land, the sooner it's out of our lives the better. The mistake is yours. Accept it. There is no going back so you will have to learn to live with the consequences of your actions—however painful that will be.'

Beatrice looked at him for a long time and then she

nodded slightly. 'Yes—yes, you're right, Julius. The mistake is mine.' Without another word she turned from him and went to the door.

'Where are you going?'

'To have a bath and a change of clothes.'

Julius's strong mouth began to smile. It turned into an audacious grin, his temper replaced by something else. 'That's the first sensible thing you've said since coming home. It will be my pleasure to get you out of those clothes.'

Chapter Eight

Beatrice spun round, shocked by the implication of his words and that he expected her to tumble into bed with him after all the hurtful things he had said to her. 'Shame on you, Julius,' she retorted, her cheeks aflame. 'I have not been in the house two minutes and already you are thinking of...'

His black brows crept upwards and with a defiant look he sauntered towards her with the predatory grace of a panther. When he spoke his voice was silky smooth. 'What, Beatrice? Of what am I thinking?'

'Of—of bedding me after all you have just said... Can you not think of anything else?' Her heart was pounding with wild confusion and she was flustered now he was so close.

She was determined to deny him, but inside her that treacherous spark ignited. Trying to deny her attraction to him was useless. There was a churning sensation in her stomach, like the fluttering wings of a captive butterfly, and a mounting heat swept through her and her body began to stir.

Julius chuckled softly, wondering why, from the very first, she'd had the power to attract him—wondering why he felt this consuming, unquenchable need now to possess and gentle her without breaking her spirit.

Placing a finger beneath her chin, he tilted her face to his. 'I'm afraid not, my love. But then after an absence of four months and relatively a new bridegroom, it is not unusual.'

She swallowed and quivered when his finger ran over the curve of her cheek, knowing that in no time at all she would lose her ability to resist him. 'Please allow me to leave, Julius.'

'I will,' he breathed, his whisper fraught with wicked seduction, 'in a moment.' He bent his head to kiss the place where his finger had been before, teasing her senses into a wild awakening for him. Beatrice closed her eyes, unable to move. 'I know you want me.' Taking her arms, he drew her against the solid wall of his chest. 'I intend to see if I can still make you respond to me as you did before I left your bed on our wedding night.'

'Please don't,' she gasped, turning her head aside, drowning in humiliation at the brutal reminder of how wantonly she had behaved then.

By the time his lips caressed her earlobe, she was overcome with the need for his kiss. Unable to stop herself, with a low moan she turned her face to his and offered him her mouth. He claimed it immediately and she revelled in his embrace, despite her earlier determination not to let this happen. Ending the kiss, he held her fevered stare before lowering his head to her breast. She watched in hazy silence as he gathered her waist in his hands and gently kissed her breast through her gown, his warm breath permeating the fabric. Her heart slammed into her ribs and she could not have uttered a word of protest if she had wanted to when his lips moved on to the V-shaped neckline and he pressed fervent kisses on the exposed flesh.

She rested her hands on his wide shoulders as his mouth travelled upwards, brushing along the sensitive column of her throat, her ear and the curve of her cheek. She made no effort whatsoever to stop him when he pushed his fingers through her hair and held her head firm, taking her lips once more. All thoughts beyond this moment and this man fled. His lips moved over hers with a flowing, demanding passion, an insistence that she kiss him back that was almost beyond denial.

What he was doing to her was more than Beatrice could withstand. With a silent moan of despair, she yielded to his kiss, parting her lips beneath the sensual pressure and, at that moment, his tongue slid between them, invading her mouth and taking possession of her. Lost in a stormy sea of desire, confusion and yearning, she felt him relinquish his hold on her head and splay his hand across her lower spine, forcing her closer to him, moulding her melting body to the hardening contours of his. She could feel the taut strength of his legs and thighs pressing intimately against hers. His other hand cupped her breast, his thumb brushing back and forth across her sensitised nipple, an action that was overwhelming. He could do with her what he willed. Her body was open to him. He could take her there and then, and he surely knew it.

The ardour with which Beatrice was responding to his kiss had a devastating effect on Julius's starved body. Desire flowed through his bloodstream like wildfire, pounding in his loins. Fighting back the urge to lay her down on the carpet and ravage her there and then, he dragged his lips from hers and drew a long, steady breath.

Her heart still pounding, her mind still reeling with pleasure, Beatrice closed her eyes and rested her head weakly on her husband's chest and felt him press a gentle kiss on her hair. At last she found the power to raise her head and open her eyes; she looked at him with a haziness similar to that of drinking too much wine.

Julius took a step back, satisfaction in his eyes and a worldly smile. 'You are an exceptional woman, Beatrice. No more foolish talk of not wanting me. I think I have just proved a point. Now go and get your bath. I will be up to see you shortly.'

Beatrice turned from him and somehow made her legs carry her to the door. Slipping out, she went to her bedchamber, spent and breathless, and even more confused than she had been before. She leaned her back against the door and closed her eyes, trying to regain her wits. Julius had uncovered a wanton streak in her she never knew existed and there was nothing she could do. Beneath the caressing boldness of his hands and his lips, she was his woman, and though she was honest enough to admit her treacherous woman's body came alive—not against her will, but willingly—it was with a heavy heart. As intoxicating as it was, she realised it was a completely separate thing from what she really wanted—an intimacy of the heart with Julius.

Her feelings for her husband overrode all else. Everything else faded into insignificance—even Larkhill didn't seem so important any more. She could already feel his control closing around her, suffocating her. His rank, his strength, his intelligence, his power, his ability to still her protests with his lips—all this made Julius a powerful man indeed. She could feel herself sliding into his grasp and was steadily losing the will to control her own destiny.

Julius sauntered into his wife's bedchamber. Having bathed and dismissed her maid, Beatrice was seated at her satinwood dressing-table, her elbows on the surface, her forehead resting on her hands. Even with her hair shining like newly minted gold in the sun, she looked the picture of heartbreaking dejection. She hadn't heard him enter. He started to turn away and leave her to her privacy, then, with a sigh, he changed his mind and went further into the room. Closer now, he realised her shoulders were shaking with sobs and he felt a surge of remorse, cursing himself for behaving like an insensitive, blundering idiot.

He was barely able to believe his own selfish

callousness. He should have been gentler with her, more of a husband than a hard-bitten businessman with a bitter past. His churlish display had upset her, alienated her, and he regretted that. He hadn't meant to make her cry. Being the cause of her misery, he knew he was in for a delicate round of diplomacy.

'Beatrice?'

She started violently at the sound of his voice. Snapping her head up, she dashed her tears away with the back of her hand and, picking up her hairbrush, began brushing her hair vigorously.

'What do you want?' she managed to say, her voice flat.

'To apologise.'

This was not what Beatrice had expected. Her eyes met his in the mirror and her lips twisted wryly. 'You? Apologise? Is the callous attitude you used on me earlier supposed to be endearing? Is this what I am to expect in the future if I unwittingly transgress?'

'This is how I am, Beatrice. I am not perfect.'

'No, you're not.' She sighed despondently, tired of the argument. 'It doesn't matter. You were right. I've been a fool, a stupid fool for thinking that by marrying you I would bring Larkhill back into my life, and now I shall have to live with the consequences of my stupidity.'

Julius's heart turned over when he looked at her reflection in the mirror and saw the wounded look in her glorious green eyes. Going to stand behind her, he stilled her hand and took the brush from her, taking on the task of brushing the long silken mass himself.

Beatrice made no move to stop him. She just sat quietly, watching him through the vanity mirror. The image of his tall, masculine frame occupied with such a feminine task enabled her to manage a weak smile.

'You missed your vocation, Julius. You would have made a good lady's maid.'

He grinned leisurely. 'I would be only too happy to stand in when your maid is absent.' He paused and gazed into her eyes. 'Why were you crying?'

'Because I couldn't help it. I am ashamed of myself. I was crying for my own ineptitude, my incompetence and my inability to manage my own life.'

'I don't agree. I think you have a natural talent for all three. You're being too harsh on yourself, Beatrice. Your aunt made it clear that you were not particularly welcome in her house, therefore you had no desire to stay where you were not wanted. But without means where could you go? You yearned for your old home, which was the only place where you had known happiness, and you saw me as a means of getting it back. I cannot blame you for that.'

'You don't?'

'No, I don't.' He experienced a feeling of comprehension, for while he had been struggling with his own life, her world had also been falling apart. At least now he had an insight of what lay behind her fear and dread, and what had driven her to do what she had.

'Nevertheless, I can see how, by my actions, I have humiliated and embarrassed you. I should not have done that. I thought of no one but myself. You can divorce me if you like. I wouldn't blame you.'

Julius stiffened. 'Is that what you want?'

She sighed dejectedly, looking down at her hands. 'It no longer matters what I want. The choice is yours, Julius.'

Putting the brush down, Julius turned and walked slowly across the room to the window, where he stood looking out. Divorce! It was unthinkable. He could not imagine having to go back to the way his life had been before he had met Beatrice—back to the darkness, the loneliness, the endless isolation, the despair, though he would never admit it to anyone. To be with Beatrice now, to have known her as a husband knows his wife and then to have her walk away, that would reduce him to a wretched creature who had been cast out. Whatever it took, he knew he would do anything to keep her with him.

Recovering his composure, he said firmly, 'There will be no divorce.'

Beatrice stared at her image for a moment as relief washed over her. Closing her eyes, she tried to gather her thoughts, to know what to say, what to think. Julius had never spoken of how much he cared for her, not even pretended to. She wasn't certain of his feelings—she wasn't certain of her own, either. All she really knew was that the sight of his hard, handsome face and the bold amber eyes never failed to make her entire being feel tense and alive. She liked being with him, she liked it when he kissed her and when he made love to her. Added to his other attractions, she knew that Julius had a depth of character other men lacked. She was confused as to how she should feel and think, but that didn't really matter one way or the other, because she *was* going to love him. It was happening and she couldn't stop it.

Julius came up behind her and his hands settled on her shoulders. In the mirror she watched him bend his dark head, felt his warm lips against the curve of her neck sending tingling sensations down her back.

'You're very beautiful, Beatrice. I suppose you don't want to hear it, but it's true. I feel we are well suited to help each other. A rare jewel. That's what you are.' She was very still, unable to move as he drew her hair aside and placed a kiss lightly in the nape of her neck, before whispering in her ear, 'And quite irresistible.'

She wanted to contradict him, but her tongue remained silent. The rest of her body began to sing and her pulse raced at the warmth of his breath on her neck.

He looked deeply into her eyes, wanting to show her what he felt when he looked at her, not just what he saw. 'Will you do something for me?'

The raw emotion in his voice registered on Beatrice and she felt her bones begin to melt. 'What? What is it you want?' she asked with a nervous tremor in her voice.

Julius raised his head and his lips curved in a smile, while striving to keep his raw hungry need to be inside her at bay. 'I know exactly what I want; if you come to bed with me now, I'll show you. I want to see you naked on the bed with your hair spread across the pillows. I want to look at your face while I touch you and make love to you, because I badly need to know how you feel.'

Mesmerised by the seductive invitation in those eyes and the velvet roughness of his deep voice, Beatrice stood up and wrapped her arms around her husband's neck, knowing that, for him, this was a moment of atonement. Julius swung her into his arms, driven to try to make amends to her in the only way he knew how. Carrying her to the bed, he lowered her gently onto the quilt and followed her down, his lips finding hers in a long, deep kiss.

When he could finally tear himself away from her to remove his clothes, Beatrice watched him unashamedly, glorying in his magnificent body. Slipping out of her robe, she slid beneath the covers and waited for him to join her. When he did, he gathered her to him.

'You're trembling,' he said in the gentlest of voices.

'I know,' she admitted nervously. 'I don't know why.'

'Don't you?' he asked softly. 'Perhaps this might help,' he murmured, placing his hungry lips on hers to still their tremor, tasting the hot sweetness of her mouth.

Feeling as if her heart would surely burst with what was inside her, Beatrice made a tiny, smothered sound of desire and answered him with a melting kiss of her own. It was enough. Julius gathered her tightly to him, pulling her against his full length, clasping her against his rigid thighs while his lips were both rough and tender. When he lifted his mouth from hers, she felt an aching sense of loss that was replaced by sweet torment as he slid his mouth down her neck to her breasts, nuzzling them slowly before his lips closed tightly over her taut nipple. She moaned in helpless pleasure, desire streaking through her, her hands tangling in his hair, her back arching in helpless surrender.

Deliberately taking his time, Julius slid his hands over her like a connoisseur, caressing with skilful reverence, claiming every inch of her for his own, heating her skin and making her ache with soon-to-be-fulfilled yearnings. Eager to do some exploring of her own, Beatrice heard the quickening of his breath as her fingers inched tentatively over his bare flesh, savouring the sculpted hardness of his chest and abdomen. His hands slid lower, curving around her hips, his lips trailing lower and nuzzling closer to the curly triangle between her legs. Beatrice gasped, tilting her head back, her hand gripping his shoulders, her head pounding like a maddened thing, filled with a mixture of excitement and impatience for him to take her.

Julius felt her escalating desire. All his cool control stripped away. Desperate for her, he pulled her beneath him as though he could not withstand another second of denial. Lifting her taut buttocks to receive him, he entered her.

Beatrice opened completely to him, moulding her hips to his as he began to move, presenting him with a gift of surrender, unwittingly driving him to unparalleled agonies of desire, her surrender answering something deep within his soul. Wanting all he had to give, something wild, raw and primitive and savage built inside her, racing through her veins with wrenching pleasure, the undulant waves of his taking increasing to a crescendo of resounding power. Nothing either of them felt was suppressed or hidden, there was just exquisite joy.

They reached their climax in wild, wonderful, burning unison. Julius's body jerked convulsively again and again, and he clasped her to him, feeling the tiny, shudders of her body as she rung the last pleasure of her orgasm from him. Breathing hard against her cheek, his heart raging in frantic tempo with hers, his body merging into hers, his seed deep inside her, he was more pleased by what had just happened between them than by any other sexual experience of his life. It was also, he thought, the most profound moment of his life.

When reality returned and his breathing evened out, he moved on to his side. Beatrice's hair spilled over his naked chest like a drift of satin and he raised a hand to smooth it off her face, feeling humbled and blessed by her unselfish ardour—and relieved that this time she didn't turn from him. Content and sated, their bodies succumbing to the dreamy aftermath of complete consummation, they remained that way for several minutes, then Beatrice stirred and draped a leaden arm around his waist. Julius tipped her chin up so that he could gaze into her eyes.

'How do you feel?' he asked softly.

Beatrice's long, curling lashes fluttered up and her eyes like two languid green pools gazed into his—this man, her husband. She had not sought his love, she did not expect it, and she certainly had no right to it, but at that moment, more than anything she had wanted in her life before, she wanted it.

'I feel like a wife,' she whispered. 'Your wife.'

He laughed huskily. 'Which is exactly what you are, my love. My wife in every sense. And I feel like a husband,' he said, with tender solemnity. 'To think I actually believed there was no such thing as marital bliss.' Relaxing against the pillows, he revelled in the simple joy of having her in his arms, her head resting on his shoulder. 'How incredibly stupid I have been.'

'No, you are not stupid,' his wife declared loyally, turning her face up to his. 'Although I would dearly like to know what has given you reason to think that.' She observed a tightening of his features and something in his eyes warned her not to press, but she was not to be put off. Placing her lips against his shoulder in the gentlest caress, her heart aching, she wished he would open up to her. 'As your wife I would like to know something of your past, Julius—your parents. Will you not tell me?'

'Time enough for that,' he replied, closing his eyes.

Beatrice wriggled on to her stomach and propped herself up on her arms, her face only inches from his. 'Please be open with me, Julius. I want to know the nature of the man I married. I have always been forthcoming about myself—and you witnessed for yourself the misery of what my life was like at Standish House. I too find it hard to speak about my deepest feelings, but I would willingly do so with you. Despite all my efforts to keep you from seeing my many insecurities, you have a habit of pulling them out of me. I think that is because now I am your wife, I want you to know who I am. I know you are a very private person, Julius, and I respect that, but if you cannot open up to me as I am willing to do with you—even if it's just a little at a time—then we have no chance of happiness until you can begin to share yourself with me.'

For a moment he did not move, nor did he reply. Then he opened his eyes and met her direct gaze. From the very start, despite her outward show of confidence, as he had gazed into those soft green eyes he had sensed in this brave, unspoiled girl a great capacity for love that made him hope that in time his own most secret yearning would be fulfilled. It was a yearning he had never known and never thought he could have until Beatrice had thrust herself forwards and challenged his spirit. He now felt that he could tell her something of his past without revealing the dark secret he kept locked away in the furthest corner of his mind.

'It is the way I've always been,' he said in answer to her question. 'I cannot change the way I am.'

'I would not expect you to do that, but it is not unnatural for a wife to want to know about her husband. I know you've had a difficult past—indeed, we have both suffered because of what our fathers did,' she said, knowing that whatever she said now might determine their whole future. 'Lady Merrick has told me a little about your life, and you, if you remember, when you brought me to London. I know of your achievements and how they made you rich, but your family remains a mystery to me. Why, Julius? Why won't you tell me? I know it is largely down to your father. Is it because you are ashamed? Because if so, I will tell you now that I don't care who your parents were.'

Rage blazed in Julius's eyes for a moment, but then he sighed resignedly. 'Yes, Beatrice, I suppose I am ashamed, but there is more to it than that.'

'Please tell me?' she asked softly.

'If you insist on knowing, I will tell you. Until his demise my whole life revolved around my father. He was a greedy man. It was not in his nature to live his life in modest comfort. He was the Marquess of Maitland, once a name to gain admittance into the highest political and social circles. He was also the worst in a long line of gamblers, falling deeper and deeper into debt running into tens of thousands of pounds. Everything of value was stripped away to pay the bills and his gambling debts. It was sheer hell for my mother. She was constantly at her wits' end. He was not a good man, nor was he kind—especially not to my mother. He also drank heavily and treated her very badly.'

Beatrice watched, her beautiful eyes wide with shock as pain slashed across his features. 'That must have been awful for her—and for you, having to witness it.'

Reaching up he pushed her hair casually over her shoulder. 'He was a brute. The banks were threatening foreclosure on loans he could not hope to cover. Nothing remained against which capital might have been raised. I had a personal income, but Father took it all. He stole and gambled away every penny. Even the properties were gone—pledged against loans he could not hope to repay.'

'Lady Merrick told me it was some money given to you by your grandmother and your own intelligence and good sense that enabled you to succeed. I admire you for that.'

'Yes, God bless her. Without her—without that money—I could not have done it.'

Beatrice smiled. 'Oh, I'm sure you would have found a way. Is your grandmother still alive?'

He hesitated, and for a moment Beatrice thought he wasn't going to say more. When he did, his deep voice was strangely hesitant, almost as if he was testing his ability to talk about it. 'She died shortly before...'

'Before what?' Pain slashed his features once more. She touched his cheek. 'Julius, please tell me.'

He turned his head to one side and quietly said, 'Before my mother.'

'There—was a fire—at Highfield. Your parents...'

He turned and looked at her once more, a fierce light having entered his eyes. It was so hard to say these things, even harder than he had thought it would be, each word an ocean of pain, and he felt as if he were a youth all over again.

Beatrice did not say anything, but simply listened as the words carried on pouring out of him.

'Both my parents perished. Only days before, Father had suffered badly on the stock market and it went from bad to worse when he tried to recoup his losses at the tables. On the night of the fire, finally realising his dreams of greatness were shattered, he returned to Highfield. Arriving late at night, he thought he was alone in the house. My mother was supposed to be visiting a friend. Unbeknown to my father, she was feeling unwell and decided to put off her visit. She was asleep when he returned.'

Beatrice's heart quaked and her soul was beginning to hurt at the forlorn air around him. 'Julius, what are you saying? Surely you don't think he set fire to the house deliberately—that he—'

'What? Committed suicide? That he killed my mother?' He spoke with glacial calm. 'How would I know? How would anyone know that? Some say it was started accidentally. Some say it wasn't. The fact that he dismissed all the servants before the fire started speaks for itself,' he finished grimly.

'I'm so sorry,' Beatrice whispered through a blur of tears, and all the sympathy and warmth in her heart was mirrored in her eyes. Once she had foolishly thought she knew what a broken heart was like. How wrong she had been, for it was only now breaking for this man who had to live with the knowledge that his father might have killed his mother. 'You must have been out of your mind with shock and grief. I can understand why you didn't want to talk about it.'

'All their married life my father crushed my mother. I loved her down to the depths of my soul and could not forgive him for the hurt he dealt her by his actions. I was appalled by the enormity of his debts and that, along with what he might have done to my mother, was the moment when I truly think I began to hate him. Can you imagine what it is like to do that, Beatrice? That was also the moment when I began to hate myself for harbouring such feelings.'

He fell silent and after a moment he looked at his wife, as if remembering she was there. He saw some of the horror in her eyes, and said, 'Now you know my deepest secret. You are right. You are entitled to know all this, but God help me, Beatrice, until this moment I could not tell another living soul how I felt.'

Beatrice didn't know what to say. How could any words suffice? 'Thank you for telling me, for sharing that with me.'

'Thankfully I was then in a position to pay off my father's debts and lost no time in having the part of the house damaged by the fire rebuilt. As far as I was concerned, that was the end of it.'

He said that, Beatrice noted, with deadly finality. It was as if he'd resolved matters to his complete satisfaction in his own mind, and nothing and no one could ever intrude on the place where he had put his parents to rest.

'After that I threw myself into my work, travelling east and west to try to forget.'

'And—Larkhill?' she whispered tentatively. 'You haven't mentioned how my father came to lose it to you.'

Apart from a tensing of his body, Julius's face remained expressionless. 'I would prefer not to go into details of that night, Beatrice. Suffice to know that after paying off the mortgage I placed the estate in the hands of an agent to run in my absence. The first time I saw Larkhill was when I went to assess it for myself. In all honesty I had no idea you existed. I didn't know your father had a daughter. If I had known it would bring me face to face with you and the pain of your loss, not for the world would I have gone down there.' He met her gaze. 'How do you feel now you know the whole sorry story?' he asked, gently smoothing the tousled curls with his hand. 'Are you wishing you'd never laid eyes on me? I wouldn't blame you.'

'Please don't think that. I'm glad you've told me. I cannot imagine what would have become of our marriage if you had not shared this with me. It's too big, too important to have let it stand between us for the rest of our lives.'

'And there will be no more talk of divorce? In for a penny, in for a pound?' he murmured, encouraged that she didn't pull away.

Beatrice swallowed the lump that had risen in her throat and, lifting her head, she gave him a wobbly smile. 'Yes, something like that.'

'And you have no concerns about the position of being my wife—about what that entails?'

'Tell me what it is you expect your wife to do.'

He upturned her face to his, gazing deep into her eyes. 'Always remain by the side of the marquess and desire him as you do now with all the passion you are capable of—all the days of your life.'

Beatrice tilted her head to one side, her heart pounding so hard she believed he must hear it. 'I already do that, but will the marquess continue to desire his marchioness with the same amount of passion he asks of her?'

He cupped her cheek in his hand, loving all the subtle nuances of feeling conveyed in her expression.

'I believe I could manage that—in fact, I believe the marquess already does.' He wiped a tear away with his thumb. Only then did she realise she was crying.

'Oh, Julius! I pray God you are sincere, for I could not bear it if you weren't. I—I love you, you see…'

His face hardened and he pressed his finger to her lips, silencing her. 'Don't say it, Beatrice,' he said with quiet, implacable firmness and a caution he had always maintained when it came to affairs of the heart. 'Already you have given me far more than I could ever expect. Do not give more than that.'

Beatrice lowered her eyes and said no more about it, but his rejection of her love hurt more than she imagined possible. She accepted that she loved him, that he gave her great joy, and it broke her heart to think he might never reciprocate her love. Looking at him once more, she put her face close to his, studying it intently, looking to see if there were any more secrets. As though he suspected that she was trying to see into his mind, there was a darkening to his eyes which after a moment seemed to disappear like a cloud blown away by the wind. There was nothing to see, but she could not explain the tiny *frisson* of doubt that would not leave her.

'Please don't lie to me or hold anything back, Julius. We must both agree to set a pattern of honesty and frankness for the future. You married me because I made it difficult for you to refuse—and I married you because I wanted to bring Larkhill back into my life.'

'What are you saying?'

Raising her head, she met his gaze. 'That things

change in the most peculiar way. Not for one moment did I think I would end up feeling like this when I challenged you to that race. When I first realised I had feelings for you I told myself I was deceiving myself and continued to do so. I do not know when those feelings began, but what I do know is that they are feelings so much stronger and deeper than anything I have ever felt before.'

'You are right,' he murmured. 'Things do have a way of changing. But I'm beginning to like the result of your scheming. I would like you to know that from the moment when I first laid eyes on you I wanted you—badly, my love.'

Beatrice jerked her head back and gave him an indignant look. 'You did? You should have told me.'

Julius chuckled and rolled her on to her back. 'What? And spoil the fun? Not in a million years,' he said, kissing the tip of her nose.

Beatrice laughed at his unprincipled determination to get what he wanted and his complete lack of contrition for it. 'Shame on you, Julius Chadwick. Have you no principles at all?' she demanded.

He pulled her further down the bed and covered her body with his own. 'None whatsoever,' he told her before taking her lips in a kiss that she was unable to resist, and their bodies joined once more in a dizzying union of delight.

After their loving, with a feeling of well-serviced bliss lingering in his body, Julius was enjoying looking at his wife seated at her dressing table. She had slipped into her robe, which was nothing more than a wisp of satin and lace and ribbons in a delicate shade of peach. His eyes lingered on the thrust of her breasts as she raised her arms and attempted to bring her tousled hair into some kind of order. He admired the long graceful line of her back and the fall of her golden hair. As he watched her his throat went dry. Dear Lord, she had been beautiful before, but now she was glorious. Before they had married she had seemed wholesome and innocent, but now she seemed different, like a young woman who had come into her own. She glowed and bloomed and seemed softer somehow. In the mirror her eyes were drifting, dreaming, and she looked like a woman whose senses were fulfilled, physically and emotionally.

When she stood up and stretched languidly, like a cat beneath the sun's warmth, the slender, graceful length of her was outlined beneath her robe. The fabric strained over her breasts, rich and full. Her figure was taut and trim, yet he saw the slight roundness of her belly as her robe clung to her.

All at once Julius felt unbalanced by the strength of his emotions. Was it possible that his wife was with child? Doubting his suspicion, he cautiously looked again. No, the swelling was there, noticeably. He was perfectly still as though the slightest movement might disturb his thoughts. He wondered if she knew she was with child and, wondering if she did know, why she wasn't telling him of his impending fatherhood?

He did his best to calm himself. Should he tell her he knew her secret? Should he wait for her to tell him of her own accord? The child would make a difference to their marriage, he realised that, and he and Beatrice must try to shape some solidity into their lives—for the child. *The child.* The mere thought of a child growing inside Beatrice warmed his cold heart until it glowed with something sweet and loving. He felt a thrill of anticipation race through him and his heart gave a leap of excitement. He wanted to reach out for her, to touch and caress that little mound, but his pounding heart told him to be cautious, not to rush things.

He glanced at her face. She seemed preoccupied, troubled, suddenly, and he wondered if she might be considering how best to tell him of her pregnancy.

'Is there something you wish to tell me, Beatrice?' he prompted with peculiar gravity.

On a sigh she turned and looked at him. 'Yes.'

His heart soared. He waited in hope and expectation for what she was to say.

'It—it's Astrid, Julius. I am so concerned about her.'

Dumbfounded, Julius stared at her. 'What? Astrid?' He sounded stupid. That wasn't what he'd wanted to hear. 'What about Astrid?'

'Aunt Moira is forcing her into marriage with a man almost old enough to be her grandfather. Oh, Julius, I have to help her.'

Julius swallowed down his immense disappointment. 'You may speak freely. Please tell me the facts. What is the name of the prospective bridegroom?'

'Lord Alden. I am sure you are acquainted with him.'

'I am. And has Astrid asked for your help?'

'No.'

'Then do you think you should interfere?'

She stiffened. 'Interfere? I would not call concern for a dear cousin interfering. I'm at my wits' end trying to work out what to do.'

'Have you spoken to her?'

She shook her head. 'No, I have not. Aunt Moira will not let her see me. I've seen George on occasion and he is powerless against his mother.'

'Lady Moira cannot force Astrid to marry against her will.'

'Yes, she can. Astrid is terrified of her. She is cowed by her mother. She will do what she is told to do. But George tells me that she is suffering greatly. She is making herself ill.' Moving towards the bed, she sat beside him, moving closer when his arm came round her, and in a small voice, she said, 'Julius—could you, perhaps…?'

Annoyed that she should feel such concern for her cousin when he was riven with questions about her condition, he lifted his head and looked at her in that lofty manner so characteristic of him. 'And what would you have me do? Leave it, Beatrice. Do not interfere in this.'

Beatrice held his gaze, stung by his words, but determined to stand her ground to the bitter end. She felt that she was fighting for Astrid's very life. 'Do you doubt the seriousness of my cousin's plight?'

'I think it might have been exaggerated. Married to Lord Alden, Astrid will be mistress of one of the finest houses in the country and she will find him a generous husband. Beatrice, I will not become involved in this. I will not be used.'

'And so Astrid will have to suffer a miserable marriage to a lascivious old man so that your good name might be preserved? Shame on you, Julius.'

He looked at her through narrowed eyes. Beatrice stared back at him, outwardly calm while her emotions became a turmoil of anger, fear, exasperation and compassion—and a deep, abiding love for her husband.

Julius scowled, knowing that what she said was right—Alden was a lecherous old man and he couldn't blame Beatrice for wanting to prevent her gentle cousin from marrying him. 'All right, Beatrice,' he said more agreeably. 'You win. I promise I will give the matter some thought.'

Gently pushing her away, he tossed back the covers. Swinging his long, muscular legs over the side of the bed, he stood up and proceeded to dress, a reluctant smile tugging at his lips when he saw his wife's face light up with joyous delight. Utterly defeated in this, laughing softly, he strode round the bed and caught her to him, kissing her lips before turning for the door.

'But think on, my love. Do not strain the bonds of husbandly affection beyond this. Now I will leave you to dress and see you at dinner.'

On a sigh Beatrice sank on to the bed. 'Julius,' she said softly. With his hand on the door handle he turned and glanced back at her, hearing the emotion that clogged her voice. 'Thank you.'

He smiled. 'For what?'

'For everything.'

The smile faded from his face, replaced by an expression so intense, so profoundly proud that he could not speak.

Over the days that followed, instead of repairing to Highfield, Julius decided to stay in London for a few weeks to be close to the offices where he conducted his business and for Beatrice to enjoy the position of prestige in society she was entitled to. For the first time in his life he enjoyed the company of a woman—taking her places, showing her off and lavishing expensive gifts on her.

When the novelty of their unconventional marriage had run its course among the members of the *ton*, they became a favoured couple, much sought after for any social occasion. Invitations arrived at the house in large numbers. They went through them together, laughingly inventing excuses to decline some of the invitations so they could spend their time together in serenity and seduction.

Beatrice's days were filled with contentment. Her nights were spent in Julius's bed and the primitive, wild splendour of his lovemaking. He would linger over her with painstaking tenderness, making love to her slowly, prolonging her release, until she had to plead with him to end the wonderful sweet torment. Other times he would reach for her in hunger and take her quickly. She came to learn there was a baseness to him, too, when he would take no denial, when his kisses could be fierce and demanding, his passion all-consuming, leaving her breathless but thoroughly content in the warm security of his embrace.

He taught her many things, one of them being to show him what she wanted. He also taught her the power she had over his body—and how to use it. Always an avid learner, Beatrice put her new-found knowledge into immediate and highly effective use; but, when not stirred to impassioned heights, she would simply nestle in her husband's arms, feeling the brush of his lips on her brow or a nuzzling kiss against her ear. He was the husband that women dream of having for their own and Beatrice was still stunned by the realisation that he was hers.

Among a society where it was considered unfashionable for husbands and wives to spend all their waking hours together, the Marquess and Marchioness of Maitland—who were rarely seen apart and were clearly very much enamoured of each other in a way that went beyond wedlock—made it fashionable. With collective sighs of envy, society had to admit that they made a striking couple, the marquess incredibly handsome, smiling that lazy approving smile at his beautiful young wife, who seemed to have the ability to make him laugh in a way no one had ever heard him laugh before. And the marquess clearly adored his wife and didn't care if the whole world knew it. Theirs was a most unusual marriage.

Chapter Nine

Ever since Julius had noticed Beatrice was pregnant he had floundered in a sweet morass of unbelievable joy and hope that would not let him rest—hope that this child would give them an anchorage to settle down. It was so unbelievable. Some instinct warned him not to let her know he knew her secret—if she knew herself. If she did, he was waiting for her to tell him of her own accord.

It was on their wedding night when she had conceived—over four months, yet still she had not said a word. For the first time in his life he was completely bemused by what went on inside a woman's head. Why hadn't she told him? A woman must know when she was pregnant—surely? He had been waiting for two weeks, scarcely leaving her side—not that he wanted to—so he might be available when she finally revealed her condition, which couldn't be long.

The matter came to a head when her horse was brought from Larkhill and she came into the drawing room in her riding habit, her face lit up with excitement. She intended taking Major for some exercise in the park, despite the fact that rain-filled clouds covered London and already heavy splashes could be heard against the drawing-room windows. Julius came alert instantly. He could imagine his wife's idea of exercising her mount—more like a break-neck gallop clearing any obstacle that confronted her.

'I don't think you should,' he said, putting his newspaper aside.

'Why ever not?' Beatrice said, pulling on her gloves. 'Major will be feeling so frustrated after the journey. A good blow out will do him the world of good. We both need the exercise. Come with us if you like. I'd love it if you would.'

'No, Beatrice, not today. Besides, it's raining.' He spoke softly, patiently, while squaring his broad shoulders and preparing to do battle, knowing his refusal to allow her to ride would more than likely send her back into the stubbornness, the mutinous obstinacy she had shown at the beginning of their relationship.

'Don't be ridiculous, Julius. Since when did a little rain put you off?' Picking up her crop, she walked to the door.

'Beatrice,' he said, getting to his feet. 'I said I would prefer it if you didn't ride today.'

Hearing a warning note in his voice, she turned and looked back at him, her dark scowl telling him not to start ordering her about—or trying to. 'But I must ride.

I can't sit about all day, as you have had me do ever since I came back from Larkhill. I shall go out of my mind if I don't get out of the house. You can't deprive me of the pleasure I get from riding.'

'I have no wish to, but what if your horse takes it into his head to bolt?'

'He won't—and if he did I can deal with it. I do know my horse, Julius. You of all people know that.'

'Nevertheless I would prefer it if you did not ride him,' he told her firmly, tempted to say that he didn't want her gallivanting about Hyde Park taking risks. This was his child and, by God, he was going to see it born. 'I've told the grooms they are not to saddle him. When he needs exercise they will do it.'

'Goodness me, aren't you the fierce one today,' she remarked crossly. 'I might as well tell you now that I will not take orders from you or a groom, and if necessary I shall saddle my horse myself.'

'I don't think so,' he said, going to stand in front of her, trying to put some warmth into his voice so as not to antagonise her. 'What if you were to take a tumble?'

'I won't.'

No, he thought, she wouldn't. She was the best horsewoman he knew, but his judgement was tempered not with admiration, but with fear.

Perplexed by his refusal to let her ride and his strange mood, Beatrice frowned up at him. 'Julius, what on earth is the matter with you? There's nothing unusual in my riding out—and I promise to take one of the grooms with me if that's what's worrying you.'

'No, it isn't that,' he replied sharply. 'You can hardly

expect to get up on that horse and go galloping in the park when you are in a delicate condition. Have you not the sense to safeguard your child—our child?'

She stared up at him in disbelief, then laughed, thinking he was being ridiculous. 'Forgive me, but I'm not sure I take your meaning. Child? What are you talking about?'

'That I know you are pregnant, Beatrice.'

'I am? How do you know?'

'Your own body provided me with the announcement of my impending fatherhood.'

'A baby? But—I can't be. I mean—I feel so well. In fact, I've never felt better in my life. When you're having a baby you're... Oh dear! I think I may have put on a little weight but—a baby?'

Slowly shaking her head, feeling as if her legs were about to buckle under her, she sank into a chair, trying to get her head round what Julius had said. Could it be true and, if so, how could she possibly not have known? Her monthly fluxes had always been irregular—although now she came to think of it she'd seen nothing for—how long?—three months. Her breasts were tender, but she had thought that was just blooming womanhood. Her stomach was still taut, yet her clothes had seemed a little tight of late.

'Dear me, if I am with child then—then I must be four months,' she whispered. 'It must have happened on our wedding night.' She placed her hands to her scarlet cheeks. 'I cannot believe I didn't know.' Her eyes flew to Julius, who was gazing down at her with all the love and tenderness he felt for her there in his eyes. 'But I might not be. It's not certain.'

'We'll get the doctor to confirm it,' he murmured, squatting down beside her and taking her hand. 'But I do think you are, my darling. You really didn't know?'

Smiling while close to tears, she shook her head. 'No—but you did. How stupid is that?'

Getting to his feet, Julius laughed softly, pulling her up and gathering her to him. 'Not stupid, my love. Just a little—naïve, I think. But think about it—how wonderful it will be,' he murmured into her sweet-scented hair, the mere thought warming his heart.

'How long have you known?' Beatrice asked, her cheek against his hard chest, still unable to believe it and yet at the same time feeling a thrill of anticipation race through her. Her heart gave a leap of excitement in her chest, for Julius was acknowledging it and, even more wonderful, was saying he did not mind.

'Since the night you came back from Larkhill. I wanted to ask you, but I felt you might want to choose your own time to tell me. You would have told me, wouldn't you—had you realised it yourself?' He smiled wryly when she turned her face up to his in dreaming contemplation.

She returned his smile tremulously. 'I could hardly not, could I?'

'And you are not unhappy about it?' he said, as he traced his finger along the elegant curve of her cheek.

'Deliriously happy,' she murmured, her eyes aglow

with love. 'And you were right to tell me not to ride. I would not wish to harm the baby.'

'You won't—if you ride at a gentle pace. I'll accompany you tomorrow. Hopefully the sun will be shining by then.'

'It already is,' she said, wrapping her arms around his neck and pulling his head down to hers. 'For us.'

'I have something to give you.' Disentangling her arms, he went to a table. Picking up a flat packet which looked as if it might contain papers, he brought it to her.

Beatrice took it, looking at it and then at him in bemusement. 'What is it?'

'My belated wedding present to you.'

Tentatively she opened it and pulled out some papers, yellow with age. She was hardly able to believe what she saw. 'But—these look like the deeds for Larkhill. But I—I don't understand.'

'They *are* the deeds, Beatrice. I told you I had no intention of keeping the estate. I have made the property over to the person to whom it rightly belongs. You.'

When Beatrice realised what he had done, she was overwhelmed with gratitude and love. Reaching her arms around his powerful shoulders and burying her face in his neck, she murmured, 'Thank you so much. I can't find the words to tell you how much this means to me. I really don't deserve you.'

The naked anguish in her voice brought a constriction to his throat. Threading his fingers through her hair, he framed her face between his hands and gazed at her. '*I* don't deserve you, my love,' he whispered hoarsely. 'Dear God, I don't.'

Some days later, Julius had business to attend to at his offices, so Beatrice was alone when an unexpected and unwelcome visitor arrived. It was mid-morning, too early in the day for visitors, so Beatrice was surprised to see her Aunt Moira. Beatrice felt a chill steal across her heart when her aunt breezed into the room. She gave no greeting, save a slight inclination of her head.

Beatrice received her with the utmost politeness. 'Aunt Moira, this is an unexpected surprise. I hope you are well. I had no idea you were in London.'

'Why should you?' Lady Standish began in her authoritarian, yet ladylike way. Without being invited to do so she sat, stiff backed, her hand resting on her brass-knobbed walking cane. 'This is not a social call, Beatrice. I am here out of necessity, not because I choose to be. You will understand the reason why I am here.'

Sitting stiffly opposite, Beatrice looked at her aunt with unaffected astonishment. 'Forgive me, Aunt, but I don't.'

'I have come to fetch my daughter home. I assume this is where she is hiding out.'

Beatrice stared at her in disbelief. 'Astrid? But—she is not here.'

'No?'

It was clear her aunt did not believe her, but if Astrid was not at Standish House and she had not come to

Beatrice, then where was she? 'No, Aunt Moira, she is not. When did she leave home?'

'Three days ago. She left the house to visit a neighbour for a musical afternoon and did not come back.'

'Then—is it possible that she might have met with an accident?'

'No. Enquiries were made. Some of her clothes are missing, which tells me she has run off.'

'But—this is alarming. Where is George? Did she not confide in him?'

'George has been in Brighton for the past two weeks. He is due back tomorrow. As yet I have not informed him that Astrid is missing.'

'Then I think he should be told. But—why would you assume she has come here?'

'Where else would she go?' Lady Standish said in an angry tone. 'Don't pretend to be ignorant of it,' she accused scathingly. 'She is here, isn't she? You are hiding her. I know it.'

'Indeed you are mistaken, Aunt Moira,' Beatrice answered. 'When I left Standish House you forbade me to see Astrid and I swear I have not.'

'Do not trifle with me, Beatrice,' Lady Standish said. 'You may have married a marquess, but you are still a nobody.' Her eyes had taken on a wildness as she looked around at the luxurious green-and-gold room. 'Just look at this place—look at you. Your scheming has paid off admirably.'

Beatrice bristled with indignation at the affront. 'My father was a gentleman as well you know, Aunt Moira. I do not consider myself beneath Julius. In our marriage we are equal. Astrid is my cousin and I am worried about her.'

'Astrid is not your concern. Untrustworthy, that's what you are. You are together in this. I know you have been down to Larkhill. I am also aware that George visited you there. You are all in it together—scheming against me—all part of the same wicked conspiracy.'

'There is no conspiracy.'

Lady Standish banged her cane with impatient outrage, her voice rising. 'Do not contradict me. If you know anything at all, then I demand that you tell me. I am entitled to know where my daughter is.'

'Clearly Astrid doesn't think so, otherwise she would have told you. If you do not believe me when I say she is not here, then please feel free to search the house. May I remind you that this house also happens to be my home and should Astrid come here for whatever reason, I would not turn her away.'

Lady Standish looked as though she had been pole-axed. Both hands gripped her cane fiercely, the knuckles white, her eyes staring icily at her niece.

'Perhaps if you had not insisted that she wed Lord Alden,' Beatrice went on, 'she would not have run away.'

'But they are engaged. It is an excellent match and it is my wish that they wed.'

'Clearly Astrid has an aversion to the match—as great an aversion as she had when you aspired that she marry Julius,' Beatrice told her tightly, struggling to keep her anger under control. 'Julius has spoken to

Lord Alden on my behalf—since George told me what you intended I have been exceedingly worried about Astrid. Julius has explained to Lord Alden Astrid's fondness for another man. From what Julius has told me, he is reconsidering the marriage.'

Lady Standish's face was chalk white, and when she next spoke her voice shook with fury. 'And you denied there was any conspiracy. Lord Chadwick had no business, no business at all, to interfere in a matter that does not concern him, and neither have you. How dare either of you disregard the arrangements I have made for my own daughter? This is too much.'

'I did so because I happen to care for Astrid. I was deeply concerned when George told me you were forcing her to marry a man she does not care for. Where have you looked for her? Have you seen Squire Talbot? That is the obvious place. Is Henry at home? If he is absent and his father ignorant as to his whereabouts, then I would say that is a clear indication they have run away together.'

Her aunt's body was visibly shaking with anger. 'If that should prove to be the case, then believe me when I say that her ambition will never be gratified.'

'Astrid's ambition has always been to marry Henry.'

'And I forbid it,' she replied, her voice brittle. 'Any alliance between Astrid and Henry Talbot will be seen as a disgrace. She will be censured and slighted by everyone connected to us. I will not have it. You do know her intentions, don't you?'

'No, Aunt, I do not, and if I did I would not tell

you—not if it meant Astrid would suffer further heart-ache.'

'Your defiance does you no credit. How dare you address me in this impertinent manner? You will pay dearly for this,' she warned Beatrice with a fixed stare. 'God help me, you will pay the price of what you have done to me. I will not be beaten.' Struggling to maintain her composure, she stood up and crossed regally to the door, where she turned and looked back, her piercingly cold eyes regarding the beautiful young woman, whose eyes were filled with contentment. 'So it's true what everyone is saying,' she sneered. 'Your union with Lord Chadwick is working out against all the odds. I believe you have put on a little weight, Beatrice. Marriage clearly agrees with you.'

Beatrice lifted her head and met her stare for stare, reluctant to disclose her pregnancy to this cold woman. 'Yes. Julius and I are very happy.'

'And so you should be—after the trouble you caused securing for yourself a most advantageous marriage, you despicable, scheming girl. I know he sent someone to assess Larkhill for its value, which implies he might be going to sell it. It will serve you right if he calls your bluff. You should have thought he might do that when you propositioned him.'

'Julius no longer owns Larkhill, Aunt Moira. He has made it over to me. So you see, I have achieved everything that I set out to do.'

'Really? Your scheming is not worthy of congratulations. You think you know Julius Chadwick, don't you? Perhaps you would not be so cocksure if you knew what the man you married is guilty of.'

Perplexed, Beatrice stared at her. 'What do you mean? What are you saying?'

'Ask your lying, two-faced husband,' she uttered viciously. 'He knows.'

'Knows? Knows what, Aunt Moira?'

'The truth. The truth about how your father died.'

Beatrice laughed a little nervously, then her heart began to beat with a new intensity, as though perceiving she was about to be told something that had been hidden from her. 'What are you talking about?'

A slow smile stretched the older woman's mouth, a smile that was pure evil. 'Why, Beatrice, that your husband is a murderer. After he took Larkhill from your father and found the estate was mortgaged up to the hilt, he killed him.' Her smile became one of satisfaction when her niece's eyes widened in deepening incredulity. 'There, you have it.'

Pain and disbelief streaked through Beatrice and a tiny hammer of panic began to pound in her head. 'No. You are lying.' She swallowed past a constriction in her throat. Something inside her had begun to die. 'This is preposterous,' she uttered shakily as terror began to hammer through her. Everything in her recoiled from believing Julius was capable of such evil. She knew in her bones he would not do something so wicked as to kill her father and then marry his daughter. None of it made sense. Julius couldn't do that. He wasn't a murderer—but then, how would she know?

'I know you are bitter about what I did, when I challenged Julius, but to say...that—why would you say such a cruel thing?'

'Because it's true.'

Her entire body vibrating with horror, a scream of hysteria and denial rose in Beatrice's throat. But then she recalled what her aunt had said before Julius had taken her from Standish House, that when she came to know the true nature of the man she aspired to marry, how he dealt with those who dared to cross him, she would learn to hate him. Was this what she had meant?

Facing her aunt, she felt each of her enraged words as if it was a blow to her head. 'I do not believe you. Unable to live with what he'd done, my father killed himself.'

'If that is what you want to believe, then do so—it's what your husband wants you to believe—but do you know that for a fact?'

'Yes,' Beatrice answered implacably.

'And I have reason to know,' her aunt said with equal implacability, 'that the man you married shot him.'

Beatrice was trying so hard to concentrate and not to give way to the terror of her aunt's accusation that she dug her nails in her palms. 'I cannot—will not—believe this. I will speak to Julius. He has to have a chance to deny this—this slander, to explain.'

'He has no defence. Your mother knew—in one of her more lucid moments she told me when she came back from London, before she took to her bed and turned her back on the world.'

Beatrice's blood already ran cold, but those words froze her heart. 'My mother,' she whispered. 'She told you that?'

'She was there. She saw Julius leaving the house. I promise you, Beatrice, I do not lie.' Her smile was one of venomous satisfaction. 'Think about it. How does it feel knowing you are married to the man who killed your own father?'

Lady Standish made to leave. Beatrice watched her, feeling quite ill to have confirmation of something she had sensed, but could never put her finger on—that when Julius had opened up to her he had not told her everything. His betrayal of her trust was like a stab in the heart.

A tremor of fury rippled through her, and with a sudden spurt of anger, she said, 'And what does that make you, Aunt Moira? If, as you say, Julius is a murderer, how could you bear for him to marry Astrid? Was your greed for title, wealth and power so great you were prepared to sacrifice your own daughter on the altar of matrimony with a man who is capable of such evil? Where were your principles then?'

Lady Standish looked at her hard before raising her head and leaving the house.

Drowning in a black pool of despair, Beatrice couldn't stand it. She understood everything her aunt had said, but she could not seem to move or feel. Was it really true that Julius had killed her father? If he had, how could she bear it? She was in pain, a constant searing pain that would not ease.

Mechanically she moved to the window, her arms wrapped round her waist in an agony of suffering, staring blankly at nothing. Feeling sick to the stomach, she tried to collect her wits. What on earth should she do? She didn't think she could confront him just yet, to look into the harsh, handsome face she adored and hear that beautiful baritone voice. And yet could she stand the uncertainty of not knowing the truth? Could she go on living with him, spending days and nights together, pretending—living with the lie that would be their lives? Or could she bear the torment of living without him?

But as she considered the awfulness of his crime, she could not believe he had done this to her. Anger began to burn in her breast. If what she had been told was indeed true, how dare he make a mockery of her faith in him? Little wonder he had been so secretive. Little wonder he had wanted to conceal what he had done. She told herself to be fair and give him the benefit of the doubt, but deep down she knew there was some truth in it.

She had half a mind to seek him out at his place of business and demand that he tell her what he was playing at, but no doubt he would prevaricate and lie and continue treating her like the stupid idiot he took her for. If he had gone to great pains to conceal the mystery, then how could she think he would oblige her and tell her the truth now?

Resentment burned through her. They had an agreement to be open with each other, to be on equal terms, to tell each other the truth in all things, yet, despite his promise, her husband had persisted with his deception. How dare he conceal something as important as this from her? There was nothing equal in what he had done. She wanted answers and explanations and nothing would stop her from finding out exactly what had happened.

When Julius arrived home he went into his study to look over some papers. He was seated at his desk and just about to raise a pre-dinner brandy to his lips when the door was flung open and Beatrice came in like a hurricane.

'Good Lord!' he spluttered, dabbing his chin where the brandy had splashed. 'What's got into you? Beatrice? I'm always glad to see you, but could you not knock or…?' His voice died away in bewilderment at the sight of the expression on her face and he placed the brandy glass on the desk.

Beatrice knew she must look odd. How could she help it when the words she wanted to speak—shout—at him were roiling at the back of her throat in an effort to get out, to tear him to pieces in her fury?

'What have you done?' she managed to say at last.

Julius's face showed astonishment. 'Done? What have *I* done? What can you mean? I have merely come home after concluding a successful day's business and come in here and poured myself a drink, which, if I am allowed to, I shall relax and enjoy.'

'Stop it, Julius. Don't you dare pretend you don't know what I mean.'

'My love, believe me, I haven't the slightest idea.'

'Then you should.'

'You do seem to be annoyed about something...'

'*Annoyed!* Dear Lord, annoyed doesn't half-describe what I'm feeling right now you—you blackguard, so will you stop prattling on and tell me the truth or I swear I shall scream,' she uttered vehemently.

He was getting annoyed and it showed in the narrowing of his eyes and his scowl. Julius Chadwick was not accustomed to being called names of any sort or brought to task about anything; though he adored this woman and knew he always would, he was not about to let her throw her weight about like a street woman looking for a fight. He didn't know what had awoken her temper, but something had and it seemed it was aimed at him.

'It's you who are prattling on, Beatrice,' he said irritably, 'and unless you tell me what all this is about I cannot answer your accusations over something I know nothing about. Is something wrong?'

'Yes—yes, you might say that.' Looking at him across the desk, she rested her hands on its surface and leaned in, her face on a level with his. 'It's about honesty, openness and trust. Stupidly I thought we had agreed to that in our marriage. I now find I have got it so very wrong. How can I trust you when you are up to your eyes in deception? This is not the marriage I agreed to when I came back from Larkhill.'

'And why is that?' His voice was icy.

'My father, Julius.' She met him look for look and her eyes were green ice. 'I want the truth about the manner of his death, and who better to ask than the man who killed him.'

For a moment his face took on an expression of total incomprehension. He frowned as though he were doing his best to unravel her words, make sense of them, then his face hardened when realisation of what she was accusing him of hit him.

'Who told you?' He spoke mildly, but his amber eyes had sharpened.

'Aunt Moira.'

'And when did you see your aunt?'

'A short time ago. She came to tell me that Astrid is missing and accused me of hiding her here. She also told me that not only did the man I married take Larkhill from my father, but that he also killed him. I have to ask you if there is any truth in this, Julius. And please don't lie to me.'

'Do you believe I am capable of such an act, Beatrice?' He was watching her warily, having schooled himself well in the necessity for restraint in trying circumstances like the one he now faced.

'Before my aunt came here I would have said no, never in a thousand years would I have believed you could do anything so—so vile. I don't want to believe it, but it would appear that my mother bore witness to the whole sorry affair—and my mother was not a liar.'

'I'm sure she wasn't, but perhaps she mistook what she saw.'

'Did she? Then perhaps you can explain what did

happen that caused my father to lose his life. Either he shot himself or someone murdered him. Tell me the truth—if you can.'

Julius got up and walked round the desk to stand in front of her, where he stood looking down at her upturned face. Despite the fact that they were hurling daggers at him, her eyes were also full of hope that he would deny he'd had any part in her father's demise. But he could not alleviate her doubts. Telling her about her father and the manner of his death would change the whole picture for her and he knew she would not be pleased with what she saw. It might make it worse. Maybe she would be better off not knowing the burden that lay so heavily on him, that there had been times when he thought he would be crushed by it. Unfortunately after her aunt's visit, she now knew half of the story and would assume the rest and assume wrongly.

His face became tense and he looked away. 'I'm afraid I can't do that.'

'Then tell me this—did my mother see you leave the house that night?'

Julius pushed his hand through his thick hair. His face was becoming dangerous and the gentleness, the concern, was replaced by grinding anger. His eyes darkened and he spoke through gritted teeth. 'Damn it, Beatrice. Can't you leave it?'

'No, Julius, I cannot. Don't you understand? Ever since my father died I believed he had killed himself and that my mother—who found his body—was so shocked she retreated into herself because she couldn't bear to live without him and the knowledge of what he had done. Now I know that she couldn't bear to live with what she had witnessed—that he did not die by his own hand—and, being the gentle person she was, she was too afraid to speak out. I have a right to know what happened and I demand that you tell me. Were you there? Did she see you leave the house shortly after my father was killed?'

Julius looked at her hard, seeming to consider very carefully what to say next. At length he said tightly, 'Yes, Beatrice, she did.'

Beatrice stared at him with eyes wide with horror. She had hoped and prayed he would deny it, that he would tell her there was no truth in what her aunt had told her and that what she had said was merely the rantings of a vicious old woman.

'Then you have deceived me most cruelly,' she uttered with a rage that was buried bone deep. She stepped back from him, as if she couldn't bear to be near him. 'How could you? When I married you I did so for no other reason than to gain access to Larkhill. The opportunity was too beautiful for me to resist. Suddenly you were more to me than the whole world, more than my own future, more than fortune. I would have been a fool to turn away from what you could offer me—and then I fell in love with you.' She gave a hard, contemptuous little laugh which bordered on hysterical. 'How stupid was that? I now find that the one man I have ever loved is worthless, utterly vicious and corrupt, without principle and without honour—a man who killed my own father. Do you think I could ever forget that? No, Julius, that memory will burn within me as long as I live.'

Julius's hand went out to her. His face was strangely gentle and his amber eyes softened and were filled with compassion and warmth. They told of his own regret, not that her father was dead and that she truly believed he had killed him, but that it should give pain to her.

But Beatrice would have none of his concern and her cold, narrowed eyes told him so. 'Don't touch me,' she spat.

He drew back his hand. 'Your father did not shoot himself—I can tell you that—but there is more to it than that, Beatrice.'

'Then tell me.'

'I—I cannot tell you,' he said haltingly, finding it almost impossible to think of that night when his whole world had fallen apart, let alone speak of it. For a moment his mask slipped and Beatrice glimpsed fleetingly his inner pain, that he seemed deeply troubled and genuinely at a loss. But then the mask was back in place.

'But if you want me to believe you, you must.'

'I—cannot.'

'Then if you cannot defend yourself, I am not interested in anything further you have to say.' She turned from him and walked across the room to the door. 'There is nothing more to be said. I want to be by myself—to think about what I'm going to do—away from here. Away from you.'

Julius's eyes narrowed. 'Just exactly what is that supposed to mean?'

'That I'd rather die than live in the same house as the man who killed my father. I am going to Larkhill—without you. I suppose it was your guilty conscience that prompted you to return it to me.'

'No, it was because I wanted very much to give you back the equivalent of what was taken from you.'

'Then I suppose I must be grateful for that at least.'

'I am sorry, Beatrice, if I have hurt you. I regret that, but please believe me when I say that I desire only your peace and happiness. Do not forget that.'

She turned and looked at him. 'It is not enough to say you're sorry, to try to make amends, hoping to wipe out everything you have done,' she said, stiff with pride and anger. 'You should have thought of all this before you robbed my father to add to your own fortunes and then killed him. Now it is too late, do you hear, too late! How can I possibly remain married to you knowing this? I will keep Larkhill, but I would rather die a thousand deaths than take anything else from you! Can't you understand that I hate you?'

She flung the last words in his face and had the bitter satisfaction of seeing him whiten. She triumphed in it, rejoiced in it, hoping for some sign of weakness which would put him absolutely at her mercy, but Julius Chadwick was a man of steel and did not know how to weaken. He merely shrugged and turned away from her.

'I shall leave for Larkhill at first light. Please don't try to stop me.'

'I won't.' The fact that she had been so quick to believe the worst of him cut through his heart like a knife, leaving him with a dark sense of having been betrayed. He knew that by not telling her everything he was being unreasonable, but he just couldn't help himself. Even if their marriage had been a travesty at the beginning, he had become comfortable with the idea of her being his wife and was reluctant to let her go.

'Go if you feel you must—after this I am sure you can't wait to leave me, but I will never divorce you,' Julius continued dispassionately, immune to the wrathful expression on her beautiful face. 'We will discuss the course of our future at a later date, but until then we have a child to consider and it will be raised by both a mother and a father.'

One look at his face convinced Beatrice that he was absolutely furious with her. Not only were his eyes glinting with icy shards, but the muscles in his cheeks were tensing and vibrating to a degree that she had never seen before.

She drew an infuriated breath. 'As you said, we will discuss the course of our future another time. Goodbye, Julius.' With that she swept out of the room, leaving him staring after her. She did not see the move he made towards her, or his look of angry pain and suffering, or hear the sigh of bitter defeat he uttered when she closed the door.

With a sense of burning betrayal and seething anger at her husband's terrible crime, fighting back scalding tears of hurt, Beatrice hurried to her room—to pack, she decided, for if he wasn't going to tell her the truth, she would not remain in the same house as a liar and a murderer.

In her wretched suffering she lay awake, hearing sounds of her husband moving about his room behind the closed connecting doors. It went on all night, which told her that he too was unable to sleep. She wanted to call out to him, wanted desperately to feel his arms around her, but she could not do it.

Dawn found her huddled in the comforting warm refuge of her cloak as the coach left the house. On the point of leaving, a letter addressed to her was delivered. It was from Astrid. Not until the coach had left London behind did Beatrice open it. It was as she had expected. Astrid had run away with Henry Talbot. They were in Scotland, at Gretna Green, where they had married. Astrid went on to tell her that they were deliriously happy. Things would be hard for a while since they had no money, but Henry's parents had agreed that they could live with them for the time being.

Beatrice was happy for Astrid and sincerely hoped her cousin would find happiness wed to the man of her choice. She could well imagine how the news would be received by her aunt and had no doubt that she would turn her back on her daughter and cut her off without a penny.

It was raining hard and clouds the colour of pewter brushed the rooftops of London, the streets blacker than midnight. The roads were bad, as bad as Beatrice had expected when she'd embarked on this journey, and the rain showed no sign of relenting. But she was oblivious to the cold and the discomforts of the journey the closer she got to Larkhill.

She had closed her eyes and listened to the pounding hooves of the horses and the pounding of her heart. The familiar pain of betrayal was still present, but after hours of thoughtful contemplation in a more rational frame of mind she had the feeling that something was not quite right. Had she really married a monster, a murderer? In her mind she could see Julius smiling down at her, hear his voice filled with need. Could the man who had held her so tenderly and loved her with such unbridled passion really have killed her father? Was he really capable of doing that and then making that man's daughter his wife?

Nothing rang true. In the confused and heated aftermath of her aunt's disclosure, when her emotions had veered between hysterical panic and shaking irrationality, when she had questioned him and accused him so fiercely, his replies had been tentative, almost painful, and she began to suspect that there was something he had not told her—that even now he was deliberately keeping something from her. He had not denied murdering her father, but then, he hadn't admitted it either. He had admitted being there at the time, but that didn't mean he was responsible.

Recalling the moment when the mask had slipped from his face and he had seemed at a loss to know how to answer her questions, she asked herself why. She knew it was not out of coldness.

It was out of fear.

But what was he afraid of? Himself? It was strange

how that one look she had seen on his face could cause everything to shift, to put everything into place. Julius wasn't a murderer. She wasn't mistaken in that. She had been too ready to judge. Had she misjudged him? And if she had, would he ever be able to forgive her?

As the coach swung up the drive to Larkhill, she vividly remembered her confession to him of how she had fallen in love with him and how quickly he had silenced her. She had known he did not love her, but there were times when he made love to her that gave her reason to believe he was coming to that conclusion. She wished she hadn't left him. She wished she was with him now so that she could tell him she was mistaken and apologise for being too ready to condemn him.

By the time the coach stopped in front of the house, so convinced was she of Julius's innocence that she was tempted to tell the driver to turn and head back for London, but out of consideration for the tired horses and driver, she decided against it. She would spend one night at Larkhill and then she would take a leap of faith all the way back to her husband.

Chapter Ten

The man who stood at his bedroom window watched his wife climb into the waiting coach. The hood of her cloak protected her head from the driving rain, denying him one last look at her lovely face. As if she sensed he was there, she paused and raised her head in that regal way of hers, the crisp wind flirting with the cluster of curls escaping their confines, before dropping her eyes without looking back, gathering her cloak about her and climbing inside.

His face impassive, Julius watched the coach pull away, but inside everything was shattering, bleeding, draining the life out of him, for without Beatrice it had no meaning.

He had been a fool not to tell her what she wanted to know, but, dear Lord, apart from James and Constance Merrick, he had never told another living soul about what had happened on the night Beatrice's father had died. He would tell her, that he had decided. He would tell her every sordid detail, no matter how painful, because he now realised that he wanted her more than he had ever wanted anything in his life.

Beatrice had become a part of him which he could not deny. She was like burnished steel, strong and audaciously bold—her eyes blazing with defiance, fighting him, challenging him. daring him with her outrageous forfeit, determined not to have what was hers denied her. Her heart was the sweet centre in the headlong strength of her mind and body and, quite simply, now that he knew her and could see her for what she was, he loved her. He would fill her days and nights with joy and pleasure, until she loved him as much as he loved her. For he did love her, and his heart swelled as he admitted the truth to himself. He could not lose her as he had lost his mother.

Telling her the truth would be difficult, for he found it hard to expose his inner self, but Beatrice would understand—like no one else she would understand. It would take a while to earn her trust after this, he decided, but some day she would surely find him worthy of it.

Driven by a fierce eagerness to see his wife, it became clear to him that if he did not go after her, his energy would be spent in waiting and tearing himself to shreds.

The night was dark and Beatrice was restless in her bed. The wind was high, but the rain that had been falling for two days had temporarily abated. A figure made its way with stealth-like caution towards the house, halting when it reached an iron gate that opened on to the kitchen yard. The figure paused to take stock of things before proceeding. A deathlike stillness hung over the house, which seemed to moan in sorrow over its impending doom. A chain was lifted from the gate and the earthbound shadow slipped through the opening and dashed towards the outbuildings that joined on to the house.

The night's depth of darkness was impenetrable, then the wind changed direction, and the clouds allowed a shaft of moonlight to sweep across the yard. Concealed beneath an enveloping cape, the figure scuttled into the interior of a shed. Gloved hands hastily struck flint to steel over a small mound of gunpowder, and sparks shot outwards and upwards until a sudden blaze flared up. Several minutes later the figure re-emerged and ran the way it had come, looking back only once to watch flames leaping from the building, the wind whipping them towards the house.

Having been travelling for hours, impatient to be at journey's end, Julius willed the coach to go faster. The well-matched team lunged forwards, taking their duties seriously, as the driver drove them at a breakneck pace along the mired roads, swerving madly around bends and not even checking their stride when the wheels caught a rut. Only a couple of miles and he would be at Larkhill. A deep sense of relief surged within him. The wind rushed by the coach and once again heavy splashes of rain began pelting the windows. Pulling up the blind and gazing out, Julius wondered at the reddish glow of heat in the night sky, while a rolling mass of grey billowed above it.

Cold, congealing horror suddenly seized him as memories of another fire—a fire that had robbed him of his mother—almost overwhelmed him. The fire was in the direction of Larkhill. Dear God, he prayed silently, don't let it be the house—don't let Beatrice have come to harm. His fears were confirmed the closer they got. He was relieved to discover it was the outbuildings that were on fire, but being connected to the house, it was only a matter of time before the whole lot went up if it was not checked.

Spurred to action, he leapt from the coach and ran towards the blaze, ignoring the searing sting of flying ash. Along with members of the small staff Julius retained at Larkhill, men from the surrounding area, alerted by neighbours who had not retired for the night and had seen the blaze, were trying to fight the flames to stop them reaching the house. There was no hope in saving the outbuildings. They were succeeding, for mercifully the rain aided them in their task as it came sheeting down once more.

The urgency of the moment pressed upon him and his tone conveyed his growing anxiety for the occupants of the house as he enquired as to their safety. On being told they were still inside, he ran towards the front door.

Torn from her uneasy dream, Beatrice came upright with a gasp and stared about the dark room in wide-eyed panic. Something had disturbed her. A sudden chill shivered along her spine as she pressed back upon the pillows, trying to listen above the howling of the wind. Her heart suddenly lurched. Was that smoke she could smell?

'Beatrice…Beatrice…'

'Julius!' The name flared through her brain as she realised it wasn't part of any dream. It was Julius! She threw herself from the bed and ran out of the bedroom. As she reached the top of the stairs her eyes swept the hall, anxiously searching for the man who had called her name. Someone was pounding on the locked front door; a moment later it crashed open—and there, right below her, was a very tall, dark-haired man. Her heart gave a leap, missed a beat, then began to thump madly as a pair of penetrating amber eyes looked straight into hers. Momentarily stunned by his arrival, she saw the bitter regret carved into his handsome features and the aching gentleness in his compelling eyes.

'Julius!'

Immediately she flew down the stairs and ran across the hall towards him. He caught her up hard in his arms and listened as the words came tumbling out.

'Thank goodness you've come. But why did you? I intended to leave in the morning to return to you. I couldn't bear it, leaving you like that. I know you didn't do it, Julius. I know you didn't kill my father—you couldn't do that, and I don't know why you said you did, but…'

'Hush, Beatrice,' he said, holding her away from him to look into her face. She was flushed and breathing hard, her hair dishevelled from sleep and utterly lovely. He saw tears shimmering in her magnificent eyes; one of them traced unheeded down her smooth cheek. 'What is this?'

'I know you're innocent. I know you didn't do it.'

Gently he traced his lean fingers along her cheek and, with a raw ache in his voice, said, 'What made you realise that?'

'I worked it out for myself.' Her heart in a tumult of emotion, Beatrice clung to him once more, burying her face against his chest. 'I do believe in you, Julius,' she whispered fiercely. 'Forgive me for doubting you—I didn't mean to, I didn't want to, but I was so angry and confused. I will support you in anything you do. I trust you implicitly. I love you so much.'

'That's all I need to hear.' His arms tightened round her, his impassioned whisper strained with feeling. 'We'll talk later, Beatrice. Then you can cry in my arms all night if you wish and, while you do, I'll tell you how sorry I am for everything I've done and said that has hurt you. And when I've finished doing that, you can help me find a way to forgive myself.' He held her away from him. 'I have to go. I promise I'll explain everything, but in the meantime there's a fire to put out.'

She sprang back in alarm. 'What? A fire? Oh—I thought I could smell smoke. Where? Is it the house?'

'It's the outbuildings. Hopefully it won't get to the house. Men from the village were already working on it when I got here. Thankfully the wind's changed direction and it's raining hard. With a bit of luck it will be put out.'

'But how did it start—do you know?'

'Not yet. The time for questions will come later, but I would like you to get dressed all the same. Best to be prepared should the wind change direction again.'

A part of Julius's urgency seized her and when he disappeared through the door she took the stairs at a frantic pace.

The fire was put out and the night grew still once more as Julius went to join Beatrice in the master bedroom. She was in his arms before the clock had spent another second. Lowering his head, he kissed her in stormy tenderness before closing his eyes and burying his face in her sweet-scented hair as his arms fairly squeezed the breath from her. When he raised his eyes to meet hers, his lips smiled.

'I thought I told you to get dressed.' His voice was hoarse with emotion, for Beatrice was attired in nothing but her nightdress, her wonderful wealth of golden hair tumbling down her spine. 'Do you intend to spend your life disobeying me?'

Beatrice leaned back against his arm and smiled with joy as she caressed his soot-smeared cheek. 'I did not disobey you. When I saw the fire had been put out I decided to get undressed again.' Her dark eyes took on a pleading look. 'Come to bed, Julius.'

The sound of her voice was so sweet, Julius almost pulled her down on to the bed. Instead he sighed and gently disengaged her arms. 'Later. I want to talk to you first. There are things I want to tell you.'

Feeling an unexpected lurch of dread, Beatrice swallowed her disappointment. 'Can't it wait until morning?'

'I would prefer to get it over with. Until you know the truth it will always be there, lurking between us."

'How did you become so wise?' she asked with a tender smile.

'If I were wise, my darling, I would have told you everything at the beginning. Keeping it to myself has only made matters worse between us. I can see that now.' Removing his coat and loosening his neck linen, he took her hand and drew her to the fire. Sitting beside the hearth, he drew her on to his knee, sliding his arm about her waist. 'I want to tell you everything about the night your father died. I promise it will be the truth.'

Beatrice gazed at him, warding off an icy chill. 'I sincerely hope so, Julius. You didn't kill him, did you?'

'No. And before we go any further I want to tell you that Constance was right. I never gamble. I never have—only with business investments. The game of cards that was to be the destruction of both of our fathers took place at a private gentlemen's club. There were few present to witness the outcome. Your father lost Larkhill to my father—not to me.'

'I see. Were you present?'

'I arrived when the game was over. My father was more excited than usual. I didn't know why until later. I was deeply shocked and wanted him to return it. He wouldn't hear of it and told me not to interfere.'

'You should have told me this. I'm sorry that I made you suffer for it. My father should never have put Larkhill on the table.'

'Don't forget that he, too, was desperate. Nor did I kill your father, Beatrice. My father did.'

Beatrice didn't say anything. She simply sat on his knee, listening as the words began pouring out of him.

'My father couldn't believe his good fortune when he won Larkhill. He genuinely believed it would be the answer to all his problems. When he checked its value and found it was heavily mortgaged he became demented. He began drinking—in fact, he became a walking, drunken nightmare. He swore revenge on your father. I arrived at the house when he was about to leave with the intention of confronting your father with a loaded gun. He was so drunk he didn't know what he was doing. He became violent, so violent that I had to lock him in his room. I don't know how he got out—his valet, I suppose, though he denied it.'

Combing his fingers through his dishevelled hair, he looked at Beatrice. He must have seen the horror in her eyes, for he said, 'I think you can guess what happened next. I knew where he had gone and hurried after him. Your parents had rented a small house in Charing Cross. The hour was late and when I arrived the deed was done. Your father was dead, shot in the head, and my father stumbling out of the door. He had thrown down his gun. I left it there. The house was quiet—I had no idea your mother saw me and would naturally believe I had killed him.'

'That was what she told Aunt Moira, on one of

the rare occasions that she spoke. She had found my father's body, you see, and so deep was the shock that it affected her health.'

'And your aunt told no one?'

'No, I don't think so. Why she kept quiet about it is a mystery—unless she meant to use the knowledge against you at a later date.'

'She could try, but there are people who would testify that your mother was an ill woman, that her mind had become somewhat unstable following the suicide of her husband. I have restored the Chadwick good name, earning the respect of those in the upper echelons of society. I doubt anyone would listen to the rantings of an aged and bitter woman.'

'I sincerely hope not. Now that we have resolved matters between ourselves, I would hate to have you cast into prison.'

Julius kissed her forehead. 'I am not going anywhere, my darling, I promise you. After leaving your father, when I got back to the house, James and Constance were there. They had seen my father arrive home and were worried by the blood on his clothes and the state of his mind. He was quite demented, almost boasting of what he had done to your father. I told them everything that had happened and swore them to secrecy. The next day when my father was sober, he remembered nothing. I did. It was like a nightmare, like a dream in a delirium, so infamous I could scarcely believe it.'

Beatrice stared at him in horror, hardly able to take in what he had told her. 'I knew there was something you weren't telling me, but I had no idea it was anything as shocking as this,' she whispered. 'But—I don't understand. Why did you let me go on thinking it was you? Why did you let me go on thinking the worst of you?'

'Because I was ashamed of what my father had done,' he answered, choosing his words with care, his conscience smarting with the irony of trying to protect the reputation of his undeserving father while—at least where Beatrice was concerned—damaging his own. 'Everyone believed your father had shot himself because he could not bear the shame of losing Larkhill. No one stopped to question whether or not the weapon found at the scene might not be his. It was assumed that it was. Nothing on earth would have compelled me to reveal the truth about what had happened and only my determination prevented an almighty scandal at the time of your father's death. Some scandals dim with time—that one wouldn't.'

'So you covered it up and were prepared to let me— and my mother—live the rest of our lives believing my father had killed himself.'

'In that, my love, I am guilty—and deeply ashamed for my weakness. I am truly sorry and beg your forgiveness.'

'You have it, Julius, for I understand why you acted as you did. But do you realise what could have happened to you had my mother spoken out?'

He nodded grimly. 'I can only thank God that she didn't. I couldn't tell you. I thought you'd be better off not knowing the burden that lay heavily on the man you married.'

'What I don't understand is why you felt you had to protect your father, after all he had done to you and your mother? He was undeserving of your sacrifice.'

'Like I said, I was ashamed—and at the end of the day he was still my father,' he said, speaking quietly, the pain of his father's crime evident in his eyes. 'It was hard enough for me to accept he had been a failure, without having to tell the whole world he was a murderer. Shortly after that he, too, was dead. As far as I was concerned it was over—I had no wish to resurrect a time that was painful for me. I saw no harm in letting the world go on believing I was the culprit who stole your home—things might have been different had I known about you. As things turned out, it was fortunate for you that Larkhill was one of the few properties I managed to save being taken over by the bank. That was the only good thing that came out of it—and meeting you.

'The behaviour of my forebears—their addiction for liquor and gaming—has been difficult for me to take. I hoped it was not hereditary—that I would not turn out like them or any offspring I might sire. When I agreed to marry you I knew you were entitled to know all this, but dear God, Beatrice, I could not tell you. I cannot blame you if you hate me for what I've done. I deserve it.'

With tears clogging her throat, Beatrice wrapped her arms around his neck. 'I don't hate you, Julius. Never that. I know I said I did, but I didn't mean it. I love you so much—more than anything on earth.'

When she drew back her head, Julius reached out

and wiped a rogue tear away with the tip of his finger. 'Bless you for that.' He took a deep breath. 'I can't remember when I came to love you. I think it was from the very start—when you challenged me to that damned race. You were feisty, stubborn, an outrageously brave and gorgeous girl who challenged my spirit, blithely incurred my displeasure and refused to yield to my authority—and, much, much worse than that, you mocked my equestrian skills. That was unforgivable,' he said with a teasing smile. 'But despite all this your smile warmed my heart and the touch of your lips heated my blood. So you see, my love, I have loved you from first sight and cannot imagine my future without you.'

Beatrice's eyes filled with tears as she gazed at him and smiled tremulously. 'I'm glad you've told me at last. I wanted so much to believe you were innocent. I wanted it so badly to be true, and in my heart I knew it. I love you, Julius Chadwick, and I don't know what I would do without you.'

'I'll see that you never are, sweetheart.'

Suddenly she moved slightly and a look of wonder lit her eyes. Her hand went to her stomach and a smile touched her lips. 'Oh,' she whispered, 'how odd.'

Julius frowned, bewildered by her remark. 'What is?'

'Our baby. Oh, Julius, I do believe it moved—like a butterfly fluttering its wings.'

A lump of emotion swelled in Julius's chest as she took his hand and pressed it against her stomach. With a feeling of awe, he, too, felt the gentle movement of their child.

With her cheek against his chest, she whispered, '*Now* will you take me to bed?'

Without saying a word he swung her into his arms, cradling her tenderly against him, brushing his lips against her forehead. He carried her to the bed and laid her down, intending to give her so much pleasure that she'd be able to forget the misery he'd caused her.

As dawn settled its pinkish shroud upon the land, the circling, confused wind that had battered the earth with a sheeting rain for most of the night had abated. The countryside grew quiet in hushed relief. The very air seemed to hang in breathless suspense, while wraith-like vapours shifted aimlessly among the trees and shrubs and filled low hollows on the land. The house, bounded on three sides by tall, gaunt trees, seemed to merge with the landscape. Apart from a tired, thin spiral of grey smoke rising from the outbuildings to the rear, nothing moved and nothing stirred, not even the lovers, their bodies entwined beneath the covers.

Now the truth was out at last, the shadows between them had gone away. After all their years of loneliness, they were no longer alone. They had each other now. They were together, in spirit as well as in flesh—as one, as though they had found the bits that were missing from themselves in each other.

They remained at Larkhill for a further week, during which time Julius arranged for work to begin on rebuilding the outbuildings. The cause of the fire remained a mystery, until a grim-faced George paid them a visit.

'It was my mother,' he said without preamble. 'I'm sorry, Beatrice, but unable to bear the thought that you had finally got what you wanted, she paid someone to destroy the house.'

Beatrice, seated on the sofa, was clearly horrified. Though she knew her aunt wished her ill, she could not believe she would go so far as to want to destroy Larkhill. 'Does you mother really hate me as much as that?'

'She couldn't stand knowing you had won, that you had indeed secured Larkhill for yourself. She wanted to hurt you the only way she knew how. I'm so sorry, Beatrice.'

'Aunt Moira can be very cruel.'

'Yes, yes, she can. When she learned her scheming had failed to destroy Larkhill, she could not hide what she had done. In her fury she could not stop herself telling me. I could not believe it myself. I can only thank God that apart from the destruction of a few outbuildings, no one was harmed and the house is still intact. I—would appreciate you not taking this further, Beatrice. No good would come of it.'

'We won't,' Julius answered for her, 'providing Lady Standish stays away from my wife.'

'She will—I shall make sure of that. It may surprise you to know that she regrets her actions and is more than a little ashamed. She didn't mean to harm you, Beatrice. Having seen you in London earlier, she had no idea you had come down to Larkhill. She knows how much Larkhill means to you. She meant to hurt you by destroying it. I have her word that she won't try anything like that again. You need not fear. She—will shortly be moving to the dower house.'

His hesitancy and the sudden warmth that lit his eyes brought a knowing smile to Beatrice's lips. 'Then that can only mean one thing. You are to be married, George?'

He beamed at her. 'I am. Leonora has consented to be my wife.'

'That's wonderful news, George. And does your mother approve?'

'Leonora has all the requisites that are important in my mother's scheme of things. But whether she approves or not is neither here nor there. I chose my own wife, not my mother.'

'Then I wish you every happiness, George. But what of Astrid? Has she returned from Scotland?'

'She has, although I haven't seen her yet. Henry and Astrid are living with Henry's parents. It's just a temporary situation, until they've found somewhere they can afford to live. As you know, the Talbots are not wealthy. Astrid's dowry will help, but she will find that her standard of living will be somewhat reduced and nothing like what she has become accustomed to.'

'She is happy, George. That is what counts.'

He smiled at her. 'So it is, Beatrice. So it is.'

The following morning Julius didn't accompany Beatrice when she went to call on Astrid and put his wife's excitement down to her eagerness to see her cousin. In fact, she had seemed strangely preoccupied and somewhat secretive ever since George's visit, which puzzled him. Everything became clear when she returned and told him she was ready to leave Larkhill, that she wanted him to take her to Highfield where she was impatient to take up her new life.

He gazed at her suspiciously. 'Of course. We'll leave right away if that is what you wish. You'll have to decide what you are going to do with Larkhill. The house shouldn't be left empty indefinitely.'

She hesitated, searching his face. 'It's not mine any more,' she told him. 'It belongs to Astrid. I wanted her to have it.'

Julius nodded slowly. This was the last thing he had expected her to say, but he knew she would have given the matter serious thought and that the decision to part with her beloved Larkhill would not have been taken lightly. 'You are sure?' he asked.

Beatrice took a deep breath. 'I'm sure. I know it will be safe in Astrid and Henry's hands.' And she was sure. She would always remember the look of joyous disbelief and gratitude on her cousin's face when she had offered Larkhill to her. That alone made it all worthwhile. 'I would be grateful if you would take care of the legalities, Julius. You know all about these things. All I want is you—to live with you wherever that may be.'

'And you will not regret it?'

'No. There is nothing that can be bought or sold or bartered that I would want. The only thing I want cannot be bought—and it is not the ownership of Larkhill. It is you, Julius. Only you.'

Overcome with emotion at what she had done, he put his arms around her and drew her close to him.

She lifted her face to his kiss and breathed in the warm, masculine smell of him, tasted the warmth of his mouth as it came down on hers. All the love that had been accumulating through the lonely years of her childhood was in that kiss. Julius felt it in the soft lips. With unselfish ardour she offered herself to him and Julius took what she offered hungrily, feeling it flowing through his veins and mingling with his blood until the joy of it was shattering.

'I love you,' she whispered. 'I belong with you—wherever that may be.'

He sighed, his eyes adoring her. She was everything he'd ever dreamed she could be—and more.

The next six months were spent in wedded bliss at Highfield Manor in Kent—a magnificent estate that surpassed anything Beatrice had ever seen. It was at Highfield where Julius and Beatrice's son was born. It was also at Highfield where they received news that Lady Standish had died in her sleep. Beatrice did not grieve for her aunt and chose not to return to Standish House for the funeral.

After twelve months of mourning, Julius and Beatrice did attend George's wedding to Leonora Fenton and they stayed at Larkhill with Astrid and Henry.

With its acres of corn and green meadows filled with cattle and sheep, Larkhill looked loved and well tended and prosperous. Beatrice's heart soared with affection and gratitude to Henry, who had done all this, but she no longer considered it her home.

When George and Leonora stood at the altar to speak their vows, Julius's gaze riveted on his wife standing next to him. The sight of her still continued to have a devastating effect on him, but here, in the church, caught in a shaft of light piercing the stained-glass windows, expecting their second child, never had she looked so radiantly beautiful or so serene. Every muscle of his body strained to endure the torment of her nearness. But it was a torment he welcomed, an agony he didn't want to be spared. And he knew that having her beside him was all he could ever want for the rest of his life.

* * * * *

Don't miss Pink Tuesday
One day. 10 hours. 10 deals.

PINK TUESDAY
IS COMING!

10 hours...10 unmissable deals!

This Valentine's Day we will be bringing
you fantastic offers across a range of
our titles—each hour, on the hour!

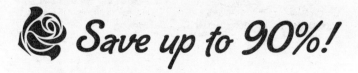

Pink Tuesday starts
9am Tuesday 14th February

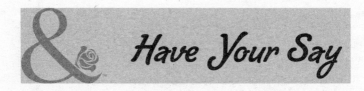

Have Your Say

You've just finished your book.
So what did you think?

We'd love to hear your thoughts on our
'Have your say' online panel
www.millsandboon.co.uk/haveyoursay

 Easy to use

 Short questionnaire

 Chance to win Mills & Boon® goodies

Visit us Online Tell us what you thought of this book now at
www.millsandboon.co.uk/haveyoursay

YOUR_SAY

"Perfect for fans of
Downton Abbey"
—*Now* magazine

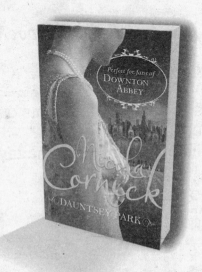

Jack Kestrel is the dissolute and dangerous son of the
family of the Dukes of Kestrel, who finds himself
in London, not to enjoy the many temptations on
offer, but to uphold his family's honour. But it's
Sally Bowes, owner of the fashionable Blue Parrot
nightclub, where the upper echelons of London
society come to sparkle under dazzling chandeliers,
who has all of his attention…

Set in the bustle and boom of Edwardian London,
Dauntsey Park captures the roar and glamour
of the early twentieth century.

www.mirabooks.co.uk

M241_DP